For the Fishbowl, whose endless antics will fuel my imagination for a long time to come

Chapter 1

'Uh, a latte, please,' I say, not even looking up at the waiter. I don't know why I ordered that. I don't even *like* coffee. I'm an iced or herbal tea kind of girl.

But sitting here in this smart café with its posh name – Langlois – makes me feel so . . . I don't know – cosmopolitan? Upper class? Cool?

'Coming right up.'

The barista walks off, and I focus all my attention back on the cell phone in my hands. It's some swanky new model – it has a slide-out keypad, 3G internet, unlimited texts, stores tons of music . . . It sounds like a good phone. It looks like a good phone. The woman in the store *said* it was a good phone.

Shame I have no idea how to work it.

The manual is on the table beside me, but the spine is stiff, the book unwilling to stay open at the page telling me how to set up the internet.

I mean, it's not like I know what I'm doing. Not only

am I kind of useless when it comes to technology – unless it involves downloading and converting music files – I've never had a cell phone before. I've never really needed one. It's not like I got out much back in Pineford.

I don't think of it as 'back home'. Why should I? I don't miss it.

We've been here in Florida for ten days and counting. And I love it already. It isn't just a chance for me to turn over a new leaf; it's a chance for me to have a whole new life.

A throat clears, distracting me just as I think I've worked this internet thing out.

I realize why the guy doesn't just put the steaming white mug down on my table: my purse, the empty cell-phone box, wires, and the tiny manual are covering every inch of space.

'Oh, sorry!' I apologize automatically. I sweep my bag off and bundle the wires haphazardly into the box.

He sets the latte down, and for the first time I really look at him. He isn't anything special. You wouldn't look at him and think *Omigod!* because he's so hot. But he is, I have to admit, kind of cute.

The black uniform and dark green apron probably make him look a little paler than he really is. He has a long bony nose and really bright green eyes with thick, dark eyelashes. His dark hair is short, in tight half-curls. If he ever let it grow longer, I bet he'd have a mass of springy ringlets most girls would envy. He's tall, but not insanely tall. A few inches more than me, maybe? His long limbs make him look kind of gangly, though.

'Thanks,' I say.

'Anything else I can get you?'

'No, thanks, that's fine.'

I look back at my new cell, then at the manual again – I'm holding it open with my elbow. It sounds like a bunch of mumbo-jumbo, to be honest. But there is no way I'd ever figure out this darn thing by myself.

'Do you, uh, need a hand?'

I blink, looking up at him. I hadn't even realized he was still there.

'Don't you have people to serve?' I probably sound like a snob, but I don't mean to; I'm just getting frustrated with the phone. I've been here for at least ten minutes already trying to work out one tiny thing.

'We're not that busy – I think I can spare a few minutes.'

He sweeps a hand around and I see he's right: a group of three gossiping girls, a couple tucked away in the corner, and a man typing away on his laptop.

'Everybody's at the beach,' he carries on by way of explanation. 'Enjoying the last few days of summer before school kicks in. Usually this place is heaving.'

I nod.

'So – you want some help, or not?' He gives me an easy, friendly smile. It's kind of lopsided, going up higher on the left, but it looks quirky and cute on him.

I don't know if it's the smile or just that I really do need the help, but I give in.

'Please?' I say, laughing sheepishly.

He scrapes out the chair opposite me, dropping into it. 'What're you trying to do?'

'I'm not a hundred percent sure. It said something about having to set up the internet before you can use it, and there's some kind of code on the box, but I don't know what I'm supposed to do.'

He holds out a hand and I pass the cell phone over. I hover over the manual, wondering if he needs it, or if I'm just an idiot.

He doesn't need the manual, as it turns out.

'What's the code?'

I read it out off the box, and after a few taps on the cell phone he hands it back. 'There you go. All done.'

I smile. 'Thanks! I swear, technology has a vendetta against me. I almost broke the microwave last week.'

It was a bit of an exaggeration, sure. I'd put it on the wrong setting and my pasta had exploded, and then the microwave shut itself off automatically.

The guy laughs.

That's nice too – somewhere between a big, hearty laugh and a chuckle. But it makes me want to smile.

Now he's closer to me, I see there are freckles scattered all over his face, clumped around his nose and thinning out as they spread over his cheeks.

'You're new around here, then? I'd have seen you before, otherwise.'

'We just moved here. From Maine.'

'Nice. My cousins live up there. I've been a few times for Thanksgiving.'

'It's okay.'

'You prefer Florida?'

I nod, maybe a bit too enthusiastically, since he gives a chuckle. 'Better weather, for one thing.'

'You haven't seen the storms yet.'

'Can't wait,' I say, semi-sarcastic, and he smiles again.

I'd been so worried that it would be hard to make friends here; that things would be just the same as they had been in Pineford; that people just wouldn't want to get to know me. Especially being the new girl: that could go one of two ways, as I see it. They'd either be fascinated by the shiny new toy, or they'd shun me automatically.

It's not that I can't talk to people, or that I'm not

5

friendly. I'd just never had people interested in talking to me. Years of that makes a person a little shy, to say the least.

But making friends is easier than I'd anticipated.

'What school do you go to?' I ask, feeling brave. He looks around my age, but maybe he's a senior.

'Midsommer. I guess you're enrolled there too, right?'

I nod – yet again. 'I'm a junior. Well, I will be, in a couple of days, anyway.'

He laughs again. 'Same.' He holds out a hand. 'I'm Dwight.'

Dwight?

Now, that is *a weird name*, I think. I have never in my entire life heard of anybody called Dwight. But somehow, it fits this guy.

'Madison,' I introduce myself, shaking his hand. 'Nice to meet you.'

'Likewise. How come you're not at the beach, then? Catching some last-minute sun, checking out the guys?'

'I didn't really fancy going on my own. Plus, I needed a new cell.'

I say 'new' on purpose. I thought it'd seem weird if I told him I'd never owned a cell before now.

'Ah.'

'What about you?' I counter.

'The waves are no good today,' he says, 'but I had to cover a shift anyway.'

'Waves?'

'For surfing.'

'Oh. Cool.' I scrutinize him a little. He doesn't look like a surfer. I'd always pictured surfers as broad-shouldered, muscled guys with shaggy blond hair. And I'd have thought surfers would be tanned from being out in the sun so much. He looks too pale and gangly.

I sip the latte to fill the silence a little, and can't stop myself pulling a face.

Yup. I will definitely never order a latte again.

'Too hot?' he assumes.

'Uh, yeah . . . Thanks for the help,' I say quickly.

'Give me a shout if you need anything else, okay? I've got to get back to work before the boss tells me to stop mingling with the customers.' He smiles at me again. 'I'll see you around?'

It sounds like a question rather than a statement, so I reply, 'Yeah, sure.'

'Nice meeting you, Madison.'

'Nice meeting you too, Dwight,' I say to his retreating back.

Looks like you just made a friend.

And I feel all light and bubbly inside. Maybe fitting in here won't be so hard after all.

Chapter 2

Great-Aunt Gina's death is probably the best thing that ever happened to me.

Now don't get me wrong – I loved her, and I miss her now. But she had her 'favorites' in the family. I mean, okay, so my dad's brother and his family live over in Nevada, so they were too far away for an old lady to visit. But it was us who Great-Aunt Gina came to for Thanksgiving and Christmases. She'd send my cousins a check in the mail instead.

When I was little, I'll admit I was totally scared of her. She was eighty-nine when she croaked. A tall, bony lady with thin gray hair and false teeth that always fell out and clacked together noisily when she spoke. But when I saw the photos, I realized why she'd been some big-shot model in her younger years. Despite her scary old lady appearance, though, Great-Aunt Gina had been a genuinely nice person.

She'd lived in Florida, in a big house by the sea. And when she died, she left us everything.

And I do mean *everything*. A massive inheritance, her house, and all the vintage clothes and jewelry.

At first we weren't sure what to do about it. Sell the property and maybe upgrade to a nicer house in Maine? Keep it as a holiday home?

I still don't remember who suggested moving to Florida. But whoever it was, I owe them big time.

Dad looked into it. He found a private clinic near the beach where Great-Aunt Gina's house was, and they were looking for a new doctor. Mom found a nice three-bedroom house with a big garden, and even a small pool, in the suburbs, near a high school. Being a teacher in elementary school, my mom didn't have too hard a time getting a new job in Florida.

Jenna, my elder sister, was already out of Maine by then; she currently attends NYU, and she didn't care if we moved from Pineford, Maine, or not. She was out of there, and she planned to stay out.

'It's so boring. Nothing happens here,' she'd told Mom and Dad when they asked why she didn't apply to college closer to home. 'Besides, the course looks better in New York. Plus, I want to get out, see the world. That's not happening if I stay in Pineford.'

The only thing that might've stopped them from

going ahead was me. And I could not *wait* to move.

There was just nothing for me in Pineford. By the end of my sophomore year I'd pretty much stopped trying in class, and it wasn't like I had a million friends and a busy social life I was leaving behind.

So when Mom tentatively asked me, 'Madison, honey, do you think you'll really, really be all right if we move to Florida?' my reply was instantaneous:

'Can I start packing now?' Because moving to Florida meant I could have a whole new life.

My sister Jenna was the girl everyone knew back at my school in Pineford. She was on the homecoming committee, she was class president, the blonde cheerleader who got the beauty and the brains. The All-American It Girl.

Then there was me.

And I just . . . I wasn't Jenna.

I tried, though. And I was happy enough to keep to myself – though it wasn't out of choice that I'd never really gone to parties, been part of high-school gossip, had a boyfriend . . . I didn't make myself the lonely loser; it was a spot in high school designated for me by other people.

But moving to Midsommer, in Collier County, Florida, was my big chance for a completely new life. Nobody was going to judge me by the standards my sister had set. Nobody had to know what I'd been like in the last couple of years.

I could be me.

Just, you know, a better version of me.

I pick up the little spoon that rests on my coffee saucer, and turn it over in my hands, angling it so I can see my distorted reflection in the back of it. I'm still getting used to seeing a stranger when I look in the mirror.

When I realized I could build a whole new life for myself by moving here, I also realized that this was really the perfect time for a makeover. Because that's what people did, right? They moved someplace new and recreated themselves to be a whole new, better person, didn't they? So that's what I wanted to do.

Okay, I didn't have to do anything too drastic. Fatty Maddie had disappeared over a year ago – it was just that nobody had cared enough about me to notice. I lost the braces last Christmas. I'd had contacts since February too, and lost those hideous glasses.

But when people have this opinion of you, it's very hard to change it. They've judged you, and they like to label you, and they like you to stay with that label for ever. You've been allocated a place in their society, and that's where they want you to stay.

So even when I lost weight, even when I had my

braces taken off, even when I started wearing contacts simply because they were more convenient than glasses, nobody cared. People can be shallow and superficial, but sometimes they're too selfish to care about you.

It got to the point where I stopped caring. Once you build up walls, it's hard to tear them back down.

Now, though, I do care, for once, what people are going to think of me.

The new Madison is cool, spontaneous, daring.

Looking at my stretched-out reflection in the spoon, I can kind of believe I'm on my way to the new Madison.

I touch a hand to my hair – not out of vanity, but because I'm still getting used to having, like, no hair. It's a pretty drastic change, actually: I had long hair my whole life. On anyone else – like Jenna – people might've envied it. But considering my hair was a bland shade of dishwater blonde, and I didn't even have layers or bangs to liven it up a little, then you can see why I cut it all off.

Well, not *all*. But close enough.

Mom had flipped when she saw what I'd done at the little salon in our town. She'd gone all bug-eyed and gawped at me. 'I thought you said you were just going a *little bit* shorter!'

But now I smile at myself in the tiny silver spoon, because I love my new hair. I opted for a short bob, the hair longer at the front so that it framed my face. I got some lowlights as well as highlights to try and make it look a bit less dull. Oh, and the sweeping side bangs that almost obscure my left eye give me a kind of 'rock-chic edge', according to Bobby, my hairdresser. I took his word on that one.

The main reason I did it, though, was so I wouldn't have something to hide behind. Not so I'd look better – although that *did* factor into it. Back in Pineford, I could duck my head and hide behind my hair, put in my earphones and do my best to be invisible. I wanted to change, be the new Madison. So by hacking off my hair, I'd *have* to try. It'd be harder to back out.

I'm not particularly pretty – I know that, and I've never expected any haircut or makeup or whatever to change it. Still, compared to how I used to look back in Pineford, with the ugly glasses and braces and extra pounds, I look good – not so drab. And that is good enough for me.

One thing I did strike lucky on when it came to the gene pool was inheriting my mom's flawless skin. Well, all right, mine isn't *that* flawless – teenage hormones don't allow that. But it's close enough.

The new Madison is cool, daring, spontaneous.

Daring was the haircut. Cool was covered by my buying a new wardrobe – you know, one that didn't just consist of plain, baggy T-shirts and shapeless jeans to obscure my figure. My parents were only too happy to finance all of this and see me finally behaving a bit more like a normal sixteen-year-old girl.

I had yet to tick off *spontaneous*, but that's something I can't really plan out.

I set the spoon down and pick up my mug, swallowing enough of my lukewarm latte that nobody will know I don't actually like it.

Then I pack away, putting the phone box back in the carrier, and my swanky new cell phone, now fully functional (and with no more help from Dwight the barista, I'm proud to say), into the back pocket of my jean shorts.

Dwight is cleaning out a coffee pot when I go up to the counter. 'Thanks again,' I say to him. I hand over the check, leaving a ten-dollar bill, which is a huge tip for only a latte, but I feel like I owe him for the help with my cell phone.

When I speak, he looks around and then smiles at me. 'No problem. You're heading off now?'

I nod. 'I need to be home for dinner, so . . . Well, um, I'll . . . I'll see you around,' I stammer. Then I flash another smile and give an awkward wave before heading for the door.

'Hey! Uh, Madison?'

One foot is poised to step through the open door, and I swivel around to look at him. 'Yeah?'

My voice is shockingly calm, seeing as how my heart is suddenly racing, my palms clammy. I clutch the plastic carrier tightly. My mouth turns dry, and I swallow hard.

Because for a moment I think: *Oh my gosh, is he about to ask me out?*

Don't be so ridiculous, Madison. You don't look that good. You just met. He wouldn't ask you out.

Then Dwight speaks, calling a halt to all my inner ramblings and bringing me back to reality.

'What're you doing tomorrow?'

I blink.

Was that . . . Did he just . . . ask me out?

'Nothing. At least, I don't think I'm doing anything. Why?' I think I'm babbling, so I clamp my mouth closed.

'Well, I was just thinking, since you're new to town, if . . . Have you been to the beach yet?'

'No, I haven't had a chance.'

'I've only got the afternoon shift tomorrow,' he says, with that easy lopsided smile. 'There's a party there –

on the beach – tomorrow night. They do it every year – you know, like an end-of-summer thing. I just thought maybe you'd like to go. You can meet some new people.'

All those rambling thoughts are gone; now my mind is blank, and it takes me a couple of seconds to respond. Because a) this guy has just asked me to a party and I've never been to a party before, and b) this guy, who's actually quite cute, has not asked me out on a date. 'Sure,' I manage to say eventually, with a smile. 'I'll have to check with my parents first, but . . .' I trail off. Was it too dorky of me to say I had to ask my parents?

He grins back. 'Awesome. Is your cell phone working okay now?' When I nod, he adds, 'I'll punch in my number. I'll meet you somewhere before, so you don't have to turn up totally alone.'

I know he's just being friendly, but I can barely suppress a massive grin. *He's giving me his number!* I think as I hand over my cell.

'It usually starts up around eight,' he tells me.

'Okay. Um. Okay. Thanks. I'll, uh, see you tomorrow, then.'

Would it make me look like even more of an idiot if I slapped my forehead? Jeez, can't I just form a sentence?

'Bye, Madison.'

'Bye, Dwight.'

As I leave, I'm on Cloud Nine. Seriously.

I'm going to a party (as soon as I clear it with Mom and Dad)!

I bounce down the road. Here, on the outskirts of the town, there's a small strip of shops: the Langlois Café, and the hair salon, and the library; then a drug store, and a couple of independent record and clothes stores too.

I'm not sure what it is that catches my eye, but all of a sudden I stop to look at the shop. It's not very big, and it's a bit dark and not exactly high-brow, like the rest of the street. In big cursive writing on the window, I see: *Bette's Urban Body Art Parlor.* And the windows are covered with photos of body piercings and tattoo templates. I stand there staring, totally mesmerized by it.

I jump when there's the noise of a door opening, almost dropping the carrier.

There's a woman standing in the open doorway, arms crossed, looking at me. I gulp. She's like a catalogue for the place – piercings all over her ears and face, and tattoos on her arms. The soft, slightly tinny sound of an old Guns N' Roses song plays from inside. She's plump, with graying wavy hair to her shoulders.

'Can I help you with anything, hon?' she asks me politely.

I stare at her, and I know it's rude, but I can't help it. She looks like she should have pit-bull terriers at her feet, and a huge Harley Davidson; she sounds like a really sweet mom who's always baking her kids cookies.

'Um,' I say, 'I'm just looking . . .'

I turn back to the window. Out of the corner of my eye I can see her scrutinizing me, and it makes me shift from foot to foot uncomfortably.

'Ever thought of having your nose pierced, hon?'

I shake my head. 'No.'

'It'd suit you,' she tells me, and there's a smile in her voice. 'On the right side, though, because of where your bangs are.'

'Oh. Well, I never really thought about it.'

'Well, you know where to find me if you ever change your mind – okay, hon?'

I turn to look at her and she gives me a warm smile.

A nose piercing? Mom and Dad would kill me. Didn't it hurt? What if it got infected?

But the new Madison is meant to be spontaneous, right?

And it does sound kind of cool . . . Plus, it'd suit my new 'rock-chic' hair, wouldn't it?

I haven't even finished thinking it through when I hear myself saying, 'You know what? Sure. Why not.'

The lady (I'm guessing she's Bette of Bette's Urban Body Art Parlor) raises her eyebrows at me. 'You sure, hon?'

And I smile and nod before following her inside, despite the fact that I'm pretty much freaking out – because a) I have the feeling it's going to hurt really bad, and b) I'm so dead when I get home . . .

Chapter 3

The nose piercing hurts like heck.

When I first see myself in the mirror, I can find barely any resemblance to my old self. The 'rock-chic' haircut and the sparkly blue stud in my nose are one thing, but the artfully ripped Abercrombie shorts and a cute blue tank top with matching flip-flops are also hugely different to the old me.

I picture myself as I was back when I started out in high school. Chubby, and with thick lenses in my wiry glasses, and braces I'd had for at least a year. A shapeless jumper and jeans, to make it less obvious that I was far from a size zero.

It would've been better if I'd been invisible. But I wasn't. It would've been better if I was really smart; but I only got A grades when I worked for them, so I wasn't a nerd. It would've been better if I was a band geek or in the chess club – but I wasn't.

I shake my head, because none of that matters now,

not here. I don't have to be that person anymore. I'm forgetting about her.

I smile at my reflection. Definitely cool, daring and spontaneous.

I'm pretty pleased with myself as I walk home. Not just because of the piercing, and not just because a cute guy put his number in my cell phone, but because everything is finally looking up for me.

Well, until I get home, at least.

'Is that you, Madison?'

'Considering I'm the only other person in this state who has a key to the house, no, Mom, it's not me,' I call back.

The house smells of cooking, and I automatically know that Dad's been making pasta. I breathe in deeply: Dad's cooking always smells amazing. Mom's cooking often smells a little more . . . burned.

'You're just in time for dinner,' she says, popping her head around the kitchen door for a moment. As I take off my shoes she carries on, 'Did you find a cell phone?'

'Yeah. It has internet and stuff.' I don't specify the 'stuff' because I'm not entirely sure what the 'stuff' consists of just yet. I only know how to send a text, make a phone call, and open Google.

'That's good.'

She doesn't even ask me how much it cost. She's just glad I'm acting like a normal teenager.

I walk into the kitchen, which is all wooden units and ceramic tiling and beige walls, as Dad is dishing out pasta. I grab a plate and sit down at the table.

'Did you finish putting the rest of the boxes in the attic?' I ask.

'Yep,' Dad tells me smugly. Mom's been bugging him to move all the old photo albums and toys from when me and Jenna were kids – you know, the usual kind of junk you keep in attics – out of the spare room for *days*.

They sit down, and I realize just how fast and hard my heart is beating. They haven't noticed the nose piercing yet. Maybe they won't – at least for a couple of days. Or maybe they've noticed and miraculously just don't care about it. I don't know, but I'm not going to question it.

After a couple of minutes Mom says, 'You were out a long time.'

'I went to the café. To try and set up my cell phone. There was this guy who works there, though, and he had to help me work it.'

'There was a guy?' Mom's ears perk up at that. I knew they would.

'Yeah. He said he's – well, he's *going* to be a junior at the high school, same as me.'

'Really? What's he like? Was he cute?'

Yes, I think, *he's very cute.*

But I shrug and say, 'Sure. I guess. He was really nice, anyway. He said there's a party at the beach tomorrow night. Like, a back-to-school thing . . .'

'Did he ask you to go?'

I nod, but hastily add, 'He just meant as friends, though. So I can meet people before school starts.' I have to specify it's not a date; Mom would go crazy if she thought her daughter, who was finally breaking out of her shell and becoming a normal sixteen-year-old, actually had a date.

'Oh.' She sounds a little disappointed, but then adds, 'But that's nice! He sounds lovely. What's his name?'

'Dwight.'

'Dwight . . . ?'

'I don't know.'

'Where does he live?'

'Around here somewhere, I guess. I don't know. I didn't ask for his autobiography.'

'More to the point,' Dad says, pointing his fork at me, 'what about this party?'

'It's on the beach. It sounds like it's a bunch of the

kids who go to the high school. Dwight said it starts around eight.'

My parents exchange a brief look, and then my dad tells me sternly, 'No drinking, Madison, you hear me? We don't want you going out and being stupid. You don't know these people, and I don't care if they're all drinking, you're not.'

I'm of half a mind to argue, just because. But the truth is, I'm too excited about this party – *an actual party!* – to argue. I just nod and smile and say, 'Yes, of course. Got it.'

Dad nods and gives me a stern warning look. 'Good. And you can be home by eleven-thirty.'

'What if nobody else leaves then? What if it finishes at twelve, or one?' *I don't want to give anyone cause to think I'm a loser*, I add silently.

'You can be home by eleven-thirty, Madison,' Mom tells me. 'Like your father said, you don't know these people, and we don't want you staying out till tomorrow morning with them.'

'Fine,' I grumble, but I don't make too much fuss. Eleven-thirty curfew is better than them telling me I couldn't go.

We eat in silence for another minute or so, and then Mom says, 'Madison, look at me a moment.'

So I do.

And her cutlery clatters to the plate, almost flicking pasta over the table. 'What the hell have you done to your face?'

It takes me a moment to realize what she's talking about.

I bite my lip, and I can feel my stomach fall away.

'We trust you to go out and buy a cell phone and you come home with – with that?' she cries out. She's turning red in the face with anger now. Mom rarely gets mad. She's that loveable kindergarten teacher who adores children. Jenna and I always knew that when our mom was mad, we were not going to get off lightly.

Once, Jenna smashed an antique vase Mom had inherited when her grandma died. It was completely by accident – Jenna had tripped and smacked into the table. Mom got so angry about it, though, Jenna was grounded for a week.

So right now, I want to turn to dust and I wish I'd never gotten the piercing.

'It's only a piercing,' I mumble defensively. 'It's not like I got a tattoo—'

'You got a *what*?' Dad shouts, more shocked than angry. '*Why?*'

'Yes, Madison.' Mom's seething. If looks could kill . . . 'Why don't you tell us exactly why you disfigured your face like that?'

'I don't know,' I mutter. The smell of pasta, which seemed delicious when I walked in, suddenly makes me feel sick. 'I just wanted to . . . I thought it'd look cool . . .'

'Oh, Madison, you stupid girl!' Mom says, and in that instant all the anger seems to go out of her. She doesn't sound mad anymore; more like she's upset. Sympathetic, even. It's almost as though the anger directed at me was the only thing keeping her upright; she collapses back into her chair like a rag doll.

Then she sits back up and leans over the table, putting her hand over mine. 'Honey, I know it's been hard for you. I know. It's killed me inside. And I know you want to make a good impression here, and make friends – but you don't have to do something like that just . . .' She trails off with a sigh.

She thought I'd done it so people would like me more.

Maybe she's right. I mean, I thought it'd make me look edgy and cool . . . A conversation starter. Something that would stop me from being relegated to the background. So, yes, maybe my mom is right – except I'd done it for that reason on more of a sub-conscious level. Who knows? I'm not in the mood to psychoanalyze my actions right now.

I open my mouth, starting to argue that it wasn't

that, but she cuts me off. 'Well, you can't take it out now. It might get infected.' She sighs. 'I'm not happy about this, you know, Madison.'

'I know,' I mumble.

I expect her to say that I'm not allowed to go to the party tomorrow, and maybe even ground me. I've never been grounded before. But then again, if I'd done anything worth being grounded for, what difference would it have made? Back in Pineford, when everyone else went to a party, I just stayed in my room anyway.

But now, when I think I may actually get grounded for the first time ever, I kind of panic inside a little.

Then Mom says, 'Have you thought about what you're going to wear to this party?' and that's when I really, *really* begin to panic.

Jenna phones that night, and after about ten minutes Dad yells up to me, 'Madison, Jenna's on the line for you!'

I pull the earphone out of my left ear and lean over to my nightstand to pick up the extension. 'Hi, Jenna.'

'Nose piercing, huh? I've gotta say, Mads, I did not expect that from you. Mom's so not happy about it.' She laughs. 'Good for you, though. I bet it looks hot.'

'Heck yeah.' I say it sarcastically, but I actually kind of hope it does look 'hot', now she's said it.

Jenna laughs again, and before I can ask how the Big Apple is, she dives right in and says, 'Tell me all about this coffee-shop guy!'

'His name's Dwight. He's a junior, same as me, and he'll go to the high school with me too. So that's good, you know, 'cause I kind of have a friend already. He's really nice too – he has a great smile.'

'Aw,' my big sister coos. 'What's he look like, then? Is he tall? Buff? Cute? Does he look like he plays football or anything?'

'Well, he's kind of cute . . .' I twirl a piece of hair around my finger as I say it, and there's a smile playing on my lips. 'He's tall. Dark hair. And he surfs,' I add. 'But he only invited me to the party as a friend. He wasn't even flirting so it's not like it matters.'

Jenna totally ignores that last part. 'Really? He's a surfer? Wow. That's . . .' She laughs. 'That's actually pretty cool! Sounds like you've got yourself a very nice guy in the bag there! And what's this Mom said about a party?'

Jenna says party like 'part*aaay*', which makes me giggle and shake my head.

'Dwight told me there's a party on the beach tomorrow night. He gave me his number so—'

'*He gave you his number?*' Jenna shrieks. '*Omigod!* Are

you serious? And you said he was just being friendly. Pfft.'

'Yeah, but only so we could meet up beforehand. He *was* being friendly!' I insist.

'Um, Madison, no, he was not, trust me! A guy who gives you his number like that' – I hear her snap her fingers sharply in the background – 'likes you.'

'I don't think so,' I say, picking a piece of loose cotton from my comforter. 'I really, really think he was just being nice. You know, so I wouldn't have to show up on my own and stand there like – like a lemon.'

'Mm,' she says thoughtfully. 'Do you want it to be a date?'

'Kind of,' I mumble. I wouldn't have told my mom that, but Jenna is different. 'But it doesn't even matter because *it's not a date.*'

'All right – well, next question: What are you wearing?'

'Right now, shorts and a tank top and the sweater Gran knitted for me last Christmas.'

'I mean tomorrow, to the party, doofus.'

We both laugh then. I say, 'I honestly don't know.'

'Well, then, what are big sisters for? Shorts, definitely. Do you have any, like, distressed shorts? And when I say shorts, I mean really short shorts. The kind Mom would not approve of.'

I giggle, and roll off my bed to go open my closet. Jenna and I talk for over half an hour and she talks me through what she thinks is appropriate wear for a beach party. Considering she never went to a beach party when we lived in Maine, she seems to know an awful lot about them.

When I point that out, Jenna just laughs and says, 'Madison, just trust me on this.'

And I do.

Chapter 4

Ever had that nauseous feeling when you text a guy you like for the first time?

Well, imagine that: the twisting in my stomach so bad I almost need to pee, the clammy hands, the racing mind. Deleting and retyping one text at least a dozen times.

Except it's even worse – since I've never texted a guy before, period. I have no idea what the protocol for this is.

I spend about twenty minutes trying to compose a text to Dwight. Right now, the screen on my cell phone reads: *Hey! How're you? I was just wondering what to do about meeting you later for the party* ☺ – and all I can do is stare at it, and wonder if it's all right. Should I delete the *How're you?*, and should I add a kiss on the end?

I don't know, I don't know, I don't know!

I drop the phone on my bed and run my hands

through my hair, biting down on my lip to muffle a little scream of frustration.

Ping!

I freeze. Then I drop my hands, open my eyes wide and stare at my phone. I think my heart actually stops beating for that moment.

I lunge for my phone, snatching it up and staring helplessly at the screen.

It's sent the message.

When I threw my phone down I pressed the send button. I hear a little whimper of worry escape my mouth, and my heart starts beating again, and beating hard.

I double-check the screen of my cell – yep, it *definitely* sent the text to Dwight.

It takes a couple of minutes for the panic and anxiety to subside. It was probably the kind of thing I would've sent him anyway. It isn't even such a big deal. I was being stupid.

Now all I have to do is wait for him to text back.

I remember he's working the afternoon shift, so maybe he's still at work and won't reply for a while.

So in the meantime I go to my closet and find the outfit Jenna helped me to pick out. It's a pair of teeny tiny shorts that only reach a third of the way down my thigh, light blue denim and kind of torn at the hem.

Then a white camisole, with a low neckline decorated with black lacy stuff. A pair of black sandals, some gold bangles, and a thin white hoodie – because according to Jenna, people won't be too dressed up, and it might be cold, but I still want to look good.

I'm not sure about the camisole. I mean, I haven't got much in the way of curves. Jenna always teased me (and actually still does) about being as flat as an ironing board. Which is a bit of an exaggeration, but not much.

But hey, Jenna may not have been to any beach parties, but she sure knows a heck of a lot more about parties and what to wear than I do.

I'm so busy contemplating how the outfit will look that when my cell phone goes *ping!* again, I jump.

Oh, gosh, he's replied!

I hastily put my clothes back into the closet as tidily as possible, not wanting them to be creased tonight. Then I pick up my cell.

One new message: Dwight.

I grin, but at the same time I'm feeling hideously anxious. But I do it – I open up the text.

Hey ☺ *Where do you live? I can meet you at your house at eight, if that works for you?*

I text him back with my address, and say that works out great, thanks! I throw in a smiley face and hit send;

then I fall back amongst the cushions on my bed, and I smile.

A mixture of excitement and fear courses through my veins. I honestly don't know what I'm thinking. I can't stop smiling, because I'm finally being the person I want to be, and getting out there in the real world; I'm not being left behind in the shadows, or laughed at. My stomach has just totally disappeared, though, because I've never been to a party before and I have no idea what I'll do there. I don't know anybody except Dwight, and I can't expect him to spend the whole night with me.

I know I'll have to talk to people – I'll have to face most of them at school on Monday. What if they don't like me? What if I can't find anything to say to them, or I make an idiot of myself? I feel like I'm being thrown in the deep end without anyone to toss me a kisby ring.

I know this is probably better than me just turning up at school on Monday, a lost sheep in a pool of piranha. At least with this party, I'll get the chance to meet people, maybe even make a good impression.

And before I know it, it's almost seven o'clock.

I jump in the shower and then take extra time to fix my hair, get dressed, and put on some makeup. Since moving to Florida, Mom had convinced me to buy a whole load of makeup.

'Not that you even need it,' she said. 'You're beautiful, sweetie. But when you just want to look that little bit better, you're going to want it, I know. Jenna was exactly the same.'

Lately, I'd only worn mascara, since my lashes were so blond they looked almost nonexistent, and not bothered with much else. If I was going to the mall with my mom, I'd maybe add some concealer under my eyes. But that was it.

Tonight, though, I stand in front of my dresser and carefully apply it all: eyeshadow and eyeliner, foundation and blusher, mascara and lip gloss. I go all out.

And again, I'm so glad I grew up with Jenna for my older sister; I'd never worn much makeup, but at least I knew how to apply it properly.

Once I'm dressed and ready, I step back and take a good look in the mirror. I'm getting used to seeing this strange version of myself, but I am shocked by what I see this time.

I look . . .

I look *good*. I don't look anything – anything at all – like I used to be. I stare at my reflection and wonder what happened to Fatty Maddie; wonder how the heck I got from being bullied and alone and, if I was lucky, ignored, to looking like . . . like this.

I would never admit it out loud, but I look more

than good. The new Madison is supposed to be cool, daring and spontaneous. And I sure look like the new Madison.

A smile spreads over my face. I feel confident, like I can handle this party, like I can go out there and talk to people. Then I switch my bangles from my right arm to my left, because I don't want anybody to see my scar and ask about it.

The doorbell rings.

I gasp. *He's here!*

I laugh out loud, wondering how excited I'd feel if the guy ringing the doorbell was here for a date.

'It's not a date,' I tell myself quietly, looking the Madison in the mirror right in the eye. 'He's only asked me because he's a nice guy. It's not a date.'

I exhale sharply and then realize I've totally forgotten that Dwight is downstairs, waiting at the door, until Dad yells up, 'Madison! Your friend's here.'

I practically sprint down the stairs in case Dad embarrasses me – or Dwight. I don't want to look eager or anything, but seriously . . . When Jenna brought guys home, I saw how embarrassing my parents could be when they wanted – though they were usually pretty good. Even so, and even if Dwight is just a friend, I wasn't about to put either of us through that experience.

But Dad decides to embarrass me anyway and says, 'Shouldn't you go put some pants on with those, Madison?'

I clench my teeth, and suppress a blush. Over the years I got quite good at not letting my cheeks burn after being humiliated at school.

'And eleven-thirty curfew – I've got it,' I reply. Then I turn and shoot Dwight a smile, looking at him for the first time.

He's wearing khaki pants and a white T-shirt. It's not a fitted tee, so it makes him look even more gangly and thin – but not in a bad way.

He smiles his lopsided smile back at me. 'Ready to go?'

I nod. 'Yep.'

'Got your cell?' Dad asks me.

'Yes,' I say, kind of testily, because I just want to go.

'Good.' He turns to Dwight then and nods briskly. 'You kids have fun.'

'Bye, Dad,' I say, and move towards the open door. Dwight has to back up outside so I don't ram into him. I pull the door shut with one hand and then stop, looking at him and letting out a puff of air so my bangs fly off my face for a moment.

He laughs. 'It's almost like you're embarrassed by your father, Madison.'

'What?' I say, pulling a face like I haven't a clue what he's talking about. 'Wherever did you get that idea?'

He laughs and smiles at me again. 'Don't worry – he seems nice. I know my mom's the worst. She decided to show my friends baby pictures once. And I mean the kind of baby pictures that should stay gathering dust in the loft.'

I laugh, and remember when my parents did that to one of Jenna's boyfriends.

'Cool piercing, by the way. It suits you.'

'Oh, thanks!' I beam at him.

We start off down the sidewalk.

Walking next to him, I realize how much taller than me Dwight is. I'm a little on the short side, and since I lost the weight I'm kind of petite.

'Thanks for asking me to come tonight,' I say, filling the silence a little.

'No problem. I figured you might want to try and meet some people before school starts.'

I smile, grateful.

'It must be scary,' Dwight carries on as we turn a corner. 'To be starting a new school, I mean.'

I shrug. 'Can't be any worse than my last school.'

'What happened at your last school?'

I'm silent for a moment, beating myself up inside. I can't believe I just said that! How stupid can I get?

38

'Sorry,' Dwight says. I guess I paused long enough that he figured out it was a sensitive issue. 'I didn't mean to pry.'

'No, it's fine. Just . . . me and my big mouth,' I joke, and force a laugh. 'It's just that, um, I wasn't really . . . My school in Maine didn't exactly have the nicest people.'

'Oh.'

'I'm sorry. I didn't want to make things awkward. I just have a big mouth sometimes – it's my own fault.'

I'm babbling. I don't have a big mouth; I know when to shut up. I'm very good at shutting up. I'm also good at keeping my emotions bottled up inside. I'm extremely good at not having a big mouth. I'm talking total trash.

Dwight smiles, oblivious to what's going on in my head. 'It's fine, don't worry. I know the feeling – when you say something without thinking. I'll forget it if you want . . .'

I shake my head. 'I've said it now . . . it doesn't matter. So, anyway, how was your day?'

He chuckles, and then we talk. I've never really talked to people before, so it's weird how natural it feels with Dwight. He tells me about a rude customer and how the toaster nearly exploded; I tell him how my parents flipped when they saw I'd gotten a nose piercing, and how much I like Florida.

It doesn't take long to get to the beach. There are already a lot of people there, all around my age, and I'd guess all in high school. The sky isn't totally dark just yet, but it's getting there. The sun's still setting, and it throws red and pink and purple streaks across the rippling sea. I've never seen anything like it. If you removed the litter and driftwood, and the partying kids, it'd be even more of a breathtaking sight.

As it is, I don't spend very long gazing out at the gorgeous sunset. My attention is quickly drawn to the masses of people. There has to be something like a hundred kids here. Most of them are drinking. They're all talking and laughing, hanging out, some of them making out . . . The kind of thing I guess happens at parties.

And I'm scared.

Like, seriously quite terrified. I want to grab Dwight's hand, just to reassure myself that I'm not alone, I have a friend here, that everything will be totally fine. But I don't, because he's still walking and I've stopped in my tracks.

Before he notices I'm not beside him anymore, I hurry forward and fall into step with him again. I wring my wrists and flex my fingers; my hands are sweating.

My confidence from earlier is slipping away pretty

darn quick now. I'm scared I won't be able to talk to them. I'm scared they won't like me. I'm scared it'll be just like Pineford all over again.

'Hey,' Dwight says softly, all of a sudden, making me jump a little. 'You don't have to look so scared. They won't bite. Well, some of them might, but I'll warn you if any of them approach.'

I laugh, but there's a nervous ring to it. Dwight bumps his shoulder against mine, our arms pressing together, and smiles at me encouragingly. Somehow I smile back, and take a couple of deep breaths as we go towards a campfire.

There are logs arranged around it, and some kids are sitting on them, talking and drinking. One guy crumples an empty beer can, making me look over. He tosses it into the fire and then slings his arm around the girl next to him.

'Are any of your friends around?' I ask Dwight. I feel kind of bad, wondering if maybe he'll think he has to spend all night with me because I don't know anyone.

He's already scanning the party, though, and then I see his eyebrows lift when he spots someone. He raises a hand and then nods, and I guess whoever it is must've seen him too. I go up on my toes and crane my neck, trying to spot them, but I'm too late – there's no one waving over now.

'I'll be back in a sec,' Dwight tells me. 'Do you want a drink or anything?'

I shake my head. 'No, I'm fine, thanks.'

'I swear, I'm not ditching you,' he laughs, then grins at me reassuringly. 'See you in a minute.'

I let out a breath of laughter and say, 'Sure,' shooting a smile at him. I stare at his retreating back for a second or two, but then I feel stupid, standing here alone. I take a few steps towards one of the logs around the fire, and flop down onto it.

I fiddle with the zipper on my hoodie for a moment. It isn't cold, but I'm tempted to zip it up, just so I can feel like I have something to hide behind. I half wish that I hadn't cut all my hair off: I feel totally exposed.

My iPod is in my back pocket. I don't like to be without it. It was an extension of me the past couple of years when I was at my last school. I'm tempted to put in just the one earphone, but I can't. I *won't*. I refuse to give in so soon.

I clasp my hands together and rest them on my knees, staring at the fire. I know I should talk to someone, but who? Who are the 'right' people to know? Is sitting here alone waiting for Dwight to come back the wrong thing to do? Should I be mingling?

I decide to just wait till Dwight returns. It's safest. Easiest.

The chatter and laughter around me are so loud, but the crackle of the fire sounds louder. It feels hot on my face and neck, and my legs.

I don't even notice the guy until he speaks.

'Now, you can't just leave a pretty girl on her own at a party without a drink,' says a voice that's deep, friendly, and most definitely not Dwight's.

Chapter 5

I look up, and the guy who snuck up on me is holding out a red plastic cup. Then I realize that he is seriously hot. He's broad shouldered and tanned, and his hair is blond and a bit wavy. He has these chocolate-brown eyes and they're looking right at me.

Oh, and then I realize he called me pretty. And this is one occasion when I just can't stop a blush.

I eye the drink he's offering, while inside I'm kind of freaking out (in a good way) that this guy called me pretty, and I know I should try to flirt – because this hot guy is talking to me. *Me!*

Instead, I blurt, 'Didn't your mom ever tell you not to take things from strangers?'

Even as I am saying it, I know it's not the kind of thing I should say, but by then it's too late.

However, he laughs like I just made a good joke. Then he sits down beside me. I'm shocked, but so not complaining: for the first time in my life, a hot guy is choosing to sit beside me, laughing like I'm actually funny. He's starting to talk again, but without thinking I blurt out more words:

'Do you always use that pick-up line on girls?'

I want to slap myself in the face. Then turn to dust. I am just *such* an idiot!

'Only on the lonely ones,' he jokes, and winks at me. The blush rises in my cheeks again; I can't stop it. I gulp at how close he is to me, but my heart races at the thrill of having someone like him interested in me.

'I'm Bryce,' he tells me, and offers me the drink again. 'There. Now I'm not a stranger.'

I laugh, and this time I take the drink. I'm tempted to take a sip, but I know my parents would kill me – and besides, I don't even know what it is. I think it's cider, or beer, but who knows? So I don't. I just hold the cup.

Bryce. I bet he's, like, the quarterback or linebacker on the school football team or something. He just emits that kind of social standing – the confidence, the winning smile, the way he carries himself. It all screams Mr Star Football Player, and Mr Popular. It makes me wonder why he's sitting here, talking to *me*.

I wonder where Dwight is. Shouldn't he be back by now?

Then I realize that this guy, Bryce, is waiting for me

to give him my name, and I think, *I'm such a dork*. I must've paused too long, though, since he carries on.

'So where are you from, Lonely Girl? I haven't seen you around.' He says it like he knows everyone. And he probably does.

'Maine,' I answer. 'I'm from Maine.'

'Really? Oh. That's cool.'

'No, it's not. LA is cool. New York City is cool. Where I'm from, it's boring.'

He laughs again. 'I'll take your word for it. So you're gonna be coming to school at Midsommer?'

I nod. 'I'll be a junior,' I say, when Bryce doesn't fill my silence again.

'Cool. Maybe I'll see you around sometime.'

'Sure.'

Flattered as I am that this hot, obviously cool and popular guy is talking to me of all people, I feel like a complete and total dork.

I know they say 'be yourself' around guys, and 'never change for a man', or whatever. But the thing is, I don't really know how to be myself. I've hidden myself away for so long. This is my big chance, my once-in-a-lifetime opportunity to start over again. And I want people to like me. I want guys to ask for my number at a party. I want a busy social life. I want to have friends. I just don't know how to do it.

And I'm scared.

So I sit there, feeling like a dork, and give Bryce a smile, because a) I have no idea what to say now, and b) why not? I can barely believe it when he actually smiles back at me.

He even has dimples.

Of course he does. Go figure.

The firelight makes his teeth sparkle. I bet if the sun hit him just right, he'd be like some cheesy mouthwash ad.

'Hey, Bryce! Get over here, man! You've gotta check this out, it's totally gross!'

I follow the voice and so does Bryce. There's some tall guy with spiky hair waving him over: a group are clustered around something. They shuffle a little, and I catch sight of it for a moment. I think it's a jellyfish.

I stand up first, though, again wondering where Dwight is. He shouldn't have been gone this long, should he? What was he doing anyway?

'Nice meeting you,' I say to Bryce awkwardly, and start walking off, hoping I'll spot Dwight around somewhere.

'Wait,' I hear him call after me. 'I don't even get a name, Lonely Girl?'

'I think "Lonely Girl" is good enough for now,' I tell him. Not that I mean it to – but I bet if anybody else said it, they could make it seem like they were flirting. Bryce appears to think I *am* flirting, though, from the way he raises one blond eyebrow at me and smirks.

I just wave and say, 'Bye, Bryce.'

He's laughing when he calls out, 'I'll catch you around, Lonely Girl.'

As I walk away, I'm smiling inside and out. A rush of adrenalin and relief courses through me. I just talked to a hot, undoubtedly popular guy – and I didn't even make too much of an idiot out of myself. In fact, I think he may have even been flirting a little at the end there . . .

Probably not. But I like to think he was.

First Dwight being friendly, and now this guy, who was maybe flirting too. Things are really looking up for me already.

'Oh, hey, there you are!' I exclaim all of a sudden. I've been scanning the party, and now I run up to Dwight and push a hand into his shoulder – only playfully, though. He stops talking mid-sentence for a moment.

I take a quick look at the guy he's talking to – messy brown hair that sticks straight up in the air, defying gravity. It's not even gelled, I don't think. He's got glasses too, and he raises his eyebrows behind them, looking from Dwight to me, and back again.

'Hi,' I say, because there's a bit of an awkward pause. I smile at the guy with the gravity-defying hair. He looks a bit . . . I don't know, really. *Shocked* isn't quite the right word. *Stunned*, maybe. Yeah. He looks kind of stunned, before smiling back at me.

'Hi, Madison.' Dwight gives a smile, but it doesn't quite reach his eyes.

His friend clears his throat pointedly.

Dwight sighs and says, 'Madison, this is Andy. Andy, this is Madison. She just moved here from Maine.'

'Hello.' Andy smiles.

'Hi.'

'How do you know this guy, then?' Andy jerks his head at Dwight, who takes a sip of whatever he's got. It reminds me that I'm holding a drink too, and I haven't drunk any of it.

'I met him at the café.'

'Ooh, the *café*,' Andy says teasingly. When I give him a wondering look, he explains, 'We all call it the coffee shop. *Café* sounds posh. No offence. It just seemed kind of funny when you said it, is all.'

'Andy talks a lot when he's had a drink,' Dwight says matter-of-factly.

'Oh,' I laugh to Andy, and shake it off, but I know my cheeks are threatening to burn up a little.

49

'Um, so you, uh, you go to Midsommer High, right?'

Andy nods. 'Uh-huh. I guess that's where you're going.'

I nod. 'I'll be a junior.'

'Same as us, then!' Andy claps Dwight on the back. 'Cool. Hey, has Dwight introduced you to Carter yet?'

'Uh . . .' I shake my head.

'What? Oh, you've got to meet Carter. Come on – I think he was over there, last time I saw him.' Andy starts walking off, like he assumes we're following him.

I glance at Dwight. 'What's up?' I ask. I can't help but feel that somehow I've done something wrong.

'Huh?' He shakes his head slightly, a barely perceptible movement, and says, 'Come on, or we'll lose Andy.'

We catch up just before Andy has the chance to completely disappear into the crowd. There's a heck of a lot more people here now than there were earlier; it makes me wonder just how long I spent talking to Bryce.

'There you are.' Andy glances over his shoulder, then starts striding off through the crowd. Dwight and I hurry to chase after him.

When he suddenly stops, I actually run into him – like, bump right into his back and bounce off. Dwight catches me and gently pushes me back, but by then it's too late. My drink has already slopped all over me.

'Oh, shoot,' I mutter irritably, pulling at my soaked camisole. 'I hope whatever is in that cup doesn't stain . . .'

'Madison,' Andy says, oblivious to my mishap and gesturing to the skinny boy standing in front of him. 'This is William Maverick Carter.'

'It's just Carter,' William Maverick Carter tells me. He sounds a little embarrassed, and he can't quite make eye contact with me, but he smiles anyway.

He's not much taller than me, and his short mousy hair is a bit scraggly and uneven. I don't think I'm making the best impression, considering I'm covered in beer or something. I pluck at my top. Then I notice something: he only has one and a half eyebrows.

Like, he's actually missing half of his left eyebrow. I know I'm staring, and I know my jaw has dropped a bit, but I can't help it. It's not every day you see someone who's missing half an eyebrow.

And, because I'm oh so socially adept, I blurt out, 'What happened to your eyebrow?'

'I was saving an old lady's cat from a burning building,' Carter tells me, and now he looks me dead in the eye, very serious.

'Oh my gosh!' My free hand claps over my mouth automatically. 'Really?'

All of a sudden Dwight snorts with laughter. 'Carter! Seriously, you think anyone is going to buy that?'

'Well, *she* just did,' Carter defends himself, with a laugh. Then he looks back at me. 'Had you going for a minute there, didn't I?'

I'm not sure whether to frown or laugh, so I do some strange mixture of both.

'What happened to your top?' Andy asks me, only just noticing the wet stain.

'I spilled my drink.'

'Someone's clumsy,' he says, laughing. But he doesn't say it in a mean way, so I laugh too.

'Just a bit,' I admit sheepishly.

'So, Carter, this is Madison. She's Dwight's friend. She's from Maine. A soon-to-be junior like the rest of us.' Andy turns to me. 'Anything to add?'

I have a lot to add to that, I think. But I just grin and shake my head no, like I'm a totally normal, carefree teenager and this isn't my first party ever . . .

'Well, I'm Carter. I'm also Dwight's friend. And, uh, I'm from around here. Orlando, actually, but we moved here when I was about three years old.'

'Oh, cool,' I say. And I shift from foot to foot, then smile.

'I'm going to get another drink,' Dwight says, excusing himself.

52

Impulsively I hold up a finger to indicate 'one minute' to Andy and Carter, and say to Dwight, 'Hold on a sec – I'll come with you,' despite the fact that I have no intention whatsoever of getting a drink.

He doesn't stop, but I manage to catch up to him. 'Is everything okay?' I ask nervously.

He turns to me. 'What was Bryce talking to you about?'

I shrug. 'Just stuff, I guess.'

'*Stuff.*' I look at Dwight, and he's raising an eyebrow at me, one side of his mouth quirked up higher than the other so it's half a smile and half a smirk. 'Care to elaborate?'

I shrug again. 'Well, we just . . . talked.'

'About . . . ?'

'Why does it matter, anyway?'

I guess I come off as a bit snappy, because Dwight holds up his hand, palm out, as if in surrender. 'I'm just curious, is all. Bryce Higgins doesn't exactly have the, ah . . . the best reputation when it comes to girls.'

'Huh?'

Dwight shrugs. 'I don't know if any of it's true – it's only what I've heard. Rumors. You know, the usual high-school gossip that gets around. It's just that he's not really the *nicest* guy out there, from what I've heard. Could be wrong, but you can never be too careful.'

'What difference does it make? I was only talking to him.'

Dwight makes a noise that I think is a grunt, but it could be a sigh; it's some strange in-between thing. What with that, and the look he's giving me – the raised eyebrows and sympathetic expression – I get the impression he doesn't think Bryce is the kind of guy to 'only talk'.

And maybe he isn't. What do I know about guys? And for that matter, what do I know about Bryce? A few minutes' talking to him makes me an expert on what kind of person he really is?

'Watch it,' Dwight says all of a sudden, throwing an arm out to stop me. I stumble back, dropping the cup I'm still holding so that the contents slop over my feet and flip-flops.

'Darn it,' I mutter under my breath. Great. Now I will definitely stink of booze when I get home. I just hope my top and shoes aren't ruined.

Wow. I never thought I'd find myself thinking something like that.

I shake that off, though, and turn to Dwight. 'What did you stop me for?'

He nods at the ground. 'Jellyfish.'

I look down and, sure enough, there's a dead jelly-fish lying on the sand. I think it's what all those guys with Bryce were looking at, before. I wonder for a moment if it was alive when they found it, and they didn't do anything to help it out.

People are like that sometimes. They don't want to think about the consequences. And why should they? They're having fun. Sometimes they don't even realize somebody's in trouble until it's too late.

I stare at the dead, sand-covered jellyfish a heartbeat longer before going round it. Dwight falls back into step beside me, and tells me a little about his friends, making me laugh and smile. And when I'm laughing and smiling and chatting, it's almost like the old me never existed.

Chapter 6

Don't judge a book by its cover.

We all do it, I guess. You turn your nose up at the mangy cat by the dumpsters, or you think that guy, with his Prada suit and Rolex, and the BlackBerry clamped to his ear, is some snooty businessman who thinks he's better than you.

People know not to judge a book by its cover. But people also say it's important to make a good first impression.

Which is why I spend almost my entire weekend trying to decide what to wear on my first day of school.

The suburbs around here are all the higher end of middle class: big houses, pristine front lawns and shiny cars on the driveway. I get the feeling that a lot of the kids around here are rich. But Midsommer High is a public school.

I kind of wish it was one of those schools that made you wear a uniform. You know, where you have to pay, and the science teachers are all 'Doctor' or 'Professor'. At least then I wouldn't have to worry endlessly about what the heck I should wear.

I never used to worry. I mean, there was that one year when I did try, after I lost all the weight. I made an effort to look good, to show everyone that I wasn't Fatty Maddie anymore. Needless to say, it didn't work – nobody noticed, and if they did, they didn't care.

Monday morning, I get up an hour and a half before school, so I can do my hair and put on a little makeup, leaving loads of time to decide what to wear.

It's hot out, and humid. What're the other girls going to wear? What if I'm too dressed up? What if I'm not dressed up enough? What if what if what if?

Mom knocks on my door and pokes her head in. 'You're up early,' she says, but comes in and puts a mug of herbal tea on my nightstand.

'I have nothing to wear!' I cry in frustration, tugging at the ends of my hair.

Mom takes in the clothes I've thrown back into my wardrobe and the 'maybe' pile scattered over my bed . . . and she laughs.

I grit my teeth. She's so not helping!

Then she tells me, 'I never thought I'd hear you say that, Madison.' But she sounds almost . . . well, she sounds practically *proud* when she says it.

I just huff loudly, and turn back to my closet. Surely there's something in here that's perfect. There has to be. Something casual, but something that looks good.

'I'll leave you to it,' Mom says, backing out of the bombsite that is my bedroom. 'I have to leave for work in a minute. But make sure you clean this up before you leave.'

'Yes, Mom,' I say testily.

Before she leaves, though, she gives me a kiss on the cheek and squeezes my shoulder. 'You'll be fine, Dice – don't worry about it. You're a tough girl.'

I smile, but it's a sad kind of smile. 'Thanks, Mom.'

Dice has been my nickname since I was tiny. I couldn't say my own name, apart from the middle bit, which came out as 'Dice'. Kinda embarrassingly, it stuck.

I'm thirty-six minutes early.

Dad drops me off, because I don't really know the way – I might get hopelessly lost and turn up late on my first day.

But I'm genuinely shocked when I check the time on my cell phone and find out I'm so early. The gate across the main entrance is open, but as I walk up to the front door, there's nobody around.

There's a field on one side, with a whole bunch of

painted black wooden picnic benches. On the other side is a parking lot. There are a few cars there, but I guess most of them are the teachers'.

The gravel on the main path is uneven, and I teeter in my one-inch black stilettos. They're not excessively fancy or high, but I don't walk in heels. Even little ones. It's harder than I anticipated.

In the end, I opted for a pair of denim cut-offs and a white tank top. I'm wearing a delicate pink scarf too, just to add something to my outfit. I figured if it seemed too fancy, I could always take off the scarf.

I'm over-thinking it – I know, I know.

But I'm scared.

And when you're as scared as I am, it's hard not to be totally paranoid about every little thing.

I have an earphone in my left ear with my iPod in my pocket. I may be a heck of a lot happier and more confident here than I ever was in Pineford, but I'm still too insecure to go without my 'security blanket'.

Back in Pineford, I'd taken to wearing an earphone all the time, even in class. I wouldn't necessarily be playing music, but it just made me feel a little better. When I had music on, I could tune out the rest of the world, ignore the sneering, joking comments thrown my way, the people pushing into me.

I am determined not to have the earphone in all the

time here. But I need it right now. At least, just for this morning.

I let the guitar and bass and drums and vocals fill my ear. The music covers up how hard and loud my heart is pulsing.

I don't even know the car's there until the horn blares.

Jumping, I yank out my earphone and spin around. I barely even noticed I was walking in the middle of the road – I was just trying to stay on my feet in these darn heels.

'Didn't your mom ever tell you to look both ways before you cross the street?'

Just my luck. It's Bryce.

'Yeah,' I say, because he's waiting for a response. 'What's your point?' I automatically wince inside at my sarcastic response. Why do I have to be so blunt? Why am I such a complete dork around people? I wish I could just act cool for once in my life.

Bryce laughs, though, still leaning out of his window. I take a look at his car. It's silver, and really shiny. It's a convertible Lexus, and it looks like it cost a lot of money; but the rust on the front bumper and the scratches I notice on the door make me think it's second-hand.

'You're early,' he says eventually, after a long pause.

I stand there awkwardly, one hand clamping my bag to my shoulder, the other holding my earphone. I feel a blush start up, and I try to fight it back – though my heart is hammering erratically at actually being checked out. I retort, 'Guess so. Looks like I'm not the only one, though.'

Bryce twists in his car seat, looking behind him, and it strikes me that maybe he's not the sharpest tool in the box.

Or maybe he's just trying to be funny.

Either way, I blurt, 'I meant you, you know.'

'Yeah, I am a little early . . .' He laughs sheepishly, looking back to me. He's kind of adorable, I think distractedly. 'But, hey, at least I can show you around the school a little!'

'Uh . . .'

Come on, say yes! He's interested! Guys like him don't talk to girls like you unless they're interested! Say yes!

I smile. 'Yeah, sure, that'd be great!' I say it so fast he looks confused for a moment, trying to decipher what I've said. I bite the insides of my cheeks in annoyance.

'Awesome. I'll meet you by the steps at the front of the school.'

'Okay.' I get off the road so he can drive past, and once he's gone I carry on up to the doors.

Midsommer High is a big brick building, four stories high. I read on its website that it was built around the 1800s. Grey stone steps lead up to the huge wooden doors with big ornate black iron handles. The windows gleam in the early morning sunlight. It's pretty impressive – and totally intimidating.

I don't walk quickly, since I don't feel safe walking on the loose gravel in these shoes. I only make it to the bottom of the steps when Bryce is suddenly standing next to me.

'What're you listening to?' he asks as we head up. Before I can tell him, he's grabbed hold of my spare earphone. I try to yank it back, but I'm too late. He's already recognized the song.

'Jessie J?'

'It *was* My Chemical Romance,' I mumble. Louder, I say, truthfully, 'My sister bought the album and she—'

Before I can finish telling him that she snuck it onto my iPod and I actually found I liked one of her songs, Bryce cuts me off.

'Nothing wrong with a bit of mainstream, Lonely Girl.' He gives a hundred-watt smile that probably gets girls swooning over him. It sure makes my heartbeat pick up.

'Sure,' I reply sarcastically. 'Say that to the transfer from Maine.'

Bryce laughs again, realizing just how funny 'mainstream' is. 'Mainstream. I think I like that better than Lonely Girl. You still haven't told me your name, you know.'

'I know.'

I feel more than see him looking at me. Out of the corner of my eye I glimpse him smiling at me, amusement glimmering in his big brown eyes.

I actually feel kind of . . . kind of *cool*. Almost flirty. Like someone who knows how to talk to a guy like Bryce, Mr Popular.

I stop watching my feet carry me uncertainly up the steps and turn to smile at him; I open my mouth to say something when—

Smack.

I groan. 'Ouch . . .'

I knew I should've just worn flats to school. Darn heels!

I push myself up off my face, and check my nose for blood. I do *not* need a broken nose today!

Bryce's hands are on me – in the small of my back and at my elbow – supporting me as I get to my feet again. 'Are you all right?'

'Beyond humiliated,' I laugh shakily, still prodding my sore nose, 'but I think so . . .'

'You sure?'

'No.'

I say it so bluntly, we both laugh. I catch sight of his dimples again. I notice then that he's still holding me up – except now there's no reason for it, and I glance at his hand on my elbow. He has to get the hint, but he doesn't move away or drop his hand.

Bryce takes me to the office, telling me that everyone will get timetables for the year in their homeroom.

There's some middle-aged lady sipping coffee and sorting papers behind the desk we walk up to.

'Hi, Mrs Willis,' Bryce says pleasantly.

She looks up, startled, and then smiles. 'Hello, Bryce. How was your summer?'

'Not too bad,' he says politely. 'This is, um . . . a new student. Transfer from Maine?'

'Madison,' I tell the lady quietly when she looks at me. 'Madison Clarke.'

'Oh, yes, I know! I'll be back in a minute,' she says, smiling encouragingly – I guess I must look a bit shy, or nervous. 'I just have to find your transcript and make sure everything's in order.'

'Okay,' I reply. She walks off into the office and rummages through the filing cabinets, which clank and clatter noisily.

'So.' Bryce leans on the desk and twists

around, raising his eyebrows at me. 'Madison Clarke.'

'Yup.'

He holds my eye for a moment, and I look away, and run a finger over the shiny edge of the desk.

'I think I'll stick to Mainstream,' Bryce tells me, and I glance back up at him. 'It's cute.'

'Whatever floats your boat,' I say with a shrug, but my heart does a strange skittering thing in my chest, and I bite back a smile at the thought that I've got a nickname. Not a derogatory nickname, either. It is, like Bryce said, kind of cute.

'You seem pretty friendly with the secretary,' I carry on, nodding my head in the direction of the clanking filing cabinet.

He laughs sheepishly, and shifts his stance slightly. 'Yeah . . .'

'Care to elaborate?'

He laughs again. 'My stepdad's the school principal. How's that for family connections?'

'Oh. Guess the teachers can't give you too many detentions, then.'

Bryce laughs louder at that, shaking his head. 'I wish! Nah, my stepdad wouldn't stand for any of that special treatment stuff.'

'Oh. Right,' I reply awkwardly, not knowing what sort of response I'm supposed to give.

'All right! Here you go, Madison.' Mrs Willis reappears behind the desk with some papers in a neat pile for me. She staples a couple together before putting them back in the pile and pushing them across the desk.

'So here you've got your class schedule . . . And a map of the school. This is a list of all the extra-curricular activities, in case you're interested, and the school rules . . . And your locker combination.'

'Okay.'

'Bryce, will you show Madison around? Or at least to her homeroom?' Mrs Willis asks. To me, she adds, 'I'm sure you'll make friends, no trouble, and someone will be able to show you to your next class if you need help.'

I nod, but I'm feeling pretty dubious about the whole 'make friends, no trouble' part.

I scan my schedule, just to see what subjects I've been given: Art and Photography, Algebra II, French, English Literature, AP World History, Gym, Biology and—

'Oh, crud,' I whisper.

'What?' Bryce asks.

'Is something wrong?' Mrs Willis turns back to me curiously.

'Yeah, I have a slight problem . . .' I put my schedule back on the desk and turn it around so she can see. 'AP Physics.'

'Yes,' she says, nodding. 'On your transcript it said—'

'No, you don't understand,' I interrupt. I can feel panic beginning to settle in the pit of my stomach. 'I don't do Physics. I barely scraped a B last year. I can't do AP Physics.'

The secretary frowns, and then says, 'Two minutes . . . I'll see if there's space in any other classes at that time.'

'It'll be fine,' Bryce tells me. 'There's bound to be something else they can fit you into, don't worry.'

I gnaw on my lower lip. I can't do Physics – let alone AP Physics. I'll fail class. I'm not the smartest person, but I promised myself I'd put in the effort here. Problem is, I don't think I can even pass AP Physics, no matter how much effort I put in.

If Bryce says anything else to comfort me, I don't hear him over the blood rushing in my ears. I don't hear anything until the secretary clears her throat. But it's an ominous kind of throat-clearing, like she's preparing to give bad news.

'I'm sorry, Madison, it looks like there was a mix-up

on your transcript. The only other classes I could fit you into at that time are AP Trigonometry and American History, but you're already taking History, and—'

'I got a C in Trig.'

'Well, I'm sorry, Madison, but there's really nothing I can do for you without redoing the entire schedule, and with most classes already oversubscribed ... I may be able to fix something up for next semester, though by then I'm not sure it'd be wise for you to switch ...'

I want to hyperventilate and freak out and insist that she works out my class schedule somehow so I don't have to take AP Physics (or Trigonometry), no matter how long that will take or how busy she is, but I don't do any of that.

Instead, I take a deep breath, I smile politely and say, 'That's okay. Thanks anyway.'

I start walking off, and a moment later Bryce falls into step with me. 'Damn,' he says. 'That sucks.'

'Mm. Whatever. There's not much I can do about it now, so no point in making a fuss.'

Bryce laughs. 'You're a very strange person, you know.'

'Is that bad?'

He stops walking, and so I stop walking too. He

considers me for a long moment, just looking at me with a small smile playing across his lips that just hints at his dimples. I stand there staring right back into his eyes, like I'm fearless and confident and not still freaking out inside about AP Physics.

'No,' he said. 'It's definitely not a bad thing.'

Chapter 7

School seems to get very busy very quickly, with hordes of students pouring through doors and along corridors.

Bryce and I haven't reached my locker yet. Other kids are filling the hallway rapidly; the sound of excited chatter and laughter bounces off the walls. Lockers clatter open, but most people just lounge against them and catch up with friends.

It's the kind of scene I've seen every year. Everyone's excited to see their friends again, to talk and exchange stories and laugh and joke. And every year I'd stand by my locker and scroll through songs on my iPod, trying to look occupied, and remaining pointedly oblivious to everything going on around me.

Now, though, my earphones aren't in, and I'm with someone who is willing to talk to me. I feel lost. And I'm getting kind of claustrophobic.

I can't help it: at the familiar sight of a hallway full of lockers and kids on the first day back at school, I freeze up. Even if I am in a whole different state, the scene is all too raw. I remember that first day back at school when Jenna wasn't there anymore.

I'd been running late to homeroom. I'd been so nervous about the first day back, without my older sister looking out for me, I had hidden out in the bathrooms, locked in a toilet cubicle. I didn't care if I got a tardy mark on the register; I just wanted to avoid people.

It hadn't worked.

I was bumped into my locker, an elbow digging into my spine. 'Watch it,' said the guy who barged into me.

I shouldn't have said anything. I didn't mean to say it aloud, really, but I muttered, 'You could've gone around me. You don't have to walk right through me.'

Unfortunately they heard me. Some girls started giggling. I didn't care who the guy was, because they were all the same. Bullies. I caught a glimpse of the letterman jacket, though, telling me it was a jock. Of course it was.

'Go around you?' he said, laughing in a way that made my stomach churn. I was glad I hadn't eaten any breakfast, so I had nothing to throw up. 'Pretty hard to do when you're taking up the whole freakin' corridor, Fatty Maddie.'

My cheeks almost flamed, but I kept my gaze fixed

on my locker, taking steadying breaths. I wouldn't let them see how much they got to me. I wouldn't. That was what egged them on – tears wouldn't help me now, and they'd certainly gain me no pity from anyone.

'Oink, oink,' he snorted, imitating a pig. I cringed, and balled my hands into fists. My one earbud wasn't enough to drown them all out, oinking and snorting at me, trying to get some kind of reaction. When they saw that I wasn't about to burst into tears, they gave up, and sauntered past. Shoulders and elbows dug into my back, and one hooked a foot around mine, so that I fell forward against my locker. I was on the verge of hyper-ventilating. All I wanted to do was run to the bathrooms, or maybe home. But I didn't. I collected some books I'd left over the summer, closed my locker door, and put in my other earbud, turning up the volume on my iPod.

Now, I am overwhelmed by the urge to flee to the bathrooms, or maybe even our new home.

I don't.

I take a breath and fall back into step beside Bryce, who is greeting people and hasn't even noticed I've lagged behind.

'Bryce! Hey, man, how's your summer been?'

'Yo, Bryce!'

'Hey, Bryce!'

I expect him to ditch me and talk to these people, but all he does is nod and call hello back, saying he'll catch them later. He stops at what I assume is my locker. Since I don't have anything to put in it, I don't bother to open it.

The bell goes, and the throngs of kids start to disperse to homeroom.

Bryce looks at my schedule and then says, 'Up the stairs and take the corridor on the left. Room 27B.'

'Um, okay . . .'

'You don't sound very sure,' he laughs.

'I'm not.'

'Do you want me to walk you there?' he offers.

'N-no,' I stammer, and then someone bumps into me and I lose my balance, toppling over into the lockers. I gulp. 'No,' I repeat. 'It's fine.'

Bryce grabs my forearm. 'Come on, I'll walk you there.'

I let him guide me towards a staircase off the hallway. The crowds thin out as we go up the stairs and turn down the corridor, and he stops as we reach 27B.

'This is you.'

'Thanks,' I say, a rush of relief spreading over me. 'Seriously, I really appreciate it.'

'No problem. Hey, I'll, uh, catch you around later, yeah?'

He shoots another of his grins at me, and I find myself grinning right back at him. 'Sure. Yeah. Thanks again.'

'Anytime, Mainstream.' There's a chuckle in his voice when he says that, and then he walks back the way we just came. As I turn around to watch him go – though I'm not entirely sure why – I find that there's a girl standing right behind me.

The first thing I think is how intimidating she is. It's in her stance – one perfectly manicured hand on her hip and the other hanging gracefully at her side, with one hip tipped to the side, head held high – and in the way she looks. This girl somehow manages to make a pair of cut-offs and a plain tank top look like something from a fashion magazine; I look more like I'm lounging around the house.

My second thought is how pretty she is – the kind of pretty that girls are jealous of, while wanting her for a friend. She's got deep brown skin, and big brown eyes, and her face is soft and round so she looks like a doll. I get the vibe that, whoever she is, she's popular.

'How do you know Bryce?' Even her voice rings with the haughty tone of the elite crowd.

'Um . . . I, uh, I met him at the – at the party at the beach . . .' I stutter, and gulp hard.

I can't tell if she's mad that I was talking to Bryce, or if she's just curious.

'You're new, aren't you?' This time, her voice is softer, more amicable.

I nod, and swallow the rising lump of anxiety in my throat.

Then the unexpected happens: her face breaks into a wide smile and she says, 'I'm Tiffany.'

'Madison.'

'Where're you from?'

'Maine. I moved here over the summer.'

'Cool.'

'It's really not,' I say. 'I don't know why everyone thinks that.'

She laughs, and flicks her hair over her shoulder before hitching up her handbag. I think it's a designer bag. I try to see the metal clasp on the front – I'm pretty sure it's Gucci.

Tiffany notices me looking at it, and she smiles again, twisting around so that I can see it better. 'You like? I got it in Milan in July. It's the real thing, before you ask. Late birthday present from my aunt.'

'I don't doubt it,' I tell her honestly. I wouldn't be surprised if everything from her earrings to her jeans is expensive and designer. She nods her head at me.

'Cool piercing. It's cute. Especially with your hair. It's, like, so punk-rock. Totally chic.'

'Oh.' I grin widely, flattered by her compliment – and also relieved that the nose piercing and getting my hair cut was totally worth it. 'Thanks.'

All of a sudden we hear a throat being cleared, and we both look around to see a teacher standing with his arms crossed and gray eyebrows raised at us.

'Are you planning on coming into homeroom any-time today, ladies?'

'This is Madison,' Tiffany says, in a bubbly, bright voice, grabbing my arm like we're old friends. 'She's new.'

'Ah, I see. Well, Madison,' the teacher addresses me, 'let's not make a bad impression on your first day by dawdling outside classes, shall we?'

'Sorry,' I say quietly, ducking my head a little. I never got in trouble back at Pineford – but then again, I never really did anything at all back in Pineford. But I don't want to make a habit of annoying any teachers this year, even if I am the new Madison.

The classroom is full of enthusiastic chatter, which hushes slightly as I walk into the classroom with Tiffany right behind me. It's not the hideous, pregnant pause I'd expected. No staring, or whispered remarks, or sneers. There's just a lull in the conversation: people looking at me and wondering who I am. The thing I hate most is them looking at me; it makes my heart thud against my ribs sickeningly. But then the chatter picks back up and I'm not so much of a focus point anymore.

'Tiff! Over here!' a girl calls brightly, and I look over to see her pulling out a desk chair in the middle of the classroom. There's an empty desk in front of it too.

'Come on . . .' Tiffany walks past me, beckoning. She falls gracefully into the seat pulled out for her, next to a blonde girl. I follow, but slowly, hesitantly. My legs are shaky, and they feel unsteady. The heels definitely aren't doing me any favors so far.

'This,' Tiffany announces, her voice loud and clear enough to carry across the whole class, even though she's only talking to the blonde girl, 'is Madison. Madison, this is Melissa.'

'Uh, hi,' I say, and give her a smile.

Melissa has perfect curls and sun-kissed skin, and she's dressed almost as well as Tiffany. I'm a little jealous that they make casual look so . . . so *wow*.

She looks me up and down, and I can see her taking in every detail. I'm suddenly super-aware of the fleck of mud on the front of my shoes, and I sit down on the chair at the desk in front of Tiffany, but stay facing them.

'Hi,' Melissa says. 'Welcome to Midsommer High. Home of the Hounds.'

'Right, everyone,' says the teacher. I turn back around in my seat. 'I have your class schedules here. Hand these out,' he tells the boy closest to him, setting down a pile of papers.

The boy sighs and gets up to give everyone the schedules. People immediately start comparing, and either grumbling about their teachers or sighing in relief that their schedules are all A-okay.

Lucky for some.

I just sit there until the bell rings for first period, wondering exactly how I ended up sitting in homeroom with what must be two of the most popular girls in school, with AP Physics on my timetable.

I can't decide if the new Madison's life is going to suck, or turn out seriously awesome.

Chapter 8

I make it through the entire morning without falling on my face again, at least.

When I walk into Art and Photography third period, I see the familiar sight of scraggly, mousy brown hair and one and a half eyebrows amidst the circle of easels and the tables set up with vases of flowers or bowls of fruit, ready for a still-life drawing.

'Carter!' I all but bound across the classroom towards him. In the process, I bump into a table with a wooden bowl containing two apples and some grapes. I hop, trying to keep my balance, and manage to save the table and an apple. Everything else falls to the floor.

'Sorry,' I mumble, and duck my head – but of course, I no longer have the long curtain of hair to hide behind. I feel so exposed: everyone who's already in class is looking at the strange new girl who just destroyed a display.

I hear a chair scrape and footsteps head towards me as I pick up the grapes. The person kneels down to grab the bowl and the other apple for me.

'Way to make an entrance,' Carter says.

'How many people saw that?' I mumble, shaking my head at myself as he sets down the bowl and I add the grapes and the apple.

'Pretty much the whole class. Miss Augustan isn't here yet, though, so you're safe.'

I pick at the grapes, shifting them so that they sit better, before I follow Carter back to his seat. I take the easel next to his.

'How's your first day so far?' he asks me.

'Um, okay, I think.'

'Made any friends?'

'I think so. There're some girls in my homeroom who seem nice. Tiffany and Melissa?' I say their names like a question, because I want him to tell me about them.

'Whoa . . . wait.' Carter turns his whole body to face me. 'Tiffany? As in, Tiffany Blanche?'

'Um, I think so . . . Dark hair, really pretty . . .'

I trail off, because Carter looks shocked. And slightly confused. There's no other way to describe that expression: wide eyes, furrowed brow, mouth half hanging open, like he's deciding whether or not to say something to me.

'Why? What's—'

Before I can finish asking my question, and before Carter can say anything about Tiffany, someone claps their hands together, and a musical voice rings out, 'All right, class, settle down, settle down! Another new year lies ahead, and I'm expecting great things from you all!'

Miss Augustan is tall and willowy, with long wavy hair. She's wearing jeans and a paint-flecked white T-shirt – her clothes don't really scream teacher.

She looks around with a big smile, taking everyone in, and pauses at me. 'You're new, aren't you?'

'Yup.'

'Name?'

'Madison. Um, I mean, Madison Clarke.'

Miss Augustan nods. 'Do you do much Art? Photography? PhotoShop?'

'Not really. I guess I liked it in my old school, though.'

'Good enough for me,' she says brightly. 'Welcome to my class, Madison. Okay, everyone, we're going to break y'all in easy this year. I set up fruit bowls and vases. Paint them. Draw them. Abstract, watercolor, pastels, biro – anything at all! Whatever and however it takes your fancy! But at the end of this double period, I want your interpretation of one of those displays on that canvas!'

There's a heartbeat of silence before the class bubbles with conversation and the clatter of pens and pencils and paints being taken out.

I look at the small desk beside my easel. There's a paint pallet of about a dozen colors, a couple of black biros, varying grades of B and HB sketching pencils, a couple of paintbrushes and an eraser. My hand lingers over them before I pick up a biro.

I don't start to draw, though; I twirl the biro around my fingers a couple of times, and then I turn in my seat to look at Carter, who's drawing a green curve with a pastel.

'So,' I say pointedly. 'About Tiffany?'

Carter sighs. His hand pauses, but he doesn't turn towards me. 'Tiffany Blanche,' he tells me, 'is more or less the Queen Bee of the school. If she were a senior, that would be indisputable. She's . . .' His mouth twists like he's finding it hard to pick the right words. 'She's . . . bitchy, but most of the time she puts up a front as a nice person. Like, she smiles at everyone in the corridor, but you know it's a front. Which is the worst part, because then you feel bad for hating her. But she's got her place in this school and that's where she likes to stay, just like the rest of them. The rest of *us*,' he corrects.

I know what he means, and I nod. But then I reply,

'She seemed really nice when I spoke to her. I mean . . .
she was talking to *me*.'

'Then you've got your place now too,' he responds,
not unkindly. He gives me a small smile to soften his
words.

'If she was talking to you,' he carries on, 'then I'd
suggest you don't talk to me. One of her *minions* might
see you.' His ominous tone makes me throw my head
back and giggle. But he just stares at his canvas, slowly
forming an apple, without even a hint of humor in his
face.

'What're you talking about?' I ask, a little nervously.

Carter shrugs his shoulders. 'Do you need me to
bring out the dictionary definition of "minion", or are
you okay on that?'

'No,' I say, frowning in confusion. 'I just – I don't
understand.'

'What's there to understand?' he says. 'Like I said, if
you want to be friends with Tiffany, stop talking to me.'

'But *why*?'

'I don't think you really need me to answer that,
now, do you?' Finally he turns his head, and the look on
his face is still grave, but there's something sad about it.
Almost pitiful. 'You're a smart girl, Madison.'

And then I twig: Tiffany's pretty much the most
popular girl in school, from the sound of it. Carter is

probably not the kind of guy who hangs out with the popular crowd. And if I want in with the popular crowd, and Tiffany, then I don't want to be around Carter.

But I don't know anyone else in this class, and I don't know if any of Tiffany's friends are here. And anyway, I kind of like Carter. He seemed like a nice guy when I talked to him at the party.

So I say to him, 'How exactly did you lose half of your eyebrow?'

He laughs a little, but there's still that pity in his eyes when he shakes his head at me. 'My fourteen-year-old cousin had a blowtorch and decided to get all up in my face with it.'

'Oh, ouch,' I reply, and turn back to my work.

After a couple of minutes Carter says, 'You know, the blowtorch incident isn't true.'

Slowly I turn my head and stare at him, my eyes narrowing a little. 'I've fallen for your fake stories twice now.'

There's a smirk on his face, and he laughs at me. 'I know. I'm very convincing.'

'Are you ever actually going to tell me the truth?'

'Nope.'

'Why not?'

'Because it's not half as cool as the other stories.

Plus, it's damn hilarious when someone believes it. Like you did.'

'Ha ha.'

But then I laugh too, and we only stop laughing when Miss Augustan suddenly appears behind us.

'Some may say that laughter is the music of the soul,' she tells us, 'but it's not helping your productivity.'

'Sorry,' I mumble, and she says, 'Mm,' before wandering off to look at other people's work.

Carter catches my eye, though, and I bite my lip hard. He snickers, and I concentrate on my biro sketch, trying not to laugh again. I don't want to get into trouble on my first day. Face-planting on the steps in front of Bryce was bad enough.

As I'm leaving class, someone cries out, 'Madison!' and I whirl around to see Tiffany at the far end of the corridor, with a few other people. She waves me over with a smile, and I hesitate uncertainly, but then I head towards her.

I'm not entirely sure why I'm so nervous; Tiffany seemed friendly enough in homeroom. My palms turn sweaty, and my hands are trembling, but my chin is up and I put on a casual sort of smile, like I'm totally confident.

'Hey,' I say, mostly to Tiffany, since I don't know any of the others. There's a tall, lean guy with dark spiky hair, an arrogant look on his face. The other two guys have dark brown hair; one of them has an arm slung around a slim redheaded girl.

'Everyone, this is Madison,' Tiffany announces, waving one of her French manicured hands in my direction. Seeing her pristine nails makes me very aware of my own bitten ones, and I curl my fingers up a little, self-conscious.

'Madison, this is Kyle, Adam, Marcus, and Summer.'

She points to each of them when she says their name. The redhead is Summer, and the guy with his arm around her is Marcus. Kyle is the one with black hair and the smirk, and Adam is the other guy. I now notice that Adam and Kyle are wearing identical letterman jackets – it tells me instantly that they're footballers or something for the school team.

'Hey,' they all say, in terrifying unison.

'Hi,' I reply, hitching my bag higher onto my shoulder.

I'm saved from an awkward pause when a voice that's already all too familiar calls out, 'Yo, guys, there you are! I've been looking all over for you.' Then, as he comes closer, he adds, 'Aw, look at that, Mainstream – making friends already.'

Chapter 9

'Hey, Bryce,' Tiffany says, flicking her hair back.

'So you guys met Madison,' Bryce says, nodding at me.

'Yeah,' Summer says. 'How'd you know her?'

'We met at the beach party,' he answers. 'What's up?'

Kyle says, 'Nothing new.'

Tiffany says, 'Ann-Marie Thompson totally hooked up with Jason Wills over the summer, even though she was still dating Sam. Like he was never gonna find out. They broke up,' she added, as an afterthought.

'I don't suppose you guys know anyone else doing AP Physics?' I ask hopelessly, partly because I feel I should contribute to the conversation, and partly because I think it'd be nice to know *somebody* in the class.

Kyle and Tiffany laugh. 'No way,' Kyle tells me. 'Sorry, Madison, think you're gonna be alone in a sea of nerds in that class.'

It's the way he says 'nerds' that makes me frown a little. Like it's a bad thing. Like he means it in a derogatory way.

'The worst thing about being in a sea of nerds is that I'm definitely going to flounder,' I say, instead of asking him what's so bad about being a nerd. In my mind, 'nerd' always seemed synonymous with 'smart'.

They laugh, though. 'Loving that pun,' Adam tells me, and the silent guy, Marcus, nods appreciatively. Even if I was going to voice my thoughts to Kyle, the bell rings, meaning the ten-minute break between classes is over.

Tiffany links her arm through mine. 'Biology next, right?'

'Um, yeah. Right,' I say. To the others I add, 'Bye.'

'I'll see y'all at lunch!' Tiffany calls as we all start to head separate ways.

We're halfway down the hall when she sighs and says, 'So. *Bryce.* What's the deal with you guys?'

'I'm sorry – *what*?'

'You know . . .' She laughs, and bumps my shoulder. 'You guys talked at the party, and he walked you to homeroom this morning . . . And what was it he just called you then?'

I think for a second. 'Mainstream?'

'Yeah, that. So what's the deal? Do you *like* him?'

'What? Oh, no! No, we're – we're just friends. I mean . . .'

I trail off when Tiffany laughs again. She says, 'All right, well, I'll ask you this: do you think he's cute? C'mon, be honest with me now.'

'Well . . . yeah. I mean, of course he's cute.'

'He's the star soccer player for the school, you know,' she informs me. 'He's on the football team too, but soccer's the big thing here.'

'Oh, okay. Well, that's cool.'

But in my head I think, *Duh. Like I didn't already guess he was Mr Big-shot Jock?*

'He's totally going to end up with a soccer scholarship too.'

'Really?'

'Mm-hmm, everyone says so.' She pauses. 'And I think he's pretty interested in you.'

We walk into a room I assume is our biology classroom, and it looks like nearly everyone's already there, but the teacher hasn't started yet. Tiffany guides me towards a lab bench with a couple of empty spaces, and I sit down next to a girl who's doodling in her notebook. Out of the corner of my eye I see her glance up at us, then shuffle over to make a little more room.

I laugh in response to Tiffany. 'Yeah, right. I barely know the guy. He's not interested in me.'

Tiffany smiles like she's holding onto a secret that only she knows. 'Whatever you say, Madison, whatever you say.'

I give a careless kind of laugh. Meanwhile, my mind races, trying to process everything. Because a) Tiffany, one of the most popular girls in school, seems to be my friend. And she introduced me to her friends, which should mean that b) I may actually be part of the elite clique, and that's something I'd never even have considered before. I just wanted to make friends here, and not be miserable and lonely. Being one of the popular crowd wasn't part of my plan.

And then there is the small matter that c) Bryce, who from the sound of things is Mr Popular and quite possibly considered the cutest guy in school, could be interested in me. At least, according to Tiffany. And that seems totally crazy to me. He's out of my league, and I don't expect him to be interested in me.

I'd like him to be interested, of course.

But I don't think he is.

And frankly, I'd rather not get my hopes up.

For the next forty minutes Tiffany tells me everything and anything about all her friends. She, Summer and Melissa have been best friends since third grade.

Marcus, who I met earlier, is the 'strong, silent type'. And totally loved up with Summer – they've been dating for fifteen months now. 'It's so totally adorable,' Tiffany gushes. The last of the guys they usually hang out with is Richard. 'But everyone calls him Ricky.'

The teacher shoots us a glare before carrying on explaining the PowerPoint presentation about natural selection we're supposed to be taking notes on. Mine are disjointed and I know I've missed some stuff as I listen to what Tiffany's telling me.

I'd wanted to try and focus on my schoolwork here, but right now I don't really care that I'm not paying attention. I'm flattered Tiffany wants to be friends with me – it seems like an easy pathway right to the summit of the high-school social hierarchy. I don't want to mess it up. And they seem like nice people, taking me in without question like this. Besides, it's not like I can afford to turn down the offer of friendship. And I know better than anyone that it's best to stay on the right side of the popular kids.

Once the teacher turns back to the projector screen, Tiffany rolls her eyes and carries on, lowering her voice only a little. 'Of course, we'll hang out with the rest of the jocks – and the rest of the squad, but—'

'What squad?' I interrupt.

She arches her eyebrows slightly. 'Oh, did I forget to mention? Cheerleading squad. Every Tuesday. Coach managed to free up the afternoons.'

'Ah,' I say, nodding. *Of course they're cheerleaders.* 'Can I take a wild guess here, and say you're head cheerleader?'

Tiffany laughs loud enough to have the teacher turn around. 'Miss Blanche, please.' Then he goes back to teaching.

'Sadly, no. Seniors only. Ditto for vice head cheerleader. But I've got a pretty good shot at it next year, Coach told me.'

'Cool.'

I'm really glad Tiffany is being nice to me, but it makes me anxious. Like, what if I do something to mess it up? I'm not the best person when it comes to social skills. I cannot afford to screw this up.

I know there's that reputation popular people have: that they're shallow, and conceited, and self-centered. But I know it's not always true; Jenna wasn't like that. Not everyone fits the mold. I'm giving these people the benefit of the doubt.

Ambling out of the biology lab, Tiffany leads the way to the cafeteria. There's the usual hustle and bustle of kids trying to grab their food and get a seat. There are two queues, one at each side: one for salad and sandwiches, the other for a hot meal – looks like today is taco day.

Tiffany heads for the salad queue. I'm not surprised that this is the shorter of the two lines. I stand there too, but I'm not hungry – all the anxiety that's been building up has made my stomach feel unsettled. I know I should eat something, though, since I was way too nervous for breakfast, so when we get to the counter I grab an oatcake and a banana.

Tiffany, much to my surprise, has a can of (full fat) soda, a BLT sandwich and a Three Musketeers bar. She turns to me and says, 'Don't tell me that's your lunch.'

'Um, yeah.'

'Seriously?' She goes kind of bug-eyed when I nod my head.

'Well, what about you?' I say, nodding at hers. I would've thought – and call me stereotypical – that the future captain of the cheerleading squad would at least eat a healthy lunch.

'Oh, this?' She laughs. 'This is nothing. Seriously, my metabolism is so high, I could eat a Big Mac every lunch time and keep this figure. Well – with a little exercise. But that's totally covered anyway.'

'Lucky,' I say – and I say it enviously, but if she notices she doesn't let on; instead, she just laughs good-naturedly. I start to think she's really not the horrible, conceited kind of popular girl. She's nice.

'Summer! Marcus!' she hollers, holding her tray in

one hand and waving across the canteen with the other.

I recognize a guy from earlier – Kyle – coming over. Bryce joins us, along with Melissa, and some guy I haven't met yet. I think he's Richard – or Ricky, I suppose – since he seems to be the only guy I haven't been introduced to yet.

I follow them all across the huge cafeteria, feeling like the black sheep in the herd. I know people are looking over – at me. I hate it. I'm itching to get out my iPod – but I don't want them to think I'm antisocial or anything.

As we all drop into seats – with me on the end, opposite Ricky and next to Melissa – I get the feeling that this lunch hour is going to seem very long. I fiddle with the strap on my bag, and keep tucking a strand of hair behind my ear. I'm totally flattered and more than a little excited that I'm at the 'cool table' with the popular kids, practically one of the elite. But I have no idea how to act, what to do, what to say, and it feels so surreal. Dream-like. It's just not right.

I mean, come on. I'm Fatty Maddie. The outcast, loner, weirdo girl from Pineford. I can change the way I look, but seriously, things like this are only supposed to happen in movies. They don't *actually* happen in real life. I'm literally expecting Ashton Kutcher to jump out and tell me I've been Punk'd.

'Madison?' someone prompts as I nibble my oatcake.

I jump, realizing they've all been talking and I've not been listening. 'Huh? Sorry – totally zoned out.'

'Cheerleading tryouts? Are you up for it?' Tiffany asks.

'Come on,' Melissa says. 'It'll be so cool!'

'Plus,' Tiffany adds, 'you're little. I bet you'd be really easy to throw around.'

I actually snort. It's a proper snort – the kind that nobody should ever hear you do. But I can't help it, honestly. The thought of me, cheerleading . . . Me being part of the popular clique is ridiculous enough, but me at cheerleading tryouts?

As if.

'Um, no,' I say bluntly, my voice flat and unequivocal. 'No way in heck will you ever get me doing *that*.'

There's a moment of silence.

Bryce is the first to break it. 'Why not? What's wrong with cheerleading?'

'I didn't say there was anything wrong with it,' I tell him, breaking off a piece of oatcake and popping it in my mouth. 'It's just not for me, at all.'

'Too mainstream?' He puts a teasing emphasis on the word *mainstream*, which makes me bite back a smile and lean forward to look down the table at him.

'Ha ha,' I say, laying the sarcasm on thick. 'So anyway, what's everyone got after lunch?'

I say it to shift the focus off me; it works.

I'm right about it being a long lunch hour. I'm so nervous and fidgety, time passes all the more slowly. About fifteen minutes before the bell is due to go, we all begin to get up, grabbing the remnants of our lunches and the trash.

What happens next is a blur.

'Whoa,' says Kyle loudly. I recognize the two people he is talking to in a heartbeat. 'Watch where you're going next time.'

I just stand there, my mouth open in a small circle, as I stare at Andy and Dwight. Andy has something wet all over his green sweater – I assume it's orange soda from the open can he's holding.

'Gee, thanks,' Andy says sarcastically, muttering it more than saying it to Kyle's face, and he pulls at his sweater. 'Jackass.'

Most of our little group have gone; it's just Kyle, Adam and me. I stay rooted to the spot.

'Get a life, losers,' Kyle mutters, purposely barging into Dwight, with Adam following.

'Get some brain cells,' I hear Dwight retort under his breath.

Then he catches my eye. I don't know what it is, but there's something in his expression I really don't like – something similar to his look at the beach party, after I'd spoken to Bryce. 'Uh,' I stammer. 'I – I have to . . . Bye.'

I hurry away. I have this sick, twisting feeling in my stomach; I know I should've said something, done something, told Kyle to shut up, or at least stayed and talked to Dwight. I haven't seen him since the party – don't I at least owe him a 'hello'?

But no, I just scurry off after my new friends, because I genuinely don't know what to do. And for the next fifteen minutes or so, until the bell rings, all I can do is ponder what I should've done, and think about that awful expression on Dwight's face.

Chapter 10

Physics is three rooms away from where I had biology class earlier, so it's easy to find. But I still turn up late, dragging my feet because I'm so reluctant to go to AP freaking physics. The bell has already rung when I finally reach the door to Room 31: PHYSICS DR ANDERSON.

Pausing for a minute, I gulp slightly. My teacher's not just a Mr or Mrs Anderson. It's *Dr* Anderson. *Doctor*. Who is *so* going to give me detention for being late . . . Great. Detention on my first day – it just doesn't get any better . . .

I take a deep breath, and then sigh heavily as I push at the door.

Except it doesn't open.

I sigh again, this time a heck of a lot more frustrated, and jiggle the handle, twisting it, and finally shoving my shoulder into the door. And, of course, when I do that, it flies open. Typical.

Today is really just going totally *swell*.

I fly into the room, clutching the door handle so I don't fall on my face for the second time. In the sudden silence my heels sound unnervingly loud on the laminate tile flooring.

'Late, as well,' says a voice. It doesn't sound too pleased, either. 'Miss . . . Clarke, isn't it?'

'Um . . .' I pry my shaky fingers off the door handle. It's stupid, but my hands are trembling at the thought of a teacher being displeased with me. So I may not have been a model student in Pineford, but heck, I never got detention!

'Um, yes . . .'

The teacher looks like a Dr rather than just 'Mr', I think. His hair is thick and white, and his thin silver-rimmed glasses are perched on top of his head. He has a bony, crooked nose, and he wears a long white lab coat. 'You're late, Miss Clarke,' he repeats.

'Sorry,' I say, then add in an undertone, 'Nobody ever said I didn't know how to make an entrance, though . . .'

I say it quietly enough that I think he can't hear me, but a few people in the front row nearest me stifle a laugh, which makes me feel a little less nervous. However, even Dr Anderson chuckles – he must have superhuman hearing or something.

'Um, Dr Anderson?' I say, edging closer to his desk after pushing the door shut behind me. 'There was a mix-up with my transcripts . . . I'm not actually meant to be in this class.'

'Then what are you doing here?'

'Apparently there aren't any classes for me to move into.'

'Hmm. And how good are you at physics, Miss Clarke?'

'Not very.' I smile innocently, just to make it clear that I'm not being modest, I'm perfectly serious.

Dr Anderson closes his eyes, pinching the bridge of his nose like he's got a headache. 'Perfectly capable students and they can't fit them into the class – and no wonder, if they keep messing up schedules.' Then he says, in a louder voice, 'All right, Miss Clarke, you'll have to grin and bear this class for the time being.'

'I really don't think there's much chance of me being moved,' I tell him miserably.

He scans the classroom. 'Mr Butler, please make space at your desk. Miss Clarke . . .' He waves a hand for me to go sit down.

And at this, I suddenly see Dwight's head snap up. He doesn't so much as glance at me. 'But can't—'

'Mr Butler. Move.' The teacher looks back to me again. 'You'll have to try and muddle through, I'm afraid. I'll speak to the office at the end of the day and see if there's anything they can do, but I'm sure Mr Butler over there will help you out. Worst comes to worst, you'll have to think about extra classes, or a tutor.'

Then Dr Anderson claps his hands together. 'Now, after that lengthy interruption, back to the *matter* at hand . . .' He chuckles at his own joke.

I don't even listen to the rest of the 'matter at hand', though; I'm too busy making my way to my designated seat next to Dwight. He doesn't even acknowledge me as I drop onto the stool next to him.

'Hi,' I say quietly. I have to say something, just to fill that empty void. It feels so incredibly tense, and I'm not even entirely sure why.

Okay, okay! I *know* why. I should've said something to him at lunch time rather than stammering incoherently and running off.

But it stings: he was so nice and friendly to me the other day. Now he won't even answer me and say 'hi' back. Nor will he look at me, for that matter. So I try again: 'Dwight.'

'You know, some of us are trying to learn here.' He doesn't sound like the friendly, easygoing Dwight I met in the coffee shop. He sounds irritated. Not mad or snappy; it's more like I'm a pesky fly.

'Sorry,' I mutter. And I don't try to talk to him again.

It's not until we're told to discuss the answers on page 180 of the textbook that I speak to him again – and not about question 2a. Dwight reaches across to pull the textbook closer, and flips it open to the right page. I watch him for a moment before I blurt out the sentence I've been trying to perfect for the past twelve minutes:

'So what, you suddenly hate me now?'

I see his eyebrows go up a little, but he doesn't turn to look at me. Though he answers this time, at least.

'Right, because you were just being so friendly earlier, weren't you? Let's just be *best buds*.'

'What did you expect me to do?'

It's the only reply I can come up with, and I know it's a lousy one.

But I'm not about to tell him the truth, to explain myself. And how can I say that I didn't know what to do because I'm no good around people, that I chased after the people who wanted to be my friends because I didn't want to jeopardize my shot at actually *having* friends? I can't tell him that without giving him my life story and sounding like a complete loser.

And no way in heck is anybody here going to find out about Fatty Maddie. I won't let it happen.

Dwight shrugs in response to my rhetorical

question. 'I thought you were better than that, Madison.'

I don't need to ask what he means: he thought I was better than someone who would run off after the popular people instead of staying to at least say hi to him and Andy.

But the only reply I can come up with is: 'Well, I guess we can't all be perfect, can we? Or geniuses at Physics.'

'Don't expect me to do your project for this semester for you.'

'I didn't ask you to,' I snap – but I'm not so much angry as hurt by his comment. 'I barely scraped a B in Physics last year. Sorry I can't keep up with you AP brainiacs. Sue me.'

'We prefer the term nerds, you know.'

I cast a sideways glance at him, and I'm surprised to find he's biting back a smile.

'Sure,' I say. 'That's what I meant. Nerds. Gotcha.'

Dwight lets the smile he's holding back slip onto his face. Then he says, 'Are you going to switch classes?'

'I can't. Looks like you're stuck with me for the rest of the year.'

'Whoopee.'

He uncaps his pen with his teeth, and starts writing the answers to the questions. I look at him for a moment – the freckles, the gangly arms and skinny frame, the curly black hair . . .

It didn't even cross my mind when I met Dwight that he could be a nerd. I didn't want to stick a label like that on him. I just thought he was a really nice, cute guy. Now he says it, though, it seems so obvious that he's on a different social level to Tiffany, Summer, Kyle, Bryce – all of them. Like he's just turned on a flashing neon sign over his head.

Jeez. Spend years with people not wanting to be your friend, and then this kind of thing happens. But I just . . . I don't know what to do. How am I supposed to know what to do?

I don't want to not be friends with Dwight. I like him. And if he gets over being mad at me, I think he'll like me too.

And on the other hand, Tiffany and the rest of the girls seemed really nice, and I could almost – almost – picture myself being friends with them, and the guys. But it's darn near impossible to see myself hanging out with the popular kids.

'I'm sorry,' I blurt out. 'About earlier, I mean. I don't know why I didn't say anything to you.'

He's silent for a moment, but then he says, 'It's okay. I get it. New school, you get straight in with the popular crowd . . . I get it.'

He says it so sympathetically, so understandingly, that for a minute I almost believe he really *does* get it. But he doesn't. He doesn't know the half of it.

Dwight carries on, 'At least you're a big enough person to apologize. Just remember, the higher you climb, the harder the fall.'

I have no reply to that, because I know it's true.

I struggle through the rest of the lesson, but at least I manage to survive it. I have a free period next, so I figure I can go home. Mom and Dad are still at work, but surely I can find the way by myself. It shouldn't be too hard . . .

'What class are you in next?' I ask Dwight, just to make conversation.

'Nothing,' he tells me, shoving his notebook into his over-stuffed messenger bag. 'Study period. How about you?'

'Same,' I answer.

'Are you staying in school, or going home?'

'I guess I'll go home, if I can remember the way.'

'*If you can remember the way?*' he repeats quizzically, with a frown. I hold the door open for him as we leave the room. 'How'd you get here this morning?'

'My dad gave me a ride,' I say. 'I'm pretty sure I can remember. It's not exactly too far to walk, right?'

'Well, no, it's not,' Dwight says. 'Where're all your friends?'

I shrug. 'I don't know. How am I meant to know where they are?'

'Uh, your cell phone?' he suggests, like it's totally obvious. And once he says it, it *is* obvious. Except, you know, I'm not used to using a cell phone for everything, and it didn't even occur to me earlier in the day to ask for anyone's number.

'Oh, good point,' I say. 'I don't have anyone's number, though. It doesn't matter, I'll just head on home.'

'Hang on,' Dwight says. I pause, and turn back to look at him. He fishes his cell out of his back pocket. 'I'll just see if Carter is around and we could all hang out—'

'Madison!' trills a voice, and we both turn to see Tiffany and Summer at the end of the corridor; Summer waves at me.

'Um . . .'

'It's fine,' Dwight says. 'Go talk to your . . . friends. I'll, uh, see you around.'

I start stammering at him that he doesn't have to go, I'm happy talking to him, but he's already walking briskly down the hallway, so I'm left gaping, speechless, staring after his retreating back.

'Madison,' calls Summer, and I turn round to see them coming towards me.

Dwight's sudden departure leaves me feeling confused. And strangely hollow. But I smile at them anyway. 'Hi.'

Tiffany nods her head in the direction Dwight took. 'What were you talking to him for?'

'Dwight? He's in my physics class.'

She nods and goes, 'Mm-hmm,' and she and Summer exchange a glance. But neither of them says anything, so I just smile innocently at them.

'What do you guys have now? I have a free period,' I say, just to move the conversation on.

'Free,' they both chorus. Summer adds, 'We're going to the mall – you in?'

'Sure,' I say enthusiastically, excited that these girls are inviting me to go to the mall with them. It's, like, an actual everyday social activity!

'Cool,' Tiffany says. 'Come on, I'm driving.'

Chapter 11

It turns out that going to the mall basically involves sitting on the edge of a fountain sipping milkshakes, and talking for about an hour. No actual shopping is involved, which is good, since I only have twenty-three dollars (and a nickel).

I mostly just drink my strawberry milkshake; they mostly just talk about people I don't know.

'So, Madison,' Summer says, turning to look at me. 'Are you really stuck in AP physics?'

I nod. 'Yup. Sucks, huh?'

'You're lucky you've got that Dwight guy as your lab partner. He is your lab partner, right?' I nod my head 'yes'. 'Well, shouldn't be too hard. He's such a geek – it's kind of sad, actually. I bet you can get him to do most of the work for you.' Tiffany smiles innocently, like she didn't mean anything horrible by it.

'Why's it kind of sad?' I ask. 'That he's a geek?'

'Well, just, you know,' Tiffany says vaguely. 'Sad.'

'Oh,' I say. 'If you say so.' I make it clear that I disagree with her.

'Are you interested in Bryce?' Tiffany suddenly asks me, grinning broadly. 'I should totally set you two up.'

'No, I'm not interested in him. How about you, though? He's the star soccer player or whatever, you're the cheerleader . . . I just thought you guys might be . . . you know . . .'

I trail off, feeling idiotic, because Tiffany looks like she wants to laugh. She's halfway through putting her hair up into a ponytail, and pauses to look at me. I can see her trying to decide if she's going to laugh or not.

Tiffany does laugh, but it's not in a mean, condescending way, like I expected. 'Bryce is hot, and he's a total sweetheart, believe me. But me and him? It's just not going to happen. We've known each other since kindergarten.'

I nod, not knowing what to reply.

'Besides,' she carries on, inspecting her nail a moment – I see there's a slight chip in the lilac nail varnish – 'I've totally sworn off guys. Right, Sum?'

Summer nods. 'You mean after the Steve situation?'

'What's that?'

'So, freshman year,' Tiffany begins, 'I started dating this guy, Steve, and we were totally loved up. And then, the winter of sophomore year, he just – whoop! – up and left. His parents moved to somewhere in Idaho. Idaho! Totally broke my heart. Sworn off guys entirely since then.'

'Entirely?' Summer raises an eyebrow and giggles.

Tiffany smiles sheepishly. 'Okay, okay, *almost* entirely.'

I don't say anything much, but then she exclaims, 'Oh, no, no! Not like *that*. I don't, like, hook up with every hot guy who comes my way. Not like that! *Making out* with every hot guy who comes my way, though – that's a different thing entirely . . .' She winks, and she and Summer laugh. 'But yeah, I don't sleep around.'

'I didn't suggest you did.'

'I know, I'm just sayin'. You might've been thinking it.'

'Oh. For the record, I wasn't.'

She laughs, and slurps the last of her milkshake. 'How's your love life been, then, Madison? Come on, tell us a little gossip about yourself. Any sex scandals? Games of truth or dare gone awry?'

I snort, and shake my head. 'Yeah, right.'

'Oh, come on,' Summer says, giggling. 'Spill it all.'

'There's really nothing to spill,' I say. 'No . . . sex scandals, no truth or dare games gone bad. Nothing.'

'Never had a boyfriend?' Summer sounds like she seriously doubts that, almost like it shocks her. I'm kind of flattered she thinks I could've had a boyfriend, actually.

I would've stammered some vague answer, but why should I lie to them? It's nothing to be ashamed of, but I can't help it. When you spend years being ridiculed and trying to keep to the shadows, you kind of learn what people want to hear from you.

But I steel myself and say, 'Nope, never had a boyfriend.'

'But you've kissed a guy, right?' Tiffany asks.

I laugh, hoping it doesn't sound as nervous as I feel. 'Why?'

They're not going to let me stall though; Summer elbows me playfully. 'Just answer, already – we're not going to judge you or anything.'

I close my eyes briefly and take a deep breath. 'No. I've never kissed a guy, either.'

The two of them exchange glances and look surprised. I'm flattered that they look so shocked, like they legitimately think I could have kissed a boy.

'I'm totally setting you up with Bryce,' Tiffany announces happily. 'Summer, don't you think they'd be cute together?'

'He's totally into you,' she agrees. 'Go for it. It's not like there's anything stopping you.'

I shrug. 'I barely know him.'

'Then you *get to know him* . . .' Tiffany pulls out her phone, tapping away at it as she carries on talking. 'I'm all over it, don't worry. A little get-together at my place Friday night. My parents are out then – some conference out of town. I wasn't planning on doing anything, but I cannot resist now. It's perfect.'

'How little are we talking? Like, fifty people?' asks Summer.

'Yeah,' Tiffany says. I don't bother to point out that fifty people hardly seems like a small get-together. 'I've got this all under control, Madison, don't you worry. You and Bryce will be the Brangelina of Midsommer High in no time.'

'Hey, quick question,' Summer says. 'Madison or Maddie?'

'Madison,' I say quickly. 'Madison. *Not* Maddie.'

My instant reply is the only thing that might betray the horror I feel at the name 'Maddie'. I don't want to be associated with the old me.

'Madison's cooler. Totally chic,' Tiffany says distractedly. 'Okay . . . done. Oh, and Madison, you need to accept my friend request on Facebook.'

Chapter 12

During the following week, I get introduced to a few more people – most of them friends with the popular clique – and spend my lunch times with Tiffany and Summer.

I carry on talking to Carter in art and photography, even when he suggests I don't.

'Your friends won't be too impressed if they discover you hang out with me in art class.'

'I don't really care, to be honest,' I tell him. I do care a little, but not enough that I'd rather not speak to him at all. That just seems stupid.

By the time Friday morning finally rolls around, though, I can't stop fidgeting all through double AP physics.

'What's eating you?' Dwight asks, a chuckle in his voice. 'You can't sit still.'

'Tiffany's having a party tonight.' Even my voice sounds nervous and fidgety – jumpy.

'Ah, I thought it was that. I heard about it the other day,' he adds by way of explanation. 'Why are you so worried?'

I shrug my shoulders. 'I don't know. I just – I didn't do parties much in Pineford.' He's the only person I've told that to. I clamp my mouth shut instantly. I shouldn't have said that.

But it's Dwight, I think to myself. *Dwight's . . . different.*

'Everybody, listen up.' Dr Anderson claps his hands together and leans forward over his desk, looking out at us all through his glasses. The class falls silent, as always. 'I'm about to announce your projects for the semester, so you'd better be quiet and listen to what I have to say.' He pauses for a minute, just to make sure he has our attention.

'I will be officially giving you your projects next week, but I'll tell you what you'll be doing now. It will count for twenty percent of your final grade, so I recommend you take it seriously. You will create, with your partner, a presentation on a scientist of your choice. You will tell us all about their contribution to the scientific world. It must be a physicist. We are not especially interested in Gregor Mendel's pea experiments, however useful to our understanding of genetics they may be. Thomas Young. Willebrord Snell.

Wherever possible, you will carry out experiments related to your chosen scientist's findings. But if you are going to choose Newton, please don't attack your partner's head with apples. We don't need to cause anybody concussion.'

There are a few chuckles at that.

'As I said, I won't set this project formally until next week, but you may begin to think about it now. Remember, twenty percent of your final grade.'

A few moments of silence pass before Dr Anderson says, 'There are only a few minutes left – you may all pack up and leave.'

There's a collective scraping of stools as everyone gets up, shoving their things into their bags.

I, on the other hand, turn to Dwight with a look of dread consuming my face. 'Experiments? You mean, I can't just copy and paste from Wikipedia?'

Dwight laughs. 'We're doing it with our lab partners, Madison, so I really hope you're not going to copy and paste from Wikipedia.'

I sigh melodramatically and say, 'I'm destined to fail . . .'

He gives me a shrug and a comforting smile. 'It's an AP class, so of course he's going to make us do experiments. Nothing lethal, or even remotely dangerous, though – don't worry. Besides, you're buddied up with me, so I don't know why you're looking so scared.'

'Well, it's just . . .' I trail off, then run a hand through my hair, frustrated. 'Ugh, I hate Physics. I hate Science. I suck at school.'

Dwight laughs and bumps my shoulder with his as we head out of the door. 'Calm down, Madison, it'll be fine.'

'I can barely keep up in class,' I say miserably. 'You'd be better off doing this project by yourself, believe me.'

'Look, I already have a couple of ideas, and it won't even be too hard once we figure out what we're doing. It'll be fine.'

I make a strange noise to express my doubt. It comes out as 'Nngaaah,' but Dwight seems to understand me just fine anyway, and laughs a little.

'See you 'round, Madison,' he says.

For Tiffany's party, I decide to make like my new friends and wear a dress. I choose a white lacy one that's not actually too short – though I feel so hideously self-conscious that I trick myself into thinking it *is* short.

It doesn't take me long to do my hair and put on a little makeup. As for jewelry, I find a pair of simple faux-pearl studs and a thick cream bangle with floral patterns, which I put on my left wrist. I'm ready in half an hour – which is just as well, considering Summer's picking me up in ten minutes.

I grab my overnight bag and jacket, and then head downstairs into the lounge. Dad's working late, so it's just me and Mom.

'Oh, Dice, you look lovely,' she tells me with a proud smile. 'What time do you think you'll be home?'

I shrug. 'Remember, I told you Tiffany said I can stay over. That's what Summer and Melissa are doing.' I pat the small overnight bag I packed to emphasize my point.

'If you want to come home earlier, just let me know.'

'Yeah.'

'And I spoke to your dad,' Mom carries on. 'We were both thinking, if you do want to take something to drink – not much, of course, but we trust you. And if you are thinking of drinking there, if the others are, we'd both rather know you were drinking safely.'

'Really?'

She nods.

'Well . . . thanks,' I say. 'But I wasn't going to drink, so it's okay.'

Mom sighs and smiles, the look on her face telling me there are no secrets kept from a mother. She says, 'Dice, I'm not an idiot. I know what the parties Jenna went to were like. If there's going to be drinking—'

'If there's going to be drinking,' I interrupt, 'I don't really care. I don't want to drink. But thanks for the offer, Mom.'

She looks a little dubious.

'I'm a hundred and thirty-eight percent sure, before you ask.'

'Mm.'

I hear a car pulling up outside and give my mom a quick kiss on the cheek, then head to the door, hurrying down the drive as fast as my one-inch heels will let me. I say hello to Marcus, who's taken shotgun, and slide into the back of Summer's blue Ford.

Lucky for me, Marcus turns up the music, so I don't have to make conversation; I'm too excited to formulate a coherent sentence right now. But can you blame me? I settle back into the seat with a grin. *Here I come.*

When Summer slows before pulling onto Tiffany's long driveway, I get my first glimpse of the house.

It doesn't let me down. For one thing, there are gates outside: big electric gates that keep unwanted guests out, and have an intercom at the side. They're already open so we drive through.

Neat lawns line the long gravel driveway, and I can make out sprinklers set into the grass. The house itself is an impressive sight – there are huge glass windows, and everything is modern and expensive.

'Welcome to Chez Blanche,' Summer tells me with a giggle as she and Marcus climb out of the car. I grab my bag and slide out of the back seat.

I'm glad I didn't opt for bigger heels. I don't know how Summer manages to reach the front door in her three-and-a-half-inch stilettos.

There's music thumping from inside the house, and it gets louder as Summer throws open the door. Marcus follows her, and I trail in behind them. There are people milling around in the hallway. A couple sit on the spiral mahogany spiral staircase. I can feel the bass reverberating through me like an adrenaline rush.

Marcus drifts away to talk to some guys I recognize from the soccer team, and Summer grabs my wrist and drags me up the stairs, weaving in and out of people gracefully as I stumble in her wake.

'We'll toss our stuff on Tiff's bed,' she tells me. 'Then we'll find the girls.'

'Okay,' I call back over the noise of the party.

Tiffany's room is enormous. Probably three times the size of mine.

'Hang on two secs,' Summer tells me. 'I'll just hang my jacket in the closet.'

She slides back a mirrored door that I thought was

part of the wall, to reveal a walk-in closet lined with shelves of shoes and bags and sequined trinket boxes – and rails and rails and rails of clothes.

'Pretty cool, huh?' Summer laughs when she sees my expression – which is partly amazed, a little envious, and also kind of horrified at how someone could spend so much on clothes. 'That's Tiff for you. Now come on, Madison, let's party!'

Again, she grabs my wrist with a surprisingly strong grip for such a slim girl, and hauls me out of there. As we get to the top of the stairs, I see a group of people coming in, and all of a sudden fear takes hold of me, blocking out the adrenalin, and even the bass pumping through me. I start to panic at the thought of being at a house party with all the popular kids. Oh, and not forgetting that Tiffany's trying to set me up with Bryce. Yeah, that's pretty darn scary too.

'Hold on,' I say frantically to Summer. 'I need to run to the bathroom.'

'Oh, okay. Use the one in Tiffany's room,' she instructs me. 'I'll meet you in the kitchen, okay?'

I nod, even though I have no idea where the kitchen is. But I turn and walk as calmly as possible back to Tiffany's room. I go into the en-suite bathroom and lock the door.

The music isn't so loud now, more of a muffled

background noise. The entire bathroom is white. White sink, white bath, white toilet, white towels. It's kind of soothing, actually. I sit on the edge of the bath and lean over, my elbows resting on my knees and my forehead resting on my palms.

My hands feel clammy, and they tremble against my head. My knees quake a little too, and my breathing is shallow, but I'm not hyperventilating – well, not yet, anyway.

My iPod is tucked in my pajamas in my bag, on the other side of the bathroom door. But I can't summon the will to stand up and go get it.

I couldn't tell Summer because I knew she wouldn't understand, but the fact is, I'm scared.

Normal people my age probably take parties for granted. They always know a bunch of people there. Sure, I know a few here, but so what? I've known them for a week. And I'm so used to keeping myself out of it that I don't know how to get in.

I don't want to drink at this party; I was telling Mom the truth. But I'm pretty sure everyone else will be drinking, and I don't know how drunk people act, or even how to behave around drunk people. What if this all completely sucks, and I'm just scared and lonely and shy and silent all night? I can see myself ringing my mom to come pick me up, like a total loser.

I put my hands over my ears and squeeze my eyes tight shut, like that will block out all my thoughts. It's all too loud. Too much. I can't do this. I *can't*. I don't belong here, with these people. I'm too different. Too weird.

I heave myself up from the bathtub and lean over the sink instead, looking into the big bright mirror.

And it's only when I see my reflection that I remember I don't have to be scared and shy and lonely and silent all night, because that's not me anymore. That was the old Madison. The new Madison is confident; she can handle herself at a party – even if she does end up phoning her mom for a ride home.

I stand up a little straighter and push my bangs out of my eyes. I lean closer to the mirror to check my makeup. Then I stand up again and smile at myself, a big, bright, confident grin. If I can pretend I can do this long enough, maybe I'll trick myself into believing it.

I can totally do this.

I look at everything from the other angle: I'm at a party hosted by one of the most popular girls in the school – after only a week I'm in with the popular crowd, so even if I don't know everybody yet, I guess you could say I know the 'right' people. And one of my new friends is trying to set me up with a hot guy because she thinks he likes me.

When I look at everything that way, the grin on my face doesn't feel as forced and the fearful anticipation is replaced by excitement. I steel myself with a few deep breaths, and head out of the bathroom before I can think about it anymore.

I walk with my head held high, exuding confidence like I'm not faking every bit of it. I even make it all the way to the bottom of the spiral staircase without tripping. I smile at people I don't even know as I try to find the kitchen.

I don't know how long I was up in that bathroom, but jeez, there are tons of people here now. The entrance is rammed and there are people spilling into all the rooms. I wonder if Tiffany invited them all, or if they just turned up, but either way – 'small get-together', my butt.

Eventually, after weaving my way to the end of the hallway and then through the dining room, I reach the kitchen. It has granite worktops and everything is silver and chrome, from the refrigerator to the waffle iron. Just like everything else in the house, it is – surprise, surprise – very luxurious. People are hanging around and cracking open bottles or beer cans, and there's a keg in the corner with a stack of plastic cups next to it – red ones, same as at the beach party. I reach the big chrome refrigerator and pull a door open to grab one of the silver Diet Coke cans.

Leaning against the kitchen counter, I take a sip of my drink, and assess my situation. I should find Tiffany, or Summer . . . Even Kyle or Adam, or Ricky. At least Bryce. Then I'd have someone to talk to, and hopefully they'd introduce me to some other people so I can make it through this party without looking like a complete outsider.

The one flaw in that plan is the simple fact that I have no idea where any of them are.

Only one thing to do, then, isn't there? Look for them, idiot.

I push myself off the counter and start making my way through the rooms, keeping my eyes peeled for a friendly face I can put a name to. It's harder than I anticipated, though, trying to weave past the writhing bodies dancing to the pounding music. I shove my way through a couple of gossiping, tipsy girls, and burst free into the hallway.

'Ricky!' I cry in relief, when I spot him standing by the spiral staircase. He looks over, startled, and then smiles when he sees me waving a hand to him. 'Hey,' he says. 'Why are you looking so happy to see me all of a sudden?'

'Don't I always look happy to see you?'

He laughs and shrugs. 'I knew you'd fall for my charm eventually.'

'Sure. I'm practically swooning all over you.'

'Honey, you can swoon over me any time you want,' he says in a low, slow, suggestive voice, waggling his eyebrows. I don't know how he manages to joke around and keep such a straight face. I burst out laughing (being careful not to snort), but feel my cheeks have grown slightly flushed.

'Not drinking?'

I shake my head.

Ricky arches an eyebrow, but smiles. 'I'm sure Tiff won't complain – one less person likely to upchuck.'

And then that's when someone smacks my butt, hard.

Chapter 13

I stand there for a moment, unable to react.

Then, when it registers that, yes, someone *did* actually smack my butt, my mouth falls open and I whirl around. I don't know what I'm going to say, but I'm sure as heck going to say *something* to them, and it's not going to be anything nice.

But whatever sharp retort I was about to blurt dies on my tongue before I say it, and I freeze.

Tiffany cracks up, giggling hysterically, and relief floods through me, deflating my chest and making me laugh too.

'You should've seen your face!' she giggles. She dabs a finger at the corner of her eye, wiping away any smudges of mascara or eyeliner. 'Oh, sweetie, I'm sorry, but that was funny.'

I don't say anything at first, because we're both still laughing.

Then she jumps in, asking, 'Where've you been all

night? I haven't seen you! Don't you know you're meant to greet the host?'

'I tried to find you, I swear.'

'Not very hard.'

'You're right, I *have* been completely ignoring you all night, actually. Totally avoiding you.'

She laughs again, and then puts a hand on her hip. 'Nice dress. And you didn't want to wear it why?'

I shrug, smiling. 'Thanks.'

'Seen Bryce yet?' She waggles her perfectly sculpted eyebrows at me teasingly, and I shake my head, feeling a little embarrassed. 'Don't worry, I've got it all planned.'

She drags me off, linking her arm tightly through mine. I trail after her, doing my best not to fall over.

We go into Tiffany's room, where a few people are sitting around. There's Ricky and Kyle, and Owen from my algebra II class. Melissa's there too, and a couple of girls Tiffany introduced me to earlier, Nicole and Ann. There's another guy slumped next to the bed. I think his name's Jay, but it could be John. And there, giving me his hundred-watt smile, is Bryce.

'Awesome – this'll do!' Tiffany exclaims excitedly. 'Great!' She takes a swig from a bottle of wine, draining the last of it.

'*Truth. Or. Dare.*' She enunciates every word like it

deserves its own sentence, and we're all silent for a few moments – no sound except for the distant hubbub of the party and the dulled thump of the music.

'Cool, I'm in!' says Nicole, and drops gracefully down to a spot on the floor near the empty wine bottle.

There are a few more mumbles of 'Sure, cool, okay, I'm in,' and then we're all sitting in the circle, and I find myself next to Bryce. I'm hesitant, not sure whether I really like the idea of truth or dare. I don't know what kind of dares these people will come up with, but I'm more scared of having a truth.

'No, Madison, you're sitting with me and Summer!' Tiffany instructs me. I get up again and walk around the circle to a spot that's almost exactly opposite Bryce, and take my place next to them.

'I'll start off,' Ann announces, and leans over to spin the bottle.

It lands on Marcus.

'Truth or dare?'

'Truth,' he says.

'If you had to kiss one guy here, who'd it be?'

He sighs slightly, and looks around at the guys for a few moments. Raising a finger, he points at Jay/John. 'Let's go with Jay.'

Noted.

Marcus spins the bottle. This time it lands on Kyle. 'Truth or dare?'

'Dare.'

'Hmm,' Marcus says thoughtfully, thinking up a good dare for him, and we all wait patiently. 'Hey, Tiffany, mind if Kyle tries on some clothes?'

'Not at all.' A sly smile slips over Tiffany's face; then she hiccups.

'Wait – *what*?' Kyle's eyes bulge.

'I dare you,' Marcus says slowly, as though he's savoring the words, 'to wear some of Tiffany's clothes. There will be photographic evidence taken.'

We all start to laugh – either at the horrified look on Kyle's face or the thought of him dressed up in girl's clothes.

But he doesn't back down. He goes into Tiffany's walk-in closet with an old miniskirt and woollen sweater she finds him, and dresses up. Ann leaps up, crying, 'Wait! You need lipstick!'

My sides ache from laughing: Kyle looks arrogant; he's tall and lean, with short spiky hair and a soccer player's build – and he's wearing a denim miniskirt.

When Summer gets out her phone to take a photo of it, Kyle strikes a pose, his hand on his hip, and pouts at the camera, a caricature of a model. It's hilarious.

'Now get out of my clothes,' Tiffany demands, once Summer's taken the photos.

The game carries on. A couple of people pick truths, which surprises me – I'd have thought all the guys would go for dares. There's nothing too bad, though. Owen is dared to kiss Ann; we find out that Summer's celebrity girl-crush is Megan Fox; and that of all the girls at the party, Ricky would make out with Tiffany.

I've been lucky so far: the bottle hasn't landed on me.

'My turn,' Tiffany announces loudly, and leans forward to spin the bottle. As she straightens again, she nudges my side. It's so slight, I'm not sure if it's an accident, so I look at her. She catches my eye and winks.

Slowly I turn my gaze back to the wine bottle, which spins slower, and slower . . . and slower . . . and stops.

And it's pointing at me.

I don't know how she managed it, but she's done it deliberately.

'Ooh, Madison!' she trills. She doesn't even ask me whether I pick truth or dare. I mean, I'd have picked dare anyway, but she steamrollers ahead. 'Um, let's see . . . Oh, I know! Madison, you have got to . . . ready for this? You have to spend seven minutes in heaven . . . with Bryce.'

I stare at her for a moment that stretches out so long

and silent it feels like an eternity. I don't know what to feel – annoyed, surprised, or happy. Actually, all three. But mostly annoyed at Tiffany for putting me under pressure like this.

Then again . . . even if her plan is going to work, there's the indisputable fact that I have to kiss him. I have to kiss a guy. I've never kissed a guy before. This isn't how I imagined my first kiss. What if I'm a terrible kisser?

She interrupts my thoughts, saying, 'Well, go on – what're you waiting for?' and gives me a shove, prompting me to get to my feet. I do, but it's a hesitant and awkward movement, and I'm unsteady. A hand catches my elbow – Bryce's hand, of course. He smiles at me easily, like this is no big deal.

No big deal? I want to yell at him. *I'm freaking out over here!*

I gulp, and then Ricky says, slurring only a little, 'Hang on – if you're gonna do this dare, you're gonna do it right. Tiffany, do you happen to have one single closet in this house which is not a walk-in one?'

She laughs. 'Come with me.' She gets to her feet, sways a little, hiccups, and then drags Bryce after her. He takes hold of my wrist to pull me along too. I look over my shoulder. Melissa winks at me, and Summer gives an excited little smile, looking like she wants to squeal.

Tiffany pauses partway down the hall, and throws open a white door. It's dark inside, but I can see stacks of towels, and pipes running behind the shelves.

'In you go!' she cries, pushing us into the closet. The door shuts behind us, and we hear the key turning on the other side; my heart beats nauseatingly fast. I feel just like I did at the start of the party, when I hid out in the bathroom – scared and nervous, with sweaty palms and a racing pulse roaring in my ears – though the butterflies in my stomach are different.

This definitely isn't how I imagined my first kiss. *But it could be a lot worse*, I tell myself.

'Isn't there a light switch anywhere?' I ask. My eyes haven't quite adjusted to the darkness yet, and the only light is the thin band spilling in through the crack under the door.

'No idea,' Bryce says. His voice is closer than I expected, and his breath tickles my face a little. His fingers are still closed around my wrist, and as I remember they're there, my hand twitches involuntarily. Instead of letting go, Bryce just loosens his grip so his fingers brush against mine.

'What, you're not even going to try and look for one?'

'I wasn't planning on it, no.'

I roll my eyes, even though he can't see me doing it. 'I don't suppose there's a way to unlock this door from the inside, either, huh? I don't—'

'Madison,' Bryce says, talking over me a little. His voice is hushed, though, and I feel him moving towards me. I don't know why I do it, but as he steps closer, I step back – not that I can go very far. The closet is so small, my back immediately hits the shelves.

My eyes are still adjusting, but I can make out Bryce looking at me. He's standing right up close to me now.

'If we're going to be in here for the next seven minutes,' he says, his voice still quiet. 'I'll just do what I've been waiting to do all night.'

And then he kisses me.

It's a cheesy line, and I roll my eyes at it – but it almost makes me blush, and I wonder if it's true; if he actually *has* been waiting all night to kiss me.

It's kind of a weird feeling, being kissed. But a good kind of weird. I don't know what I'm doing at all, but I just follow Bryce's lead and press my lips back against his. He puts one hand on my waist and the other twines our fingers together.

His lips are soft and warm against mine, and the kiss is kind of tentative at first. But once I start to kiss him back, he kisses me harder, and his hand slides around to the small of my back, so he can pull me closer.

At first my arms just hang there, because I don't know what to do with them. When I'm kissing him back, though, I forget all about how awkward and inexperienced I am, and my arms snake up around his neck, my hands resting on his broad shoulders.

I'm the one to pull away first.

'Don't tell me kissing is too mainstream for you,' he says teasingly.

I laugh. 'No.'

'Good,' he replies, and then he's kissing me again.

Chapter 14

We decide, once we're all up the next morning, to go shopping for a while, and have some lunch. Melissa's still complaining of a hangover that Advil hasn't cured, but she still looks better than me; I have huge bags under my eyes from a sleepless night.

I couldn't stop thinking about my kiss with Bryce. Once the party was over I'd spent ages with the girls analyzing the entire seven minutes with him, and we'd come to the conclusion that he definitely liked me. Or, at least, *they'd* drawn that conclusion – I'm still not totally convinced. And then I was annoyed with myself: maybe he didn't want to date me – I wasn't about to turn into one of those girls who kissed random guys at parties. That was not who I wanted to be.

We're in some pretty pricey Italian restaurant at the mall, when my cell phone trills with what I'm slowly coming to recognize as my text message tone. 'Oh!' I exclaim when I suddenly remember that, oh yeah, that annoying chirping noise is my cell. I apologize, thinking I must seem rude answering it when we're out at lunch. 'Sorry.'

'Don't worry 'bout it,' Melissa says.

Wiggling my phone out of the back pocket of my jeans, I tap the screen to bring it to life again.

One new message: Bryce Higgins, it reads.

I actually drop my phone, I'm so shocked that he's texted me. I mean, I hoped he would, and the girls said he would, but . . . I guess I just didn't expect him to. My cell makes a clatter as it tumbles to the floor. I hope it's not damaged – and I really, really hope I'm imagining everyone looking at me. It wouldn't surprise me if they're shaking their heads at me, the foolish klutz on table nine.

Hoping for the best but expecting the worst doesn't seem like the best way to live, but it's worked for me so far.

My cell phone has fallen underneath the table, and I reach for it. When I come back up, I whack my head on the table. Of course I do. 'Ouch!'

If I wasn't making a scene before, I sure as heck am now. Wonderful.

'Shoot,' I mumble to myself, rubbing my temple as I sit back up. I smooth my hair out.

'You okay?' Tiffany asks, biting back a laugh.

'Mm.' I turn my cell phone over, inspecting it. It doesn't look scratched or broken. That's good. Then I bring the screen back to life again. I let out a sigh of relief when I see I haven't just killed it.

It's still there on the screen: *One new message: Bryce Higgins.* Like it's teasing me or something. My breath catches in my throat as I open the message.

'Who is it?' Summer asks me.

I don't answer at first. I can't. I can see the message Bryce has sent me, but I can't seem to read it. I see the words, but they're not making any sense to me. I shake my head to clear it.

'Madison, who is it? Is it Bryce?' Tiffany prompts.

I nod. 'It's Bryce, yeah.'

I tune out their excited babbling and try to focus on the screen. Eventually the words make sense:

Hey there, Mainstream. How was your night? XXXX

'Um, does it mean anything if he put kisses at the end of his text?' I ask, feeling totally stupid, looking up at the girls helplessly.

'How many?' Melissa asks.

'Four.'

'What did he say?' Summer demands, grinning.

I read out the text and add, 'You know, 'cause he calls me Mainstream sometimes?' The girls nod. 'What do I say?'

'Pass it here,' Tiffany tells me. Which just makes me clutch my cell phone a little tighter in my sweating palms. She sighs when she sees I don't want to give it up. 'Ask how his night was and put a wink face.' She demonstrates the wink face as she says it.

'Can't I just say I had a good time, how was his night?'

'Well, you could,' she huffs. 'If you don't want to take my advice . . .'

'No, I do. Um . . .' I look at my phone for a moment before typing in a reply – *It was good thanks* ☺ *How was yours?* – and then I turn my phone round for Tiffany to see. Summer and Melissa lean round to look too. 'How's that?'

Tiffany smiles. 'Perfect!' She pulls the cell phone out of my hand and quickly hits a couple of buttons – but she does it all so fast I only have time to stammer incoherently.

'There, sent. Don't worry,' she laughs, seeing the worried expression on my face, 'I just added some kisses and pressed send, I swear.'

I give a doubtful 'Mmph' and she hands my cell phone back. I check and see she was right, though, and relax. But I start to stress out again as I wait for him to text back. It's the longest minute or two of my life, I swear.

When he does reply, I open the text straight away and the girls lean in, trying to see. 'What did he say?'

I read it aloud to them. '*I had a great night too. What're you up to?* and then there's a smiley face and four kisses again.'

That one doesn't seem so scary to reply to, so I just tell him I'm at the mall with the girls and ask what he's up to. I hesitate before I do it, but I type a couple of kisses at the end and hit send. I let out a big gush of air.

'Told you so.' Tiffany gives me a big smile and leans back in her chair. 'I told you he liked you, didn't I? And who didn't believe me?'

I laugh. 'All right, all right, you were right, okay! But he could just be being polite. Or friendly. He's a friendly kind of guy, right?'

Melissa giggles. 'Madison, he *likes* you. Duh. We went through this last night.'

'Trust me on this,' Tiffany says, leaning across the table with a look that's so open and honest I wonder how I *wouldn't* trust her on this. 'I've known Bryce for years. He definitely likes you. He doesn't put kisses to just anyone.'

I laugh nervously, not entirely reassured.

The text conversation that follows between me and Bryce is pretty casual, so it doesn't stress me out too much. He's not being flirty or anything, so I don't have to panic or look like an idiot when I ask the girls how to reply.

About ten minutes later, the food turns up, and I tell Bryce that I can't talk for now.

His reply comes through almost straight away – *Okay, talk to you later then. Have fun shopping* ☺ *XXXXX* – and I suppress a smile, and the blush that threatens to spread over my cheeks.

Silly as it might sound, I feel kind of excited seeing the kisses at the end of Bryce's text. It makes my heart skitter in my chest. I've never got texts from a guy – unless you count Dwight: his texts certainly didn't come with Xs on the end, and I hadn't made out with him in a closet the night before, either.

'What was Bryce saying?' Summer asks as she begins to dig into her steak and I put my cell phone away again.

'He's cleaning his car – one of the guys threw up in it last night.'

'Oh, ew.' Melissa scrunches her nose up. 'Did he say who?'

'Jay.'

'Ah. Yeah, Jay doesn't hold down alcohol too well,' Summer says. 'Especially vodka. God, he knows he can't do that shit. I don't even know why he bothers.

I puked my guts up last time I had vodka. Haven't touched it since.'

'Jay didn't look that drunk when we were playing truth or dare,' I say.

'He seems relatively sober' – Tiffany shrugs – 'but he's usually totally wasted.'

'Oh.'

'Yeah. I'm just glad he didn't puke in the house.'

'You were so lucky with all that,' Melissa says, pointing at Tiffany with her fork. 'I mean, there were only, what, two people who threw up, and they both did it in the bathroom. Remember the last party I had?'

'Oh, yeah. God, that was awful,' Summer says. She turns to me and adds, 'Some girl puked on the couch.'

'Oh, gross!' I pull a face.

'Going back to the subject,' Tiffany says, 'what's going on with you and Bryce? Are you seeing each other again?'

'Other than school, you mean?'

'Duh.'

'I don't know – he hasn't said anything.'

'Whatever you do, don't ask him to go somewhere. Not even to the movies,' Melissa tells me. 'Play hard to get and keep him on his toes.'

'Hard to get?'

'Please tell me you know what that means, Madison,'

Summer says – but she laughs a little as she says it, so it comes across as a joke.

'I know what it means,' I say, mumbling only slightly. I shift in my seat. 'I just . . . don't . . .' I clear my throat, then take a bite of pasta, chewing it slowly so as to stall. I swallow hard. 'I just don't know if that's me, you know?'

What I mean is, I have no clue how to 'play hard to get' – I'll only make an idiot of myself.

Even last night, when I was kissing Bryce, I felt awkward, inexperienced. I let him lead because I didn't really know what to do. But with this – playing hard to get so he'll be even more interested in me – nobody's there to guide me every little step of the way.

Sure, the girls might advise me on how to act – but I'll only feel stupid doing it, and mess everything up. I'd much rather just be myself and hope I don't come off as too much of a fool.

I mean, I must've done something right since I met him at the beach, given that he seems to like me.

The girls must see I don't want to talk about it anymore – or maybe they just give up when I start eating and ignoring their prompting sentences.

We get the check and leave. I go to hand it to the guy who served us and tell the others to head on out, I'll meet them in a minute.

'You just want an excuse to talk to the cute waiter,' Summer teases, laughing.

'Why are you after the waiter? You have Bryce now to keep you warm at night,' Tiffany joins in, hugging herself and giggling.

I laugh too, and roll my eyes at them. The guy who'd served us *was* kind of cute, I guess. He looked like he was in college, but couldn't have been much older than us. I didn't think he was really anything special – but hey, what do I know?

I clear my throat slightly to get his attention. He looks round and I smile, holding out the check with our wad of crumpled notes.

'Everything okay with the meal?' he asks.

'Yes, thanks.'

'Good.' He prints a receipt, and then scribbles on the back of it before handing it over – signing it off, I assume. 'Come again.'

'Uh, thanks,' I mumble. I've always found it awkward talking to waiters and salespeople. I'd only offered to sort the check because it didn't look like the others were going to, and I didn't like to leave it on the table – a pet peeve of my dad's I'd inherited.

'Flirt with the waiter?' Summer asks jokingly, elbowing me lightly in the ribs when I finally emerge from the restaurant.

'Hardly,' I reply. I realize I'm still holding the receipt. As I turn it over, I see the scribble on the back. Then I laugh.

'Anyone want his number?' I say, completely shocked. He gave me his number; I'm flattered, but at the same time I know I'm not going to call him – I'm just not interested.

'He gave you his number?' Tiffany looks at the scrawled digits, and shakes her head. 'Hold on two secs.'

'What're you doing?' Melissa asks as we watch her take out her cell phone.

'Posting on Facebook that Madison just got a cute waiter's number.' She looks up at me with a wicked grin. 'Bryce is definitely going to see it. He'll be so jealous. This is, like, perfect. Ah, thank God for social networking. It makes the whole dating game so much more fun.'

'He might not believe it,' I point out. I barely believe it. I'm still a little stunned, actually.

'Why wouldn't he?' Melissa asks. 'Besides, he's bound to ask you out even sooner if he knows you're in demand.'

'But I'm *not* in demand.'

'Some random waiter has just given you his phone number,' Tiffany tells me.

'Well, yeah, but—'

'Madison, chill, it's all part of the master plan.' Melissa shoots me an encouraging smile.

'What master plan is this exactly?'

'The master plan to get you and Bryce together, duh.'

'Oh, right, okay . . .' I say hesitantly. I shake my head, deciding to simply go with the flow and leave them to their 'master plan'. I just doubt it'll work.

'Was he a good kisser?' Jenna asks, grinning into the webcam. She's so excited about me getting my first kiss. 'I remember my first kiss – it was Hank Phillips, at the school prom at the end of middle school. He was such a sloppy kisser, it was totally gross. I kind of avoided him after that . . . Never mind about me, though – tell me all the details.'

'He was a good kisser, I guess. I don't know. It's not like I have anyone to compare him to, is it?'

'Mm, I guess. But hey, you've had your first kiss! You're getting yourself out there a little more! You've made friends and you have a maybe boyfriend! I wish I was down there right now so I could give you a big old hug, Mads.'

I smile wryly. 'How is college? So far we've only talked about me.'

'And we're not done talking about you, so don't you dare try to change the subject! College is college, New York is New York – but Maddie, you're no longer the same old you! So we're still talking about you, and if you don't like that, tough shit.'

'What if I just hang up, huh?'

'Then I will call you back and call you back and call you back until you answer, and then we'll carry on talking about you.'

'Oh . . .' Then I laugh. 'Well, I don't know how much more there is to say.'

'Has he texted you or anything since lunch?'

I shake my head. 'No, not yet. But I don't expect he'll—'

That annoying chirping sound interrupts me. Jenna laughs. 'Is that your cell? Christ, that's spooky. Is it him? If it is, that's even spookier. I'm like, psychic, huh? Is it him?'

One new message: Dwight.

'It's not Bryce . . .' I shake my head at the webcam. 'It's Dwight.'

'Dwight? Nerdy Dwight from your physics class?'

'Yeah.'

'Well?' she asks, leaning into the lens of the webcam eagerly, her blue eyes wide. It's the same look she used to get when she heard new gossip from one of her friends. 'What's he said? Tell me, tell me!'

Laughing, I load the text message and read it out. 'He said, *What's this I hear about you and a waiter? And there's one of those smileys with a tongue out.*'

Jenna laughs. 'He likes you, doesn't he?'

'Who, Dwight?' I ask doubtfully.

'Yeah.'

'He doesn't *like* me.'

'Well, at least as a friend. He sounds so cute. Like, a really nice, sweet guy. Unless, of course, you like him as more than that?'

'No,' I say hastily. 'No, we're just friends.'

'Mm,' Jenna says, with that confidential kind of smile that tells me she's in on my secret.

'I'm serious,' I reiterate. 'He's only a friend. I'm lucky he's that. I told you – he was mad when he saw me hanging around with all the popular people. I mean, I get where he's coming from, but they're not that bad. They're all pretty nice, actually. Well, Kyle, not so much, but the others . . . I don't know why Carter said—'

'Hold on, which one's Carter?'

'Carter is Dwight's friend – the one with half an eyebrow missing. He's in my art class. Anyway, he'd said I shouldn't really hang around with him even in art class because Tiffany and the others might get annoyed.'

'That's high school for ya,' Jenna says with a bitter kind of twist in her smile. 'It can get pretty shitty.'

'Like I don't already know that,' I mumble. She hears me; I can tell by the way her expression softens and turns sympathetic. But she doesn't say anything. 'Hold on a sec, let me just reply to Dwight.'

'What're you saying?'

I tell her as I type, but I speak slowly, struggling to multitask. *'It's nothing much. Just some waiter gave me his number.* Then I've put a laughing face at the end,' I add.

'Any kisses?'

'No. I don't usually put any kisses to him.'

'Usually?' Jenna picks out. Then she laughs a little. 'How often do you text him?'

'Not much at all. I texted him, like, Wednesday about something, I don't remember what. It wasn't a particularly long conversation. Then he's just messaged me today.'

As I'm talking, a text comes through.

It's not Dwight replying, though. This one is from Bryce.

Jenna assumes it's Dwight, and doesn't ask what he's said. But I do see the expectant, slightly impatient look she's giving me through my computer screen.

Movies tomorrow night? I'll pick you up at six. XXXX,
it reads.

'Uh, Jenna?'

'Yes?' she replies, drawing the word out.

'Bryce . . . Bryce just asked me on a date.'

Chapter 15

'What're you wearing?' Tiffany asks. I've got her on loudspeaker, and my cell phone sits face-down on the bed.

'Jeans, I guess?'

'*Uh!*' she says, making a noise like a buzzer. 'Wrong.'

'Shorts?'

'*Uh!* Try again.'

'What, then? What do you suggest I wear? We're only going to the movies.'

'A skirt,' she says. 'Duh. And a cute top. Make sure it's casual.'

I know I should take her advice. Tiffany knows a heck of a lot more about what to wear on a date to the movies than I do. Jenna told me to wear a skirt too, so I know it's legit advice.

So I say, 'Okay.' And I take a pair of dark denim cut-offs out of my closet and step into them, simply because I don't want to wear a skirt.

'You want a girly top to go with it.' Tiffany's carrying on talking. I'm barely listening, though. I texted her this morning to tell her I was going to the movies with Bryce, and she insisted on coming over. I managed to stop her from doing that much, but she still phoned me up.

I rifle through my closet, but I've already got a good idea of what I'm going to wear. I'm really worried about my first date, and I want to look good. But I know I don't want to wear anything I feel awkward or uncomfortable in, so I have to try and find some sort of balance.

I'd have explained to Tiffany, but that would have given away too much. She and Jenna might have the confidence to wear anything at all and look good in it, but I don't, and I know that.

'Have you found anything?' Tiffany asks. 'Maybe something pink?'

'Um . . .' What I picked out is a long-sleeved black sweater that's kind of baggy, with gold decoration around the neckline. 'Yeah, I've got something. It's . . . uh, it's pink.'

I describe it to Tiffany, and leave out the fact that it's definitely not pink; but it's cute. And it's what I want to wear. So who cares what Tiffany says?

'Don't wear heels,' she says. 'Wear some cute

pumps. Or – no, wait, you're kinda short, aren't you? Maybe you *should* wear heels: Bryce is pretty tall. You couldn't tell so much at the party, 'cause you had heels on then. Not big fancy heels, though – you don't want to go overboard, especially since you're wearing a skirt . . . Ah, screw it, wear heels.'

While Tiffany's talking, I'm trying to decide between my Converse and a pair of plain black pumps. But I pause, because okay, she may be right on this. So I find a pair of sandals. They're gold wedges, so they match my top perfectly, and they're not very high, only about an inch and a half. Plus, I find wedges much easier to walk in than stilettos.

'I have shoes.'

'How high?'

'Inch and a half, I think.'

'That's great. Okay, so protocol for the first date: he's going to pay. This is Bryce we're talking about, and he's definitely going to insist on paying.'

'But I'll offer to pay anyway,' I say, because it's true. I'd feel bad if he paid for everything.

Tiffany seems to think I'm just finishing her sentence or something, though, because she says, 'Exactly!'

I know I'm not taking Tiffany's advice when it comes to my outfit, but I'm listening attentively now she's talking about what to do on this date. The beach party was bad enough, but then Dwight had asked me purely on a friendly basis, so I was more relaxed. This is different.

Plus, what if he tries to kiss me when we're at the movies?

This is different to the usual first date, since we've already passed the first kiss barrier. Ugh, why does everything have to be so awkward and confusing? And why do I have to overreact to the smallest things? I'm such a dork.

I just hope Bryce hasn't noticed.

Not long after I hang up and finish doing my makeup, I hear a car door outside, and the doorbell sounds.

Taking Tiffany's (and Jenna's) advice not to look too eager, I don't hurry down, and let one of my parents get the door instead.

Then I wander down and see Bryce standing there. He's wearing a pair of khakis and a blue button-down shirt with the Abercrombie and Fitch logo. His wavy blond hair catches the early evening sun and looks practically gold. He sees me on the stairs and smiles broadly, his dimples showing. I smile back, except I know I look awkward and self-conscious.

'I won't have her back too late,' Bryce tells my mom. I know she wouldn't care if I didn't get in till midnight, because I've actually got a date, and with a really cute jock at that. She was beyond ecstatic when I hesitantly asked her if she minded if I went to the movies with Bryce. Even Dad didn't have a problem with it.

Mom laughs, but says to me, 'Ten-o'clock curfew. Let me know if you're going to be any later than that.'

'Okay,' I promise.

'You kids have fun!' The huge grin on her face makes me shake my head and roll my eyes.

'Bye,' I say testily, and pull the door shut behind me. Then I smile at Bryce. 'Hi.'

He laughs. 'Hi yourself.'

We climb into his car and I ask, 'So what movie are we gonna see?'

'That new film with Bradley Cooper, I thought,' he tells me. 'It's got really great reviews. Is that okay with you?'

'Yeah, sure, that's totally fine.'

'Aren't you too hot in that?' he asks, nodding at my sweater. It is pretty warm, but I shake my head, picking at the cuffs of my sleeves, pulling them down.

There's a silence just hanging in the air between us. I wait a few moments – but they're long, endless moments that drag out with the silence. I don't know what to do. I think I'm supposed to say something, but no small talk springs to mind. There's no way I'm

154

resorting to talking about the weather. There's not much to say about school, since we're only a week in and nothing's really started up properly yet. Football and soccer practice has barely started, and tryouts aren't until next week. Barely any classes have had homework.

So what do I talk about?

Around the girls, if I don't have anything to say, I just listen to their conversation and pitch in where appropriate. But guys are different. They don't talk about the same things as girls. I don't even know much about Bryce— Actually, scratch that: I know next to nothing about Bryce. Sure, I know what people have told me, but I don't know much about him personally.

And I don't know what to ask him to find out.

It's different with Dwight. I seem to be able to talk to him effortlessly – though admittedly half our conversations are physics-related. But things are just easy around him. I don't feel anywhere near as un-comfortable as I do right now.

I start to wonder: what if Bryce doesn't actually like me, as everyone claims he does? What if the only reason he's asking me on this date is because we kissed, and he's being polite? Thinking that makes my palms turn clammy, and my stomach ties itself into knots.

'Can I ask you something?' I blurt.

'Uh, sure. Go ahead. Shoot.'

'Why did you ask me on a date? Is it just 'cause we kissed at Tiffany's?'

We're at a stop sign when I say this, so Bryce takes the opportunity to look at me. His handsome face is serious, and his brown eyes pierce into mine. I shrink a little inside, scared of his answer.

'No,' he tells me quietly. He pulls off, and after a pause, his eyes trained on the road, carries on: 'When I met you at the beach I thought you were cute. Different. You weren't like all the other girls. You're a very interesting person, Madison – you know that? It's like . . . you don't care what people think of you.'

How wrong that is.

'But at the same time nobody knows anything about you.'

There we go – now you're back on track, Pretty Boy.

'I don't know,' he says. 'But there's something about you that made me want to get to know you. What happened at Tiffany's . . . Well, that was just an extremely convenient coincidence.' He laughs. 'But knowing Tiffany, she had something to do with that, and it wasn't a coincidence at all.'

'Mm,' I say, laughing, but then I add, 'And it had absolutely nothing to do with some random waiter giving me his number?'

'Um...' He clears his throat with deliberate sheepishness that makes us both laugh. 'Maybe. OK, here's a question for *you*, Mainstream. What made you say yes?'

I don't answer him for a moment; I've already spoken without thinking once tonight, I don't want to mess up my chances with Bryce. Why *did* I say yes?

He's cute, and he's nice, and he's funny, and he's that guy in high school who all the girls have a crush on. I like him. And it was great kissing him the other night...

Or is it just that I'm flattered?

I mean, he wouldn't have looked twice at me if I was the old Madison. But this guy's taken an interest in me, he's got a nickname for me, he kissed me at a party. I don't know if I like the *idea* of all that more than I actually like *him*.

But I tell him, 'Because I wanted to say yes.'

He laughs. 'That's not much of an answer. Care to elaborate?'

'How about if tonight goes well, then I'll elaborate?'

'And how am I going to know if you think it goes well?'

I shrug, and answer vaguely, 'If it goes well, I'll tell you why I said yes. Then you'll know it's gone well.'

Bryce sneaks a sideways glance at me, a smile

playing on his lips, his dimples not quite showing. I smile innocently back at him, and he chuckles quietly, shaking his head. I bump up the volume on the radio, and he shoots me another look.

'What, you don't want to talk to me?' he says. He has to raise his voice because of the level of the stereo.

I shake my head. 'No. I just like this song.'

'No.' Bryce puts a hand over mine and pushes my wallet back down into my purse before I can finish getting out a ten-dollar bill. 'I told you, I'm paying for this. Consider it my treat.'

'And I told you, I'll pay for myself – it's fine.'

'Come on, Madison, you don't really expect me not to pay on a first date?' He laughs, smiling at me, and as he does so, his eyes bore right into mine, making my cheeks warm.

'I can go on some kind of feminist rant if you like.'

'I don't doubt you would,' he says, so seriously I don't think he's joking. *Do I really come off like that?* I wonder briefly. 'But seriously, it's fine. I'll pay.'

'Yeah, but . . .'

'But nothing,' he tells me, pushing my purse away again as I start to bring my wallet out for the third time. 'I'm going to pay and you're going to say thank you, and then we're going to have a nice evening and watch the movie.'

'Do you want popcorn or anything?'

'If you do, sure. I don't want to look like the pig I really am and eat a whole thing myself. I will do that, you know.'

I laugh. 'Salted or sweet?'

'Toffee,' he says, waggling his eyebrows like toffee popcorn is the most daring thing in the world.

'Wild man,' I say sarcastically. 'I should just start calling you Tarzan. I'll go grab popcorn now,' I tell him. 'Just so we don't have to wait for the next twenty minutes and miss the commercials.'

'Can't go missing the commercials.' He shakes his head slightly, a grave look on his face as if to say that this would be truly tragic.

'Exactly.'

'Here,' he says, handing me a five-dollar bill. 'I told you, I'm paying for tonight.'

I step back and clasp my hands to my purse so he can't give me the money. I shake my head at him and take a couple of steps back. 'Toffee popcorn it is. And this one's on me.'

'Madison,' he sighs, stepping towards me.

I cut him off hastily. 'Uh, uh, uh! You can't move or

you'll lose your place in the line. And then we may actually miss those commercials.'

'Damn, you're right,' he says with a melodramatic sigh. Then he smiles at me. 'You will get this five-dollar bill by the end of the night.'

'No, I really won't. Large popcorn all right?'

'Whichever one you want.'

I join the queue at the snack stand. I get a large Diet Cola since I know popcorn makes me thirsty – but I grab two straws, just in case – and when I eventually turn round with my snacks, Bryce is standing waiting for me, smiling.

'Come on – we wouldn't want to miss those commercials now, would we?'

Chapter 16

I'm acutely aware throughout all 108 minutes of the movie that Bryce's knee is pressed against mine. It sounds kind of sad, I know, but it's all I can think about. He doesn't put his arm around me, but whenever our hands brush reaching to get some popcorn he twines our fingers together, until I begin to think he's waiting for me to get some popcorn to take some too.

He was right about being able to eat plenty, though; I have a few handfuls, but Bryce eats most of the box himself.

I wonder if he'll be cheesy and yawn before putting his arm around me. It seems like the kind of thing he'd do, in a jokey and cute way. He doesn't, though, which makes me all the more aware of how our knees and elbows are touching.

When the movie's over – and it was a pretty darn good film – we stand up. I grab the popcorn box, and shake it so the kernels in the bottom of the box rattle around. I take a peek inside, and then look back up to Bryce, putting on a shocked expression. 'Are you really going to leave all that popcorn?'

He laughs and bumps my arm playfully with his as we walk down the aisle. 'Maybe that explains why I'm so ravenous. Do you want to grab a bite to eat somewhere?'

Given that yes, I'm hungry, and yes, I want to prolong this date with Bryce as much as possible, I nod and try not to smile *too* enthusiastically. 'Sounds good to me.'

'What do you feel like?' he asks, pausing as I ram the popcorn box into a trash can. 'Pizza? A burger? Someplace really nice? It's entirely up to you.'

I think for a moment. 'Pizza sounds good to me.'

'Everything sounds good to you,' he jokes, laughing. 'I know this place that does really great pizza.'

And fifteen minutes later, we're being seated in a restaurant that smells of melted cheese and a delicious mix of dough, vegetables, and tomato. The carpets are red and the lighting is dim, so the whole place has a cute and cozy feel to it.

We slide into a booth the waiter directed us to. 'What can I get you guys to drink?'

'Water, please,' I say.

'I'll have an orange soda,' Bryce says.

'Okay. Here are your menus . . .' the waiter says as he hands one to each of us, 'and I'll be back in a few minutes to take your order.'

I open the menu up, and put it down in front of me. The first thing my eyes flit to is the prices – I let out a small, silent sigh of relief when I see that it's not expensive. Not that I couldn't afford it, but if he insisted on paying again, then I'd feel terrible.

I don't check out the food on the menu, though; instead, I look around. It's not a big restaurant, but there're enough people to make a nice background buzz of conversation that mingles with the low, soft mood music.

I turn back to study my menu, but I feel Bryce staring at me. I look up under my bangs, which almost cover my eyes now that my head is tilted down, and see that he's smiling at me. 'What?'

He shrugs. 'Nothing.'

A minute later, the waiter comes with our drinks, and takes our orders. I'm shocked when Bryce orders exactly what I want: a chicken and vegetable pizza. So I say, 'I'll have the same, please.'

When the waiter's gone, Bryce says, 'Was that purely coincidental, or . . . ?'

I laugh. 'I wanted that pizza. What, do you think I picked it just because I couldn't decide for myself?'

'You might've,' he jokes. 'I have good taste in food – it wouldn't be the first time.'

'Right.'

There are a few heartbeats of silence before Bryce takes a deep breath, lets it out again, and leans closer. 'So, Madison, tell me something about you. Anything at all.'

I think for a moment. Surely there's something that doesn't betray what I used to be like back in Pineford?

'I have an older sister. Jenna. She's studying at NYU.'

'Really? Cool. What's she studying?'

'Art.'

He nods slowly, thoughtfully. Then he sips his orange soda and says to me, 'You know, that's not telling me something about you personally. How am I supposed to get to know you if you don't tell me about yourself?'

I laugh, but I sound a little nervous – I hope it's only to my ears it sounds off. 'Okay then, how about . . . *America's Next Top Model* is my guilty pleasure.'

'That's the kind of thing.'

'Now it's my turn to ask you something,' I say. 'How come you're such a big soccer star?'

'It's a good sport,' he tells me with a smile. 'I was in Pee Wee Soccer Pals when I was a little kid. Went to soccer camp a couple of summers. I'm hoping it's going to get me a scholarship to a good college.'

'What do you want to do at college?'

'Law. But a couple of colleges would take me on with a sports scholarship. I've heard it's pretty competitive . . .' He looks at me and asks, 'What do you want to do at college, then?'

I shrug. 'I haven't thought about it much. Maybe history? It's one of the few subjects I'm good at.'

'Unlike AP physics?' he teases, smirking over the top of his glass.

'Very funny.'

'Sorry. Still no chance of you getting moved out of that class to somewhere else?'

I shake my head. 'I went to the office to ask again. Apparently Mrs Willis tried to shuffle my schedule around, but for some reason it wasn't working. I've given up. I've got Dwight, so I'll be able to cope.'

'Dwight?'

'Yeah. Dwight Butler,' I add, when Bryce gives me a prompting look to tell me he doesn't know who I'm talking about.

He thinks for a moment. I can see his eyes darting around like he's trying to picture him. Then he says, 'Oh, yeah. Hangs out with a kid missing an eyebrow?'

Half an eyebrow, I correct him mentally. Aloud, I say, 'Yeah.'

'Since when did you hang out with that guy?'

'I met him before the party at the beach. And he's my lab partner for physics.'

'Oh.'

'Why? Is there some kind of problem with that?'

'What? No, no!' he exclaims hurriedly, wide-eyed. 'I didn't mean it in that way. I just wondered because, you know, he's . . . kind of a nerd.'

'So?'

He shrugs. 'I guess it's not a bad thing. He's just – well, a loser.'

'I didn't get that impression.' My stomach churns; I should be defending Dwight, but I'm too scared to risk damaging Bryce's – and everyone else's – opinion of me. I cringe, thinking how shallow I've become.

'Something tells me you don't really care all that much whether it's socially acceptable for the popular new girl to be all buddy-buddy with the nerdy guy.'

I shrug, avoiding answering the question. Heck yes, I care. But if he thinks otherwise, I'll let him think that.

He smiles wider, chuckling under his breath. 'See, that's what I meant about you earlier. You're interesting.'

'I think *weird* might be the word you're looking for,'

I mumble. I instantly clamp my mouth shut, unable to believe I actually just said that.

Bryce heard me; but he laughs, like he thinks I'm joking. 'No, that word definitely doesn't describe you. *Pretty. Intriguing. Funny.*'

I blush – I can't help it. I bite my lip as though I'm trying to stop smiling, and duck my head because I don't want him to see me blush. Then I remember – oh yeah, no curtain of hair to hide my face. I laugh. 'Is this you trying to be cute on the first date?'

'That depends.'

'On what?'

'Is it working?'

I giggle. 'Yes, it's definitely working.'

Bryce leans back in his side of the booth with a confident kind of smile. 'Good.'

Over the rest of dinner we talk about all kinds of things. Miraculously, I manage to avoid telling him too much about myself before I moved to Florida.

But we chat, and it's not as uneasy and forced as I'd feared. In fact, it's just nice. I laugh and smile, and even though I occasionally panic about what to say, I find I'm having a good time.

Bryce gives in eventually when I insist on paying for my half of the bill. It does take a while to convince him, though; at first he wouldn't even let me give the tip.

He gets me home about quarter of an hour before my curfew.

Except he doesn't park right outside; he parks two or three houses down. I know what's coming: the goodnight kiss at the end of the first date. I may not be very up to scratch on date etiquette and guys, but I've seen enough movies and read enough books and magazines to know that much.

And I don't blame him. I bet my parents – okay, my mom in particular – will be peeking out of the window to check it was me.

'I had a good time tonight,' I tell him, unbuckling my seatbelt. 'Thanks.'

'It's no problem,' he replies. That smile must have girls' stomachs filled with butterflies. I know mine is. 'I had a great night too.'

There's a moment that seems endless; I wait with bated breath, wondering if he's going to kiss me or not. I don't want to move in first in case I look silly.

Then Bryce leans towards me and presses his lips gently against mine. I kiss him back, and all of a sudden feel light and warm inside.

We both break the kiss at the same time, but Bryce doesn't move away; his forehead rests against mine, his breath mingling with my own.

'I said yes because you were nice to me,' I whisper.

'Sorry?' His voice is as quiet as mine.

'You wanted to know why I said yes. I said yes because you were nice to me and you didn't even know me.'

He doesn't say anything for a couple of seconds. I count seven heartbeats thudding heavily inside my ribcage before he reacts; and then he puts a hand up and tilts my face up towards his so that he can kiss me again.

'Madison,' he breathes softly, staying close so that his lips brush against mine, 'I'm very glad you said yes.'

Chapter 17

Bryce is waiting for me after my world history class first period the next day. At first I think he's just waiting to go in to see the teacher, or something, so I smile and say hi, then carry on walking.

'Whoa, don't leave so fast,' he laughs, jogging a couple of steps to catch up to me. 'I wait for you outside your class and you walk off?'

I laugh, but then I do a double take and pause, my pace slowing. 'You waited for me?'

'Well, yeah.'

'Oh.' I smile brightly up at him. 'Thanks.'

'What class do you have next?'

'Art and photography,' I tell him. 'How 'bout you?'

'English literature,' he sighs, not sounding very enthusiastic, and rolling his eyes. 'Tell me why *The Catcher in the Rye* is such a great book?'

I grin at him. 'It's not that bad. We looked at it last

year, in my old school. I liked it. I loved the whole thing with Holden and his hat—'

'It's not that bad?' He raises an eyebrow. 'It sucks.'

I shrug. 'Whatever. To each their own. I maintain that it's one of the best things ever to grace my book-shelf.'

He laughs, and we round the corner, turning into the bustling main corridor. Usually I'd be shoving my way through people, but everyone seems to just part for Bryce like the Red Sea. Like he has some kind of force field clearing his path.

When we finally reach my art room, I pause before following some of the kids inside. I turn to say goodbye to Bryce, and as I do, I see Carter behind him. I shoot him a smile, and he returns it – but quickly stops when Bryce turns to see who I'm smiling at. Carter ducks his head and doesn't look back up at me.

For a moment I'm frozen in place, staring at Carter, feeling shocked, and a little hurt. What's up with him?

I shake myself mentally as he goes into the class-room, and turn back to Bryce. 'Uh, thanks. For walking me to class, I mean. Um. Yeah.' I shut up before I stammer and babble any more, and settle for a smile instead.

'No problem. I'll catch you later.'

'Okay.'

He gives me a kiss on the cheek, and then carries on down the corridor towards his English classroom.

I sense a few people looking at me as I walk into class. They're whispering too – loud enough that I can make out what they're saying:

'Are they dating?'

'I heard they totally hooked up at Tiffany's party on Friday. Jane told me all about it.'

'She's been here, like, what, a week? And she's already getting together with *him*?'

'I'm so jealous – he's totally hot.'

'... don't you think? I mean, just look at that nose stud. So gross.'

I clench my jaw, breathing deeply. They're only talking about me because of Bryce. They can judge me for that all they want – it's only a few stupid rumors, it doesn't mean anything. What matters is that I've got some friends, and they're only too happy that I'm with Bryce now. Moreover, *I'm* happy. So they can carry on; it's all a load of trash anyway.

I know it'll be all over the school by the end of the day. News travels fast here. But at least it's not exactly bad news ... Actually, I think, it's pretty darn good news.

So I lift my chin, instead of looking down at the floor. I make my way to my usual spot next to Carter, and drop into my seat, pretending to be absolutely oblivious to the gossip.

'Hey,' I say to Carter, smiling.

'So, you and Higgins, huh?'

I shrug my shoulders alternately. 'I guess so.'

'When did that happen?'

'Um, I . . .' I clear my throat. 'Tiffany's party? We were all playing truth or dare, then . . .'

'Ah, truth or dare,' he says, nodding knowingly, looking me right in the eye. 'I see.'

'We only kissed, though,' I say hastily, making my voice deliberately loud, in case he'd heard I'd slept with Bryce. I didn't want that kind of reputation. 'Then we went to the movies last night and . . .'

'And then you lived happily ever after,' he finishes for me with a wry smile.

I laugh. 'Oh yeah, totally. Planning the wedding and everything. Would you like to see some sonograms?'

Carter laughs, and I see him relaxing.

'You still think it's weird that I talk to you even though I'm friends with them, don't you?'

I have to say it: I know it's why he looks kind of uncomfortable around me sometimes; why, when he saw Bryce, he pretended to ignore me.

The look on his face and his few seconds of silence are enough to tell me I'm right.

'That's stupid. You're just being silly.'

He laughs. 'You're a very blunt person, aren't you?'

'Sorry, I didn't mean it like—'

'Oh, no, I didn't mean that in a bad way. It was more of a statement. It's good that you don't believe that you can't talk to certain people because they're not at the same level in the social pyramid. Although, I think you pretty much rival Tiffany now. Dating the most popular guy in school does give your own popularity a boost.'

I laugh. 'I suppose so.'

Then Carter says, 'Dwight likes you.'

I don't say anything – just knit my eyebrows and tilt my head to the side, giving him a questioning look.

'You know,' he says, shrugging. 'He likes you. Not *likes* you likes you,' he clarifies hastily. 'But he likes you as a friend, at least. Even if you are too good for him now.'

I snort. 'Yeah, sure. Just because I hang out with some cheerleaders and jocks?'

'Madison, come on. Don't tell me you don't know that nerds and jocks don't mix.'

The way Carter says 'nerds and jocks don't mix' makes it sound like it's some kind of universal law. It sounds so incredibly ridiculous that I burst out laughing. Carter grins back at me, chuckling – although

174

I'm not sure if he's responding to the fact that I find it funny, or to the fact that what he said is actually ridiculous.

'If everyone's done talking, I'd like to begin the lesson,' Miss Augustan announces loudly, her voice carrying so that everyone shuts up pretty darn quickly.

I glance away from her once to look at Carter, though; and wonder if what he's just said means I'll have to choose between my two very different sets of friends.

Chapter 18

I'm right: the news that Bryce Higgins is dating that new girl, the one with the nose piercing – yeah, that's it, the short blonde one, Madison Something – is all over the school. It spreads like wildfire, and I only have to walk down a hallway to hear people say, 'That's the one who's dating Bryce.'

I don't exactly want to be known by who I'm dating, but I'd rather be 'that girl dating Bryce' than 'that weirdo loser', or 'Fatty Maddie'.

As soon as the bell rings after lunch, I head off to AP physics with Dr Anderson; I turned up about a minute late to the previous lesson and was told that since it was my first week he would let it slide, but if it happened again I'd have detention. I don't want to be late for a single lesson now.

On my way there, I spot the back of a familiar head of curly black hair in front of me, turning towards the staircase.

'Dwight!' I call, but he doesn't hear me over the noise of kids going to class. I jog up to him, glad now that I'm wearing my Converse today rather than heels (even if Tiffany turned her nose up at them earlier). He doesn't hear me come up behind him, so I jump at his back, my hands clapping down on his shoulders, and he stumbles forward slightly.

'I called and you didn't hear,' I tell him before he can ask what the heck I'm doing.

He blinks two or three times, like he's a little shell-shocked and confused, but then shakes his head rapidly and smiles that easy, infectious smile at me, his sea-green eyes lighting up. 'Hey, Madison.'

'How's it going?' I ask.

'Not too bad,' he replies. 'How about you?'

'Okay.'

'Only okay? If what I've heard through the grapevine is anything to go by, things are better than okay for you right now.' He nudges his elbow at my ribs, and I laugh.

'So you heard about me and Bryce.'

'Uh-huh.' He nods and smiles at me again. 'When were you planning on telling me? I'm truly hurt by this betrayal, Madison. How can you not tell your AP physics lab partner that you're dating the hottest guy in school?' The feigned hurt is so melodramatic he can't

177

keep up the façade for more than a few seconds; then he breaks out in a grin and laughs with me.

'Please, I'm begging you, don't go giving me every single detail of your relationship. Personally, I'm not that bothered whether or not he's a great kisser. Or if he's got, like, the hottest abs you've ever seen in your whole *life*.'

I laugh, and push open the door to Room 31. 'Don't worry, I'll spare you the details, Dwight.'

'Thank God for that.'

'Hand these out,' Dr Anderson tells a girl near the front, handing her a stack of papers. As she gets up to distribute them, he carries on in his slow voice: 'What you'll be receiving now is a copy of the basis of your projects. You'll all remember, I hope, that you will be working with your partner on a project to investigate a physicist who changed the science world in his or her own unique way . . .'

He carries on – the same stuff he told us last week about the project counting for twenty percent of our final grade. Then he starts to read through the sheet we're being handed, which is the most pointless exercise.

As the girl approaches our table, she pauses. 'Are you really dating Bryce Higgins?' she whispers to me.

'Um . . . yes,' I whisper back.

'Omigod,' she breathes. 'You're one lucky girl. Do you know most girls in this school would kill for a shot with him?' She smiles and puts two sheets on our desk before heading to the next table.

'Has it been like that all day?' Dwight asks, a chuckle in his voice.

'Sadly, yes.'

He bites back a laugh, but smirks. 'You poor thing. Popularity is such a burden.'

'Is that supposed to be you taking a dig at me?'

'Not really. Just a dig at popular kids in general.'

I roll my eyes and shake my head at him. My eyes glaze over when I scan the sheet, and in the end I slump over the table, my elbow on the desk and my cheek resting on my fist. I suppress a yawn as Dr Anderson drones on. Dwight's taking notes, like most of the class, so I take out my notebook too. Part of me thinks that if it weren't for Dwight, I wouldn't make any effort in this class at all.

As we pack up our stuff, Dwight and I are talking about the project. It has to be handed in by Christmas break, so we have a couple of months, but with the amount of work Dr Anderson expects us to put in, we need to get started as soon as possible.

'How about this weekend?' Dwight says. 'We can

meet up at your place or mine and have a look. I've already got a couple of ideas, so it won't be too difficult.'

I nod. 'Sounds good.'

I do wonder briefly if I might see Bryce this weekend, but then I shrug it off. I can see him another time. I'll hang out with him in school too. It's not that big a deal.

'Hey,' says a voice I recognize as Andy's as we leave the lab. He's waiting outside. 'Double math got cancelled,' he says, by way of explanation.

'Lucky,' I giggle.

'Lucky? It's terrible! We were doing integration today.'

I laugh again, but then realize he's kind of serious, so I stop.

'What're you guys doing now?' he asks, pretending not to acknowledge the brief awkward moment.

'Um . . .'

'I don't know what Madison's doing, but I was going to finish off some work from trig—'

'How 'bout we go grab a milkshake?' Andy suggests. 'You guys up for it?'

'Uh . . .' Dwight looks at me uncertainly.

'Sure,' I say, grinning. I haven't hung out with them since the party on the beach over a week ago, and it'd be nice to have a bit of a change. 'That'd be great. I could kill for a strawberry milkshake right now.'

We start to head off, wandering down the corridor. Suddenly I see that Tiffany and Summer are heading towards the stairs too, and we all meet on the landing, neither group heading down. I don't miss the way Tiffany's nose scrunches up ever so slightly at the sight of Andy and Dwight; like she's looking down on them.

'Madison, what're you doing?' she asks, turning to look at me.

'Um . . . going for milkshakes?'

'It's fine,' Andy mumbles quietly to me. 'You can take a rain check.'

'Yeah, but—'

'Madison,' Tiffany says. Her voice holds a certain ring of command. She arches an eyebrow at me, almost daring me to object – but there's a calm smile on her face, and I squirm inside, torn.

I open and close my mouth, trying to say something, anything, when Dwight decides for me.

'See you around,' he says quietly, and gives me a fleeting smile before heading down the stairs with Andy, leaving me with the girls.

They wait until the boys are out of earshot to say anything. Summer speaks first: 'Were you *really* going to go with them for milkshakes?'

'Yeah.'

Tiffany sighs. 'Honey, I know he's your lab partner so you guys have gotta get along and everything, but . . .'

'What, hanging around with him is bad for my social standing?' My voice is derisive and blunt. I immediately regret saying anything.

Tiffany just looks at me like 'duh'. 'People like them don't mix with people like us. You think I haven't heard what people say behind my back? A bunch of people at this school think I'm a total bitch, and quite frankly, I couldn't care less about those people. Half of what they've heard about me isn't even true.'

'And what, you think Dwight and Andy are like that?'

'I didn't say that,' she replies. 'But you know how these things work. Not everything is rainbows and butterflies. There's a certain way things are done and—'

'Save it,' I say, but I try not to say it in a mean way. Tiffany wasn't being horrible, or even patronizing, really, but I don't care to hear about the social airs and graces of the popular clique. 'I get it – it's fine.'

And I *do* get it, but it's not fine. It's not fine at all.

I know I'm acting stupid. And shallow. And awful.

But I can't help it.

I don't want a repeat of anything like what happened to the old Madison back in Pineford, Maine. The new Madison has friends, and she's popular, and the best thing is: she's not the victim this time. And I plan to keep it that way, whatever it takes.

'So, where are we going?' I ask instead, putting on a bright smile to let them know I'm not mad, even though I sort of am.

'Back to Summer's.'

'My mom found out this morning that she has to bake two hundred cupcakes for my little sister's school fundraiser,' Summer explains. 'So we've been enlisted to help.'

'Two hundred? All by herself?'

'Well, the other moms are working, so my mom volunteered. She likes doing this kind of thing,' Summer says.

We begin heading down the stairs, and Summer and Tiffany tell me all about the time Summer's mom offered to make all the animal costumes for the nativity play when they were in fourth grade, and how some of the costumes hadn't been big enough, and none of the sheep could move, and they'd fallen down like dominoes on stage.

There's a nagging feeling at the back of my mind telling me that I should've just gone for milkshakes with Dwight and Andy, whatever my friends thought about it.

But I know that's just the way high school is. There are the people you hang around with, and the people you don't. And that hierarchy is not to be disturbed. And that is exactly why I push away the feeling and don't say anything – and why I don't reply until I'm home later that evening to the text Dwight sends me as we're getting into Summer's car: *Any chance we can start the project at yours this weekend? My sister is having a sleepover. . . I am declaring my house off limits for my own sanity.*

Chapter 19

As Summer drives down my road later, I see brake lights ahead of us, but I can't quite make out the car – I just know it's not my mom's or my dad's.

'Whose car is that?' I ask.

Summer shrugs, but as we draw closer, she exclaims, 'Oh! That's Bryce's car.'

She pulls to a stop behind it, and he gets out.

Summer winks at me as I turn to thank her for the ride home. 'And you said he wasn't interested.'

I laugh. 'Shut up. See you!'

'Talk to you soon!' she replies, and leans out of her open window. 'Hey, Bryce!'

He raises a hand. 'Hey.'

Then I close the car door, and Summer ducks back into her car and pulls off.

And she leaves me standing there, with flour, a bit of dough, and some icing smeared over my T-shirt and the front of my jeans, with my incredibly cute boyfriend, who is most definitely not covered in cake. My arms hang awkwardly at my sides and, partly for something to do, I wrap my right hand around my left.

'Um, hi.'

He reaches a hand up to brush my cheek. 'You have a little icing on your face.'

I laugh, and raise my eyebrows. 'Just my face?'

'I figured you wouldn't be too impressed if I brushed the flour off your boob.'

I laugh again. Then the front door opens.

'Madison,' Dad says. 'I thought I heard a car pull up.'

Then he takes in the state of me, and Bryce. He looks from one to the other a couple of times, mouth open like he's about to say something, but he's not sure what. Then I remember that Dad hasn't met Bryce; and Mom only saw him briefly.

And once I realize that Dad will be acting like he did whenever Jenna brought a new boyfriend home, I immediately begin to get nervous.

But Dad opts to go for me first. 'Madison, what happened to your clothes?'

'Me and Tiffany were helping Summer's mom bake cupcakes.'

'Right . . .' he says slowly. Then he stands up a little

straighter and crosses his arms. 'Aren't you going to introduce me to your friend, Madison?'

'Um, maybe. Two seconds.'

Dad raises an eyebrow at me, and Bryce starts to say something – he's probably about to introduce himself and sound super-polite. Except I elbow him in the ribs and say, 'Dad, I'll be in in a minute.'

And Dad says, 'Fine. Nice meeting you, Madison's friend.'

Once the front door is shut again, I turn to Bryce. The corner of his mouth twitches up in a smirk and he says, 'Are you too ashamed of me to introduce me to your dad?'

'No, but—'

'So what, I'm gonna have to sneak in your bedroom window at night to see you?' He pretends to consider that for a minute. 'I can live with that. Nothing wrong with a bit of excitement.'

'Shut up,' I laugh, prodding his arm, and he laughs too. 'What're you doing here anyway?'

'I came to see my girlfriend,' he answers simply. 'Or didn't you want to see me?'

'No, no, I do! It's just ... well, you could have warned me! How'd you know I'd even be home?'

'You didn't answer your phone earlier, but Tiffany told me when you'd left Summer's.'

'Oh, right.'

There's a silence.

'Aren't you going to invite me in?' Bryce asks, but not rudely.

'Right. Yeah. Sure. I, uh . . .' I clear my throat. 'Come on in.'

With that, he follows me inside.

I lead him into the lounge, where both my parents are watching TV. I'd bet anything that they wouldn't be here if they didn't think they were about to see my boyfriend. Dad would've been on his computer; Mom might've had her feet up reading a magazine.

'Mom, Dad, this is Bryce. Bryce, these are my parents, Carrie and Greg.'

That's when Bryce puts on one of his hundred-watt smiles that I find incredibly cute. 'It's really nice to meet you.' And then he puts his hand out.

Dad shakes it. 'Nice to meet you too. Are you staying for dinner?'

'I don't want to impose . . .'

And I just stand there thinking, *Man, he is really playing the part of the perfect boyfriend, isn't he?*

'Oh, no, you're not imposing at all!' Mom says, with just the appropriate amount of enthusiasm. 'It's no trouble at all, don't worry. Madison, why don't you go clean up before dinner?'

That's when I remember I'm covered in cake mixture.

I turn to Bryce. 'Give me ten minutes.' I run up the stairs, and call back over my shoulder to my parents, 'Be nice!'

I want to look good, so I should really take more time and care washing the icing sugar and flour out of my hair and choosing clothes; but I don't want Bryce to be left alone with my parents for too long: with Jenna's boyfriends they tend to tell funny (or as Jenna saw it, embarrassing) stories from her childhood. More than once they've cracked open an album of baby photos.

I get back to the lounge and Bryce says, 'Wow. I've never known a girl get ready so quickly.'

'Is that an insult?'

He laughs. 'You think I'm complaining because you didn't spend forty-two minutes on your hair? Not that you need to,' he adds quickly, with a wink. 'You look great.'

'Oh. Thanks.'

'Your parents are in the kitchen,' he tells me before I can ask.

'What were they saying?'

'Nothing incriminating.' He smiles warmly. 'They're really nice, don't worry. And I *think* they like me . . .'

'I'm sure they do.' My parents would be happy with almost any guy I brought home. The fact that he's nice, and a cute jock, means they probably love him already.

I leave Bryce in the lounge while I pop my head around the kitchen door.

'Dinner will be ten minutes,' Mom tells me. 'And oh, he's a lovely boy, Dice! And he's so polite too.'

'We only asked him about school and soccer – no embarrassing stories,' Dad assures me just as I start to ask. Then he adds, 'Yet.'

'Ha-ha, very funny. Just . . . be nice, okay? Please.'

'Of course we will,' Mom laughs. 'We're hardly going to scare off your first boyfriend, now, are we?'

I only sigh and shut the door, going back to the lounge.

Bryce is at one end of the couch. I flop down on the other end with a big sigh. 'My mom said dinner is nearly ready.'

'Why are you sitting all the way over there?'

'Because it's comfy . . . ?'

'It's comfi*er* here.' Bryce pats the spot next to him.

'I know my own couch, Bryce. And it's comfi*est* here.'

'We'll see about that,' he says. Then he reaches over, grabs my hips and legs, and pulls me over. I don't resist him, I just giggle – but he's probably strong enough to move me even if I'd tried to push him off. He sits me half on his lap.

I'm not entirely sure what to do, but then he kisses me, and I don't need to know what to do anymore. I simply kiss him back and lean into him as one of his arms goes around me and his hand rests on my back. I can feel the warmth through my T-shirt.

'Convinced now?' he asks in a quiet, teasing voice.

'Not really,' I answer, and I tilt my head down to his to kiss him again.

I like the way Bryce kisses. Not that I've got anyone to compare him to, but I've heard plenty of tales of bad kissers from Jenna. There are the sloppy kissers who salivate all over your face (or so I'm told), and there are the kissers who ram their tongue down your throat, and Bryce is neither of those. His lips are soft and warm, and he clearly knows what he's doing – which I'm quite glad of, because I don't really know what *I'm* doing.

Then Mom calls, 'Dinner's ready!' and we have to stop.

Over the entire thirty-two minutes we're all sitting at the dinner table, my parents don't say a single embarrassing thing about me, and neither do they grill Bryce too much – I mean, they ask him a lot of questions, but nothing too invasive. Mostly about soccer and school and college.

I'm on tenterhooks the whole time, though, just waiting for something that might send him running.

But soon enough we're all finished and Bryce is still there, and I'm not burying my head in my hands in shame. Mom collects the plates up to put in the dishwasher and I stand up to take the glasses over.

'He's very nice,' Mom says under her breath to me. 'What're you two doing now?'

'I don't know.'

'Well, your dad's going to be in the lounge – there's a documentary he wants to watch.'

For a heartbeat or two I don't say anything, because this situation crossed my mind at dinner. And by 'situation' I mean 'my bedroom'. Because what am I meant to do? There's a spare downstairs room, but it's full of odd furniture and boxes we haven't unpacked from the move, so that means my room is the only place to go.

It isn't that I'm worried about him seeing my room or anything. It's just that I've never had a boy there before. This is all new to me.

But at least I know there's no dirty laundry on my floor. By the time I turn back to the table, Dad's already excused himself, and Bryce shoots me a smile.

'Thanks for dinner, Mrs Clarke,' he says to my mom. 'It was great.'

'No problem at all, Bryce.'

I smile to him and tilt my head to the doorway. He takes the hint without me having to say anything, and stands up, following me out of the room.

I pause when I get to the bottom of the stairs, and my heart is beating hard in my chest. I'm only nervous because I don't want him to think I've got . . . other intentions in mind. I don't want to give the wrong impression, but nor do I want to sit in the lounge with my dad for the next couple of hours.

'Uh . . .' I clear my throat, and point a hand awkwardly at the lounge door. 'My dad's watching some documentary, so . . . um . . . do you want to – I mean, the only place left is—'

I stop stammering because I see that Bryce is smiling, and then he chuckles. He takes a step closer to me and then leans down to plant a kiss on my forehead, one hand resting on my shoulder.

'Chill,' he tells me, with that cute smile. 'Lead the way.'

I let out a huge, silent sigh of relief, and my heartbeat gradually slows. As I turn and head upstairs, Bryce's hand slips from my shoulder to my hand, and I lock my fingers through his, smiling to myself.

When we get to my room, my fingers seem to get stuck around the doorknob.

'You okay?' Bryce's voice jars me from whatever frozen state I was in.

'Yeah,' I answer hastily. I glance back at him with a quick smile. 'Sorry.' I take a deep breath, and it's only a little shaky. *Get a grip, Madison!*

Even though I know my room isn't that messy – well, Mom says it's a mess, but I say it's an organized mess, with everything exactly as I want it – I say, 'Sorry, I haven't had chance to tidy up . . .'

'Are you kidding?' Bryce laughs. 'You're lucky if you can see the floor of my room most of the time.'

I chuckle, but suddenly my only thought is: *Where do I sit?*

I look at my bed; do I sit there, or is that going to give him the wrong impression? I'd sit on the bench by the window, except that Bryce is there. I don't want to sit on my desk chair. So I perch on the end of my bed, looking at him.

'How come there aren't any photos of you with all your old friends?' he asks. 'It's just that I know Tiff has tons of photos of everyone, and so do my cousins. I figured it was a girl thing.'

The lie comes easily to my lips: 'They haven't been unpacked yet.'

'Ah,' he says, buying it without question. 'Do you miss them?'

'Sorry?'

'Your friends. Everything back in Maine.'

'Oh. No. I don't.'

'Really?' He sounds quite shocked, but I suppose it's abnormal not to miss everything from the first sixteen years of your life.

'Well, I don't miss it as much as I probably should' – I make it sound like a joke – 'but I like it here a lot better.'

'Why's that?' he asks, one eyebrow raised and a suggestive note in his tone.

Alien as I am to the concept of flirting, I giggle and say, 'Well, this guy might have something to do with it . . .'

'Does this guy have a name?'

'Yes.'

'Are you going to tell me anything about him?'

'For one thing, he's a really nice guy – not to mention incredibly attractive.'

I have no idea what words are spilling out of my mouth, but I can't seem to control them. Not that this seems to be a bad thing; maybe I'm doing something right for a change.

'Naturally.' He smirks slightly, unable to keep the

195

serious expression on his face. I giggle again. He's taken a few steps closer without me even noticing, and now he's only inches away; I have to crane my neck back to look up at him.

'And' – he takes another step and I put a hand on his shirt – 'I really want to kiss him again right now.'

'Well, he's more than happy to oblige.'

With that, he leans down, one hand on either side of my legs, and I reach up to kiss him, my arms around his neck. He shifts closer and forces me to lean back on the bed, until he's lying on top of me. He supports himself so that he's not crushing me, but the weight is comfortable. Soon his kisses turn harder and hungrier, and I try to pull him closer still.

I'm not sure how long we're kissing like that, but we only break apart when Bryce rolls onto his side, turning me too, so that we're lying facing each other.

We just look at one another, our breathing a little heavier than usual from the intensity of our kiss. Then, very slowly, Bryce reaches up to brush my bangs out of my eyes; his hand lingers on my cheek, and there's something about the gesture and the way he's looking at me with his clear, warm brown eyes, a smile tweaking the corner of his mouth, which makes my heart flip.

'Bryce?'

'Yeah?'

'Why were you so nice to me, that first day of school?'

His eyebrows twitch together in a frown. 'That's a random question.'

'And that's not an answer.'

He laughs. 'I don't know. I guess I'm just a nice person, for one thing. You were new, and that's hard for anyone. And you know, you're pretty, so I'd be lying if I said that wasn't a factor.'

The way he just throws the compliment out so casually makes me blush, but I don't mind because it's the good kind of blushing.

'And when I spoke to you at the beach party the weekend before,' he says in a quiet, slow, musing sort of voice, 'you just seemed . . . it's hard to explain. You weren't aloof and snobby; you were just . . . mysterious, I guess. You weren't like most girls.'

'And being different didn't make you run a mile?'

He laughs again, not realizing I'm being perfectly serious because I'm kind of shocked. I take his laugh to mean: *No it didn't* – which is good enough for me.

'I'm glad you moved here,' he says then.

I blink once, staring at him. There's a sincere smile

on his lips and he's just **looking** at me with those wonderfully warm brown eyes.

And I say without having to think twice about it, 'I'm really glad I moved here too.'

Chapter 20

I guess I always had a preconceived opinion of popular people. Which is extremely hypocritical of me, considering I know you should at least try not to judge people.

But I couldn't help it. I've seen first hand the different strains of the popular crowd.

When I was a freshman, the crowd of seniors who seemed to rule the school were some of the most horrible, self-centered girls you could ever imagine. Jenna hung around with them sometimes, but she wasn't quite high enough up on the social ladder to make them stop bullying me.

Then, during my sophomore year, when Jenna was the new It Girl, things were better; her friends were nicer. Sure, there were a couple of mean girls, because some people are just mean and you can't change that. But for the most part, everyone was okay. And they were the kind of people who'd smile at you as they walked down the halls, rather than stalking past like they owned the place and you were a piece of gum on the sidewalk. But when I say 'you', I don't mean 'me'. The best I got was being ignored.

And not just by the popular people; everybody in that place seemed to have something against the old Madison. Or at least, they couldn't bear to be associated with me.

I'd sit on my own in class. I'd sit on my own at lunch. Whenever we had to have a partner for a science lab or a project, whoever got stuck with me would get pitying looks from everyone else. I wasn't completely awful at sport; but I was always picked last in Gym class.

But yeah, I guess I always had this fixed idea of what popular people were really like.

And as it turns out, actually being in the popular clique is a very surreal experience.

By the time Friday rolls around, I'm ready for the weekend. I just need a break. I don't get any homework that day and I only have a concluding paragraph of my art essay to write. So everything is good.

It probably helps that Fridays are easy days. Well, aside from starting the morning with double AP physics. Then it's just gym, which is tolerable at the moment, and US politics, where nobody does much actual work. Then the rest of my day is clear, and by lunch time I'm free to go home. Bliss.

Once the bell rings to signal that my US politics class is over and I'm free to leave, I slide all my things into my messenger bag and head off. But I don't rush; I'm free to amble home at my own pace. I stick in an earphone and put a Fall Out Boy album on.

I go via my locker to pick up my physics textbooks – Dwight and I arranged to make a start on our project tonight. I'm not sure if I'll actually need the books, but better safe than sorry.

By the time I get to my locker, pretty much everyone else has already made their way to their next class. The hallway is almost empty; a few kids are still shuffling off to class. I spin in my combination and start loading my books into my bag.

Someone walks past me, then stops, and I hear a combination being spun. I glance up, but the door of my locker is blocking them from view. I step back to see who it is. 'Oh. Hey, Dwight.'

He turns, and seems to notice me there for the first time. Then he shoots me a small smile. 'Hello again. No class?'

I shake my head no. 'I'm free for the rest of the day.'

'Lucky.'

'Oh, come on,' I laugh, and shut my locker. 'You love school really.'

'Well. Debatable at times, but it's not all bad. I was meant to have chemistry, but the lesson's cancelled – the teacher's off on some course.'

'Ah.'

Hearing footsteps coming from the end of the hallway, we both look up. It's Bryce, wearing his soccer kit. He raises a hand to wave to me.

'What're you doing here?' I ask. 'I thought you guys had practice?'

'I forgot to tell my history teacher,' he says. 'Can't have him thinking I'm skipping class so soon.'

'Oh,' I say.

Bryce slows to a stop in front of me. 'You're off home now, right?'

'Uh-huh.'

'What're you doing later? I was thinking maybe I could come over to see you again,' he says, lowering his voice, though I know Dwight can hear every word we say.

'I'm busy,' I say, my mouth twisting downward because – no offence to Dwight – I'd much rather be with Bryce than doing some stupid project for a class I'm destined to fail. 'I can't tonight. Schoolwork.'

'On a Friday night?'

'I'm sorry . . .'

'Well, give me a call if you finish early, OK? I'd like to see you.'

I smile. 'Sure thing.'

He dips his head to kiss me, and we say, 'See you.' I watch him walk away until he glances back at me and waves, then I look at Dwight again.

He finally turns away from his locker to say, 'Schoolwork, huh?'

I pretend to look for something in my bag so I don't have to meet his eye. 'Will you still have time to fit me in around your schoolwork?'

When I look up, Dwight is smirking. I smack his arm playfully. 'Shut up!'

He lets out the chuckle and gives me that warm, lopsided smile, which makes me grin back at him. We start walking down the hallway, and he bumps my shoulder, and both of us laugh all over again.

'I'm heading to the library,' he tells me.

'Do you . . . I mean, if you've got a free period, do you want to go for a milkshake or something?'

He winces. It's brief, but I don't miss it. 'We probably shouldn't. One of your friends might see us.'

I can see how uncomfortable I've made him, so I let it drop. 'That's cool. It was just a thought. Enjoy the library. Send me a text when you're on your way over later, please?'

He nods. 'Course I will.'

'My mom will insist on giving you dinner, by the way,' I tell him. 'Part of being a good hostess, or maybe it's just the mother gene, I don't know.'

He chuckles, but says, 'It's fine, I can eat at home. Honestly. I don't want to put you to any trouble.'

'Your argument is invalid. I have no idea what we're having for dinner, but there's always takeout if all else fails.' He begins to say, 'But—' except I cut him off, and say, 'This isn't up for debate, you know. I feed you; you don't get mad at me for being a useless partner. We're square.'

This makes him laugh even more. 'All right, all right, I give in – that sounds like a fair enough trade. I'll see you later, then.'

'Yup. See ya.'

And with that, we part ways: I go one way, and he goes the other.

Chapter 21

'Now, be *nice*,' I instruct my parents.

'Are we ever anything but, Dice? Anyone would think you're ashamed of us.' Dad tries to keep his poker face, but he's not doing a great job. I roll my eyes.

I smooth out a nonexistent crease in my black tank top. I haven't taken any special trouble with my clothes. I mean, I showered and fixed my hair, but I'm just in a pair of thin jeans with a tear in the knee that wasn't there when I bought them, and a plain black top. Nothing special at all.

I don't know why I'm so nervous . . . It's a different kind of nervous to when Bryce made his surprise visit earlier this week. That was very different: it was my boyfriend meeting my parents for the first time, and I've never been in that situation before.

This is much simpler: a friend coming around to work on a project. But I've never been in any kind of situation like this, either. I haven't had a friend, full stop, so there was never anybody to meet my parents. And I'm just (more than slightly) worried they will embarrass me.

I fidget with my belt buckle and look at the clock. The second hand has moved on an entire eight seconds since I last looked. Why is time going so slowly all of a sudden? It's like when you're in a dream and your limbs won't move as fast as they should, and you can't run or anything. It's frustrating, because you know there's nothing you can do about it.

I glance up again. Five seconds. I squeeze my eyes shut until bright spots of light dance across the inside of my eyelids. Then I look again at the clock. Six seconds.

I wonder if I take the clock off the wall and shake it, that'll make it move faster?

Dinggg-donnnng . . .

The doorbell sounds, followed by four rapid knocks. Mom starts, making a move and opening her mouth to say that she'll get the door, but I'm there before she has a chance to say anything.

I pause, run my fingers over my hair, straighten my tank top. Then I open the door wide, a smile ready on my face.

'Hey!' Dwight greets me with his lopsided, warm smile. A backpack is slung casually over his shoulder –

the zipper is not done up properly, and I recognize the corner of our physics textbook poking out.

I step back and gesture for him to come inside. I notice that he wipes his feet on the welcome mat outside on the porch, though. Mom would approve.

'Dinner will be ready soon,' I tell him. 'If you want to just dump your stuff down there for now . . .'

'All right.'

We've decided to do our project on Isaac Newton. Dwight wasn't too enthusiastic about this at first – he wanted to do someone more obscure, but since I know next to nothing about scientists, we agreed that someone well-known would be better.

Mom suddenly appears around the kitchen door. She's been dying to meet Dwight. 'Oh! You must be Dwight! It's so lovely to meet you – Madison's told us a lot about you.'

Dwight smiles and says, 'Thanks for having me to dinner, Mrs Clarke.'

'Oh, please, call me Carrie.'

'Carrie.' Dwight nods politely. 'All right.'

'And it's really no trouble at all, no trouble. I hope you're hungry – we've got a heap of food.'

I don't think Dwight picks up on it, but the enthusiasm in my mother's voice is bordering on hysterical. Sure, Jenna brought home plenty of friends (and guy friends, and boyfriends), but this situation is different, because it's me, and not Jenna. Mom's excited and nervous about me having a friend over to do a school project; she's more anxious than I am, actually.

And that's why I'm so terrified she's going to embarrass me.

'You may as well come and sit down,' Mom tells us, waving a hand to usher us forward. 'Dinner's almost ready.'

I nod and say, 'Okay,' and Dwight bends down to unlace his battered Converse. They're almost as worn as mine.

'So,' he says with a hint of laughter in his voice as he straightens back up to look at me. 'You talk about me a lot, do you?'

I bite the insides of my cheeks. 'I guess I mentioned you a couple of times . . .'

'Only a couple?' he teases.

'Fine, fine – you got me. I've been totally stalking you ever since I met you in the café, okay? I can't help myself.'

He laughs. I like his laugh. Just hearing it makes you feel happy. 'Come on – your parents won't be impressed if we let dinner get cold,' he tells me.

As we enter the kitchen, I see that Dad is plating up dinner. It's a chicken casserole, with extra veg in a dish on the table and a basket of bread and butter. My parents have put in just a little extra effort because Dwight's here.

'What's this project you kids are working on, then? Madison hasn't told us much about it,' Dad says, when we're all settled down.

I roll my eyes. I should've expected something like this. I've told them everything I can be bothered to about the project; they know the basics. But I have to hand it to them: it's a clever way to initiate conversation with Dwight without seeming too intrusive.

I glance sideways at him, and even though he isn't looking at me, I catch the gleam of enthusiasm in his eyes as he begins talking about our project.

'Are you interested in physics, then?' Mom asks.

He nods. 'Yeah. There's something truly amazing in discovering how the universe works. Trying to recreate the Big Bang, learning all the intricate little details of a single particle . . .' He trails off and takes a mouthful of chicken, ducking his head down.

'So is it just physics that interests you, or science in general?'

He looks back up, swallows and clears his throat. 'Science in general, but I've always liked physics in particular.'

'Guess what,' I say. 'Tiffany texted me earlier and

suggested I go to cheerleading tryouts, since they got postponed to next week.'

'Well, why don't you give it a shot?' Mom asks.

'Yeah, Madison,' Dwight says. For some reason, I get the impression he's mocking me – just a tad. 'Could be fun.'

'As if,' I snort. 'I am not – no way, no how – trying out for the cheerleading squad. I have some sanity left.'

Mom sighs. 'You should give it a shot, Dice – it's not that bad. Jenna always loved it.'

'Dice?' Dwight picks up on my parents' nickname for me. There's a small line creasing his forehead, drawing his dark eyebrows just a touch closer together. When he frowns like that, there's a little wrinkle on either side of his nose, like it wants to scrunch up. *It's cute*, I think, before I can stop myself.

'Oh,' Dad says. 'It's just what we call her.'

'*Dice*.' It's like he's testing out how it sounds, how it tastes. 'That's unusual. Why not Maddie?'

'I hate that name,' I snap, a bit too sharply.

There's a heavy heartbeat of silence hanging over the table. Then, 'Dice is cool, though.'

'Thanks,' I mumble, because I don't know what else to say.

'Do you do any sports, Dwight?' Dad asks him. 'Soccer, tennis . . . ?'

Dwight laughs, as if the idea is entirely ridiculous. 'No, I'm not much of a sportsperson, really. I do surf, though. My . . . my dad used to surf. He got me into it when I was younger.'

'Ah.'

'The great thing about surfing is that I can apply physics to the waves – there's a difference between waves in shallow and deep water . . . it's all to do with refraction—'

He cuts off midsentence, then laughs sheepishly. 'Sorry, I really shouldn't get started on this, or I could go on forever. My sister hates it when I talk science at dinner.'

'I always thought surfing looked really cool,' I say. 'I never got the chance to try it, though.'

'Really? Maybe I could teach you sometime. I taught Carter one summer. Unless you're afraid of getting your hair wet, or breaking a nail?'

'Ha ha,' I say sarcastically, rolling my eyes. He chuckles at me. 'Sure. That'd be great.'

We finish dinner with a little more easy conversation, and just as I help Mom load everything into the dishwasher, the phone in the hall rings.

'I'll get it,' I offer, and hold up a finger to signal 'one minute' to Dwight. I dash into the hallway and snatch up the phone. 'Hello?'

'Aloha, baby sis!' Jenna all but yells down the phone at me, and I have to hold it away from my ear briefly.

'Tone it down, Jen!'

'What's up?'

'Uh, you rang me.'

'Yes, and I rang with the purpose of asking what is up. And I ask this because I know for a fact that you have a study *date*.'

I roll my eyes, even though I know she can't see me. I walk around the banister and sit on the stairs. 'Would you calm down already? It's not a "study date", okay? We're just working on a Physics project.'

'Mm-hmm,' she says doubtfully. 'Sure, Mads, whatever you say. This is the cute guy who asked you to the beach party, though, right?'

'Yes, and that doesn't matter because it's purely platonic – and are you forgetting Bryce?'

'Sexy footballer boyfriend? Of course not.'

'He plays soccer, not football.'

'Oh, yeah. Sorry! How're things going with him?'

'Good. No different to when I spoke to you . . . what was it, Wednesday?'

'Yeah. Aw, I am happy about that. Now I absolutely *have* to tell you about this guy I met yesterday on campus. His name's Henry. He's *British*. How cool and

212

sexy is that, Mads? He's British! His accent is adorable. He asked me out for coffee.'

'When?'

'Yesterday.'

'No, when are you going for coffee?'

'In about an hour. He's in my art classes, but he's majoring in history.'

'Aw,' I say, smiling. Jenna had vowed to Mom that she wouldn't let any guys get in the way of college work – at least for the first semester – unless she thought they were worth it. And a year on, she'd been true to her word. But there was something in her voice that made me think she already liked this guy.

'Is Mom there?'

'Uh, she was in the kitchen . . .' I stand and lean over the banister, peeking into the kitchen, but there's no sign of my mom. In fact, there's no sign of Dad or Dwight, either.

'Mom?' I call.

'Don't worry,' Jenna says. 'Tell her I'll give her a call later, yeah?'

'All right.'

'In the lounge, honey!' Mom calls in reply to me.

'Okay!' I yell back. To Jenna I say, 'Have fun on your date.'

'Ditto to you,' she giggles. 'Bye!' And she hangs up before I can sigh and argue that *it's not a date*.

I find Dwight sitting in the middle of the couch, a familiar big fat photo album on his lap. Mom is beside him and stretches an arm to turn the page, and they look over at me as I walk in.

'Who was on the phone?' she asks.

But I just stand there, horror slowly creeping over me, as I stare at the photo album. It's the one that Jenna and I put together for Mom's birthday last year, with all her favorite photos – ones from her wedding, from when we were born, various birthdays and Christmases and Halloweens, and even as far back as her college graduation.

It's a great photo album.

But it isn't meant for other people to see.

What I should be thinking is: *Oh, gosh, how clichéd of them. They've gone down the old baby pictures route of embarrassing me. How predictable.*

But that's not what I'm thinking.

The page Dwight's on at the moment shows a photo of me and Jenna at the beach when I was about five. But I know that the next one was taken at Jenna's high school graduation: it is a photo of the old Madison.

Then the panic sets in and overtakes the horror that froze me in place.

I pounce onto the couch, half tumbling over Dwight's shoulder and knocking the album away. Mom gets up hastily and catches it before it hits the floor. I balance precariously for a second, and then collapse onto the space Mom just vacated, an arm splayed across Dwight.

'Madison!' Dad exclaims as I sort myself out and sit up. 'What are you doing?'

I turn to Dwight. 'Sorry.'

For a split second I catch the confusion on his face – and then it vanishes and he's perfectly composed again. 'Don't worry.'

'Madison,' Mom admonishes.

Still looking at Dwight, I say, 'I just don't like people looking at old photos of me.'

'It's okay,' he says. 'You don't have to explain yourself to me.'

I give him a sort of fleeting half-smile. He smiles back for a moment to let me know it's okay.

Mom lets out a sigh, but it's not one of frustration or irritation at me. It's more of a tired, sad sigh. She moves over to the bookcase and slides the photo album back into its slot between her *Collected Works of Shakespeare* and the *Complete Charles Dickens Collection*.

'Right – we'll leave you kids to work on your project, then,' Mom announces, as though I didn't just attack her photo album in a completely crazy way. 'We'll stay out of your way, don't worry.'

They close the door behind them. I hear the TV in the study, and the low hum of voices is the only noise.

'I'm sorry,' I tell Dwight again. 'I . . . it's just—'

'Don't worry about it.' He gives me a gentle smile; one that tells me he won't ask about it, and he doesn't think I'm a complete freak.

I let out a sigh of relief. 'So . . . shall we get started or what?'

'Yup. I'll just grab my bag.'

'Okay. I'll be back in a second – I have to get my laptop and books.'

I'd put my laptop and textbooks and a notebook and pen ready in a neat pile at the foot of my bed. I snatch up my laptop charger as well, just in case, and head back downstairs.

I'm almost at the bottom of the stairs when I hear: 'Dice.'

I pause for a moment, closing my eyes and taking a slow, long breath. In . . . and out.

I poke my head around the door of the study. Dad's reading the newspaper and Mom's surfing the internet – she's looking at winter coats. There's a rerun of some soap playing on the TV.

'What?'

'You didn't have to overreact like that.'

'You didn't have to show him a photo album,' I snap back, only just remembering to keep my voice low. 'I know it's your job to be embarrassing and whatever, but not – not . . . you just can't *do* that, okay?'

I don't expect them to understand properly. It's just that . . . it was so *hard*. It was hard trying to stay invisible when people wouldn't let me. And I didn't react, not once. I refused to let myself react; reacting would have made it worse, given them another excuse to laugh at me. And now I want to leave all of that behind me. I don't mind that there are occasional reminders of how I used to be – photos and home movies, stuff like that – but I don't want them to be shown to someone who I hope is my friend. I don't want anyone to know about the old Madison. I've started moving on and I'd like it to stay that way. The past stays in the past.

But it's not like I can explain all of that to my parents, exactly.

'Just . . . please don't do that to me again,' I say instead, and then I leave.

Back in the lounge, I find Dwight surrounded by books, his laptop booting up. He turns and smiles at me, and I smile back, as though everything is completely and entirely normal.

Chapter 22

'You're kidding me!' Dwight exclaims, laughter in his voice. 'You have an apple tree in your back yard?'

'I'm totally serious.'

He throws his arms up in the air and then brings his hands down to rest on top of his head, his fingers knitting together. He looks up the ceiling, chuckling and shaking his head. 'Oh, man, this is . . . this is *brilliant*!'

'Um . . . okay . . .' I frown, not understanding his enthusiasm about the apple tree. I clear my throat to get his attention again. 'Why is it brilliant, exactly?'

'Well, you know the story they tell you in, like, fourth grade, that an apple fell on Newton's head and then he discovered gravity, and whatever, right? Well, we can use your apple tree in experiments. It's perfect! We can—'

'Wait. You're not going to *actually* drop an apple on my head, are you?'

'Of course I am. It could help you pass AP physics. Look what it did for Newton.'

I stare at him for a long moment; a moment that stretches out as we both try and discern each other's thoughts. The innocent enthusiasm in his wide eyes makes me think he's serious . . . but he can't be, can he?

Eventually he starts chuckling. 'You didn't actually think I was serious, did you?'

I punch him in the arm, scowling. 'Heck *yeah*!'

He carries right on laughing at me. 'Oh God, you should've seen your face!'

I huff. 'Whatever.'

'In all seriousness, though,' Dwight continues, 'we can do an experiment to prove that acceleration due to gravity is 9.81 meters per second squared. We can drop an apple, measure the distance it falls, time how long it takes to fall . . . it'll be easy. Plot a graph, et cetera. I might be able to put together some kind of electro-magnetic timer, so the apple flips a switch whenever—'

'Yeah,' I interrupt. 'If you want to do that, it's entirely up to you. I will try to help where I can, but I can't promise I'll understand what I'm doing.'

He laughs, then cries out, 'Oh! And you know what else we can do? Drop an apple on some cornstarch and water.'

'What? Why would we do that?'

'There's something called non-Newtonian fluids . . .' he tells me, and goes on to explain about how certain liquids (like cornstarch mixed with water) can become solid (the particles form hydroclusters, whatever that means) when something hard – like an apple – hits them.

I tune out and reflect that there's something very cute about Dwight. It's hard to put my finger on what, though. I think it's mostly his smile. It's just so un-deniably happy, and the way it reaches higher on the left is quirky rather than strange. As he's talking, he gestures with his long limbs; he's thin and gangly and looks just a little uncoordinated, like he could knock a vase over at any moment.

Right now, he's just wearing a T-shirt with a faded design of a band I've never heard of, and a pair of black jeans. Whenever I've seen him at school, he's always in a plain T-shirt or polo. Maybe a pair of slacks instead of jeans. And I've never seen him wear Converse to school – it's always shiny white sneakers or polished shoes.

But I quite like band-tee Dwight. We've only been working on this project for about an hour and a half, but he's talked and laughed more than I've ever heard him during physics class. It's like a different side of him.

And yes, again, he is very, very cute.

'Madison . . . Madison . . .'

I jerk out of my thoughts. 'Huh?'

He laughs. 'Was I really boring you that much?'

'No – well, yes. I mean, no! No, you weren't boring me,' I stammer, then slap my palm to my face, blushing sheepishly. 'Sorry.'

He laughs again. 'Don't worry. I get carried away sometimes, I know. How about I just note down the experiments and how we're going to do them, and you can put in extra effort when it comes to carrying them out?'

'Deal,' I say. Then, 'Wanna take a break?'

'I think we deserve one. After all the work we've done.' He gestures at the notebooks we've scribbled in. His scribbles are more extensive than mine. There are even diagrams. My page leans more towards doodles than diagrams.

I get up and stretch my legs and arms. I pull back the blinds to check it hasn't suddenly started raining. 'Wanna check out the apple tree?'

I turn back and see Dwight grinning at me, and he clambers to his feet and stretches too, cracking his knuckles. 'Lead the way.'

It's pretty mild outside, but the sky is cloudy. The air acts as a kind of blanket, almost tangible as it presses against my skin.

Our back yard here is bigger than the one we had in Maine. Mom's flowerbeds sit on either side, against the fences that divide our yard firmly from the neighbors'. There's the pool too, of course – but that's got a cover over it because there was something wrong with the filter, and Dad hasn't managed to get someone to fix it – and a small decking area with the wooden table and chairs we brought from Pineford.

Right at the back of the garden, though, is my favorite spot. That's where the apple tree is. Whoever owned the house before us must've had a kid – or been a kid at heart – because there's a tire swing hanging from a thick branch. The rope is dark with age and a little frayed, but it's very thick and strong. There's also a bench. That's where Dwight sits; I take the swing.

Hooking my legs through the tire, I push my feet off the ground so that I spin in a circle a few times, and then rotate back until I come to a stop.

He's just smiling that crooked smile at me. 'You're such a child.'

I giggle, not bothering to deny it.

'So this is the apple tree.' He looks at it appraisingly and nods. 'It has surpassed my expectations, considering they don't grow very well in this kind of climate.'

'Oh. Um, cool.'

After a moment's hesitation he swings his long legs up onto the bench. One dangles off the end and the other is bent, and his left arm is slung over the back like it doesn't know where to go. I just rock myself back and forth. It's nice to have the company, even if we aren't touching, or speaking, or communicating in any way. Dwight is just there, and I am just here, and it's *nice*.

I'm not precisely happy. I wouldn't call it happy. But I wouldn't call it sad, or lonely, or in any way bad.

I'm . . . content. Yeah. That's the word. Content.

'Dice.'

I glance up with a 'Hmm?' It takes a moment for me to register what he just said, though. 'Why'd you call me that?' I ask before he can go on.

'It's your name, right?'

'Well, yes, but – I mean, no. It's . . . My parents call me that. Nobody else does. Nobody else ever really has.'

'Where'd it come from, anyway?'

'When I was a baby and started talking, I couldn't say Madison, I could only manage Dice. It caught on.'

'Well, I'm going to call you that,' he declares with that adorable, easy grin. 'It suits you.'

'How so?'

'It suits you,' he tells me again, but he doesn't elaborate. I give him a second, and widen my eyes, prompting him, but this doesn't elicit anything more.

'Do you have a nickname?' I ask him.

'Not really. There aren't exactly a lot of things you can get from Dwight.'

'Big D?' I deadpan.

He laughs, shakes his head at me. 'Right.'

'Can't say I didn't try. Dwight it is, then.'

'Dwight it is,' he repeats, confirming it.

And then we sit in silence a little longer, until he speaks again. 'I never had a tire swing when I was a kid. I used to have a tree house, though. Well, I say "used to", but it's still there, up in the tree in the back yard where my dad and my uncle built it. When I was a kid I used to play up in that tree house all the time, but then one day I just didn't anymore.

'Do you ever get that feeling: one day, you just wake up and you're suddenly not a kid anymore? One morning – I remember it was mid-April, when I was twelve, and it was a really sunny day. Well, that morning, I just woke up, and for the first time I didn't want to play in the tree house. And that was it.'

I feel like he wants me to reply, but I have no idea what to say. So instead, I decide to ask, 'Didn't your sister ever play in there?'

Dwight shakes his head. 'It was always my thing. Never something that interested her.'

I spin around a few more times before I speak again. 'Dwight?'

'Yes.'

'I . . . Don't feel like you have to answer this, and I'm sorry if I'm being nosy, and you can tell me to shut up, but is – is your . . . your dad – I mean, is he . . . ?'

'My dad died five years ago,' he replies to my unspoken question, his voice quiet. 'So yeah, he is.'

'Oh.'

'Please don't tell me you're sorry, okay?' he says. 'Sorry doesn't help. I've dealt with it, I'm dealing with it, I will deal with it for the rest of my conscious existence. And that's okay. But sorry doesn't make it much better.'

'I wasn't going to say sorry,' I tell him honestly. 'I know.'

'Thanks.'

'Want to go back inside?'

'My curiosity regarding the apple tree has been satisfied.' He stands up; pulls down the right leg of his jeans, and then straightens his T-shirt.

I disentangle myself from the tire swing, and we head back inside to carry on planning out our Physics project.

Chapter 23

On Monday morning I drag myself out of bed. The weekend passed far too quickly for my liking – I'd spent all of Saturday evening at Bryce's house, meeting his parents officially for the first time over dinner; I'd spent all of Saturday afternoon freaking out on the phone to Tiffany about what to wear to meet his parents and how I should act. Now, I force myself up and throw on some clothes, too groggy to put much thought into my choice.

Mom is making herself a coffee when I slump into a chair at the kitchen table with a wholegrain bagel and glass of OJ. I'm bleary eyed and my mind hasn't woken up yet; I'm just going through the motions.

'Do you want a ride to school,' Mom asks, 'or are you going to walk?'

'Nngh.'

'Okay,' she says as if she knows exactly what I've just said. I sure as heck don't.

'Dwight called last night,' she says calmly. 'While you were out at the beach with Bryce.'

I look up, suddenly a bit more awake. 'What did he want?'

'Something about the project, but he said it wasn't a big deal. I guess you can find out today.' Then she adds, 'I like Dwight.'

'Me too,' I tell her quietly. 'He's a nice guy.'

'Bryce is very nice too, though.'

That makes me frown. Why do I think she's comparing them? And why, why, why is it making me get that horrible feeling . . . like I've done something wrong?

'Yes,' I agree slowly – cautiously. 'He's great. Really great. Fantastic, even.'

Mom just nods, and then she grins at me. Maybe I'm not following things properly, or maybe she's had too much coffee, but I don't get her sudden changes of mood. 'I'm so happy for you, Dice. Making friends, getting back into your schoolwork . . . a boyfriend . . .'

I have to smile, because my mom is so happy that I'm no longer the loser outcast. I'm no longer Fatty Maddie. I'm just Madison. And it's nice.

Mom drives me to school. I'm early, as per usual. There are only a few kids hanging around outside on the field, and a few teachers ambling in.

Sunday, I'd caught up on some English homework, and then Bryce had come by in the evening and we'd walked to the beach. We'd just sat on the sand and made out and talked. I am aware that thus far in my relationship with Bryce, there hasn't been much deep and meaningful conversation. But in fairness, my past has been a closed book, so I've avoided talking about myself. Bryce likes to talk about soccer. It's totally lost on me, but I like listening to him – he gets excited and usually makes me laugh, telling me funny stories about soccer matches. But mostly, when we're together, we kiss. Not that I mind; of course not.

I reach our usual picnic bench and sit down, earphones in. I fold my arms on the table and rest my head. I shouldn't have stayed up texting Bryce till gone one in the morning. I'm dead on my feet.

I think I fall asleep – I don't know. But all of a sudden, when I sit up and rub my eyes, there's Bryce next to me, talking to Adam and Ricky.

'Hey, sleepyhead.'

'What . . . What time is it?' I ask. I pull out one of my earphones.

'Few minutes till homeroom,' Ricky tells me. 'You were crashed out when we got here.'

'Why're you so tired?' Bryce asks me. 'You okay?'

'Yeah, sure,' I say. I start to rub my eyes again, but

catch myself before I smear my mascara. 'You just kept me up all night.'

There's the slightest pause before Adam snorts with laughter and Ricky says, 'Kept her up *all night*, huh, Bryce?'

My cheeks flame red. 'That's not what I meant!'

Bryce laughs – not at the boys, but at my reaction. He holds my gaze and brushes a fingertip over my flaming cheek.

I duck my head away, and then the bell echoes out; there's a collective movement on the field as people brace themselves for a day of school.

'We're just teasing you, Madison, don't worry,' Ricky assures me with a grin as I stumble tiredly into the building. 'Everyone knows you're the sweet innocent little virgin.'

The only reply I can come up with is: 'Um.'

And then someone yells down the corridor to Bryce that Coach needs to speak to him ASAP, so he kisses me quickly and I make my way to homeroom.

I drag myself to art class; after a while I manage to wake up enough to talk to Carter properly.

'How's the project going?' he asks. 'For Physics?'

I shrug. 'Okay, I guess. We've barely started. It isn't as terrible as I expected.'

Carter raises his one and a half eyebrows at me. 'The project isn't that bad, or hanging out with Dwight isn't that bad?'

I laugh. 'Dwight's great. I was talking about the project, though.'

'Ah.'

'What's that meant to be?' I ask, pointing with my green-tipped paintbrush at his canvas, where there is a distorted blue-black blot.

'A blueberry,' he informs me matter-of-factly. 'Use your artistic imagination – jeez.'

I can't tell if he's serious and it *is* a blueberry, or if he's just being sarcastic. I'm never sure with Carter. But either way, I laugh and shake my head, and return to my easel.

'And how'd you lose half of your eyebrow?'

'We were playing truth or dare. It was either run naked down the beach or shave my eyebrows off. And there were a lot of people on the beach that evening. We were interrupted before I could finish.'

I laugh. It's about the seventh tale I've heard. I don't know if he's actually told me the truth yet or not, but it always amuses me to hear what he comes up with next.

The rest of the day blurs past; and Monday runs into Tuesday runs into Wednesday runs into Thursday . . .

The week's over before I know it.

And somehow, I've managed to sign myself up to the track team. They practice every Thursday lunch time, Coach tells me, which is totally fine with me. The girls still say I should've gone for cheerleading instead: Tiffany sighs, 'But you'd have had so much fun on the squad! The track team girls are *so* boring.'

Saturday afternoon, I check the time on my cell phone and say, 'I'm going to go get ready,' and haul myself up from the couch, where I've been doing some history homework.

'Are you going out with Bryce?' Mom asks.

I shake my head. 'He's got something planned with all the boys. Remember, I told you. Dwight said I can go over to his house and we'll work on the project some more.'

'That's good, then.' She smiles broadly. 'Do you need a ride over there?'

'Yeah, sure.'

'Go change and get your stuff, and we'll head off.'

So I change into my favorite skinny jeans, these bright blue ones, and throw on a plain white tank top. I don't go to much trouble – but I don't want to show up at Dwight's in sweatpants and an old shirt that's got paint stains on it from when I decorated my bedroom. I throw my laptop and books into a backpack, and at the last second grab my iPod too, because even though I know I won't need it around Dwight, I still can't leave without it.

Dwight's house isn't all that hard to find – two lefts, a right, and then it's at the end of a road. I tell Mom that I'll be able to find my own way home.

'Okay,' she says. 'But if it's after ten, I want you to call me, and your dad or I will pick you up. I don't want you walking home in the dark.'

'Sure, Mom.' She gives me a look, so I roll my eyes and say, 'I swear, I'll call after ten.' Then I shut the car door and yell a goodbye over my shoulder as I make my way up to Dwight's house.

It's a bit bigger than mine, but even from the outside it looks cozy. The windows of the room that juts out beside the porch are open, and the soft blue curtains billow in the breeze. The front lawn has a worn look, like someone actually uses it. There's a red ball lying there, and a frayed blue rope that looks like a dog's toy. I check the rusting brass number on the wall beside the front door: 16. It's his house all right.

I take a deep breath. I don't know why I'm so nervous all of a sudden. I hitch my backpack higher on my shoulder. My hand fidgets with the earphone that's dangling out of my front pocket. But I eventually raise my hand and ring the doorbell. I hear the sound resonate through the house, accompanied by a loud bark. After a couple of seconds of scuffling, the door is yanked open. Dwight's there, panting a little, mostly hidden by the door.

'Come on in,' he says breathlessly. There's another woof and he disappears behind the door. I guess he's trying to restrain the dog.

I slip in and push the door closed.

As I turn back to Dwight, he shouts, 'Gellman!' and then something very large, very heavy, and very fluffy pins me to the wall. I let out a little shriek of surprise.

'Sorry,' Dwight apologizes hastily.

'No, it's fine,' I say. I try to twist my face away from the giant pink tongue lolling my way, but I fail, and when the dog licks my jaw I laugh. But Dwight moves forward, grabbing the dog's collar and hauling it away from me.

That's when I get a good look at it. It's some sort of Labrador or Retriever cross-breed, though what exactly it's crossed with I don't know. But the dog is a mass of silky soft, shaggy blond hair, with big dark eyes and a lolling tongue. I lower my bag to the floor and crouch in front of it; its eyes are level with mine, it's that huge. Or maybe I'm just that small.

I stroke its head, and scratch behind its ears. It barks again, happy at the attention.

'Who's this beast?' I ask, grinning.

'Gellman. Well. Gellman-Zweig. After Murray Gell-Mann and George Zweig.'

I just give him a look that clearly conveys I have no idea who those people are.

'They're scientists,' he explains. 'Basically, they both discovered the existence of quarks.'

'Of what?'

'Quarks. Tiny particles that make up hadrons. Hadrons being protons and neutrons.'

'Um. Okay.'

'You have no idea what I'm talking about, do you?'

'Nope.' I pop the 'p', and we both laugh.

'You can tell I've always been a physics nerd,' Dwight laughs, and rubs the back of his neck like he's embarrassed about it. 'We got Gellman when I was fourteen. Cynthia – that's my sister – she wanted to call him Fluffy. *Fluffy*. Of all the names out there, she chose *Fluffy*.' He shook his head. 'I told her if she wanted to call a pet that, she could get a hamster. Anyway – you ready to make some progress on this project?'

'Not really,' I admit cheerfully. Gellman woofs gruffly at me again, asking for attention. Then he licks my fingers.

'I'm gonna put him in the back yard for a while,'

Dwight says. 'He's not usually this excitable. Sorry. I guess it's just because he hasn't met you.'

'It's okay,' I tell him honestly. 'I like dogs.'

Nonetheless, he drags Gellman off down the hallway. I slide my shoes off and place them neatly by the door, and then I pick up my bag again.

When Dwight returns he says, 'Do you want anything to drink? Eat?'

I'm about to say no, just out of politeness, but think better of it. I'm thirsty, so to heck with it. 'A glass of water would be great?' It comes out like a question.

'No problem. You sure you don't want a soda or anything though? A latte? I know you're rather partial to them.'

I laugh. 'Water's fine.'

He shrugs and shoots me his wonderfully infectious smile. 'Okay. Well, make yourself at home . . .' He gestures to a room behind a half-open door, and then disappears towards the kitchen.

The lounge is long and rectangular. At one end is the open window with its blue curtains billowing in the breeze. There's a large TV against the wall opposite me, and I notice there's an X-box connected to it; a long brown, worn leather couch sits directly in front of it, with a matching armchair, futon and smaller couch organized strategically around the TV.

At the end of the room near the window there's a desk with a computer, and a bookshelf stuffed with all kinds of books. I wander over. There are physics books galore (which doesn't surprise me), and chick lit and romances, and Jane Austen and other classics, and a very well-thumbed collection of the *Harry Potter* series. I smile, admiring the books. Some look like they've been kept well, and others look so loved – like they've been read and cherished over and over and over again.

I turn to the couches again. There's a coffee table in the middle, with Dwight's textbooks, notebook, and a laptop. I take a seat, perching on the largest couch, and start to empty my bag out slowly, methodically.

Dwight comes in through a door at the far end of the room and sets down a can of soda, a glass of water, and a giant bag of chips.

'How's your weekend been?' I ask conversationally as my laptop boots up.

He shrugs, but he's smiling. 'Okay. I went surfing earlier, after I finished my shift.'

'Cool.' Then, without even thinking, I add, 'You'll have to take me out there sometime soon. I'm going to hold you to your promise.'

He chuckles. 'I know, I will. I just – I mean, I figured you're probably busy with Bryce most of the time now . . .' He clears his throat, and something about it makes me think he's heard a bunch of rumors about me and Bryce. I know what some people are saying, but everyone I hang out with knows it's not true.

But if Dwight believed them . . .

'You should know better than to listen to what the rumor mill is churning out,' I say quietly.

'What? No, I didn't mean it like – I wasn't . . .'

'Oh.'

He smiles softly at me. 'I know you're not that kind of girl, Madison.' It makes Ricky's words from Monday morning run through my head: *Don't worry, Madison. Everyone knows you're the sweet innocent little virgin.*

I guess my reputation precedes me.

But I return the smile and open up my laptop. Dwight clicks his back to life. He's already got a couple of documents and web pages open, most of which he closes; some he just minimizes for later.

It's quiet while we click and type on our laptops. The ringtone version of *She Had the World* that I downloaded on my cell phone a couple of days ago blares out from my pocket all of a sudden, making me jump out of my skin.

I feel Dwight watching me, and I feel embarrassed as I answer the call. I stand up and turn my back on him for a moment, but I still feel him looking at me.

'Hey, Bryce,' I say quietly.

I can hear the noise of a football match in the background. 'Mainstream. How's it going?' He sounds genuinely happy to speak to me.

'Um, okay. I thought you were with the guys?' I state the obvious, my voice questioning, like a prompt for him to explain why he's calling me.

'Yeah, I am, but it's half time and I wanted to speak to you.'

'Oh.'

'So what's up?'

'Just . . . studying.'

He laughs. 'You're so studious.'

'Hardly.'

'Studying on a Saturday night?'

'You make it sound like a bad thing.' My tone is light, joking, careless; my heart is in my throat and my palms are clammy. 'It's physics,' I decide to add, and I shrug despite the fact he can't see me. 'You know how bad I suck. I have to catch up somehow.'

I'm not technically lying. It's just not the whole truth.

'Yeah,' he says with a heavy sigh. 'I guess. Still. Sucks for you.'

'Um, okay.' But I'm not so sure it does, really.

'I wish I could be with you right now,' he says, lowering his voice to an intimate level.

I shift from foot to foot. 'I miss you too,' is all I manage to reply.

'Tomorrow you're free, though, right?'

'I think so.'

'Good. Then tomorrow, you're all mine.'

I expect to feel my cheeks heat up, but instead I just feel awkward. I can't think what to reply to him. Luckily I'm saved because one of the guys yells in the background, asking Bryce where the heck that darn popcorn is, and he apologizes and says he has to go.

'Sure thing. Have fun.'

'Have fun studying,' he replies.

'I will,' I reply, and I hang up first. Then I put my phone on silent and toss it into my bag. I smile sheepishly at Dwight, but before I can offer up an apology, he shrugs and shoots me a small smile.

'Sure you've got time to work on this with me if you're so busy studying?'

He looks so downtrodden making that joke, we both have to laugh.

Chapter 24

Dwight's mom breezes into the room about an hour into our work on the project, saying, 'Dwight, I have told you a billion times not to shut Gellman outside – you *know* it upsets him.' She stops short on seeing me with Dwight. 'Oh!'

'Hi, Mrs Butler,' I say timidly, smiling politely to her.

She looks . . . I don't know how to describe it exactly. She's obviously quite young, and her hair is a dark auburn with some graying strands, but her face looks so much older; it's like she's worn down. Tired.

She's slim, and wearing jeans and a pink sweater. Her hair's tied back in a ponytail and her cheeks are flushed. I heard the front door open and close a minute ago; I guess she's been out somewhere.

'I didn't realize we had company,' she says apologetically to me, and shoots Dwight an irritated look. 'You must be Madison, right?'

'Right,' I say with a broad smile. 'Nice to meet you.'

'You'll have to forgive me for being such a bad hostess; Dwight didn't say you were here. You're staying for dinner, though, aren't you?'

'If it isn't too much trouble . . . I don't want to intrude.' I mumble it slightly, but I'm still smiling at her. Like her son, she just radiates friendliness, and an easy-going nature.

'Of course not!' She waves both her hands around dismissively. 'How's the project going?'

'All right,' we answer unanimously. I glance at Dwight, and the corner of his mouth tweaks up at me.

'Good. I'm Teresa, by the way. Right. I'll leave you kids to get on with it, then! There are plenty of snacks in the pantry if you want anything, but just try not to spoil your dinner!' She glides back out after giving us another smile.

'Sorry about her,' Dwight mumbles to me as I turn back to my notebook and laptop. 'My mom can be a little . . . scatterbrained, sometimes.'

'She seems really nice!' I reply honestly. 'She seems a lot like you.'

He raises his eyebrows at me. 'You think?'

'Yeah. You don't look like her too much,' I admit, 'but she seems to act like you do. Same smile.'

'Huh.'

'What?'

'Nothing. I just – everyone's always said I'm like my dad.'

'Oh . . .' I say it quietly because we both know I'm never going to be able to make that comparison. But then, before the silence can grow awkward, I go on, 'You're still like your mom, though.'

He laughs. 'I'm not sure if that's a good thing or a bad thing.'

'A good thing.'

'I'm inclined to think otherwise,' he says, but there's a smile in his voice that makes me sure he agrees with me. Then he glances down at his textbook – an old one he dug out from the bookshelf. 'What was I looking for again? Oh, yeah . . .'

Teresa pops her head around the door a while later to tell us dinner will be ready in twenty minutes. But we carry on working hard until she yells from the general direction of the kitchen that dinner is on the table and getting cold!

Dwight and I tidy up our stacks of notes and save the documents we've been working on. I follow him to the kitchen, and someone barrels down the staircase loudly. I look over my shoulder and see a girl of about thirteen wearing a bright pink shirt with bright purple shorts. She's got braces, and a visible gap between her two front teeth, and her auburn hair hangs in a braid down her back.

She blinks at me, and I shoot her a quick grin.

The kitchen's not very big. Or maybe it is, and it's just cramped. I think it's the latter: what with the dog basket and mess of doggy toys, and the big round table that's large enough to easily fit six people, any space would seem small.

I wait for Dwight to sit down before I pick a seat. I choose the empty seat on his left, and his little sister sits opposite me. Their mom sits between Dwight and his sister, placing a giant bowl of salad on the table as she sits, to go with the plates of grilled chicken and fries in front of each of us.

We begin to eat, and after a couple of minutes, Dwight's little sister says, 'You're that girl Dwight likes, aren't you? The one from Maine. Madison.'

'Uh . . .' My eyes flit quickly to Dwight, who's rolling his eyes. 'Yeah, uh, that's me. Hi.'

'I thought so. You're really pretty.'

'Oh.' I blink, completely taken aback. Then I smile and reply, 'So are you.'

She grins back at me.

'Feel free to ignore Cynthia,' Dwight tells me.

'Don't be so mean to your sister,' his mom chides, but she's smiling a little. 'So, Madison,' she says then, turning to me, 'how are you liking Florida so far?'

'It's great,' I answer instantly, smiling. 'I love it here.'

'And school?'

'Aside from being stuck in physics, it's good. I'm really enjoying history.'

'Is that what you think you want to do at college, maybe?'

I wobble my head – an uncertain 'yes'. 'I think so. I'd like to be able to. I've always liked history. And English is okay too, I guess.'

'Not much of a science person, then?' she says with a slight laugh in her voice.

I laugh, snorting a little as I do so. 'Not at all. I mean, biology's not totally terrible. I've never liked chemistry, though, and I just don't do physics.'

'Dwight said they messed up your transcripts. That's got to be annoying. There's really nothing you can do about it?' I shake my head, grimacing. 'That's awful.'

Conversation flows quite easily: a lot of small talk and nothing of great importance. I don't know if maybe Dwight told his mom before that I don't like to talk about myself much. I think he must have – not once does she ask me anything about my life or my school or anything like that before I came to Florida.

But I'm most certainly not complaining.

When we're all finished with dinner, I help collect up the plates before Teresa can tell me not to.

'You don't have to do that, honey!' she objects. 'Cynthia can do that.'

'It's fine, really.' I smile. 'I don't mind.'

She grins at me. 'Well, thank you very much, Madison. Dwight, this girl's a keeper, you got that?'

'*Mom.*'

My stomach gets a funny sensation in it, but I shake it off.

'Come on,' Dwight says to me, dumping the mostly empty salad bowl down beside where I put the plates. He touches my elbow, and starts out of the kitchen.

I follow him, but shoot a smile and say, 'Thanks for dinner, it was great,' to his mom, with a little wave to Cynthia.

'I apologize for my entire family,' Dwight mutters to me as we sit back at our work.

'I like them. They're nice. Your sister's nice.'

'Mm,' he says in a tone that disagrees with me.

I click my laptop back to life. Dwight's working out the intricacies of the project and the experiments we're going to do. I've done some reading on Newton's life, his work, and his inspirations, and I'm putting together the presentation about it all on my laptop. It seemed like a fair division of the work: I do the stuff that doesn't require as much knowledge of physics, and Dwight does the complicated stuff.

We're both happy with that, actually.

We work until it gets dark outside, which is around eight thirty.

I don't even notice the time flying past, though. Even though we've somehow got tons of work done, we've been joking around all evening, chatting away about all kinds of meaningless things, like that time he went to a Muse concert, and when Jenna broke her arm falling off her bike.

It's strange how calm I feel, and how easy it is to be around Dwight.

But it's a nice strange.

I'm not worrying that I sound like an idiot when I snort, or if he'll think I'm a dork if I tell him this or that story. I'm not *conscious* of how I'm being. He's good company – a good friend.

I smile at that thought. Dwight throws down his pen. I've started to get a bit distracted by this point, switching between a blog about one of my favorite bands and a Wikipedia tab.

'That's it, I'm done for the night,' Dwight sighs heavily. 'How 'bout you?'

I nod, saving the PowerPoint I was working on. 'Heck yeah.'

Dwight closes his notebook, organizes a few papers he's scattered around him and closes the documents on his computer. I follow suit.

'Do you have to leave yet, or . . . ?' He trails off, not quite meeting my eyes. Like he's almost afraid to ask me to hang out, I think – or, no, I only *hope* that's what it is. What he *probably* means is that he wants me to go but is just too polite to say so.

'My mom said she can give me a ride home whenever, really,' I say. 'If you want me to go, I can give her a call.'

I don't want to go; I want to carry on hanging out with Dwight, with or without the physics project. But one thing I haven't considered is that as much as I consider him a friend, he may not see me the same way: I could well just be someone he puts up with because he has to.

'You can stay and watch a movie or something if you want,' he offers, smiling to me. It's a hesitant version of his lopsided grin.

'Sure,' I say, smiling back – and not just because his smile's so infectious. 'That sounds good.'

'Cool.'

'You can pick a movie,' I tell him. 'Consolation for having me for a lab partner.'

He laughs, shaking his head at me. 'Strange as it

may seem, I actually don't mind having you for a partner, Dice.'

I don't know if it's what he just said, or if it's because he called me Dice, but whatever it is washes away every shred of doubt I had as to whether he likes me or if he's just been polite all this time. I can't keep the huge grin off my face.

'Still, you pick,' I instruct him.

'All right,' he laughs. 'I'll be back in a couple of minutes.'

He heads out of the room and I hear him walking up the stairs. I start to tidy my things up and put them away in my backpack. I leave the laptop out, but set it on hibernate, and wrap up the charger.

I'm still grinning like a total idiot when Dwight comes back with *Lord of the Rings*, the first movie.

'Good choice,' I say approvingly. 'The books are better, though.'

'You've read *Lord of the Rings*?'

He sounds so shocked that my reply is hesitant. 'Uh, well, yeah . . . I mean . . . Yes. I read them. Multiple times, actually.'

His dark eyebrows pull together before relaxing, and he fixes me with those sea-green eyes. 'You're very surprising, Madison Clarke.'

'And you have very good taste in movies, Dwight Butler.'

It's late when I call my mom to pick me up from Dwight's house. His own mom had already stuck her head into the room to say, 'I'm heading to bed now, kids. Dwight, make sure you let Gellman out before you come up to bed. It was great finally meeting you, Madison.'

'Nice to meet you too,' I'd said with a smile.

'Okay,' Dwight had replied.

We've made it through a giant bowl of popcorn and a couple of glasses of diet soda by the time the movie ended. Dwight takes the glasses and empty bottle of soda out to the kitchen, and I decide to follow him with the popcorn bowl. A few kernels rattle around at the bottom.

I set the bowl on the counter near the glasses. When I look up for Dwight, I see him unlocking a sliding glass door further down the room that leads to the back yard.

Gellman barks quietly and clambers out of his doggy basket, padding over to the open door. He licks Dwight's hand and then jumps onto the small strip of patio outside and over onto the grass, his nose to the ground, hunting for a place to do his business. I stand next to Dwight and we watch the dog.

The night air is cold, pinching my cheeks. I steal a glance at Dwight and see him rubbing his hands together a little against the chill.

My eyes trail back to Gellman, and then drift around the garden. My subconscious seems to know what it's looking for; I don't realize until I see it.

'Is that the tree house?' I blurt, not thinking. My voice is hushed, tentative. I look back to Dwight, watching his face carefully.

Dwight's eyes trail reluctantly to the tree house, where it's nestled in the branches of a huge tree I can't quite define in the dark. He nods slowly. 'Yeah.'

Gellman pees and trots back into the house.

Dwight pulls the door shut and locks it.

That's all we say about the tree house.

Chapter 25

October is crisp and bright, and all anyone can talk about is the party Bryce is organizing for Halloween. When I say it is all anyone can talk about, I do mean that literally. It's surreal, though, actually being *involved* in all the chatter about it. I'd always been on the fringes, and witnessed the hype over things like this, but I'd never seen why it was such a big deal. A party, so what?

But now I understood.

Because what the heck am I going to wear?

I'd gone shopping with the girls. Tiffany was going as a fairy, which meant she had a pink tutu and a skimpy, skin-tight pink corset-style top to match. Summer was going as a 'bunny rabbit' – a little black dress with white bunny ears and a bunny tail. Melissa was going as Catwoman, in a leather-look jumpsuit. And from what I'd heard all over the school, the majority of girls were turning up in skimpy, sexy outfits.

But no way in heck was I going to do that; I just wouldn't feel comfortable.

I've shoved that to the back of my mind, though, since I still have two weeks until the party and that's plenty of time to think about my outfit.

It's a Wednesday, before lunch period. With a sigh, I wander out to the field for gym class. Last night I had track till six, and my muscles are still a little sore. But on the bright side, Coach thinks I'll be able to compete for the school in the summer, which is going to be great for my college applications.

I hate gym class. Although that's nothing new. I always have. Recently, I've taken to hiding out underneath the bleachers whenever Coach's back is turned long enough for me to slip away.

I used to be the kid who was picked last; even my own team was against me. Dodgeball? Living hell. Soccer? I'd be thrown in goals and bombarded with practice shots. And don't even get me started on the number of times I got 'accidentally' whacked in the back of the head with a badminton racket.

It isn't like that here. This isn't Pineford, and I'm not Fatty Maddie anymore. Here in Midsommer, I am Madison Clarke, girlfriend of star soccer player and school heartthrob Bryce Higgins, friends with Tiffany Blanche and Co. I am a somebody. Now, I'm one of the first names called when teams are being picked.

In AP physics on Friday, Dwight suggests we meet up and do some more work on the project.

'Well, I'm free tonight,' I tell him. 'Bryce is going out of town for the weekend to visit his grandparents, and I was only going to have a lazy night in with my parents anyway. I can't do anything tomorrow, though: Jenna's down for the weekend.'

'Oh, that's great!' he says, enthusiastic for me. 'Is she bringing her boyfriend?'

'Yeah,' I laugh. 'My parents cannot wait to meet Henry, Mr Sexy Brit.'

Dwight laughs. 'Well, Cynthia's at a sleepover tonight, so my house will be free, if you want. I think my mom's out for dinner with some friends too, so it'll be quiet. Well, as quiet as it can be with Gellman.'

'It's a date. No! I mean – not a date, just . . . You know what I mean.' I laugh sheepishly.

He grins at me. 'I know what you mean.'

So later that evening, I'm at home, packing my textbooks and laptop into my backpack, holding my cell phone between my shoulder and cheek as I speak to Tiffany.

'I can't,' I say. 'I promised Dwight we'd work on the project tonight.'

I probably don't sound half as sad as I should be that I can't hang out with everybody down at the beach instead of doing my physics project.

'You're giving up your Friday nights to work with *him* on your *physics project*? Madison! Come on, you *have* to come! We haven't been down to the beach in, like, forever.'

'I'm sorry, Tiff, I really can't.'

'Why don't you just ditch him? He won't care. He can play video games or Dungeons and Dragons with the rest of his nerds like I bet they do every weekend. Come *on*, Madison!'

I pause from packing my things and hold my cell properly to my ear with my now free hand. 'I can't just ditch him like that, Tiff. I won't leave him to do the whole thing on his own.'

She pauses. 'Would you rather hang out with him than us?' There is no blunt accusation in her voice, though; she seems curious more than anything else.

'No!' I insist hastily. 'I just – I can't ditch him. I promised we could work on the project tonight and . . . I can hang out with you guys any other time.'

'Fine. We were thinking of going to see a movie tomorrow, by the way – I forgot to tell you earlier. You up for it?'

I grimace. 'My sister's coming to visit this weekend. Sorry.'

'Oh, God, yeah, I totally forgot. Well, okay. If you can spare a couple of hours from your busy schedule for us tomorrow, then let me know, 'kay?'

'Okay.'

'Awesome. Have fun working on your project,' she says pityingly, though I'm not totally sure if she's being sincere or not.

'Have fun at the beach,' I reply. The weather's great outside right now; the sun is refusing to come close to setting, there are clear skies, and it's comfortably hot. Perfect for hanging out at the beach. But I still don't sound like I wish I could be there. 'Say hi to everyone for me.'

'Will do.'

Once I hang up, I finish gathering up my things into my backpack and then text Dwight to say I'm on my way over. I call a quick goodbye over my shoulder as I leave, and follow it with an 'Okay!' when Mom tells me to call for a ride home if it gets too late.

I do my best to forget how worried I am that Tiffany is mad at me. Dwight keeps glancing at me with a crease in his forehead, like he knows something's up, but he understands I don't want to talk about it.

I try to concentrate on the project, I really do. But I have this nagging feeling in my gut that Tiffany is mad at me for blowing them off, and for hanging out with Dwight to do our project instead of going to the beach.

I know it's stupid. I'm allowed to have other friends – and we're doing schoolwork, so that should give me the best excuse in the book to be with Dwight instead of them.

But I'm so worried about it that I can't focus.

I remember all the time I spent being the social outcast and how miserable my life was, and I realize how much I don't want to give up this new life; how badly I don't want to mess up. And I push out those thoughts about wanting to ditch my friends to hang out with Dwight instead. Maybe I should've just blown Dwight off and gone to the beach . . .

'Madison? Everything okay?'

I look at Dwight. 'Huh? Sorry, I totally spaced out.'

'Are you sure everything's all right? If you want to go home or something, or take a break, just say. I don't mind.'

I shake my head adamantly. It's too late now to reverse things: I'm with Dwight, so we may as well work on the project. 'It's fine,' I insist, and he drops it.

At some point we order a pizza to keep us going, and it's about nine o'clock when I throw myself back from my scattered notes. 'Can we stop now? I'm exhausted.'

Dwight laughs. 'Sure. We haven't actually got much left to do, now. Two more experiments and the write-ups, and then we just fine-tune the presentation and we're done.'

We sit there for a few minutes, tidying our things and sorting out papers. We both go to pick up the same sheet, and his fingers close over mine. 'Sorry,' he says, and pulls his hand away.

I sit back against the sofa, and cross my legs underneath me, watching him crumple up a sheet on which he drew some rough diagrams. 'Dwight.'

'Yeah?' He turns his head to look at me.

'Can we . . . Can I see the tree house?'

We stand at the base of the tree, which I see now is a sycamore, with lots of the bottom branches cut to stumps so that the tree doesn't intrude on the rest of the yard space too much; these stumps make the tree great for climbing.

I look up to where the little wooden hut is nestled amongst the branches. Where the window is, I can make out faded green drapes.

'There,' he says, and steps back. I know he didn't look up once at the tree house; only at the base of the trunk. He steps back again, but I turn and catch his arm.

'We're not going up?'

He looks at me with an indefinable expression in his eyes, his mouth a line, jaw clenched. Then his dark eyebrows tug together until they almost meet, and he says, 'Why?'

'To see it properly,' I explain, calm and quiet.

His brow furrows even more.

'Dwight . . .' I take a half-step closer to him. 'Why not?'

I know why not.

He takes a while to answer. Or, at least, it feels like a while. It may only be a few seconds which drag out slowly, but it may be minutes.

'I haven't . . . I haven't been up there since my dad died.'

I remember what he told me that first time we hung out, working on the project: *Do you ever get that feeling: one day, you just wake up and you're suddenly not a kid anymore? One morning – I remember it was mid-April, when I was twelve, and it was a really sunny day. Well, that morning, I just woke up, and for the first time I didn't want to play in the tree house. And that was it . . . My dad died five years ago.*

I could do the math.

I squeeze Dwight's hand, and give him a tiny smile. 'So what's stopping you?'

With a heavy sigh, he pulls his hand from mine and runs his fingers back and forth through his hair, messing it up. 'Dice, it's not that simple.'

I know he doesn't want to, and I can guess at his reasons, but I don't want to let this drop. There's something tugging in my gut that makes me want him to go up there and face it.

And then I'm talking, and the words are spilling out even though I don't want them to. I can't stop. I can't control my mouth, make myself stop. I don't want to tell him, and I especially don't want him to look at me differently because of this, but it won't stop.

'You know,' I say quietly, 'back in Maine, my life was a nightmare. I got bullied all the time. I was fat. I had braces, and these thick glasses that made my eyes look the size of tennis balls. I cried before I went to school, and I cried when I got home. I didn't want to tell my parents how bad it was, because they'd only call the school, and that'd just make everything worse. People called me names. They ripped up my homework. Threw my books in the school pool. Filled my locker with ketchup. I have this scar on my wrist from when I was little and burned it on the stove – they used to make fun of me for that too. I didn't try in class, because I knew that if I did, they'd only shoot me down for it. So my teachers thought I was useless, and stupid, and a waste of space. I got the feeling that if I stopped going to school altogether, nobody would miss me. Nobody would care if anything bad happened to me.'

Dwight doesn't say anything for a while.

'I told Jenna how bad it was, once. She heard me crying in the middle of the night, when she was sneaking in from going to see this guy she knew our parents didn't approve of – she liked doing things like that. She made me tell her everything, but I made her promise not to tell Mom and Dad, because I didn't want to worry them. She kept a close eye on me after that; tried to make people stop bullying me, even though both of us knew it didn't do much good.'

There's a silence, and it's too long for comfort.

'Why are you telling me this?' His voice is hushed and his eyes are mournful, but they hold my gaze steadily, unwavering.

'Because it made me realize something,' I said. 'That there's always someone who's going to help you out, whatever it is. Even if you don't want to notice that they're there. There's always someone who, even if they don't understand exactly, is going to be there for you. And you just have to let them help you.'

There's a long pause, and the only sound is Gellman walking across the kitchen to his bowl of water, back inside the house. He laps noisily, then returns to his dog basket. A car goes past on the street on the other side of the house. A TV is playing loudly from one of the neighbors' open windows.

Then Dwight lets out a heavy sigh. 'All right. Just be careful on the way up, okay?'

And with that, he takes two large, loping strides past me and begins to climb the tree. I watch for a split second before scrambling clumsily up after him. My feet and hands slip a couple of times – it's harder than I expected – but somehow I manage to make it all the way up to the tree house.

Dwight lingers in the branches before pulling himself into the wooden building, though. Once he's in, he leans down to offer me a hand, and he's surprisingly strong, hauling me up effortlessly into the hut.

It's oddly chilly in the tree house, without the sunlight to keep it warm. It's dark too. Dwight crawls over to open up the blinds that block the one window. I look around, and see all kinds of things the twelve-year-old Dwight left here before he stopped playing in the tree house.

There are a couple of action figures, and a pack of cards; some old empty soda cans. A wooden apple box to sit on, and a threadbare, worn beanbag that sags in the corner. A string of fairy lights are hung around the window, attached to a large battery pack. A pile of books lie against the one wall, and don't seem to have been too beaten up by the weather over the years.

Dwight starts to stand, but stops when he realizes he's too tall now. I straighten, though, because I'm short enough to. I shoot him a smug smile at that, and he smiles back a little. Then he tosses me the beanbag, and sits on the apple box. His legs stretch out across the floor.

'See,' I say quietly, making myself comfortable on the beanbag. 'That wasn't so bad.'

'I forgot I left all this stuff up here,' he says quietly, picking up the book on the top of the stack and thumbing through it. It's one of the Alex Rider series by Anthony Horowitz. He looks around nostalgically, and then says, 'I didn't realize it was so dark out.' He fiddles with the battery pack, smacking his palm on the top of it, until the fairy lights flicker to life. They cast a soft golden glow over the tree house.

Dwight is quiet then. Very quiet. I see him swallow hard, and his eyes are closed.

I don't ask if he's okay. Instead, I just stretch my leg out until I can press it against his a little. It's a small gesture, but I know he appreciates it by the way the air gushes out of his lungs in a long, quiet exhalation.

I don't know how much time passes before he says, 'What you told me, before . . .' He trails off, like he's not sure how to carry on.

'Yeah?'

'You don't have to tell me if you don't want to,' he begins, and then I know where he's going with this. I'm the one who looks away first; my gaze drops to my hands, where my fingers are knotted together. But I'm not clammy and I don't feel shaky and scared like I usually do whenever the threat of talking about the old Madison approaches.

'You want to know more about the old Madison, right?'

He nods, and I take a deep breath.

'Just don't look at me differently, okay?'

'I'll do my best,' he says, and I know that's all I can hope for.

I take a deep breath and let the words pour out before I can second-guess myself: I hear myself telling him what it used to be like, back in Pineford, in much more detail. He doesn't 'Mm-hmm' or nod or 'Oh, really?' in all the right places; that's how I know he's really listening. He just captures me with that intense stare, as I look down at my hands and tell him my story.

When I'm finished, he's silent.

'Say something,' I whisper. Now I'm scared; what if he thinks I'm a freak, that I'm weird, that I'm not the Madison he knows? What if he doesn't want to know me anymore?

'Oh.'

I laugh, but it sounds kind of empty. 'That's all you can say?'

'I don't know what you want me to say,' he admits. 'Saying "I'm sorry" doesn't change things or make it better.'

My mouth twists up in a smile at that, remembering he said something similar after telling me his dad died. 'I know.'

'Now it makes sense, though,' he says. 'Why you hang out with them.'

'What?' I frown slightly. 'No, it's not . . . It's not exactly like that. They're my friends.'

My words sound like lies even to my own ears. Desperate lies I want to be true, to believe.

I clench my fists at myself. *Stop it, Madison. Stop it.*

He doesn't say anything, and he doesn't look at me. I know he's disagreeing with me.

'It isn't,' I tell him stubbornly. 'They're good people. They're my friends. They didn't know anything about me and they took me in and accepted me without question.'

He gives me a look, and the corner of his mouth twitches. I know exactly what that expression's trying to tell me: that they might not have accepted me if they had known everything about me, like he does.

I stand up. I don't know why this is making me feel so mad, but it is, and I have to argue it. 'You don't even know anything about them. They're my *friends*.'

'Are you really sure about that, Madison?' he replies dubiously, raising his eyebrows at me. 'Really?'

My scowl deepens. 'I don't have to explain myself to you.'

I *don't* have to explain myself to Dwight. Whatever he says, and whatever I think sometimes, those guys are my friends. Tiffany and Summer and Melissa. I'm not a huge fan of Kyle, but even he's not so bad, when he's not being a jerk; and Ricky and Adam are great, and Marcus. Bryce is so sweet and wonderful, and he's always so nice to me.

'Forget it,' I mutter. 'It doesn't even matter.' And I start to clamber down from the tree house.

My limbs are trembling from being angry, and my feet carry me clumsily down the tree. Near the bottom, I miss my footing and fall a short way to the ground. I land badly on my ankle but I ignore it, and start to walk back through the house.

All the while, Dwight's calling after me, telling me to be careful.

Gellman barks sleepily to me, and I pet him quickly before moving through to the lounge, grabbing up my stuff. I don't check to see if I've got all my notes. I just want to get out.

I just spilled everything to Dwight and he should've understood. He should have at least *tried* to understand. But he didn't. He just made an assumption. I think that's what made me so angry.

I don't want to fight with Dwight. I don't want to do anything to damage our friendship. I don't want to be mad at him. What I want is someone who understands. I need Dwight.

'Madison, come on,' he says, and I feel his hand on my shoulder. 'Dice, you know I didn't mean it in a bad way . . . it's just – I'm sorry.'

Too little, too late, I want to tell him, but I'm afraid that if I open my mouth I might end up crying. So I fumble with the latch on his front door and shove my feet into my Converse. My grand exit is losing its effect since I can't storm out, but I don't care. I just want to leave.

'I'm sorry,' he says again, following me down the road. 'You know I'll just follow you the whole way home.'

I stop then, and turn back to him, hiking my backpack higher onto my shoulder.

I'm about to argue when he pulls me into a bear hug.

It's awkward and hesitant. He's towering over me

and I lean my forehead onto his chest, looking down at our feet. My thudding heart gradually returns to its normal, steady *thump-thump, thump-thump*.

'Okay?' he says quietly.

'Hugs don't make everything better.'

'They make most things better,' he argues. 'And sometimes you just need a hug.'

'I'm going home,' I tell him.

'All right.' Then, 'I *am* sorry.'

'I thought sorry didn't make everything better?' I can't help but crack a tiny smile at my own joke, and he shakes his head at me, chuckling quietly under his breath. 'Okay.'

He nods. 'Say hi to Jenna for me tomorrow.'

I smile hesitantly. 'Will do. See you, Dwight.' And with that, I carry on walking home, because even though he's apologized, I just can't stay.

Chapter 26

Jenna doesn't shut up the entire weekend.

It's nice to have her back. It's almost like old times, but it's so different. Not because we're in Florida now, and she's a seasoned college student – at least in her eyes. But because she's interrogating me about things and making me talk, rather than us talking mostly about her. Despite speaking a couple of times a week on the phone or over Skype, she still wants to know absolutely *everything* about my new life here.

Her boyfriend, Henry, is really nice. He's a total gentlemen – pulling Jenna's chair out for her at dinner, showing up with some flowers for our mom, putting up with all the questions – Dad is clearly trying to work out if he's good enough for Jenna. He totally wins Dad over by helping him fix the printer, which has been broken for about three weeks now.

We're going to some fancy restaurant for dinner, and the doorbell rings when we're getting ready. I don't know who it could be at this time, but then I hear Dad shouting, 'Dice, it's for you!' and I sigh, trying to fix my earrings as I go down the stairs. Maybe it's Tiffany or Summer.

It's not.

It's Dwight.

'Oh. Hey.'

'Who is it?' Jenna yells down the stairs.

'Gentleman caller for Madison!' Dad yells back, and winks at me, laughing at his own terrible 'joke' as he goes back to the kitchen.

I tug at my black skirt uncomfortably. I'm wearing a thin green blouse with a low neck and three buttons at the top of the neckline. It's pretty, and not exactly my thing. But Mom and Jenna suggested I wear it, so I gave in and wore it to pacify them.

'What's up?'

'You left this,' he tells me, holding out the blue hoodie I took to his yesterday. It's one of the ones I like to curl up in at home, so I'm glad he brought it back. I hadn't realized I'd left it behind – my mind was too preoccupied yesterday.

'Thanks,' I say, smiling, taking it from him. 'But you didn't have to come all the way over here. You could've just given it to me Monday.'

'I wanted to say sorry again, though.' He smiles

sheepishly, and scuffs his toes against the welcome mat. 'I was being a jerk.'

'Just a little. It wasn't just you. I overreacted a bit too. Sorry. It's fine, though.' Because I knew he meant it when he said he was sorry.

'You had every right to overreact – don't worry about it. But, uh, I kind of wanted to check up on you.'

'Why?'

'I don't know. I just felt like I should. The hoodie gave me an excuse.'

I laugh, and hold it up. 'Well, thanks. And I'm fine, really.'

'Good. And hey, I just – I never said thank you, for yesterday. For making me go up to the tree house.'

I smile at him. 'What're friends for, huh?'

Someone comes crashing down the stairs, and all of a sudden Jenna's leaning over my shoulder. 'So you're Dwight. Hey! Great to meet you.'

'Hi,' he says, with a nervous laugh. 'You must be Jenna.'

'Yup! Well, I just wanted to say hi. Bye!'

She's gone again, and I can't help but laugh.

'I'll get going – I can see you're all heading out some-where. You look really pretty, by the way.'

'Oh.' The compliment catches me totally off guard,

and after a second or two I break into a huge grin. 'Thanks.'

'See you, Dice.'

'Bye!' I call, and once he's making his way down the street, I close the door. I turn around and jump out of my skin to see Jenna standing there in her dress, hands clasped behind her back as she rocks back and forth on her precariously thin heels.

'Don't do that,' I say. 'You scared the heck out of me.'

'*So . . . ?*'

'So what?'

'So that's *him*. He's cute, in a nerdy kind of way.'

'Yeah, I guess.' I shrug.

'He doesn't look much like a surfer.'

'That's what I thought. Hey, do these earrings go okay?' They're dangly silver spirals that Tiffany gave me a few days ago amongst a whole pile of other jewelry – according to her, I needed to improve my abysmally small collection.

Jenna nods approvingly. 'Sure. So do you think he likes you?'

'As a friend,' I tell her firmly. 'Don't go getting any ideas that I'm in some sort of love triangle. I'm with Bryce, period.'

Jenna laughs. 'I'm such a romantic.'

'To put it mildly.'

She laughs again and, for no apparent reason whatsoever, pulls me into a tight hug. 'Oh, I missed my little sister.'

'I missed you too,' I tell her quietly, and hug her back just as tight.

Jenna and Henry leave first thing Monday morning, so I barely see them long enough to say goodbye and how nice it was to meet Henry since I'm rushing off to school. Summer and Tiffany are giving me a ride in this morning.

After the pleasantries of 'How was your weekend?', Summer jumps straight into it, no beating around the bush.

'Have you sorted your outfit for the party yet?'

'Um . . . I kind of, uh, forgot?'

'Like hell you did,' Tiffany snorts. 'You've been putting it off ever since Bryce announced he was having the party!'

'Are you sure things are okay with you guys?' Summer wants to know. 'Are you, like, avoiding the party or something?'

'No,' I tell her, 'it's not that. I just . . . don't know what to wear.'

'We'll have to go shopping Thursday. You guys have study hall after lunch, right?' Summer and I both give affirmative answers and Tiffany says, 'Great! We'll go then. Oh, and remind me I need to get some new lipstick. I keep forgetting.'

Everyone is at our usual bench, except for Marcus and Kyle. Bryce stands up as soon as he sees me, and comes towards us. His fingers slip around my wrist and I let him tug me towards the school. I follow him inside the building, past my locker and up a staircase. We stand between the first and second floor, next to a huge window that overlooks the soccer pitch.

'Hey.' I pull the sleeves of my cardigan further down so that the cuffs reach my knuckles.

He looks good, I think: he's wearing a white tee under his letterman jacket that emphasizes his toned body and tanned skin. His jeans are slung a little low, but held up by a thick brown belt.

'Madison,' he says, meeting my eyes, 'I missed you.'

'I missed you too,' I reply, almost automatically, smiling. He texted me a little over the weekend, but only to say that he had terrible cell phone reception and that his grandma disapproved of him calling his friends when he was meant to be spending time with the family.

Suddenly he yanks me close to him, crushing his lips to mine. It takes a moment to recover from the shock and kiss him back.

Then he pulls away and says, 'I've been waiting to do that since I saw you get out of Tiffany's car five minutes ago.'

I laugh. 'That must have been so painfully difficult for you. Five whole minutes.'

'It was,' he says, so serious that I have to giggle. Then he pulls me in for another kiss, this one much softer, and the only thing that makes us stop is the sound of the bell telling us to head on off to homeroom.

He gives me another lingering kiss, though, and then says, 'I'm supposed to go see my chemistry teacher first thing. I'll see you later.' He plants another kiss on my forehead, and leaves me there to head to homeroom, so I do.

I will the week to drag by, because I'm dreading going shopping for my Halloween party outfit. But if anything, time seems to go by deliberately fast. I don't think it helps that I'm so busy – I have essays due in for art and history, a biology test on Wednesday, extra track practice Tuesday and Wednesday . . .

So on Thursday, when the bell signals the lunch period, I drag my feet to our picnic bench to meet everyone. We decided to eat lunch here before going to the mall. I'm not complaining; it'll buy me time to think up an excuse to get out of it.

I listen to them talking about the big soccer match next Friday evening, only paying attention because I know I'll have to go to it. I'm struggling to open a pack of Skittles . . . Today just isn't my day, I think – and that's when the packet tears apart and the candy flies everywhere.

'Ah, crud,' I mutter, seeing there are only two left in the packet and the rest of them are on the ground.

'Madison?' Ricky asks, leaning down the table to me. 'Why don't you swear?'

'Yeah, why don't you?' Melissa asks me. 'Swear, that is.'

I shrug one shoulder, then the other, and pop my two Skittles in my mouth. 'I don't know,' I say when I've swallowed. 'I just don't.'

'There's got to be a reason,' Kyle insists, and I see now that they're all curious. I guess it *is* kind of odd that I don't cuss, but it's never bothered me. I don't mind when people swear; it's just not something I do.

'I don't see any need to, I suppose.'

'Go on,' Adam tells me. 'Say something rude. Swear.'

I roll my eyes, laughing him off.

'Say something,' Tiffany puts in. 'Go on, Madison. *Crap.* That's barely even a swear word. Say *crap.*'

I shift in my seat. 'No. I don't see why I should.'

'Oh, live a little!' she laughs, and I squirm a little in my seat.

'Come on, guys, lay off her,' Bryce says, speaking for the first time. He bumps his knee against mine under the table and kisses my temple. 'I think it's cute that you don't swear. It's too mainstream, anyway.'

I laugh at that, and I don't even realize how tense I am until my shoulders relax. He tucks a loose bit of my hair back, and I lean into his touch for a moment, silently conveying how grateful I am to him.

'Well, I guess we'd better get going,' Tiffany says, crumpling up her Doritos packet in her delicate, manicured fist. 'Hey, Bryce, what're you wearing for the party?'

He shrugs, making some unintelligible grunt that we all translate as 'I don't know'.

'Great. Thanks, sweetie, you're so helpful.'

Bryce frowns, looking bewildered. 'What'd I do?'

'Never mind,' Tiffany laughs. Summer swings herself off the end of the bench and gives Marcus a quick kiss goodbye. Melissa tells us to have fun, and I go to give Bryce a kiss on the cheek, but he catches my lips instead.

As I buckle my seatbelt, I try not to think how much I'm dreading this trip.

I know what kind of clothes they'll pick out for me – skimpy, sexy things that barely cover my butt. Exactly what I don't want to wear.

But these girls aren't used to getting no for an answer, and I know that when they do, they won't readily accept it. They're my friends, sure, but that doesn't mean they're not just a little bit spoiled and over-concerned with appearances.

Once we're at the mall, they make straight for a costume store, but move past the tacky outfits at the front to the more pricey section.

'How about this?' they keep asking, pointing. 'This would look so hot on you. Oh my gosh, wouldn't this just look awesome with really bright red lipstick? Hmm . . . this one wouldn't work, not with your haircut.'

I reject everything they suggest, either not liking it or knowing I won't feel comfortable in it. I'm sorely tempted to turn up in jeans and a T-shirt, because I really don't care. It's just Halloween. I don't see what all the fuss is about. You get a bowl of candy for all the cute kids dressed up in costumes and maybe you watch a scary movie on the TV.

Tiffany sighs, completely exasperated with me. 'Madison, you have to pick *something*! You can't *not* dress up, it'd be ridiculous!'

'Come on,' Summer tries to coax me, 'it's so much fun!'

'Unless you were planning on turning up naked and making some kind of statement against the commercialization of the holidays,' Tiffany laughs.

'Bet Bryce would love that.' Summer winks, and they both giggle. All I manage is a weak smile that I'm sure is more of a grimace.

'Come on, seriously, you have to pick something,' Tiffany chides. 'I am not letting you turn up at this party in your jeans, because I know that's what you're planning on doing, Madison.'

I laugh at that. 'Just give me a minute to look, okay? I'll . . . I'll find something. You guys go ahead. I'll find you later.'

They exchange a wary glance. I know neither of them trusts me to get a stop-in-your-tracks-sexy outfit like they've chosen.

'Really,' I say, hoping they can't hear the hard, impatient note seeping into my voice. 'I'll call you when I'm done. I won't be too long, I swear.'

I wander around the second floor of the mall a little until I finally find a little black and purple window display that catches my eye.

Inside, I find exactly the kind of outfit I'm looking for.

I can't help but grin as I thank the shop assistant and my fingers curl around the plastic handles of the carrier bag. It's perfect. Utterly and completely perfect.

Chapter 27

The evening of the party, the four of us are getting ready in Tiffany's room. She's got some dance/pop music blasting and they're all drinking from bottles of wine. I have a bottle of cider in my bag; not a big one, though. Mom said it was in case I wanted a drink; she wanted me to drink responsibly and safely.

The others are tipsy and giggling and dancing around the room. Tiffany's standing on her bed swaying like someone at a rock concert, which makes me laugh. I sit on a chair, swinging my legs.

None of the girls could find fault with my outfit; they thought it was sheer genius.

Except for when Tiffany sighed and said, 'Well, it's not much, is it?'

Black leggings that are artfully torn all the way from my thighs to my ankles, paired with a fluorescent green tutu; my top is torn and black, and I found a green vest almost as bright as the tutu to wear underneath. I wear a pair of black strappy sandals that Summer lent me for the party. I've miraculously managed to obey the how-to guide that I found online to get my hair to flick out, and I went totally overboard with my eyeliner, so my eyes are dark and hooded and mysterious.

The pixie look is definitely a win.

I couldn't help but pair it with my old purple head-phones, which I wear around my neck with the end of the wire tucked into my tutu. The girls thought it was a nice touch.

Truthfully, I needed the headphones as an emergency resort if the party got too much for me to handle. Even if they weren't plugged into anything, they were great at muffling the rest of the world.

Tiffany's dad gives us a ride to Bryce's. If I could drive, I'd have offered; but the girls aren't planning on staying sober and I don't have my license. By the time we get to the party, just before nine, everything is just beginning, and the girls are happily abuzz with alcohol, but not so much that they're slurring or tripping over.

Bass thrums through the house, resonating in my bones. I like the adrenalin rush it gives me, like it's lending me some sort of courage to not be a complete dork at this party. The last one was different; smaller, for one thing, but I didn't know so many people then.

Now, I hear people calling my name, and I don't know which way to look.

'Hello, ladies, you're all looking very *fine* this evening,' Kyle says with a wink at us all, drawing out the 'fine'. He and Adam are with Bryce, who's hanging in the hallway so that he's there to greet people as they come in.

'Hey,' I say, sidling up to Bryce. I push myself up on my tiptoes to kiss his cheek. Even when I'm wearing three-inch heels, he's much taller than me.

I notice how none of the boys are dressed up quite as much as the girls – a couple of cool outfits, some superheroes, one guy I spot disappearing into the kitchen in a penguin suit. Bryce has gone for the (shirtless) Roman look. And I have to admit it: he does look hot.

He swivels away from the guys towards me, his eyes slowly trailing down me and then back up to my face, where I know my blush is obvious. His hands are on my waist.

'Well,' he says in a low voice in my ear, 'you look absolutely *un*believable.'

'You know, every time someone says they don't believe in fairies, a fairy dies.' *Or something like that*, I think, not quite remembering the quote from *Peter Pan*.

Bryce chuckles. 'If I applaud you, will that help?'

I laugh too, giggling like a little girl.

'Give us a twirl, then, Tinkerbell.' I do, and when I'm
back facing him, he pulls me in close and kisses me, and
I think that this is probably a much more effective way
of obliterating the party around me than the earphones
that sit snugly around my neck.

I'm first to pull away, remembering that we're on
full display here.

He slings an arm around me and says, 'You do look
incredibly hot tonight, Mainstream.'

'And you make a highly attractive gladiator,' I reply.
'I might have to borrow that deadly plastic sword to
fend off all the girls who are checking you out.'

He laughs, and so do the guys, since they heard me.

'You don't need to worry about that, Mads,' he
laughs. 'It's me who's going to need to fight the guys
off you all night.'

'He's right,' Adam pitches in, winking at me and
taking a gulp from his can of beer. 'If he's not careful, I
may just have to steal you away.'

I laugh, knowing he's being silly, because that's
what Adam does. But still – I'm flattered, and bite my
lower lip slightly, feeling shy all of a sudden.

'You're sexy when you bite your lip like that,' Bryce
murmurs in my ear. He kisses my temple. 'Why don't
you go find the girls? I'll come get you in a while, after
I've finished playing host.' He gives me a look as if to

say he's less than pleased about having to play that role, but I know he's basking in the glory of throwing such a great Halloween party.

'Sure,' I say, and kiss him briefly. 'See you guys later!'

Even if I'm not really a party person, I can tell it's a good one. There isn't too much drinking – nobody's completely wasted like they were at Tiffany's – even at ten o'clock everyone's still just tipsy. The music's not half bad, and everyone's having a great time.

I see Bryce at intervals – never for very long because one of us is always distracted by someone else. Mostly, it's Bryce, but I'm amazed to find people vying for my attention too. I'm not used to it.

It must be around eleven o'clock, but it feels more like three in the morning to me, when Bryce finally grabs my arm and says to Tiffany and Melissa, 'Mind if I steal her away from you for a bit?'

'No, sure, go for it,' they answer him, and wave us away, carrying on dancing with everyone else.

He guides me through the teeming throngs of people and weaves through the passed-out drunks and kissing couples on the staircase. Bryce pushes open his bedroom door and closes it behind him with a sigh.

'Just needed to get away from it for a while?' I guess quietly, giving him a smile when he looks up at me.

'Just a bit,' he confesses as he leans back against the door. 'But I wanted to see you. I know you're not the most comfortable with PDA.'

I laugh, nodding, and let him pull me close. I put my arms around his neck and kiss him. I wriggle my feet out of Summer's sandals, which have been killing my feet, but before I can step out of them properly, Bryce picks me up, wrapping my legs around him. One of the sandals is still dangling from my toes; it falls off with a soft thud. He pulls me a little closer as the kiss becomes more passionate. His bare chest is warm and strong against me, rising and falling steadily.

All of a sudden I'm lying on his bed and he's on top of me, his warm hands sliding up underneath my tops.

It takes me a moment to realize, and another moment to disentangle myself from the kiss, turning away. I grab his arms, but by then he's already started pulling my top off. I push his hands away, pull my T-shirts back down and keep my face out of reach when he tries to pull me into another kiss.

I'm comfortable around Bryce; but I'm not *that* comfortable just yet. I can't even get changed in the locker rooms after gym class without feeling awkward and self-conscious.

'Don't,' I tell him.

He pauses and sits up, rolling off me. 'Shit,' he

whispers to himself. 'Madison, I didn't – I wasn't—'
He looks so ashamed of himself all of a sudden; so
torn up.

I reach for his arm, but he stands up and steps away.
'Crap, I'm sorry, I didn't – I thought you . . . Never
mind. I'm sorry.'

'It's fine,' I say quietly. 'Don't worry.'

He shakes his head stubbornly. 'No, it's not fine,
I'm—'

Before he can stop me, I scramble off the bed and
shut him up by putting my lips against his. Then I
take a half-step back and take his adorable face in my
hands. 'It's fine. Just . . . maybe don't do it again for
a while, okay?'

His eyes, which are wide and sad and can only be
described as puppy-dog, search my face for any sign
that it's not fine, but he must not find anything since
he nods. 'Okay.'

I smile and kiss him again to reassure him, and he
kisses me just as hungrily as he was moments before,
but this time he's holding my body as though I'm the
most delicate piece of glass, and I try to find a smile.

We spend a while up there, just making out, and I can
tell that Bryce is making a conscious effort to be careful
where his hands go. I'm so tired that I crash out on his

bed at some point or other, and only stir when he shakes me gently awake.

I have no notion of what the time is; I can only assume it's early morning. I mumble a string of words, trying to find out what time it is . . . what's going on. I rub my eyes tiredly.

'Tiff and the girls are leaving in a couple of minutes,' Bryce tells me softly.

'Mm, okay,' I say, the words slurring together. I leave the comfort of his super-soft pillows and stand up, stretching my limbs out.

'You're really cute when you sleep, you know,' he says with an affectionate smile. 'If it's not completely creepy that I watched you sleep for a while.'

I laugh. 'Sorry I fell asleep.'

'Don't worry about it.' He waves it off with his easy, hundred-watt smile. Then he opens his mouth, closes it, and finally says, 'I'm sorry about . . . about before. You know.' He clears his throat.

'Oh.' I smile and touch his arm. 'Don't worry about it. Forget it happened.'

'Yeah, but—'

'No, no buts,' I insist. 'It's in the past. Seriously. Just forget about it.'

He nods, but doesn't look happy with himself. He couldn't look more sincerely torn up about it if he tried, which is why I was so quick to forgive him. I don't think Bryce would push me or anything, so I put his actions down to the heat of the moment.

I pick up my shoes and we head downstairs, where the girls are waiting. They look tired, coming down from the buzz of whatever they've been drinking, but are still gossiping and giggling like always. They grin at me as I drop a shoe, my reactions still too slow to try and catch it.

'Here, I got it.' Bryce leans down and picks it up for me. I smile sleepily and take it from him.

Tiffany's phone bleeps and she cries, 'Ooh! That's my dad!' She glides over to Bryce and gives him a kiss on the cheek, saying, 'This party was awesome, Bryce.'

'Thanks.'

'Totally fantastic,' Summer agrees, giving him a quick hug. Melissa does the same, telling him with a slur that she 'had a shit good night'.

The girls start to leave, and I follow them; I only stop when Bryce catches my arm. I look up at him over my shoulder.

'I don't get a goodbye kiss?' he teases, and I laugh before craning my neck up to kiss him. I only plan on a brief one, but Bryce's lips have other intentions, and he's kissing me all over my face before I finally push him away, laughing.

'I had a good night,' I say. 'You know, when I was awake.'

He brushes my hair back from my face, his hand lingering there before he bends to kiss my forehead. 'Goodnight, Tinkerbell.'

'Goodnight.'

I don't tell the girls about the almost-topless incident with Bryce – partly because I forget about it until I'm back home. Really, it isn't that big a deal, since a) nothing actually happened, and b) he apologized and nothing was going to happen after that.

Sunday appears to be uneventful once my mom picks me up from Tiffany's house.

At least, it remains uneventful until Dwight drops by – a surprise visit, completely out of the blue.

I open the door when I'm in the middle of lunch, and he's there looking flustered and excited and somewhat crazy. I stare at him for a moment, wondering why he's here, and he watches me, breathing heavily and grinning.

'I had a breakthrough,' he declares. 'On the project. I need to see that presentation quick.'

'Uh, sure.' I step aside so he can come in, and then I gesture for him to follow me upstairs, where my laptop's on my desk.

I open my door and he zones straight in on it, opening up the file, knowing exactly where to find it on my hard drive. I sit on the end of my bed watching as he searches through the slides, reads, types maniacally, and then saves and closes the whole thing.

Then, with a huge gush of air leaving his lungs, he leans back in my chair and stretches his arms above his head.

I saw him typing in equations. I don't even want to ask what he was doing.

'Okay?' I ask, laughter in my voice.

'Sorry. I was on my way to the beach and I was thinking about something and – well, I didn't have any paper on me, so I thought I'd just come straight here. Sorry for intruding.'

'It's fine – don't worry about it.'

'How was the party?' he asks amicably.

'Good . . .' I remember to smile, like I had an awesome time. I mean, I did have a good time, but parties clearly aren't my thing.

'What's up?' he asks; there must be something in my face.

'Nothing,' I tell him. 'Nothing's wrong.'

He keeps his eyes on my face another few seconds before saying, 'All right, if you insist.'

That's when I remember something I've been

meaning to tell him since yesterday morning, and I jump a little on the bed, snapping my fingers. 'Ike!'

For a second after my random outburst, I see something flicker across his face. Something that makes him look sullen and dark. But then the most baffled look comes over his face – a look that scrunches his nose up in the cutest way and makes me want to smile – and I think I must have imagined the other expression.

'*What?*'

I keep my gaze steadily on him, barely able to contain my smile. 'You said it's hard to get a nickname from Dwight, remember? Well, I've got one: Ike.'

Dwight just looks at me, his expression of confusion smoothing out and his dark eyebrows arching a little higher on his forehead, an unspoken question.

'Like Eisenhower,' I elaborate. 'President Dwight—'

'Dwight D. Eisenhower,' he finishes, talking over me.

'Exactly.' I'd been going through my History homework yesterday morning, and there was a question comparing various posters from presidential campaigns, and Eisenhower's had been one of them. His slogan had been: *I like Ike*.

Dwight's face has become a closed book. He leans back in my desk chair and splays his fingers out on either side of my laptop. Not sure what could be going through his mind, I adopt my own poker face.

He hates it, I think. I don't know why that thought makes me feel so . . . so disappointed.

But I sit and wait, and eventually he speaks.

'Ike.' Dwight says the name like he's tasting it, feeling the way it rolls off his tongue, concentrating on the sound of it. 'Ike and Dice: partners in crime,' he jokes, but there's something in his eyes, in his voice, that leads me to believe his heart's not really in it.

'Partners in *physics*,' I correct, and earn a chuckle; then, when he lifts his head to look at me again, his sea-green eyes are soft and that quirky lopsided smile of his is back once more. I take that to mean: *Okay, you can call me Ike*.

I'm already beaming back at him, and he gives a barely perceptible shake of his head, the kind that says he just doesn't know what to do with me.

Chapter 28

School is closed on Tuesday for some kind of electrical inspection. But hey, I'm not complaining: I have a day off! And the best thing is that Dr Anderson was going to have a 'word' with me today about the pop quiz he gave us last lesson (needless to say I got, like, 52 percent, disgracing the good record of his AP class), but I'm hoping that by tomorrow, he'll have forgotten all about it.

I plan on lying in, catching up on the sleep I missed out on Saturday night.

Somebody phones me at seven in the morning, though, so all hopes of getting rid of the bags under my eyes go up in smoke.

Groggy, I fumble for my cell phone. At first I think it's my alarm going off, so I stab my finger at the screen a couple of times until I realize what's going on. 'Bryce,' I groan, 'it's seven in the morning.'

'Your morning voice is very sexy,' he replies with a chuckle in his voice.

I collapse back onto my pillows. 'What do you want?' I rub my eyes, and the light streaming stubbornly through my closed drapes refuses to let me even think about going back to sleep.

'I thought we could spend the day together,' he says brightly. 'We haven't spent time together properly in ages so I thought we could do something.'

'Like what?'

'I have a plan.' He doesn't elaborate.

I sigh. 'Don't tell me – it's some kind of surprise, isn't it?'

'Yup. Now, go eat breakfast and get dressed. Nothing too fancy, though. I'll be there at eight to pick you up.'

As I shower, I think about having Bryce as my boyfriend. He makes me feel wanted. When I'm with him, I forget that the old Madison ever existed.

My parents know my life back in Pineford was far from okay. 'Bearable' might be stretching it, even. But I didn't want them to know how bad it really was. I guess I got so used to hiding from the people at school that I started doing it at home too. Now I'm with Bryce, my position in the popular clique at school is secure – no need for pretending. So why do I feel like I'm still pretending?

Bryce turns up on my doorstep at eight on the dot.

I open the door to find him in some clean, only slightly battered white sneakers, jeans and a grey T-shirt that hugs his muscles comfortably. The sunlight catches his hair and makes his eyes bright, and he flashes me that heartbreaker of a smile.

'Ready to go?'

'I think so,' I tell him. 'Come on in a sec – I just need to grab my purse.'

'Okay.'

'So where did you say we were going, exactly?' I call down as I hurry up to my room.

'I didn't!' he shouts back, laughing.

'Darn,' I mutter, but I laugh too. I'd half hoped he'd tell me – although I'm totally excited that he's planning some surprise. I pause in front of my dresser to touch up my makeup before finding my purse and hurrying downstairs again.

We get in Bryce's car and he tells me, 'You can be DJ today. Feel honored – I don't usually let people touch the stereo.'

I laugh. 'Thanks. So, how long will it take to get where we're going?'

He thinks for a moment. 'Maybe half an hour, forty minutes? I know where I'm going, though. Pretty much.'

'Pretty much? Why does that not comfort me?'

He laughs and reaches to squeeze my knee instead of moving the gear shift. Then he leans over to kiss me before starting the engine and pulling out.

We talk about all kinds of things on the drive over – shreds of gossip from Bryce's party; the soccer match on Friday.

The Hounds have already played a couple of matches. They were mostly away, or they weren't very important because they were right at the beginning of the season, but this one, for some reason or other that I can't remember, is important. The entire school is abuzz with anticipation. It's against one of our main rival schools, Buchanan High, so there's even more of a competitive edge.

'I'm really excited about this game. I really think we could win it.'

'You haven't lost a game so far this season,' I remind him.

He pauses before saying, 'They're all counting on me. They don't always say it before the match 'cause they don't want to freak me out. But I know they are. And my parents. Coach said he heard a college scout might be at the match.'

'That's a bit early in the season, isn't it?'

'Well, yeah, maybe, but they're just scouts, finding out if there's anyone worth really keeping their eye on.'

He doesn't usually talk about soccer and his scholarship like this. It's more like, 'I'm hoping to get a scholarship,' or maybe, 'My mom's really hoping I get a scholarship to this college.' Sometimes he says, 'I need to sort out my backup plan in case the scholarship falls through. Everyone needs a safety school.'

But this is different.

I can tell he's worried that he won't get it. I can't imagine the kind of pressure he's under from everyone. And on top of that he's got to keep his grades up.

He doesn't say anything more on that subject for a long minute, which I track by the song on the radio. Then he bumps the dial a little, turning the music up.

He parks the car on a small square of gravel at the bottom of a hill. It's thickly wooded and steep, but clear paths are marked out by beaten tracks in the dirt and grass. There are wildflowers too that brighten it up.

We climb out of the car and I don't regret wearing my Converse. Bryce pops open the trunk and hauls out first a blanket, and then a giant cooler bag that looks full to bursting.

'Do you want me to carry anything?' I ask first.

He laughs. 'I can handle it, don't worry. I'll carry you on the other shoulder if you want,' he offers with a chuckle, and pats his right shoulder, since the cooler and blanket are over his left.

'I'm good. So. A picnic, huh?'

'Whatever gave you that idea?'

I laugh again, and take the three steps towards him, going on my tiptoes to kiss him.

We start walking up the hill – I don't have to be a genius to figure out we're going up. We don't talk much. Not because we're out of breath, just because we're both letting our thoughts wander. It's not until we're almost at the top that it really hits me: my boyfriend has brought me out for a picnic.

Just four months ago, if you'd suggested this could ever happen to me, I'd have laughed and told you that you were completely crazy. That would never, not in a million years, happen to Fatty Maddie. The notion of any boyfriend was simply laughable, let alone one who did cute things like this.

I glance at Bryce out of the corner of my eyes, and I grin. The thought that he went to all this trouble gives me a warm feeling in my stomach. He didn't have to do anything special. We could have hung out at one of our houses; maybe seen a movie or gone out to dinner . . . But he decided to do something special.

We stop at a little clearing. The trees have thinned out and the hill dips down, but there's a semicircular area in which Bryce sets out the blanket and then dumps down the bag.

I walk over to the edge of the hill and look out. You can see the sea from here. And over there, you can just about make out the mall, with traffic zipping by. It's an amazing view. And there are birds singing somewhere. The sun is bright and it makes the trees cast a yellow-green haze around us. It's a nice kind of warm, and I hug my elbows, smiling to myself for no reason at all other than that I'm happy.

Familiar arms wrap around my waist, and I lean back and rest my head against Bryce's shoulder. He kisses my temple.

'This is nice,' I tell him quietly. I'm almost afraid to speak too loud in case it ruins the peace that has settled here. I turn around in his arms and show him my smile. 'You're amazing.'

He kisses the tip of my nose, and it makes me giggle. 'You're really wonderful, Madison, you know that?'

I don't know if it's him or me who initiates the kiss, and I don't know how long it lasts, but it's fantastic.

When we finally break away, I can't help but let out a sigh because I didn't want it to end, and then we're both laughing, because we hear my stomach growling.

Bryce pokes playfully at my belly. 'I guess we'd better get some food in you before you waste away, huh? What do you want? I have a bit of everything. There're sandwiches and chips and salad and pasta and chicken wings and—'

'Whoa, slow down! It sounds like you've packed a feast fit for the entire soccer team in there.'

He laughs and we sit on the blanket, which is a thick fleece thing, worn with age. I run my fingers over it. Bryce starts to pile food out around us, and I see that, if anything, I was underrating the size of this picnic lunch. There's just so much food!

'Well, dig in.'

And I do. We eat from plastic plates with matching blue plastic cutlery, loading whatever we fancy onto our plates and stuffing ourselves. I usually don't eat this much, but I can't help it. I'm suddenly ravenous, and the food is too good to just leave.

Bryce brings out a pot of strawberries and a bottle of chocolate sauce – the kind you put on ice creams. 'Dessert?' he asks with a grin.

I eye it for a moment, knowing my stomach can't take much more – the waistband of my jeans is cutting in a bit – but I see the look on his face and say, 'Of course,' because you can't say no to those big, hopeful, happy brown eyes.

He opens the pot and then drizzles the delicious gooey chocolate all over the strawberries, which are a bright, succulent red. I take one in my fingers and pop it in my mouth, holding the stalk.

I let out a small groan of appreciation. Bryce chuckles at me and eats one himself. I'm about to reach for another when he picks it up for me, holding it out. I look at the strawberry for a moment before leaning forward, opening my mouth and giggling slightly.

He moves the strawberry at the last moment, touching the tip of my nose with it. I feel the chocolate sauce on my nose, and then see that he's eating the strawberry himself. I wipe the chocolate off with a finger and lick it, just giving him a stunned look.

'What?' he says defensively. 'It needed something extra sweet.'

I laugh. It's not my usual laugh: I snort and throw my head back and let out this loud, long laugh that I have no control over. Eventually I calm to helpless giggles, before stopping and just grinning foolishly at him.

'I like your laugh,' he tells me.

'I like you,' I reply, and he chuckles. Then he pushes the food away and pats the space beside him; as I crawl closer he grabs my waist and pulls me over.

Bryce draws me into a long, slow kiss. His lips are gentle and soft against mine. I shimmy a little closer to him, and at some point he pulls me onto his lap, and from there we just let gravity take over until we're lying on the grass. I'm half on top of him, and our legs are tangled together.

I pull back from the kiss, but leave our noses touching. He brushes my bangs back and replaces his arm around me.

The whole time I'm looking into his warm, piercing brown eyes and thinking how perfect this day is, how wonderful it's been, how—

'I love you,' he says.

My world stops turning for a moment. At least, that's what it feels like. It feels like my heart's not even beating, and my breath is frozen in my lungs, and the birds have stopped singing, and that thin white cloud over there isn't floating away anymore.

Then somebody presses play again, and I'm staring at him. Our breath mingles and my heart is surprisingly calm in my chest.

And I tell him, 'I love you too,' because I don't know what else to say.

I think I love him. It's not the first time I've thought about it. I've lain awake at night sometimes, thinking about Bryce and smiling about something, and then I wonder if maybe that's what love feels like. But I've never been sure. It's not, like, one day I just decided that I love him.

Maybe I don't.

Maybe I don't, and I've done the wrong thing and messed everything up.

But he makes me smile and he makes me happy. And he loves me.

And so I say it back to him, and there's a mixture of relief and glee that consumes his calm expression, and he kisses me.

And as we kiss, I let all my thoughts drift apart, scattering themselves until they aren't even there any longer, and I let myself feel: feel the grass prickling against my bare shins and the warmth of Bryce's neck under my palm; feel the sunlight bathe the nape of my neck and my arms; feel his lips, so soft against mine. And I don't even give any conscious thought to the simple act of kissing him, as I usually do; instead, I just enjoy it.

There are those rare moments in life that you want to capture in a bottle, to hug close on a rainy day and cherish when nostalgia hits you.

And this, I think, would be one of those moments.

Chapter 29

Late that afternoon we're packing up our stuff. 'We can go back to my place, if you want,' Bryce offers. 'I mean, my parents are both going to be at work . . .'

'Sure,' I say.

There's a slight pause and then he clears his throat. 'Madison, I meant – well, we'll have the house all to ourselves, and . . .' He raises his eyebrows a little, and then I get the implications of what he's trying to say and my own eyebrows shoot up.

'Oh. Right. I see.'

There's another pause. I don't say anything because I don't know what to say to that. I'm tongue-tied. Then Bryce's arms come around my waist from behind and he starts kissing my neck. I can hear his breath heavy in my ear. His hand starts to trail up from my waist, sliding beneath my top, and up . . .

I push his hand back down to my waist.

And I hear him sigh. 'Madison, I thought . . .'

I step away a little, just enough that I can turn around to face him. My cheeks are still warm but I look him in the eye and shake my head. 'I can't,' I tell him. 'I'm not – I'm not ready for anything like that just yet, okay? Didn't you get that at the party?'

I think I catch a flicker of annoyance in his eyes, but maybe I'm just imagining things. 'I thought that was just because of the situation. Because I'd been drinking. And there were loads of people there.'

'It wasn't just that,' I try to explain. 'I just . . . don't want to.'

He puts his arms back around me and pulls me in close, kissing my forehead. 'Okay. Okay,' he says softly, 'I can wait. Okay.'

I sigh in relief. 'Thank you.'

'I love you.'

And I say, 'Love you too.'

After we'd both said it once, 'I love you' seems to have become the way we end conversations. Whenever it goes quiet, he says it.

And I'm still trying to put my thoughts where they belong so that I can decide if I really do honestly love him. I think I do. I'm not sure what it feels like to really be in love. You read about it in books and see people portraying it in movies – and you see people who must

305

be in love in real life too. But it's strange trying to figure it out for myself.

When I get in, I ring Tiffany and tell her all about it. Well, almost all. I leave out the bit about not being sure if I love him or not.

I ring Summer and tell her too. I think about telling her absolutely everything, but I'm worried she'll tell Tiffany. And then I call Jenna, and it's to her that I tell the entire truth.

'Well . . .' She trails off and I can picture her lips pressing into a tight line like they always do when she's thinking. She doesn't know what to say either. I'm glad I'm not the only one. 'I can't really describe it to you. I don't know . . . I guess you just *know*. Maybe you aren't, if you're doubting yourself.'

'It's not so much that I'm doubting myself,' I try to explain. 'I can't figure out anything at all.'

'Fair point,' she concedes. 'Do you like him, though?'

'Yeah. Yeah, I really do.'

'Sleep on it,' she suggests. 'Maybe by morning your thoughts will have sorted themselves.'

'Okay.'

'All right.'

'How're things with Henry?' I ask.

And then Jenna is gushing in her bubbly, on-a-high manner how wonderful things are with Henry and how much she likes him and how fantastic he is. I'm happy for her, I honestly am.

'Have you guys said the L-word yet?' I ask, interrupting her.

'Yes.'

She sounds so sure of herself, and so truly happy as she says that. I nod, even though she can't see me.

And for the first time in my entire life, I find myself being envious of my older sister. And it's not because she's the pretty, popular one who knows what she wants to do with her life and has friends and everything. It's because she knows that she's in love and she doesn't have to think about it.

'Oh my gosh!' Tiffany smacks her palm against her forehead. 'I was so busy thinking about Bryce's party I totally forgot about this!'

Summer laughs. 'We should probably start shopping soon.'

'No kidding. If we want to get our dresses tailored in plenty of time . . . Like, Alison was telling me a couple weeks back about her cousin's wedding, and they left it till, like, the month before the wedding to get the bridesmaids' dresses fitted again, and there were four of them so it was complete havoc. One of them didn't get hers hemmed properly. And if you think about all the other schools around that are going to be having a dance too . . .'

They're talking about the Winter Dance. I've been walking past posters for the past couple of weeks but haven't paid them much attention. For some reason, it hadn't occurred to me that I'd actually be going to this dance.

I'm not entirely sure I want to, given that I'm not much of a party person, but I know I will be. Because all the girls will want me to go, and I'll be Bryce's date, of course.

'Ah, crap,' Tiffany says then. 'I'm going to have to get a date for this dance.'

'It's not like that'll be hard,' I say without thinking. 'There are guys falling over themselves to get your attention.'

She laughs. 'You're exaggerating, Madison.'

'I'm not,' I say, because I'm not. 'You'll have your pick of guys, easy.'

'Well . . .' She says it with a dubious note, but we all know I'm telling the truth, even Tiffany. She's only being modest about it. 'Ugh. Last time I went to a dance was last year with Steve. Guess I'll just have to find some poor soul to put up with me for the night, huh?' She laughs.

The bell goes then. 'Come on, then, Tiff, I guess we'd better head to geography. Pop quiz today. I've never been more excited in my whole life,' Summer deadpans, and we all laugh. She turns to me. 'What do you have?'

'Gym,' I respond, and they mumble sympathetically. I shrug, knowing I'll just hide out under the bleachers with Andy again. It's still touch football; not something I'm interested in. I'm glad the teacher I have for Gym isn't the same as the coach I have for track – I'd feel guilty for missing gym then.

I linger in the hallway by the notice board, kids rushing past me on their way to class. I look at the poster for the Winter Dance.

It's pretty, and it's quite good actually. Nice and simple, in varying shades of blues and whites and silvers, with a picture of a ballroom through an archway of balloons as the background. The date of the dance, I read, is the eleventh of December. That's over a month away; we have plenty of time to look for dresses.

I wonder what it'll be like. I've seen all the photos from Jenna's dances back in Pineford. The girls all line up in their brightly colored dresses and there are the guys in their tuxedos, with ties or maybe shirts that match their date's dress. Sometimes they all pitch in and hire a limo. At the dance, they all take photos and dance and eat and look like they're having a really great time, but I wonder if I will.

It's times like this when I think maybe I'd rather not be popular. I like my friends, of course I do, and I'm so grateful to them for taking me in in the first place, but I'm not like them. It's times like this when I don't feel like I fit in.

I shake myself mentally. *You're being stupid, Madison. You'll have a great time at the dance. Worrying isn't doing anyone any good! All you have to worry about for now is getting a dress. And that's no big deal, really. So stop thinking so much and get to gym class.*

I look at the poster once more before heading to the girls' locker rooms to change for a session of sitting beneath the bleachers with my iPod.

Thursday, I've heard so much hype about the upcoming dance that even I start to feel that mixture of eager anticipation and worry that I should be looking for a dress.

In homeroom, Tiffany and Melissa are talking about dress shopping. We're all going tomorrow, to the mall.

'I'm thinking long dresses,' Tiffany declares. 'We had

short dresses for summer *and* last winter. Besides, they're going to be so overdone this season.'

'Totally,' Melissa agrees. 'What color were you thinking? I might go pink. Like, a pastel pink. Nothing too bright.'

'Hmm, yeah,' Tiffany mumbles in agreement, or maybe consent, given the way Melissa is looking at her almost like she's after approval on that decision. 'I was thinking maybe silver. You know, in keeping with the theme and whatnot. Summer's gone for eggplant purple. She was going to have lilac, but how awful would that have looked with her hair?'

'Oh, shit, yeah. Close call.'

'I know, right.'

They both look at me then, and it's not until Melissa says, 'What about you and Bryce?' that I realize they're waiting for me to tell them what color dress I want.

I shrug. 'I don't know. Blue, maybe? I haven't really thought about it.'

'Bryce looks good in blue,' Melissa says.

Like that's supposed to help me.

I shrug again. 'Yeah, he does. I don't know. I thought I'd just pick whichever dress I like best.'

'But you have to have some kind of idea what dress you want,' Tiffany says, shocked. 'Sweetheart neckline? Fishtail skirt? Train? Straps?'

I'm not even a hundred percent sure I know what a fishtail skirt is. I shrug again, because that's answer enough.

Tiffany gapes at me a moment before snapping her mouth shut, and Melissa just stares at me, all bug-eyed. I want to squirm in my seat; now I seem really weird because I'm not as excited about the dance as they are.

Don't get me wrong now, I *am* excited. I really am. Heck, it's my first dance! And I'm going to show up with the star soccer player, the cutest guy in school, as my date! Me, Madison Clarke. I'm actually going to the dance!

But yeah, I'm really worried about it too. I know I probably won't have as much fun as everyone else – I'm kind of nervous too because I haven't been to one before. The trouble is, I'm not excited for the same reasons as they are; and I don't want to let on why I am excited.

But they mistake my lack of interest in my dress for a lack of enthusiasm for the entire concept of the dance.

Of course, I don't want to explain it all to them. I can't. Not without telling them everything. And that's never going to happen.

'I mean,' I hear Tiffany say, 'you're acting like you've never even gone to a dance before.'

For a split second I think the bell is going to blare

out and save me, sending everyone back to class. I hold my breath and count: one, two, three, four . . . It doesn't happen. Of course it doesn't.

'I totally forgot! I was meant to go and see Coach first thing this morning about a track meet!' I smack my forehead with the palm of my hand and shoot to my feet, scraping my chair loudly and making heads turn my way – not that this is entirely unusual these days. 'I'll catch you guys later, okay?'

And I run out of there as fast as I can without looking like even more of a fool.

I wasn't completely lying. I am meant to go and see Coach about a track meet. But she said I could drop by between classes, which had been my plan up till now. I look up then, and realize I'm not even heading towards her office. But I don't turn around, I just carry on. Music is pumping through my ears. I didn't even notice I'd put my earphones in; it was a reflex action, I suppose. I'm close to hyperventilating too – my chest is heaving with shallow, frantic breaths; my heart is palpitating; my hands are trembling, and my legs feel so shaky I think they're going to give out.

Luckily I don't collapse until I get to the library.

Don't ask why I went there; truth is, I don't know. But it's quiet, and since everyone's in homeroom, or making their way to first period, maybe I won't be disturbed. I'm away from prying eyes. I weave my way between a few shelves, with no idea what section I'm in, and finally stop. I just . . . slump to the ground. And stay there.

I don't know if I can even stand up again. So I just pull my knees up underneath my chin and lean my forehead against them, squeezing my eyes shut so tight that I see bright splotches against the dark void. It's almost like I'm trying to block out everything else.

Which, I suppose, I kind of am.

My breathing is starting to even out again, when suddenly I feel a hand on my shoulder, which causes me to jump violently and smack my head against a shelf behind me. A book falls on me from one of the upper shelves.

'Sorry,' Dwight says, 'I didn't mean to startle you.'

He picks up the book before I can, replacing it. I rub the back of my head and stretch out my legs a little.

Then he sits beside me on the floor. His shoulder touches mine.

I look at him, trying desperately to keep my face blank. It's not hard.

His expression, on the other hand, is full of worry: the deep crease lining his forehead, the troubled shadow in his eyes, even the little wrinkle in his nose.

'Is everything okay?' he asks me.

I nod slowly, but he says, 'Bullshit.'

I laugh. It doesn't sound quite as hollow as I expected, which is a good thing. 'I'm fine.'

'Biggest lie in the universe.'

I smile wryly, but don't say anything to him. What could I say? Tell him I'm tired of running from it all? Tell him I'm sick of trying to be someone I'm not really? Tell him I'm desperately clinging to every strand of my new life here, but I'm so close to messing it up and losing everything?

I don't know what to tell him.

I don't know what to tell *myself*.

So, after a while, he says, 'Dysania.'

'Sorry?' I cock my head sideways at him.

'Dysania,' he repeats. 'The state of finding it hard to get out of bed in the morning. I read somewhere once that it was a "rare condition". It doesn't take a genius to figure out that that person clearly had no idea what it's like being a teenager on a school day.'

He says it to make me laugh. And I want to laugh, because it's funny. But I can't manage it – I don't know why. I try a smile, only the muscles in my face are reluctant, and it feels like more of a grimace.

'Alexythimia,' he tells me next. 'Difficulty describing feelings to someone.'

I manage a slight nod.

'Eccedentesiast.'

What did you eat for breakfast this morning, a dictionary? What's with all the big words, Ike?

'Someone who fakes a smile,' he defines it for me. 'And you, my friend, are being one right now.' He puts his index finger under my chin and leaves it there a moment, and the gesture pulls my gaze to meet his. His eyes are so sad, so sorrowful, so *curious*, that I have to drop my gaze. I look at my nails, which I've been trying to grow. In this light, you can just about make out the shine of the clear, extra-strength varnish stuff I put on them.

I know he wants answers. And I want to tell him. I want to confide in him because I know that even though he might not understand, he won't think I'm stupid. But I can't tell him. I just can't do it. I've left all of that behind, back in Pineford. Shut it away in a box in the back of my mind.

I can't do this right now, I want to tell him. *I don't want to do this right now. Can you just* not, *please . . .*

'Dice,' he says plaintively, leaning into my vision so that his eyes lock with mine. 'Dice. Please, just speak to me.'

And I start to cry.

Chapter 30

Last time I cried was at Great-Aunt Gina's funeral. For some strange reason it feels kind of . . . *good* to let it all out.

At least Dwight doesn't look like a deer caught in the headlights, as I imagine most guys would when a girl bursts into tears. I can't believe I'm breaking down like this, but I can't help it. Something made the flood-gates snap like a twig, and this is the aftermath – I'm sitting on the floor of the library, silently sobbing, and Dwight's arms are around me. He rubs circles on my back and strokes my hair, lets me bawl into his chest.

All I can think is: *I'm glad it's him.*

It's a good thing I'm not a loud crier; if I was, we'd probably have been discovered by now. This is a library, after all – noise is simply not tolerated.

When the sobs start to recede, and my body stops shaking, and I'm just left with tears streaming silently down my cheeks, I say, 'I got snot on your shirt.'

Dwight chuckles softly, and shifts around a bit, digging into his pocket. 'Here. It's clean, I swear.' He pushes a Kleenex into my hand and I dab my face and blow my nose – *quietly*.

'Thanks.' My voice is raw. My mouth feels gross.

He peels his arms away when I start to sit up, and then chuckles again, and pulls the tissue from my fingers, wiping at my face, under my eyes. 'You look a mess.'

'Ike, you're such a charmer.'

'I see your sarcasm remains ever intact.'

The corner of my mouth twitches in an attempt at a smile. I take the Kleenex again and wipe my nose, and dab at the last of the tears.

I open my mouth to apologize, but he must know what's coming since he says, 'Don't.'

So I don't.

We look at each other for a moment, and then he holds out an arm; without hesitation, I snuggle into him. I rest my head over the space where his heart is, and I can feel it thrumming, strong and steady. It's soothing. His arm wraps around me, and it's warm. I shiver, suddenly realizing how cold I feel in just my thin T-shirt.

It's not a romantic embrace, though; it's a friendly

one. One of comfort. He's just being nice. Being there for me. And that's all I want right now.

'Dice,' he says softly, his breath tickling the top of my cheek. 'You don't have to tell me what's wrong, but I'm here if you want to talk. Maybe it'd help if you told someone. I'm not going to judge you.'

Part of me doesn't want to tell him; telling someone would make it more real. But a larger part of me wants to tell him, wants him to use that big brain of his to come up with a solution, like I am an equation he might be able to solve if I can just define some of the unknowns for him. It seems silly, but when I think of it that way, I can fool myself into thinking it isn't so bad, it can be fixed. And anyway, I've told him a whole bunch of stuff about myself already.

Words come spilling from my lips before I can think about them. 'It's just so hard because there's the dance and I'm really excited but not like everyone else is because I've got different reasons and the girls almost caught me earlier and I came so close to messing everything up and I just can't afford to do that. I can't go back to how things were. Okay? I just can't. And then there was that whole thing about Bryce wanting to have sex, but—'

I clamp my lips together. Tears have welled up in my eyes again, but this time I refuse to let them spill. I can't tell him everything, speak my deepest thoughts aloud to him. Besides, he doesn't really care, does he? He's just being nice.

So I won't bore him with the details.

Dwight's hand stills in my hair. I barely even noticed he was stroking it before now.

'What whole thing about Bryce, Madison?' Dwight asks in a strangely cool voice. 'He didn't – did he . . . do anything to you?'

'No!' I insist quickly, only just remembering to keep my voice low. 'God, no. He just – I think he was a little . . . put out when I said no. But it's fine. He said he'll wait. It's nothing.'

I don't know why I say 'it's nothing' when we both know I don't believe that.

Truth is, I don't know how patient Bryce will be about this. I don't know how long it'll be before he asks again, and maybe he'll get tired of waiting. I know he said he loves me, and I believe him, but I just don't know. I'd like to think I'm wrong about it and I'm being stupid. But I can't quite make myself believe that. It's not like I've had much experience in the boy department. I haven't got a clue whether what I'm thinking is legit or stupid.

Dwight doesn't push me on that issue, though, and I'm glad.

He looks me in the eye, then, and his green eyes are filled with such pain, such sorrow – but no pity, I don't think. It's more that he's sad *for* me.

Then he cups my cheek before I can look away. It's strange, but I think, *I don't want to disappoint him. I need Dwight. I don't want to ruin things with him.*

So I hold his eyes with mine, and his expression softens slowly, until there's a hint of his lopsided smile.

The silence, which has been comforting up until now, suddenly feels different. Charged. Tense, even. No, *tense* is too strong; *uneasy* might be a better word for it. Yeah. It's a thick, uneasy silence.

Yet the strangest part is that *I* don't feel uneasy. And everything bad and numb which had been consuming me ebbs away. It doesn't leave me empty; like that time we were both sitting in silence in my back yard, I feel content. Not happy, exactly, but more than simply peaceful. It's a nice feeling, even if my throat is sore and I'm still a little sniffly from the crying.

I'm not sure which of us initiates it, but suddenly we're leaning towards each other, and the next second we're kissing. It's a tentative sort of kiss – a question. His lips are soft and hesitant against mine, and I know I am just the same. And then, slowly, I press my lips more firmly to his, and he kisses me back gently, one hand still holding my face and the other moving around my back. He holds me as though I'm so fragile, and in that moment I really am; but it's not just me. This moment, which feels so perfect and so blissful, is really fragile, and I think we both know it's going to shatter any second.

It does.

And it's my fault.

I shatter it.

Because at some point when I'm kissing Dwight, I realize exactly what I'm doing. I'm kissing *Dwight*. Dwight. And I have a boyfriend who is most certainly not Dwight. And when that thought comes crashing down on me, I tear myself away, frantically swiping his arms from around me and snatching up my bag, trying not to look at him. I can't. I'm a horrible, horrible, horrible person. I just kissed another guy even though I'm dating Bryce. My stomach is contorting itself into knots.

'Dice,' I hear him say, but it sounds so distant. There's a roaring in my ears.

'I – I can't. I'm sorry. I'm so sorry.'

I'm sorry for so much more than I can put into words. So I leave. I have to. I can't stay, not after what's just happened. I feel so awful. Vile.

I don't cry now; I'm too disgusted with myself for that.

Should I tell Bryce?

No.

No, of course I won't. It wasn't as though the kiss meant anything. It was just a stupid little comforting kiss. It's not like I'm about to start sneaking around with Dwight behind Bryce's back. Gosh, no. It was just one meaningless kiss. That's all it was.

Bryce doesn't need to know. Nobody needs to know. It doesn't make any difference. I'm with Bryce and he loves me and I'm happy with him, and that's what matters. That thing with Dwight – it's not going to happen again.

We don't have much left to do on the project. I'm glad. It means I won't have to see much of him any-more. I'll see him in physics class, but so what? I won't have to talk to him.

Not that he'll even want to talk to me after what's just happened, I'm sure.

I touch a finger to my lips and then shake myself.

The bell rings, signaling the end of first period. How long were we in the library? How long was I a bawling mess?

Huh, I think distractedly, *that's the first time I've ever cut class. Guess the new Madison is a rebel.*

I detour to the girls' bathroom near the art rooms. They don't get used much because they haven't been done up for a while and the mirror is tiny. I'm not disappointed: nobody's in there right now.

I breathe a sigh of relief and dump my schoolbooks on the counter by the sink. I lean into the mirror: my eyes are a little bloodshot, but they're not too bad – I can pass it off as a bad night's sleep if anyone asks – and my eyeliner's smudged. I clean that up and apply some fresh powder from the compact in my purse so that I don't look so blotchy.

Now the girl in the mirror is composed and calm, without a hair out of place.

There. Perfect.

I stand up straight again and stare at my reflection.

My mind flashes back to when I was sitting in Langlois Café that first time I met Dwight, when he helped me with my new cell. And I'd been looking at my reflection in the spoon, thinking how weird it was seeing the new strange version of myself.

I thought I'd got used to it.

I'm not even sure I know who I am anymore.

The door opens and in walks a girl from my art class.

'Oh. Hey,' she says quietly, avoiding my eyes, but probably thinking she can't *not* say hello, because it's only polite.

'Hi,' I reply quietly.

I have art now. I wonder what my excuse should be. Maybe it'd just be better to skip the second period too, to avoid questions. Yeah. That's probably best.

The girl comes out of her stall and washes her hands in the sink beside mine. 'Are you . . . ?' Then she shakes her head.

'What?'

'You just don't look like you're doing too great,' she offers, and then ducks her head and looks at the sink, scrubbing at a bit of blue paint on her thumb so she doesn't have to look at me.

I realize then that I must be sort of intimidating to her. I'm dating one of the most popular guys in school; I'm friends with all the popular kids, so am myself popular by association. And I know from seeing kids back in Pineford around the popular clique that they never really spoke to them – they always looked a little too daunted by them.

I have no idea why I tell her, but I hear myself say, 'I messed up.'

Her mouth twists into a grim smile. 'Don't we all?'

I look at her scrubbing the stubborn blue paint stain on her thumb for a split second more, then I say, 'See you in class,' and leave to go to the second half of art class.

Chapter 31

'I'm fine,' I tell him, putting on a smile that says that nothing is wrong. 'Really.'

Bryce's brow furrows dubiously. 'You sure? Tiff and Melissa said you were acting kind of weird in homeroom. They said you just ran out for no reason.'

'I had to go speak to Coach. Track team stuff.'

He still doesn't quite believe me – I can see it in his face. But I'm determined that he will believe me. I'm already blocking out everything that happened this morning. I figure that if I can pretend it didn't happen enough, I'll start to forget it myself. I know that's a pointless hope, but it's some kind of hope at least.

'Really.'

'You know you can tell me if there's something wrong, right?' He touches my elbow with his fingertips, and then draws me into his arms, cradling me close as he leans against his locker. Closing my eyes, I rest my head against his chest. I can feel his heartbeat. Slow, steady, strong.

'I know,' I say, and I wrap my arms around him.

'So you're sure there's nothing wrong? Even just a little bit?'

I nod against his chest. 'Everything is fine, Bryce.'

'Okay.'

I don't reply; I just hug him a little tighter instead, and he kisses the top of my head.

'So I heard you're going shopping for dresses for the dance tomorrow,' he says, changing the topic. 'You guys have to be back in time for the soccer match, though.'

I nod again. 'Yeah.'

He chuckles softly. 'You're not going to tell me about your perfect dress – describe it to me in excruciating detail?'

'Should I?'

He laughs again. 'I don't know. In all honesty, I'd rather you didn't. I wouldn't have much clue what you're talking about.'

I laugh too. 'I'm just going to wait and see what dresses they have and which I like best. No point in going out with high expectations and being disappointed.'

He kisses my head once more, and I hear a chuckle

rumble in his chest. 'You're very surprising, Main-stream.'

'Good surprising?'

'Perfect surprising,' he tells me, and even though I can't see it, I know he's smiling. And that's when I realize I'm smiling as well.

'I love you.'

'Love you too,' I say, and I move my head away from his shirt so that I can meet his lips for a kiss.

'Jeez, get a room!' a familiar voice shouts close by, and we both pull apart to see Adam and Ricky laughing as they walk past us. I blush a little, shaking my head at them while Bryce tells them where to go.

Friday morning Dad gives me his credit card, telling me not to go overboard, and not to get anything too short.

'Don't worry,' I assure him, 'the girls said we're all going for long dresses.'

'Good.' He nods briskly, then breaks into a smile. 'Your mom and I are really happy for you, Dice, you know that? All these new friends, going to dances and shopping trips, and that Bryce seems like a real good guy.'

'He is,' I agree, and I smile – not because of what he said, but how he said it. There used to be times when I was sure that my parents wanted me to be just like Jenna; but I know that's not true, not really. Especially when they say things like my dad just did. He didn't say, 'You're just like Jenna was,' or, 'You're getting to be just like Jenna.' He was just happy that I was happy here, that I was fitting in. That I had a life that was entirely my own. So that's why I'm smiling so much the whole drive to school.

The day passes pretty quickly, actually. And it's great because not even physics class can dampen my day – Dr Anderson is off sick so the lesson is cancelled, meaning that I don't have to face Dwight. I'm on a high all day long.

'Someone's happy,' Summer notes with a laugh as we pile into Tiffany's car.

'What was up with you yesterday, Madison?' Melissa asks.

I shrug. 'Hormones, I guess. I don't even know. Sorry.'

'Don't apologize, silly!' she laughs. 'We were just worried, that's all.'

I smile and Melissa grins back at me.

'We have to be back here by five-thirty,' Tiffany says. 'That gives us three hours of shopping. And we're mostly just scouting today. Shoes and accessories can wait too. I was working on our plan of attack in Spanish class, earlier. I figure if we start with the little boutique stores at the back, on the top floor . . .'

I tune her out and look through the window. I'd almost forgotten about the game tonight, what with everyone concentrating on the dance, and what with the whole Dwight thing yesterday—

No, no, no! Stop thinking about that! I push that out of my mind before my thoughts can wander back to yesterday morning.

'I can't believe you guys are all ditching me for the game tonight,' I say, giving them a fake, exaggerated glare.

Summer sighs and says, 'Well, that's what you get for not joining the cheerleading squad, Madison . . .' But then she laughs and says, 'You have Ricky, though – he won't be playing. And a bunch of the others will be around too. You'll be fine.'

'Oh, and don't forget, there's the after-party at Liam Kennedy's house afterward.' Liam is on the soccer team, and I'd not given it much thought – other than to pick my outfit, which is merely a plain knee-length white skirt and a red tank top with a couple of frills on. The colors of Midsommer High, of the Hounds. I thought I'd do my part.

It doesn't take long to get to the mall. We drop by Subway and grab a quick sandwich before following

Tiffany's carefully constructed plan of action to look for dresses.

The first store we go to is one I've never heard of before; it's a pretty big place, though, and I know as soon as we hit the wall of air conditioning that we're going to be here for a while.

The girls scatter immediately, exclaiming at the various dresses that catch their eye, even more bubbly and animated than usual – and that's saying something.

However, I hesitate in the doorway. Swiveling my head slowly from side to side, I assess the situation: purple dresses, flowery dresses, elaborate sparkly, frilly dresses, pink dresses, short dresses, long dresses – all of them in some sort of order, but at first glance just mishmashed together . . . It's a labyrinth and I'm not sure where to begin.

I draw in a long breath to steel myself and pick a random rack to go look at.

'Oh my God, this is gorgeous . . .'

'Melissa, look at this one! It would be so great on you!'

'Oh, gosh, this one feels amazing, it's so silky!'

'Hey, Madison, seen anything yet?'

My head jerks up to look at Melissa, who's grinning at me and waiting for an answer. I can only imagine how much I look like a deer trapped in the headlights.

'Uh . . . nope, don't think so.' Then I laugh and say, 'We've just set foot in the store – jeez, give me a sec!'

I trail my fingers over the smooth and silky fabrics, and I feel myself beginning to slip into a state of wonderment. I've never been interested by clothes, but surrounded by all of these beautiful prom dresses . . . it's easy to see how people can get so caught up in it all . . .

My hands stop on a black dress, a few racks away from where I started. I push the others away from it, the hangers scraping noisily against the metal rail. It's a floor-length dress, sleeveless, with a v-neck. The material, which catches the light and gives the dress a soft shine, is gathered at the shoulders and wraps around the bodice before falling gracefully into the skirt.

It's a very simple dress. Elegantly simple. I think that's why I like it so much – there's no fuss, no ruffles or sashes or anything, and yet it's still a fantastic dress. I grab the hanger before I even think about it.

'Ooh, Madison's found something!' I hear Summer trill across the store, and I find she's not far away. 'Let's see?'

Walking out from behind the rack, I hold the dress up in front of me, suddenly precarious, nervous, feeling as though I need their approval on this.

'*Black?*' Summer and I glance over at Tiffany, who's scrunching her nose up at it. 'Isn't that a bit . . . a bit . . .'

'Boring?' I offer up, smiling wryly. 'Depressing?'

She shrugs, not denying it. 'Well, maybe you could just look around a bit more, yeah? A bit of color never hurt anyone. How about blue? Powder blue would look great on you.'

'I saw a baby-blue dress over that way,' Melissa says.

I see Tiffany open her mouth to retort, but she decides against it and twists her mouth into a hard line instead. She turns back to pull out another silver-white dress to add to her collection.

I walk back around my rail to put my dress back, and Summer wanders over to the other side, looking at a bright purple dress.

When she speaks to me, her voice is hushed and gentle. She says, 'I liked the black one too. Don't put it back.'

I blink at her, and she smiles.

I don't put the black dress back.

When we all decide to go try on our dresses in the large changing rooms, I have the lightest load. I have maybe half a dozen dresses, while the others each have at least a dozen.

There are fairly large cubicles with curtains drawn

across, all arranged in a semicircle around a wall of mirrors and tiny pedestals, which I assume are used for tailoring. There are a few cushioned seats too.

In my cubicle, I hang my dresses around me. Three light blue ones, the black one, a peppermint-green one, and a deep burgundy one. None of them are particularly fancy, they're all quite simple. The burgundy one is probably my favorite: it's strapless, with a lacy bodice, and the skirt has these cool golden threads woven into it. I still have a soft spot for the black one, though, even though I can't explain it.

I try on the green one first, but it looks hideous on me. It gives me curves in all the wrong places, and makes me look washed out. I don't even bother showing the girls that one.

Two of the three blue ones get their approval, but I'm hugely disappointed to discover that the burgundy one doesn't look quite as good on me as it did on the hanger. I try the two blue ones on again, since the others are still working through their piles; but neither of them call out to me, particularly. I decide I'll look somewhere else rather than getting one of these, and poke my head out of my cubicle's curtain to tell the girls so.

'But that periwinkle one looked so perfect on you!' Tiffany pouts.

I nod my head at her. 'Not as perfect as that one looks on you, though,' I tell her. The shimmery silver dress she's wearing has sleeves to her elbows and a flaring skirt. I say that mostly to distract her, but it really *does* look amazing on her, with her dark skin and hair and big brown eyes. She flashes a grin at me and twirls, so that the skirt swings out around her, and I disappear back into my cubicle.

I hear Summer announce that the spaghetti strap one with the sequins makes her look frumpy, but I'm studying the black dress. I've hung the others, my rejects, on the other side, so this one hangs alone.

I decide to try it on. I haven't got anything to lose by just trying the thing on, have I?

The material slips over my skin, smooth as water, and I contort my arms around myself with the intention of doing up the zipper before I remember there isn't one. I didn't notice at first, but this dress is entirely backless, save for the two straps that crossed over my spine and join the dress at the waist.

I run my hands over it. During this whole shopping trip I've felt a bit like a kid playing dress-up, but this one feels different. I just really, really, inexplicably like this dress. A heck of a lot.

This is the dress, I think to myself, smiling at my reflection. I know I've only tried on about five, and we still have a bunch more shops left to look in, but this is the dress. This is the one I want to wear to the Winter Dance.

I especially like the way the gathered material around the bodice makes me look like I have more curves than I really do.

Even though I'm sure this is the one, I don't need to get the dress just yet. I saw a sign at the front of the store saying they can keep items on hold for up to ten days, so I'll do that.

Then I change back into my regular clothes and go sit out on one of the cushiony seats to nod and mm-hmm and tell the others how good they look in their dresses until it's time to leave, and I ask the guy on the counter at the front to keep the black dress on hold for me.

After that's done, Tiffany says to me with a reassuring smile, 'I'm sure we'll find something brighter for you, Madison, don't worry.'

And I reply, 'I'm not.'

Chapter 32

The roar of the crowds and the added noise of the school's marching band are deafening, and the atmosphere is so charged it seems almost tangible. With my small bucket of popcorn, I make my way up the stairs of the bleachers. I left Ricky and the other guys somewhere around here, I'm sure of it . . . Maybe we were a couple rows higher up?

I'd never gone to a football or soccer game before; now, I see what all the excitement is about.

'Hey, Madison!' a voice calls, and whipping my head around, I spot Andy on my left, near the end of a row with a few empty seats beside him.

'Hi!' I call back, smiling. I'd wave, but I don't have any free hands right now. Instead, I edge like a crab into the bleachers beside him. Carter's on his other side, and he leans forward to greet me too, a big smile on his face.

'I didn't know you guys were into soccer,' I say, not in a judgmental way – just curiously.

'I'm not,' Carter says. 'They dragged me here.'

'They?' Suddenly my blood seems to be running colder in my veins.

'Andy and Dwight,' he clarifies, giving me an odd look, furrowing his one and a half eyebrows.

'Soccer and football matches are an integral part of high school life,' Andy informs me, distracting me. 'You can't miss them. Besides,' he adds in a conspiratorial whisper, 'some of those cheerleaders are hot – can't deny it.'

I laugh, as do the two of them.

Then I hear an 'Oh,' from behind me, and I freeze.

'There you are!' Andy exclaims. 'I've been dying of thirst here!' He reaches past me, and in my peripheral vision I see a hand passing a plastic cup over.

'Long queue,' Dwight replies simply. He doesn't sound like his normal self. He sounds as tense as I feel.

The notion that he told them about the kiss briefly crosses my mind; but from the looks of things – like how they seem to be baffled by the edginess between the two of us – they have no idea whatsoever.

'I should get going,' I mumble, ducking my head. I shoot a fleeting smile to Carter and Andy. 'See you guys.'

'What's the rush?' Carter asks, and that's when I know for certain that they don't know anything about the kiss, which is a relief, although I don't feel much better for it.

'I just – I shouldn't . . .'

'Madison has more important things to do than talk to people like us,' Dwight says, and unless I'm mistaken, there's a patronizing note in his voice that makes my blood boil. 'Like file her nails.'

I bite my tongue – literally. I close my eyes briefly. I want to whirl around and snap at him; tell him he has no right to say anything like that; tell him to shut the heck up. But I can't. I won't. This is one of those occasions when I'll be better off trying to be invisible.

'Wouldn't want your boyfriend to get jealous now, would we?' The disdain drips from his voice.

'Dwight – come on, dude,' Andy says quietly, looking at me. There must be something in my expression that shows he's upsetting me, even though I'm fighting desperately to keep my head down and look impassive. It used to be so easy. I guess it's harder to look like you don't care when you really *do* care.

'I was going anyway,' I mumble. I raise the hand holding my purse to Carter and Andy, attempting to give them a smile. 'Enjoy the game, guys.'

I keep my head down when I walk past Dwight, but it's difficult not to catch the look on his face – I can't help myself – and the second our eyes lock, the scornful mask he wears gives way to a flash of hurt, an apologetic, sorrowful sort of look – and then the mask is on again, and my eyes are back on the floor. It's an image that will haunt me, I know.

The thunderous voice from the speakers around the pitch announces that: *It's only fifteen minutes till the match begins, folks, so take your seats! Oh, and the home school's cheerleading team will be coming out in just ten minutes!*

I shuffle up a couple of rows until I hear someone yell my name and, grateful, I make my way along and take my seat next to Ricky.

'Everything okay?' he asks, taking a few pieces of my popcorn. 'You look a little . . . I don't know. Weird.' Then he pulls a face. 'Ew, salted. Why didn't you get butter?'

I force a laugh and say, 'I didn't know I was buying the popcorn for you, sorry. You should've specified.'

He sighs, but his smile is good-natured. 'Well, remember for next time, okay?'

'Okay,' I laugh; this time it isn't so forced, but my heart's still not entirely in it.

We win the soccer match 3–1. Bryce scored two of those three goals, and one was with just two minutes of the match left to go. Even for me – and I'm not all that interested in soccer – it was a pretty exciting match. And the excitement doesn't die down after the match, since everyone will be heading to Liam Kennedy's house.

All the cheerleaders and soccer players have gone to the locker rooms to shower and change, so there's no point in going to congratulate Bryce now; I'll wait until the party.

Ricky is giving me and a couple of other guys a ride to Liam's, choosing to be the designated driver this time. We make our way out through the swarms of people – parents and teachers and students alike – to the parking lot. And I can't stop myself from looking around for Dwight.

I've been avoiding thinking about the entire library scene because of the kiss; I refused to let my thoughts linger on it. But right now, after the way he acted, I can't help it. The guys are engrossed in a verbal replay of the entire match, so I tune out when I climb into Ricky's car, already thinking about that morning.

After the way Dwight acted earlier, saying those things to me . . . I'm sure he hates me. He regrets kissing me. He regrets even speaking to me yesterday.

He wasn't exactly very warm towards me at the start of the school year, once he'd noticed me hanging out with the popular clique – though after that things had been okay. The thing is, I like Dwight. I don't know why I told him so much about my history, especially when I wanted to bury it away for ever.

Panic swims through me in an instant. He knows my whole story. And now he hates me. He could spread it around and I could end up a social outcast again. Except this time, it would be even worse.

Would anyone listen to him, though?

Yeah, I decide. Yes, people would listen to him. The slightest gossip about anyone can spread like wildfire in high school, no matter who the source is or how reliable they are.

He wouldn't really tell anyone though, would he? I know Dwight. He's a nice guy: he comforted me in the library; he didn't freak out when I started crying. A guy like that wouldn't be vindictive enough to go feeding the rumor mill. That thought finally calms me down.

Then I think back to his reaction at the match. I really don't want Dwight to hate me. I liked hanging out with him. I actually enjoyed working on the physics project, not just because he was good company, but because his enthusiasm made it so much more bearable.

I just . . .

I'd miss him if I didn't have him around.

I haven't let on to the girls just how much I like having Dwight as a friend. I know that Tiffany would call it 'social suicide'; the others probably wouldn't understand either. Summer might – like she did with the black prom dress. I just don't see why I should feel guilty because I'm friends with a guy who isn't considered popular.

Fingers snap loudly in front of my eyes, making me jump violently, so that the seatbelt cuts into my shoulder. 'What?' I snap.

'We're here,' Owen from my algebra class tells me. 'You okay? You looked a world away.'

I shake my head a little and put on a broad smile. 'I'm fine. Totally fine.'

I clamber out of the car after Owen and smooth down my skirt. There are maybe a dozen or so cars here already, and a bunch more are looking for a place to park. Liam's already here – I spot him near the door, waving people in and saying hi, accepting the congratulations for his performance in the game.

I wonder how he got here so fast – until I see he's still wearing his soccer kit.

'Hey, Madison!' he calls as I appear behind the guys at the porch of his house.

'Hey.' Even from this distance I can smell the sweat and dirt on him. 'Great game tonight, by the way!'

'Thanks. You know, I really don't get enough credit as a defender. I mean, come on, we both know I *carry* that team of losers.'

I laugh and give a semi-sarcastic, 'Of course you do.'

He winks and then yells behind me, 'Hutchins! How you been, man! Long time no see!'

I'm not sure who's arrived. I doubt the girls are here yet. It'll be ages before they're ready if they are taking showers. But this time, I don't hide in the bathroom. I want to – like at that first party at Tiffany's house – because I still don't know a lot of people here. I only really hang out with one small group, and try and keep up with who's who, and who's dating who.

But I decide that, just for a change, I'll grin and bear it, and be a little bit braver.

Following the guys to the kitchen, I see a bunch of cans in a cooler on the floor. It briefly crosses my mind that one can of cider won't hurt anybody – my parents won't know; it wouldn't get me drunk or anything . . . And everyone else does it.

But that's all that happens; I think about it for a split second, and then I grab a can of diet lemonade instead. Not because I'm worried what my parents would say if they found out. I just don't want the alcohol, period.

'Madison! Hi!'

I turn and recognize Nicole from my English class, and a girl who after a couple of seconds I remember is called Mary-Jane. I smile, glad to have people to talk to. 'Hey. How are you guys?'

The night is actually pretty good fun; the girls find me when they finally arrive so I hang out with them for a while. I think about trying to find Bryce, but I don't catch him, even though I keep an eye out, and frankly, I'm having too much fun with the girls, attempting to dance without looking like a total dork.

I'm laughing as Melissa, hiccupping and giggling, overbalances into Tiffany. I reach forward, laughing, to help steady her, when a hand lands on my waist.

I turn around to see who it is, and find myself being kissed. In a split second I recognize Bryce, and kiss him back.

We break apart eventually, and he leans to whisper in my ear, 'I've been waiting for that all night. Come on, let's go someplace quieter.'

He keeps hold of my hand as we weave through the throngs of sweaty people. Eventually we make it outside. The night air feels cool on my bare skin after the warm house. There aren't many people in Liam Kennedy's back yard, and when Bryce guides me over to the far corner, the thrumming music fades into the background. He drops down on the grass and pats the space beside him.

'Great game, by the way,' I tell him as I sit beside him. He reaches over to pull me onto his lap. 'You played really well. I don't know why you're worried about being picked up by college scouts. They'll snap you up easy.'

'I don't want to talk about that right now,' he says dismissively, and kisses me again.

'Is everything okay?' I ask him.

'What, so now I can't even kiss my girlfriend without something being wrong?' He tries to say it jokingly but there's an edge to his voice.

'Bryce . . .'

'It's fine, for God's sake,' he says, this time a little more sharply. Snapping, almost. He starts to kiss me again but I move my head back so he can't. I expect him to get even angrier, since he's obviously in such a bad mood, but to my surprise he curls his arms around me instead and says, 'I'm just – just stressing out about the whole college thing a little. Tonight's game wasn't my best.'

'Are you kidding? You were fantastic! Everyone says so.'

His mouth twists a little, and I put a hand to his face.

His shadow of stubble scratches against my palm – and my cheek when I lean forward to give him a kiss. 'Stop worrying about it so much. It's going to be fine. Everyone knows you're going to get that scholarship. Wouldn't Coach have told you before now if he thought you needed to step it up and do better?'

'I guess.'

I plant another kiss on his lips. 'Exactly. So you should be celebrating. You should be happy. You guys won, and you played fantastically.'

He gives a small laugh and kisses my nose. 'Thanks, Mainstream.'

I smile. 'It's what I'm here for.'

He kisses me again, only this time more deeply and intimately. After we break apart, we sit in silence with the background noise of the party surrounding us.

Liam's back yard has a brick wall separating it from the neighbors'. There's a flowerbed in front of it, with old-fashioned lanterns about a foot off the ground; I can make out the quiet buzz of electricity. They cast an orange-yellow glow over Bryce's face, sending one side into shadow and highlighting his wavy blond hair. His eyes seem almost hazel. He looks so handsome; he always does. I hope I don't look too terrible in this light.

'Are you having a good time?' he asks. 'You sure

looked like you were when I saw you dancing with the girls.'

The corner of my mouth tweaks up in a smile. 'Yeah, it's a good party. And Melissa can be a funny drunk.'

'You're not drinking?'

I shake my head. 'Nope,' I confirm. 'I don't see the point. Having a good time and alcohol don't go hand in hand. At least, they don't for me. I suppose I can't vouch for other people.' 'Other people' meaning, apparently, most people at this party.

'You're so different to what I expected when I first saw you. Well, OK – pretty different. Not completely, though.'

'Why? What did you expect when you first saw me?'

'That's for me to know,' he replies mischievously, kissing me briefly.

I catch his face and hold it close to mine. 'And for me to find out,' I tell him, grinning back. 'Come on, tell me, I want to know!'

'Hmm, no.'

'You're just doing this because I want to know, aren't you? You're doing it to annoy me.'

'Maybe . . .'

'Fine, be that way.' And to emphasize my point, I push his arms away and get to my feet, smoothing out my skirt. But before I step away, he grabs my ankle and gives it a tug. I cry out, but he pulls me back onto his lap. 'Bryce! Don't do that! I could've broken something!'

He rolls his eyes, a signal that tells me he thinks I'm being melodramatic. I ignore it.

Squeezing me a little tighter, he chuckles and I feel it reverberating through his chest where my arm is pressed against him. 'All right, if you really must know, I thought you were the sort of person who didn't take any shit from anybody, and who didn't give a damn what people thought about you.'

Well, that's wrong on both occasions . . .

'Which I was right about,' he carries on, shocking me. Do I really come across as that kind of person? I must make a better job of hiding my old self away beneath these layers of the new Madison than I thought. 'But I also thought you were kind of badass. The short hair, the nose stud, the attitude. So you can see why everyone was surprised when you say you don't swear and you don't drink.'

I laugh; I can't help it, but so does Bryce.

'It's not a bad different, though,' he assures me hastily.

'Good to know.'

'I love you.'

'Love you too,' I reply with a smile, and we start

kissing again – until I lose all track of time. The loose trails of thought drift around my mind before I can put them together and stow them away to pick up again later.

Chapter 33

November crawls into December, the days quiet and uneventful, blurring into one chunk of too much home-work. Thanksgiving is, for the most part, as it always is. We visit Dad's family, and all my cousins gawp at my nose stud and new hairdo and until we leave for home again. About the most exciting thing that happens is that I get a physics tutor who I see once a week on a Thursday afternoon, since Dwight and I don't speak anymore. The only exchange between us was after the soccer match, in our next physics lesson – I said hi, and he ignored me. That's it. We haven't spoken once since.

I got my dress for the Winter Dance; I bought the black one, much to Tiffany and Melissa's – and, as it turned out, my mom's – chagrin. They all wanted to know why I didn't want something more *colorful*.

The rest of the girls have their dresses sorted too, of course. One weekend, after we'd bought our dresses, they dragged me to the mall to get shoes and clutch bags and hair pins and all sorts of things I didn't even know people had to buy to go to these things.

Now that the dance is tomorrow night, I'm not sure whether to be excited or nervous.

Strangely, though, the thing at the forefront of my mind is the physics project that's due in next week. Dr Anderson wants it next Thursday, but . . . I don't even know if we've finished it or not. I haven't done any more work on it. Dwight has a copy of the whole thing, so he might've done more. Actually, no, he *will* have done, because even though he hates me, he won't risk damaging his own grade.

Should I feel guilty about that? I'm practically sponging off his hard work. It's not really fair . . . but I did contribute to it as best I could, and it's not my fault he hates me now. Whatever. It's not like I *care* about AP physics. I just have to put up with it for the rest of the year, unless it's not too late to transfer to something – *anything* – else.

'Hello? Earth to Mads! Is anybody home in that strange little head of yours?'

I jerk my mind back to reality – back to Jenna yelling down her laptop to me, raising her eyebrows to the webcam.

'Yeah. Sorry. Just . . . thinking.'

'About . . . ?'

'About the dance tomorrow,' I lie.

'Liar. You're thinking about him, aren't you?'

'Bryce?'

'No. Dwight. Oh, come on, Mads, I'm your big sister. I know you well enough to be able to tell when you're lying. And it's totally obvious when you're thinking about Dwight because you get this faraway look and you frown. But when it's Bryce it's more of a smile.'

'Shut up already.'

She just laughs. 'Have you talked to him yet?'

'No. Why should I? I don't have anything to say to him.'

I didn't tell Jenna about the kiss. I just said we had a fight and I didn't want to go into details.

She just sighs, and there's a sorrowful look on her face. 'Fine. We'll talk about something else. All ready for the dance tomorrow? Legs waxed, eyebrows plucked? Instruments of torture lined up for curling eyelashes and hair?'

I manage a laugh at that. 'Yeah. At least, I think I'm all prepared.'

'Sorry I couldn't make it down for the weekend.'

'Don't be silly!' I burst out. 'Jen, it doesn't matter, honestly. I never expected you to, anyway. I don't know why you and Mom made such a fuss about it. It's not a big deal. I'm just going to some stupid school dance.'

'Exactly why we're making so much fuss,' she argues back calmly. 'You're going to a dance, Madison. With your friends and your boyfriend. *You* are going to one of those stupid school dances. Don't get too offended by this, but it's a mile away from where you were last year. Not that there was anything wrong with who you were last year,' she tells me quickly, smoothly, 'but you're so much happier now. We all know it.'

The edge of my mouth quirks up in a teeny tiny smile, but my heart isn't in it.

Yeah, I have a better life here. I don't want to disappear and be invisible and I'm not trying to just make it through another day. But I hate that they all say things like that so proudly; that they think it's something to celebrate . . . because that makes it seem like I've done something wonderful, and I haven't.

'Whatever,' I mumble, and Jenna gets the hint.

'So how are you guys all getting there, did you say? You didn't rent a limo like we all did?'

'No, Bryce is driving us. Most people are driving, actually, I think. It's not as though anybody will drink there. The teachers all made sure to set very strict guidelines on that one. We'll meet the rest of them there.'

Jenna nods. 'Sounds good. Make sure you send me pictures, though, all right?' She sounds so demanding and forceful, for a second I think she could be our mom when she's in one of her rare bad moods. 'I want to see *tons* of photos of this.'

I laugh, shaking my head and smiling helplessly. 'Sure, Jenna. Sure thing.'

She sits back and grins broadly at me. 'Great! And you're doing your hair like we talked about, aren't you?'

I roll my eyes. Jenna had put more thought into how I should wear my hair than I had. I figured I'd do it as I normally did, since it's too short to do anything with, even curl. Jenna, however, had spoken to Mom, and they had decided I should buy cute little silver hair pins so it looks a little more special. I agreed without complaint because that was the easiest thing to do, and quite frankly, I didn't mind.

'Yes, I am wearing those fiddly little silver things.'

'Good.' Then she pauses before saying, 'So are you and Bryce going to . . . you know . . .' She pauses again. 'Has he booked a hotel room for you guys or anything like that?'

My forehead crinkles in confusion for a moment or two until I realize what she's getting at.

'Oh! Oh, no. Yeah, we're not doing anything like that. At least, not as far as I know. Besides, there's an after party that everyone's going to. But even so. No way.'

Jenna nods and says bluntly, 'Good. Don't. I know loads of girls think it's really special, and maybe it is, depending on who you are and how your relationship is, but I don't think it's a good idea for you. Now, don't get me wrong, I'm just looking out for you here. You know, doing my big sister duty and all that. Safe sex, condoms – you know the drill, Mads. But I know what you're like, and you've only been with the guy a couple of months. I just don't think it's a good idea for you.'

I don't blush; Bryce might make me blush some-times, but this sort of thing I can handle, and I bite the inside of my lower lips slightly while Jenna talks. She's quite open and frank – she always has been with me, so I should've been expecting this. But it still catches me off guard a little.

I hadn't even properly thought about ... about actually having sex with Bryce yet. Sure, it crossed my mind a couple of times when we were making out in his room, but I discarded the idea because I knew I wasn't ready. And I'm still not.

And that was what I kept telling him whenever he asked. He was always a little hard to read, so I couldn't tell whether he was okay with it or not. He always *said* he was fine. And he was going to have to be – I wasn't about to go rushing into anything. If that was all he was after, then he wasn't worth my time. But he said he loved me, so I guess he didn't mind waiting for me.

So I say to Jenna impassively, 'Okay.'

'Are you even paying attention to me?' She frowns slightly, like she's not sure if I'm just saying 'Okay' to shut her up, or if I mean it in solid agreement with her.

'Of course I am.'

She continues to frown at me on the computer monitor before finally saying, 'Good.'

I hear Mom yelling up to my room – 'Dice, dinner's ready!' – so I yell back 'Okay!' before telling Jenna I have to go, and I'll send her pictures, probably on Sunday.

'I'll text you tomorrow, before you go, but have an awesome night, okay, Mads?' My big sister grins at me widely, with such an earnest look on her face. She's genuinely excited for me – more excited than I am, actually.

'Thanks,' I say, and disconnect the web-call.

I make my way down to dinner; Mom puts a plate of beef casserole down for each of us (Dad's working late) and asks, 'What did Jenna have to say?'

'Oh, she was just going on and on – *and on* – about the dance tomorrow,' I tell her with a laugh. 'She's more excited than I am.'

Mom laughs too, but then she hesitates a second and says, 'You are excited, though, aren't you?'

'Of course!' I reply instantly. I *am*. Not quite in the same bubbly, non-stop-chatter way the rest of the girls are, but I've had a smile on my face most of the day because of this dance. I'm actually getting to go to a dance, with my friends and my boyfriend, and I'll be able to kiss him and have a slow dance at the end of the night, and then I get to go to an actual after party . . .

But I'm nervous – and a little scared too – so that's sort of balanced out the excitement and resulted in apparent indifference. *Kind of like what my physics tutor was talking about with destructive interference in wave diffraction*, I think distractedly – and I want to laugh, but I stop myself, because it's the kind of joke I'd want to share with Dwight, only we're not talking, and he hates me.

Mom smiles at me. 'I'm just happy for you, Dice. You know that, right?'

'I know,' I say with a smile, 'I'm happy for me too.'

After swallowing a mouthful of casserole, my mom sighs and says, 'I just wish you'd picked something a bit . . . well, a bit more colorful, than that black dress. Although it does look fantastic,' she adds hastily.

I shrug. 'What can I say? It was love at first sight;

that dress was The One; there could never be another one like it.'

She just laughs and shakes her head, and then tells me to 'stop being so sarcastic and eat that casserole already'.

By Saturday I'm really agitated, my palms clammy from the anticipation of the Winter Dance. I finish all my algebra II homework and answer a few biology questions, and tidy my room, and play a video game, and read some of my book for English. But it still doesn't pass the time quickly enough. Everything just drags and crawls until, after what feels like an eternity, it's two hours until Bryce will be here, and I decide that's late enough to start getting ready.

As it turns out, two hours was a little too long, as I realize just after I step out of the shower, so I prolong all the rest of my pre-dance preparations: moisturizing, and doing my hair and makeup. But even so, I'm ready a good seventeen minutes before Bryce is due to turn up.

I sit on the edge of my bed, smoothing out the skirt of my dress. I have my shoes on, and all the fiddly little silver pins in my hair, and I used a subtle sweep of silver eyeliner and shadow to brighten up my features. I have a silver clutch purse too, and my shoes are silver.

I wasn't going to go *entirely* in black – even I drew the line somewhere.

When my clock finally ticks to just eight minutes left of waiting for Bryce, I head downstairs. I have my ticket, my cell phone, some cash . . . and my iPod. I couldn't help it. It's in the zip-up pocket inside my purse. I have another bag with a change of clothes for the after party.

I get to the bottom of the stairs and Mom springs out of the lounge. I bet she's been waiting to hear my footsteps.

'Oh, Dice, sweetie!' she gushes, and a huge grin spreads over her face. 'You look absolutely beautiful.'

I smile for her, but my stomach is curling into knots. 'Thanks, Mom.'

Dad walks out of the office and brandishes his camera.

'Careful I don't break the lens,' I tell him, nodding at it. My parents laugh, and Mom adjusts one of the silver pins in my hair before holding me at arm's length and smiling at me. I could be wrong, but for a moment I think she's almost on the verge of tears.

I hug her back tightly when she hugs me, but she pulls away first. She sniffles slightly and says, 'Don't want to crease your dress, do we?'

'When is Bryce meant to get here?' Dad asks.

'Soon,' I say, and that's when we all hear a car outside. I've heard him pull up outside enough times to realize it's his. And suddenly the knot in my stomach contorts itself in the most nauseating way possible. There's a ringing in my ears that blocks out the pounding of my heartbeat and I stare blankly at the cream wall in front of me.

Dad opens the door, and I hear them talking – the usual hey-how're-you pleasantries. Then it occurs to me: I should probably turn around. He'll think I'm being rude.

I snap myself back to life, out of my dazed state, and turn around to face Bryce, putting on a smile for him.

Before I can say hi, he greets me with, 'Wow. You look . . . wow.'

I roll my eyes, but a warm blush spreads over my cheeks. I like this kind of blushing, which goes with a fuzzy feeling in the pit of my stomach. 'You look pretty dapper yourself.'

He cocks his head to the side, raising an eyebrow. '*Dapper?*' I shrug, and he chuckles at me. 'Well, thanks.'

He does look even more wonderful than usual in his tux. It's black, of course, as is his bow tie. His white shirt fits snugly on his muscular chest, and if I thought he was out of my league before, he most certainly is now.

But he's smiling at me as though I'm the only thing in the entire universe, and all I can do is look shyly back at him before dropping my gaze to his extraordinarily shiny and undoubtedly expensive shoes.

'Picture time, I think!' Dad announces.

'Oh, wait!' Bryce raises his hand, which up until now has been tucked out of sight. 'I nearly forgot. Your corsage.'

I'd forgotten all about the whole tradition of corsages.

It's beautiful, though – a white rose with white ribbons. I take off my silver bracelets and he ties it around my left wrist, and then kisses the back of my hand, which makes me giggle. Then he pulls me close and slings an arm around my waist, and we smile for the camera as my dad takes a couple of photos.

'Got your tickets?' Mom asks us.

'Right here,' Bryce replies brightly, patting what I assume to be a pocket inside his tux jacket.

'Good. Now remember to call if you want a ride home from this party afterward, okay?'

'Yes, Mom, I know,' I sigh. She's only told me about a billion times. And I've told her a billion and one times that it's fine because I can stay over Tiffany's with the rest of the girls.

I pick up my small overnight bag and then turn to Bryce with a grin. 'Ready?'

'Yep. Goodnight,' he says to my parents as I begin to herd him out of the door.

'Bye!' I call to them.

'Bye! You kids have fun!' they yell back. 'Madison, text us when you're back at Tiffany's.'

'Okay!'

And then we're in Bryce's car and the front door closes, and the silence of my anxious anticipation floods through me. With a heavy sigh, I lean back against the head rest and close my eyes.

'You okay?' Bryce says. 'Your parents aren't that embarrassing, Mainstream, don't worry.'

I laugh and go with that, because it's better than explaining that I'm really freaking out about this. I'm enthusiastic and happy and anxious and scared all at once. My hands are moist and my stomach is full of butterflies and my heart is fluttering erratically. The thing I'm most scared of is being awkward and not knowing what to do – and looking so out of place that everybody will find out that I've never done this before.

And I really, really don't want that to happen.

Bryce squeezes my hand and I look over at him, putting on a smile. 'Yeah?'

'You sure you're all right?'

'Yeah, totally fine,' I assure him, broadening my smile to a grin. 'Sorry, I'm just . . . a little spaced out today, I guess. Excited.'

He looks at me warily for a moment, but then leans over to plant a soft, long kiss on my lips. 'I love you.'

'Love you too.'

We kiss once more before he puts the car in gear and pulls off. The dance is at the school – which, considering Midsommer High is a pretty darn fantastic school, isn't as lame as it sounds.

'You do look absolutely incredible tonight,' he tells me.

'Thanks. So do you.'

'Thanks.' There's a pause, and then he clears his throat before saying, 'Listen, Madison, I was thinking earlier . . . Well, my parents are chaperoning the dance and they'll be at the school till really late, so I thought, maybe, if you wanted to go back to my place for a bit instead of the after party . . . We could go back to the party after if you wanted, but . . .'

Oh, man.

This again.

I have to admit, he is being kind of romantic seeing as it's the Winter Dance, but . . .

Well, that's exactly it. *But.*

'Bryce, I'm still not ready,' I tell him bluntly.

I catch his sigh. It's barely audible, but I don't miss it. I don't comment on it.

He says, 'It's fine, Mainstream. Don't worry about it. I'll wait.' And he sends me a fleeting smile before turning back to look at the road, then reaches over with one hand to squeeze my thigh in what's meant to be a reassuring way.

I want to ask him if he really *does* have a problem with it – with me – but I don't want to spoil the night. I can ask him another time. Maybe.

Chapter 34

The school assembly hall looks absolutely incredible. It's reserved for formal assemblies – of which we've only had two in the entire time I've been here – and holds about a thousand people. So it's not exactly a squeeze to fit in the tables and the stage for the band and the two hundred-odd students.

It's decorated with blue, silver, black and white balloons. They flood the floor and hang in bunches from the walls. The table centerpieces are simple vases with blue or white artificial flowers. At the entrance there's a balloon arch, with a professional photographer taking photos of the couples as they go in. The music isn't too loud, either, which is nice; it fills the room over the chatter, but you don't have to yell to be heard.

'I have a hunch that the dance committee has a fondness for balloons,' I murmur in Bryce's ear as we join the small queue of people waiting to have their photos taken.

Bryce laughs loudly, causing a few heads to turn our way. 'Last year it was all streamers. I swear to God we were drowning in them. People kept tripping over them too: they ended up all over the dance floor because they were too heavy to stay tacked to the ceiling.'

I laugh at the image of it. 'Then I guess we're lucky with the balloons.'

'Not if you have a fear of balloons,' he points out.

'True,' I concede. 'Well, if that's where most of the budget went, I shall look forward to our three-course meal with extremely low expectations.'

'It's a damn big budget,' he tells me.

'And it's a heck of a lot of balloons.'

Then it's our turn for a photo, and once that's done we wander on in.

Bryce starts to ask, 'Can you see anyone anywh—' when someone yells, 'Hey, guys! Bryce! Over here, man!' and we both spot Kyle waving us over from a table against the far wall. Bryce takes my hand again and I follow him over towards the others. Summer and Marcus are cozied up, ever the world's sweetest couple, and Kyle and his date – a girl I recognize from parties and school, Mary-Jane – sit next to them. The tables are of varying sizes, but ours is one of the biggest, made to seat at least sixteen, so there's enough space for all of us.

I drop into the chair beside Bryce's and say hi. Mary-Jane says, 'Your dress looks amazing.'

'Oh, um, thanks,' I say shyly. I've never really spoken to her much; she's a senior. 'You look great too.'

'Thanks. But seriously, it's such a bold choice, wearing black! It looks fantastic, though – really stands out.'

I grin, and it's entirely genuine. I thought Summer was the only other person who liked this dress. I was worried that people would think I looked weird in it – though not enough not to buy it.

'Thanks.'

'See,' Summer pitches in, detaching herself from Marcus's mouth. 'I told you it'd look hot.'

'Definitely hot,' Bryce says in a loud whisper in my ear, making us all laugh. He plants a kiss on my cheek before continuing his conversation with Kyle.

'You look really pretty too,' I tell Summer. 'Just stating the obvious.'

She laughs and grins at me. 'Why, thank you.' Her cell phone buzzes noisily on the table, the screen lighting up. 'Ooh, that's probably Tiffany . . . Yeah, she's on her way.'

'What about Melissa?'

'Oh, she should be here any moment.'

Adam's next to arrive, with his date, Ann, and then

Ricky and Alison turn up at the same time as Melissa and Owen. Tiffany's one of the very last to turn up – with some guy I've never seen before. I thought she already had a date – she'd told me she was going with Tom, one of the football guys, a senior.

I shoot Summer and Melissa a look of confusion as Tiffany makes her way over. They're just as baffled as I am, though.

'Hey, everyone!' she chirps. She looks amazing – her dress clings to her like liquid silver, and looks dazzling against her dark skin. 'Oh, this is Justin. He's an old family friend.'

Justin is tall – that's the first thing I notice. He's about a foot taller than Tiffany, so he must have a couple of inches on Bryce. From his strong build I guess he's a sportsman. He's got close cropped sandy hair that's combed down neatly, and his tuxedo is spotless.

'Dude, I remember you!' Bryce suddenly exclaims. 'Used to live next door to Tiffany, moved before high school or something, right? I'm Bryce, Bryce Higgins.'

'Oh, yeah!' this guy, Justin, says. Bryce stands up and they do that weird hand-slap-shake thing that guys always do. 'I remember you now. I used to babysit you sometimes, and Tiffany, right?'

Bryce laughs. 'Yeah, that was me. So, how've you

been? I heard you got some big scholarship playing football.'

'Yeah, I'm in my second year, up in Alabama. It's the college my dad went to.'

'Justin's just down for the week,' Tiffany explains to Summer, Melissa and me as she drops gracefully into one of the two empty seats. 'Visiting some family.'

'And not too proud for a high-school dance?' I say to him, not unkindly.

'You are never,' he tells me seriously, 'too old for a high-school dance.'

I laugh, picking up on the sarcasm.

'I don't think I caught your name.'

'Madison.'

He nods. 'Hi.'

I say, 'Hello.'

Bryce grabs my arm. 'Let's dance.'

I can tell something's bugging Bryce, but when I ask, he tells me nothing's wrong. I don't push it because I don't want to spoil the evening. It's only a short while later, when we're working our way through the absolutely delicious appetizers, that I think the problem might be Justin.

I could be wrong, of course, but Bryce just seems a

little different towards Justin now than he did when he first arrived.

Tiffany, I notice, makes sure that everybody knows Justin is hers. She keeps putting her hand on his arm, his leg, brushing a loose strand of hair back – that kind of thing. When I was up dancing and mingling with people earlier, everyone seemed to be talking about Justin: because a) he's 'totally drop-dead gorgeous', and b) he's a college student, for crying out loud! Tiffany is so totally lucky, and c) he's an awesome footballer – that scholarship he got doesn't go to just *anybody*.

Justin, for his part, seems pleasant enough: he's nineteen, in his second year of college, studying to become a sports therapist. It's not long before we're all sitting down to dinner.

'Looks like they didn't blow the entire budget on balloons,' Bryce tells me with a chuckle, pushing away his empty plate when he's done with the first course.

'Uh-uh,' I warn him. 'That was only the appetizer.'

'True. I'll reserve judgment till the end of the meal.'

I laugh, and then he takes his fork up again, and stabs it into one of the remaining pieces of chicken in my salad. I turn my head and raise my eyebrows at him. Gradually he raises the fork to his mouth and takes a deliberately slow bite of the chicken.

'Stealing my food,' I say, mock-scowling at him, and bump my knee against his under the table. 'Rude.'

He winks at me and gives me a quick kiss, and I can't help but laugh.

'You guys are all coming to the after party later, right?' Mary-Jane wonders.

There are affirmative answers from all around the table. Turning to Justin, Marcus asks, 'What about you?'

'Party?' he says. 'I'm in.'

As the catering staff collect up the mostly empty dishes and bring out the main course, conversation turns automatically to the food – it's some kind of beef dish with a red wine sauce, and it smells and looks absolutely delicious.

'I remember the last prom I had at high school,' Justin starts with a laugh in his voice. 'There was this huge disaster with the catering staff, because they'd blown most of the budget on getting some on-the-rise pop star so they had to be a little stingy when it came to the meal, but they still tried to be all fancy, and we ended up with escargots as the starter. I don't think anybody touched them. Then we got oysters for the mains, and some kind of disgusting custard thing for dessert. So we ordered a ton of pizza.'

'I can imagine how flattered the dance committee was by that,' I say.

He laughs. 'Hell yeah. My girlfriend went bat-shit crazy on me for making her look like a laughing stock.'

'Girlfriend?' Melissa picks up on what I'm sure we're all thinking.

'We broke up ages ago,' he says dismissively.

'Aw, that's a shame . . . Anyone on the scene now?' No one could legitimately think that she was interested in Justin – she sounds like she's just making polite conversation.

'Nope,' he replies. 'But that's partly because my football coach has us all working our butts off so hard there's not really much time for *dating* right now.' He shrugs like it's no big deal, but there's a mischievous grin on his face telling us that he's not really been abiding by the rules, and a few of us laugh. I notice that Bryce doesn't, so I turn to him questioningly.

He gives me a smile and reaches under the table to squeeze my thigh. I put my hand on his and squeeze back.

'Hey, I'm watching you two,' Justin says suddenly, making me jump a little. 'No funny business under the table there. Save it for the after party.'

I manage not to blush, and force a laugh. Bryce's hand tightens on mine a little – in irritation, maybe.

'You sure you're all right?' I ask quietly.

'Sure,' he replies, and smiles at me again.

There's easy conversation over dinner; after dessert everyone's so full they don't want to move . . . But gradually people begin to get up and make their way onto the dance floor, where the band have started to play again. Bryce is deep in conversation with Kyle and Ricky, so I let the girls pull me up.

'What's up with Bryce?' Melissa asks me. 'He's acting weird.'

'I don't know,' I tell her honestly. 'But I kind of get the feeling he doesn't like Justin.'

'Well, that would make sense,' she tells me with a shrug. 'I bet he feels threatened, is all. I mean, Bryce is pretty much the hottest, most popular guy here, and then all of a sudden this other hot guy *who's in college* comes swanning in.' She shrugs again. 'Just guys being guys. Testosterone wars.'

'Yeah, I guess . . .'

'You two aren't having problems, are you?' she asks.

'No!' I insist quickly. 'Why would you think that?'

'Oh, no, I didn't mean anything by it! It's just that I thought maybe that could've been why he was acting weird.'

'Oh. Well no, we're fine.'

'Good.'

'Yeah.'

But I feel strangely guilty for saying that – as if I'd

lied to her. And I refuse to admit to myself that this might be the case. I don't want to think about that right now. I can think about it tomorrow. Tonight I'm just going to forget about all that and have fun, and enjoy my first high-school dance.

Chapter 35

The night passes quickly, which I really hadn't been expecting. I guess I'm really just having too much fun to notice. Everyone seems to be eager for the after party, but even so, the original hyper excitement dies down as the Winter Dance draws to a close. The band is playing slower songs, and it's a little darker now the sun has set.

I'm over by the drinks table, getting myself another cup of fruit punch, when a familiar voice says, 'Hey.'

'Andy! Hi!' I say enthusiastically, grinning at him. His hair is just as gravity-defying as ever, and his tie is askew, and his shirt isn't tucked into his pants, but I have to admit, he does clean up nicely – although I do usually see him in his gym kit. 'How are you?'

I still see Andy when I hide under the bleachers during gym, but we never talk anymore. Ever since that soccer game, I've been keeping my distance. And

Carter and I haven't spoken much in Art for the last month. But can you blame me? Dwight hates me. I don't want to be reminded of that every time I speak to his friends; I assumed they would have something against me because Dwight hates me. Isn't that just what people – what friends – do?

I've missed these guys, I realize.

'I'm good,' he says with a nod, sipping his punch. 'How've you been? I don't see much of you lately. Since you seem determined to avoid me in gym class.' He raises his eyebrows accusingly, and I drop my gaze to the floor.

'Sorry . . .'

'That's okay,' he says. 'I'm just . . . curious, I guess. But I shouldn't pry. I'll shut up now. You look very pretty tonight, Madison.'

I laugh. 'Thanks. You look good too.'

'Of course I do,' he says jokingly, and I laugh.

'Are you going to the after party?' I ask, but I already know the answer.

He just snorts. 'Not really our thing, in all honesty. Are you having a good night so far?'

'Yeah, I am, actually,' I tell him with a grin. 'How about you? Did you come with a date?'

'Nah, a bunch of us just came as a group,' he says with a shrug. 'Hey, you know, Dwight and Carter are just over there' – he jerks his head towards the tables we all ate at earlier – 'if you want to say hi.'

I bite my lower lip and gulp. I can only imagine how horrible it would be if I did that. Dwight certainly won't want me going over to say hi. And I know it'll only make me feel terrible too, and it's been such a good night . . . I can't go and ruin it all now.

'I, uh, I don't . . . I don't think I should,' I stammer in a mumble.

'What happened with you two anyway?' Andy asks. 'I don't care if I'm prying now. Dwight hasn't been the same since you two stopped talking. And you've been really weird with us too. What happened?'

We kissed, that's what happened. I had to get out before everything crumbled to pieces. I couldn't go back to where I was before. I'm sorry.

'You mean he didn't tell you?'

'No. He just shuts off whenever Carter or I mention you.'

'Oh.'

There's a pause. 'So you're not going to tell me either?'

'No,' I reply, my voice suddenly very quiet.

Andy just sighs and shakes his head. But before either of us can say anything else, the music stops and there's someone calling down the microphone, 'Hey, everybody, can I have your attention, please! It's time to announce the King and Queen of this year's Winter Dance!'

Andy and I both turn to look at the stage. I recognize Lucy, the head cheerleader, and head of the dance committee, and senior class president.

'Guess you'd better go,' Andy says. 'Don't want to be seen with me if you're called up.'

'Don't be stupid,' I say with a slight scowl at him.

'It's not stupid. I voted for you. Lots of people did. You've got a good chance at winning.'

'That's not what I meant and you know it.'

'Just give me a yell if you're ever in need of a Court Nerd,' he tells me with a good-natured smile, and then he goes back to his table, leaving me alone.

'Madison!' I hear Summer call. I go on my tiptoes and spot her waving me over; I make my way across just as Lucy begins her dramatic buildup, announcing the King of the Winter Dance.

I always thought the whole prom king and queen thing was a bit unnecessary. I still don't see why everyone is so excited right now.

'I hear it from a very good source that you've had a lot of votes,' Summer says in my ear. 'Tiffany was really not happy about that.'

'I've got votes?' That genuinely shocks me. I'd assumed that Andy was joking when he said he'd voted for me; I knew I was a nominee, but people actually voting for me . . . ? 'Are you serious?'

'Uh, hell yes, I'm serious,' she giggles. 'I voted for you. But you didn't hear me say that.'

'. . . Bryce Higgins!' Lucy announces loudly, and clapping and cheering ensues. 'Come on up here!' A spotlight is fixed on Bryce as he maneuvers his way through the parting crowd to collect his crown. He grins and waves at everyone, and when he catches my eye, he winks, which makes Summer giggle and nudge me in the ribs.

'If you win too, it's just going to be the cutest.'

'I don't want to win,' I tell her honestly.

'You might, though.'

'Tiffany will, since Lucy isn't running.'

'She might not. You know a lot of people like you too. You're pretty damn popular, even if you've only been here a few months.'

'But . . .'

'And your Queen of the Winter Dance . . . is . . .' There's an excruciatingly long pause, and my stomach curls into knots. What if it is me? Do I want it to be me? 'Tiffany Blanche!'

More clapping and cheering. I'm clapping too, and

I can't help feeling a little relieved. Summer claps, but says in my ear, 'Don't tell Tiffany this, but I wanted you to win.'

I'm not sure how to reply to that, other than: 'Don't worry, my lips are sealed . . .' and they are.

The spotlights on Tiffany and Bryce merge into one as they are instructed to step down from the stage to dance. The crowd forms a sort of semicircle around them, and they're the center of attention. The band starts up again – a slow ballad that I recognize as an acoustic cover of a You Me at Six song.

Marcus suddenly appears beside Summer. 'One last dance, beautiful?'

'You think I can say no to that face?' she giggles. She shoots me an apologetic smile, but I just grin at them. Even after months of being around them, it never ceases to surprise me how much they obviously love each other.

Which leads me to think about me and Bryce . . . and I'm refusing to do that right now.

I look around as everyone couples up to dance. My date, however, is right in the middle of the dance floor with one of my closest friends at this moment, so it looks like I'll be sitting this one out.

I turn to go sit on the sidelines when someone taps my shoulder and makes me spin back again. It's Justin.

'Mind if I take this dance?' he asks. 'Seeing as both our dates are otherwise occupied?'

I shrug. 'Sure. Why not.'

And I let him take my hand and lead me onto the dance floor. He puts his hands around my waist and I stretch mine up to rest on his shoulders. I'm glad I'm wearing some heels; I wouldn't be able to reach otherwise.

'So what's the deal with you and Bryce?' he asks me. 'How long have you guys been together?'

'A couple of months,' I reply. 'I moved here at the end of August and we started dating a couple of weeks after that.'

Justin nods.

'What's the deal with you and Tiffany?' I ask.

'Why, are you jealous?' he asks with a flirty smile. I roll my eyes in response and he says, 'I ran into her a couple of days ago, at Walmart, and she asked me to come along. It's not like I had any other plans, so I figured, why not?'

I bite my tongue before I tell him that it doesn't seem like Tiffany thinks that. She's been making out like the two of them are an item.

Justin adds, of his own volition, 'She's a bit . . . How can I put this nicely ? . . . self-obsessed.'

I don't respond: I know how dangerous words can

be, how they can be twisted and misinterpreted; I don't want it getting back to Tiffany that I said all kinds of things about her behind her back when I didn't.

But at the same time, I don't object. She *can* be a little self-centered at times, after all.

I flounder for another conversation starter; I'm desperate to talk about something *safer*. But we're interrupted before the silence between us becomes noticeable.

'Mind if I cut in here?'

'Bryce.' His name falls off my tongue as relief floods over me. Tiffany is just behind him, and she's looking at me in a way that I can't really pinpoint but that sends chills down my spine. With that silver crown on her head, the words *Ice Queen* flit through my mind before I can help it.

'Sure, dude,' Justin says easily, and steps back, handing me to Bryce and taking Tiffany's hand. I hold onto Bryce and we walk away from them before he puts his arms around me and we sway to the music.

'What was that all about?' he asks, frowning.

'What do you mean?'

'You and him. Dancing like that.'

'He asked me to dance because you and Tiffany were dancing, and I said yes,' I explain slowly. Is he jealous, or just annoyed? I can't quite decide. 'I didn't think it was that big a deal.'

Or at least, I didn't until Justin started acting like a complete jerk.

'What, are you jealous?' I can't help but ask.

'Excuse me for not liking the sight of my girlfriend pressed up against some other guy,' he snaps back.

'I was not!' I make an effort to keep my voice low, in case anyone overhears and it causes a scene.

'That's sure as hell not what it looked like. So excuse me for getting a little pissed off when you're all over some other guy and you still don't feel comfortable enough to be like that around me.'

All I can do for a moment is gape at him.

Wow . . .

Okay.

I just . . . I literally have no words to come up with a reply to him. Does he honestly think that about me? And it's not just that . . . it's the fact that he's bringing up the whole sex issue again. Like it's going to make me feel guilty or something.

I don't like this side of Bryce at all. Most of the time he's a nice guy – sweet and funny and kind and nice. But right now . . . well, he's not that guy.

And I don't have to put up with that. However popular he is. Whether or not people think I'm the luckiest girl in school because he's my boyfriend.

So I push his hands off me and walk away. The song comes to an end at that point anyway. I hear him call after me, but I pick my pace up a little, making my way over to our table, where I left my purse.

I had wanted tonight to be good. I didn't want to spoil it at all. But that plan has gone down the drain.

One night. That was all I wanted. One night being the new Madison and really enjoying it, having a good time at my first high-school dance.

Was that really too much to ask for?

There's still the after party. And you had a good night apart from that scene just now, right? You can still have a good time without him. You'll have fun with the girls. No use getting upset over your boyfriend being a jerk now – that can wait until tomorrow.

I drill that into my head as I pick up my purse, fumbling to get the little strap over my wrist.

A hand clamps around my arm. 'Madison, come on. Please. Talk to me a minute.'

I take a deep breath and turn around, pushing Bryce's hand off my arm and refusing to look at his face.

'What was that all about?'

'*What was that all about?*' I repeat, unable to keep the frustration and anger from seeping into my voice. 'You were being a jerk, that's what it was all about! You really think I'd – I don't know – cozy up to some other guy like that when I'm still with you? If that's your honest opinion of me, then you really don't think very highly of me at all, do you?'

'Of course it's not what I think, Mainstream, I—'

'Stop it!' I snap. 'Don't call me that. Don't act like you really care about me when you so obviously don't. If you really did, then you'd respect my decision when I keep telling you no.'

He doesn't need me to elaborate on that one, but argues, 'I do respect your decision!'

'Then why do you keep asking me about it and pushing me?'

'I'm not pushing you! I never meant to do that.'

'You are, though, and you must know it. I've told you a dozen times now!'

'Madison, I didn't mean to push you,' he says. He puts a finger on my chin and tilts my face up so that I look at him. 'I love you.'

I tear my head away. 'Stop it.'

'All this time you've been saying it back,' he starts; then, 'Do you even really mean it? Look me in the eyes right now and tell me.'

'Bryce, just stop it already!' I snap at him, still not raising my voice. 'I'm not dealing with this right now.

I'm not dealing with *you* right now. Got that? Now, I'm going to the after-party with my friends and I'm going to try and enjoy the rest of my night. I'm not having this talk right here for everyone to hear.'

My voice sounds so unlike me. I sound cool and calm and confident. I don't feel that way. I feel shaken and hurt and confused; blood is roaring in my ears and my nails are digging into my palm to stop my hands from trembling, and part of me wants to cry.

'Madison . . .' He tries to catch my arm, but I shake him off again. 'Madison.'

I ignore him, and instead move around to catch up with Summer and Marcus, who are about to leave. Summer's collecting her coat.

'Hey, um, do you guys think I could get a ride to the after-party with you?' I ask hesitantly, my voice a little breathless.

They exchange a glance. Marcus says, 'What about Bryce?'

I drop my gaze. 'We . . . kind of had a, um, a fight . . .'

'Of course you can,' Summer answers me. She lays a hand on Marcus's arm and says, 'Would you mind bringing the car around, please, sweetie? Girl talk.'

'Sure,' he says, kissing her forehead. He waits and she fishes a set of car keys from her purse, handing them over.

When we're alone, she casts a glance behind me before tugging me closer to the exit and lowering her voice to ask, 'What happened?'

'He's just . . . being a tool,' I sigh helplessly. 'And I'm sick of it.'

She gives me a sad and somewhat confused look, waiting for me to elaborate, but I don't.

'Do you not want to talk about it right now?'

I shake my head. 'I just want to go to this party and try and enjoy the rest of the night. I'll fill you in on all the details tomorrow – promise.'

'Okay.'

'Thanks.'

She smiles. 'It's what friends are for. Where's all your stuff for the party?'

I groan. 'In Bryce's car . . .'

'I've got it.'

I watch her go over to Bryce and talk for a moment. He looks over at me and I pretend I'm not looking, and then Summer comes back over with his car keys.

'Problem solved. I'll go grab your clothes. Go out the front, and you and Marcus wait for me, okay?'

I smile. 'Thanks.'

'Don't thank me. Oh, but before I go – is he being enough of a dick that I need to, like, sabotage his car, or "accidentally"' – she puts air quotes around the word – 'leave with his car keys?'

I laugh shakily. 'No, you can't do that!'

She shrugs. 'Just looking out for you here . . . See you in a sec.'

I collect my coat and then make my way outside like everyone else. I spot Marcus's car and get in the back seat. 'Summer's just grabbing my stuff from Bryce's car,' I explain. 'She'll only be a minute.'

He nods, and I feel his eyes on me in the rearview mirror. I look up and meet the reflection of his gaze.

'So what'd he do?'

I shrug. 'It's complicated. He was just being a jerk.'

Marcus smirks. 'I know you don't swear much, Madison, but this is probably one of those times when it's contextually appropriate.'

I laugh, but it's a little bit humorless. 'Probably.'

He laughs too and we sit in silence – not an entirely uncomfortable silence, though – until Summer opens the passenger door and slides in, carefully holding up her dress.

She passes my overnight bag back to me. 'Here you go. And I even gave him his car keys back.'

'Thanks.'

She leans over and gives Marcus a quick kiss, and then we join the stream of cars leaving the Winter

Dance. I lean back and let out a long, slow, inaudible sigh, all the tension rushing out of me. I sit limply in the back seat of the car listening to the radio and not thinking about anything at all.

Summer and I head up to one of the bedrooms to change out of our prom dresses. Most girls, I notice, are now wearing something skimpy and revealing, which makes me feel a little out of place in my full-length skinny jeans and black blouse. But so what. Like I'd feel comfortable in something that left nothing to the imagination?

The house belongs to some guy on the football and soccer teams. I see him at parties and stuff, but he doesn't hang around with us at school much. His name is Brandon Jones. His house is huge, and absolutely perfect for a house party.

Summer and I end up deciding to fold our dresses and put them in our bags. 'They'll have to go to the dry cleaner's anyway,' she points out. 'I'll see you downstairs somewhere. I'm dying to pee. I couldn't get the dress up high enough to pee all night long.' And with a laugh she makes a run for the bathroom before anybody else can. I laugh too, thinking now how glad I am I didn't have a fitted fishtail skirt like she did.

I zip my bag up carefully and make my way

downstairs. I head for the lounge, but then I see Bryce near the doorway so I change direction and end up in a games room, where some guys are playing pool.

'Hey,' I say, walking over to Ricky and Adam.

'Hey,' they reply.

Adam notices my empty hands and says, 'Still not drinking?'

'Nope.'

He smiles. 'Good for you.'

'Did something happen between you and Bryce?' Ricky asks me. 'You guys didn't turn up together.'

I laugh and say, 'I thought only girls enjoyed a good gossip.'

'I can be extremely effeminate,' Ricky insists, making the three of us laugh. 'No, but seriously.'

'We had a fight,' I finally say.

'About . . . ?'

'About nothing that's any of your concern,' I tell Adam – though not harshly. 'Do I really have to talk about this?'

'So what, are you two . . . I don't know, are you still together?'

'I don't know,' I reply honestly. 'I guess so.'

Adam shrugs. 'Okay, then. Thank you for clearing that up for us.'

I laugh. 'You're welcome. Did you have a good time at the dance?'

We talk a while longer before I decide to go and find something to drink – even a glass of water. I find a few of the girls I know in the kitchen, and talk to them for a while. Then I decide to go find Melissa or Summer or Tiffany to hang out with for a while. I hunt for them, but they don't seem to be anywhere downstairs. So I try upstairs.

I find Ricky waiting to use the bathroom and ask if he's seen any of the girls, but he slurs that he hasn't, so I start looking through the various rooms.

Suddenly hands close over my eyes and I jump out of my skin, my heart going crazy.

'Guess who.'

'Um . . .' I rack my brain. The voice is familiar, but I can't think . . . I push the hands off and turn around. 'Justin. Hi.' My voice sounds clipped and irritable.

'What're you doing, all on your own?'

'I can't find anybody,' I explain. 'Have you seen Tiffany anywhere?'

He shakes his head and shrugs his shoulders. 'Not for an hour or something.'

'Never mind.'

'Where's your boyfriend?' he asks, not impolitely.

'I don't know.'

'Oh dear.' He looks genuinely concerned for me. 'Trouble in paradise, is it?'

'That's none of your business,' I snap, trying to step around him, but he steps with me.

'Is everything okay?'

'Not really.' I don't know why I'm telling him, of all people – but he seems sincere, and I'm fed up with saying 'I'm fine'.

'Do you want to talk about it? Impartial ears to listen here, if you want.'

I shake my head. 'Thanks, anyway.'

He gives me a half-hearted smile, and lightly clips his finger under my chin. 'Chin up.'

Before I can muster a laugh to go with my smile, we're both caught off-guard by someone very loudly and very pointedly clearing their throat.

I turn and see Tiffany; she's looking between Justin and me with an icy cool glint in her eyes. I try not to gulp.

'Tiffany! Where have you been all night?' I walk over to her, breezing past Justin. 'I've been looking every-where for you.'

'Well, you can't have been looking very hard,' she retorts.

I just smile blankly at her. She regards me a moment

longer before turning away and saying, 'Justin, sweetie, could you get me a drink please?'

'Uh, sure thing.' He shoots me another smile and a wave as he disappears back downstairs.

Immediately Tiffany wants to know: 'What happened with you and Bryce? He told me you freaked out on him and left.'

'I didn't. He was being a tool and we had a fight, and then I left.'

'Oh. Right. Okay.'

She's not the same bubbly person I'm used to seeing at parties. This is the side of Tiffany I do my best to ignore: the part that tells me I should ditch the Converse, that I should try and make more of an effort with my appearance (if I 'wanted to make the most of myself'), and that my taste in music is appalling.

Maybe, I tell myself, she's just being this way because of the whole thing with Bryce – I mean, they *have* been friends for years, and she's only known me a couple of months. If I've upset Bryce, or at least put him in a bad mood, she'd have every right to be annoyed with me on principle. Yeah. That's probably it.

But she most definitely doesn't look happy with me right now – so I make a smooth and unhurried escape to the nearest bathroom, which happens to be in the bedroom to my right.

Once I'm in there, I lock the door. I don't bother with the light. There's a small window that lets in the faint glow of a streetlight, though, and the shadows fall across my face when I see myself in the mirror over the sink.

I run the faucet and wash my hands for no reason at all. The water's warm against my skin. I consider splashing it over my face, but I spent so long on my makeup I don't want to ruin it now.

I find myself thinking about Bryce.

Should I give him another chance? I mean, he is so sweet and nice, and he makes me feel like the old me didn't even exist and—

No. *I'm going to break up with him*, I decide. *I don't have to put up with him acting like that. I don't want to, either. I'll tell him tomorrow, when he's not drunk or mad at me and will definitely remember that we're officially over.*

I don't want to stop being friends, but who knows how awkward it will make things between us? I hope everything will be okay. I don't want it to affect my friendship with any of the rest of them – that's what worries me most. But I won't stay with him just because of the others.

I think of Tiffany too – how she turned on me so suddenly like that. The accusing looks she gave me and Justin; like we'd been caught kissing or something. I wonder if Bryce told her I was 'cozied up' with Justin at the dance, and now she's just looking for things where they don't exist.

I know Tiffany can be exactly like some of the girls who used to bully me, back in Maine – but I was so happy she'd taken me under her wing, I'd ignored it. And it wasn't like she didn't have any redeeming qualities: she was smart, even if she didn't boast about it, and she was funny, and when she wasn't being horrible, she was pretty nice.

I stay in the bathroom another few minutes, taking deep breaths and trying hard not to think too much. I just have to get through the rest of this night; I can sort my mind out tomorrow. *Just this one night.*

After what must be ages but doesn't feel like very long at all, I turn the doorknob and let myself out.

And nothing – *nothing* – can prepare me for what I walk in on.

There are two people on the bed, and my first instinct is to avert my eyes and plug my ears. But I don't look away before I recognize him.

'*Bryce?*'

It comes out as some kind of mangled croak, between a whisper and a cry of shock. I clap my hand over my mouth, wishing I hadn't said anything at all. I start to back towards the bedroom door, but it's too late: they heard me.

'Madison?' he says, sounding as horrified as I feel. 'Fuck. Madison—'

He begins to scramble up off the girl on the bed and pulls his underpants and jeans back up, tripping a little because they're caught around his ankles. I'm still backing up to the door, unable to do anything other than open and close my mouth, entirely speechless.

I flinch when the door suddenly presses up against my back. In a flash, I spin around and fumble to yank the handle open and get out of there.

'Madison! Madison, wait a sec!'

I want to scream and yell at him, ask him how long this has been going on behind my back, break down in tears. I can't. I seem physically incapable of anything but getting away from him. I trip down the stairs, bumping into people, until I make it to the front door. It's open. Good. The music – and the noise of people laughing and shouting and singing and chatting – is drowned out completely by the roaring in my ears.

But I still hear him calling after me.

'Madison! Just hold on a minute! *Madison!*'

I stumble down the driveway. I just make it to the end when he runs past and stops in front of me, blocking my path. The buttons on his shirt are askew, and his jeans aren't buttoned up. Raindrops land on him and trickle down his face.

'Madison . . . Please, I can explain. Just give me a minute, Mainstream, please. I swear, it's not what it looks like . . .'

All I can do is wonder how he thinks he'll ever be able to talk his way out of this.

Chapter 36

I feel numb. Numb, and kind of sick. But mostly numb. I'm dazed, as though I'm in a dream. My legs are moving, but the movement isn't a conscious one, and my mind feels detached from my body. I'm moving – but I have no idea where I'm going.

Away. Just get out of there.

I can't call Mom; she'll freak out. I can't call Dad – he'll tell Mom.

So my legs, despite feeling stiff and leaden, keep moving.

My knees buckle as I walk, though, and my feet wobble with every step I take. It's the heels, I realize; so I take off my shoes and carry them instead. The rough sidewalk hurts, but at least I can walk now.

Oh, and it's raining.

Not even a drizzle, or a shower. Nope. Instead, it's a torrential downpour, and the raindrops ricochet off the sidewalk like bullets, and blur the streetlights so that amber smudges light my way.

I'm soaked to the bone, but too numb to really care about something which right now seems such an insignificant fact.

Madison . . . Please, I can explain. Just give me a minute, Mainstream, please. I swear, it's not what it looks like . . .

Bryce's words fill my head and I can't get rid of them. *It's not what it looks like.* Ha. I wonder what he'd have said if I'd given him time to explain himself. *It's not what it looks like . . .* What a load of complete and utter *bull*.

And suddenly I want to laugh, because I'm such an idiot.

I don't know where my legs are taking me until I've rung the doorbell.

As the ding-dong noise fades, I begin to ebb back to reality. My clothes are sticking to me, my hair is plastered to my forehead. And then I notice that my entire body is quivering – little spasms, from my cheeks to my fingers to my knees – and my feet are so cold and sore that I can barely even feel them anymore.

I can't tell if the water running down my face is just the rain, or if I'm crying.

The door opens a crack; there's a scuffling kind of noise, and a heavy panting, a bark, then –

'Gellman, sit!'

Dwight's face and a shoulder appear in the space where he opened the door. The second his eyes light on me, they darken and he frowns. I begin to think that maybe this wasn't such a good idea; that maybe I should've just called Mom and dealt with her freaking out. This guy hates me; I don't know what I was doing coming here. I don't need his pity; I don't need an 'I told you so'; I don't—

I need a friend.

He starts to say, 'What the hell do you—' but then he seems to really see me, and notice the state I'm in, because he falls silent.

The next second he throws the door wide open and drags me inside. 'Jesus, Madison, what were you thinking? Are you crazy? You could get hypothermia or something. Are you okay?'

I can hear a video game. Through the small open crack of the lounge door I stare at the flickering lights.

Dwight follows my gaze once he's restrained the mass of shaggy blond fur that is Gellman from jumping on me. 'The guys are over. Kind of like a nerds' after-party.' There's an emphasis on 'nerds' that sends a pang of guilt through my system. It hurts.

But it's good – that I can at least feel guilty. Because

it means that I'm not completely heartless, that there is something left of me.

'Madison.'

I drag my eyes back to his face. For the first time in a long while, he meets my gaze steadily. I blink. I can't seem to do anything else. So I blink again.

'Madison,' he says again, and steps closer. He lowers his voice, sounding so soft and sad and worried. 'Dice. What happened?'

And I say, 'I'm dripping all over the welcome mat.'

Dwight takes me by the hand to pull me upstairs. He leads me into the bathroom and sets the shower on hot; the room turns steamy in a minute.

'There are clean towels right there,' he says, pointing to a rail near the door. 'I'll leave some clothes by the door for you. If you dump yours outside, I'll toss them in the dryer.' His voice is still so soft. Like he really cares. Not like he hates my guts.

I nod in answer to him, because I don't trust my voice right now. He closes the door behind him, and when I hear his footsteps disappear down the hallway, I peel off my clothes. My limbs are reluctant to cooperate. It seems to take forever before I actually step into the shower.

And how long I stand in the shower is a mystery to

me. My mind is in chaos. Billions of thoughts rage through it, but not a single one of them is coherent. I want to shut them all out. It's too loud.

The shower helps me feel a bit better physically. I ache, and my feet are killing me, but I'm no longer shaking and numb and I feel refreshed. I wrap the towel securely around me before poking my head out of the door.

My sodden after-party outfit has been replaced by a red flannel shirt and a pair of grey sweatpants with a drawstring. I'm glad I had enough sense left to keep my underwear in here. I put it on the floor near the radiator, and it's almost completely dry now.

I put the clothes on and leave my hair dripping slowly down the back of my neck. I glance in the mirror to check that I've washed away all of my makeup and don't look like some cousin of Frankenstein's monster.

Only then do I venture out of the bathroom and cautiously make my way down the stairs. I'm glad Dwight's house doesn't have that giveaway creaking step.

Although it does have a giveaway barking dog.

Gellman pads over to me as I reach the bottom of the staircase. My knees click when I bend to scratch his ears. He looks up at me, tongue lolling out of the side of his mouth, fixing me with those gorgeous big black eyes, and almost managing to make me smile.

'Madison?'

I jump when Dwight says my name. Gellman turns his head too, and barks again. I stare at Dwight. I open my mouth to say something, but nothing comes out. I can't find the right words. I don't know what I can say. There's so much I need to say.

He pulls the lounge door closed a bit. Nodding upstairs, he says, 'Come on.'

'But . . .' My throat hurts. My voice doesn't sound like it belongs to me. 'You can't . . . Your friends . . .'

'They'll understand. Come on.'

I cast another look at the flickering lights coming from the lounge TV. I bet Andy and Carter are in there. Maybe a few other people Dwight hangs out with too. I don't know. I don't want to find out, either. I can't deal with anybody else right now.

So I follow Dwight up the staircase once again.

When we get to his room, he snaps on the light and pushes the door closed, but doesn't shut it completely. I stand there looking around.

It's neater than I thought a teenage boy's room would be, but messier than I'd have expected of Dwight. There are a couple of T-shirts and socks and boxes of video games strewn around the place, and an open can of soda on the desk beside his computer.

There's a bookcase that's overflowing with all kinds of books, and gadgets and gismos – like a remote-controlled metal bug, and a model WWII Spitfire, and one of those Newton's cradles – and a shelf with trophies, which I go and inspect.

Not soccer and sport trophies. Grade 3 Spelling Bee. Mathletes Championship 2008. Pee-Wee Pals Baseball too.

'Sorry for the mess,' he says distractedly, and in my peripheral vision I see him kicking a pair of underpants out of sight. I smile inside. 'I haven't . . . Okay, well, this is clean for me. I just wasn't expecting company.'

I'd laugh at that. He's trying to make me laugh. I want to.

'Uh, sit – sit down,' he says. 'Do you want me to get you a drink or anything? I should have offered earlier.'

'I'm sorry,' I say.

He stops stammering and his dark eyebrows knit together in confusion. 'Sorry for what?'

'For coming here tonight,' I explain. 'I know you hate me, but I didn't – I wasn't thinking, I just . . .'

'Whoa, wait. You think I hate you?'

Now it's my turn to frown and look confused. 'Well, yeah, I mean . . . you haven't been speaking to me or even looking at me since—' I don't finish, but I know he understands.

Dwight lets out a short, humorless laugh. 'Madison, I don't hate you. I never *hated* you. I was pissed at you, sure, but you were the one who couldn't look at me and acted like I didn't exist. I thought *you* hated *me*.'

Was that true? Had I really been doing that?

'I thought you couldn't stand to be around me,' I mumble.

Dwight gives another dry laugh and runs his fingers through his hair. 'So what, you didn't hate me, or . . . ?'

'I didn't hate you,' I say quietly, truthfully. 'I couldn't face you, that was all. And then I was so sure you hated me . . .'

'Dice, come here,' he says softly, and I take a little step closer. With a sigh, he takes one long stride across to me, and wordlessly wraps his arms around me. That's it. He just hugs me. After weeks and weeks of neither one of us acknowledging that the other exists, he hugs me, because he knows that's exactly what I need right now. I stand stiff and unmoving for a moment, before I put my arms around his thin, gangly body and bury my face in his chest, inhaling his smell. I don't cry, though.

A while later, he peels my arms away, and takes me by the wrists to sit on his bed. I tuck my legs up and fold them underneath me, and Dwight sits in the same way, facing me. There's a loose thread in his comforter, and I twirl it around my fingertip.

'What happened?'

'I don't even know where to start,' I tell him.

'The beginning,' he tells me. 'That's always a good place to start.'

Chapter 37

I tell him everything.

'And you know what the worst part of it is?' I say, my voice void of emotion as I look him right in the eye. 'I don't think I even really loved him. It would hurt more than this if I had done. And it doesn't hurt. He can go – go screw whoever he wants. I just don't care. I thought I did. But I really, honestly don't.'

'You know . . . it's okay to be upset over it,' he says slowly, holding my gaze. 'Nobody's going to think you're weak if you are upset.'

'I'm not, though. I think . . .' I search for the right words, trying to put my thoughts into order. 'I think the trouble was that I was more in love with the *idea* of Bryce than Bryce himself. I think – I think the idea of actually having this boyfriend who's so fantastic and wonderful on paper blinded me to the fact that he could be kind of a jerk in real life.' I laugh humorlessly. 'I sound so heartless and cruel.'

'No, you don't.'

I look him in the eye again. 'Yeah. I do. It's the same thing with Tiffany. I was so – so caught up by the fact that she wanted to be my friend that I could only look at her in a positive way and didn't want to think about how she made me feel two inches tall sometimes.'

After another moment I say, talking more to myself than I am to Dwight, 'They didn't suddenly just become bad people. It's more that I suddenly looked at them without a filter. I've been shrugging off the bad stuff and ignoring it. It's always been there. I just chose to ignore it.'

'I don't think,' Dwight tells me, 'that anybody can blame you for any of that. It's not your fault that Bryce would rather get laid than have a meaningful relationship. It's not your fault that Tiffany can be a complete bitch who likes to lord it over everybody, her friends included. And it's not your fault that you wanted to fit in and ignore the bad things.'

I rub a hand over my face and give him an empty smile. I shrug helplessly and look around the room. A lump rises in my throat, but I push back the threat of tears. I'm not going to cry, not over this. Worse things have happened, and to much better people than me.

The truth comes out in a helpless, fearful whisper before I can help it, before I've even really considered it myself. 'I just didn't want things to go back to how they used to be. I'm a terrible, terrible person,' I whisper. Because I am.

What have I ever done that's any good in my life? I'm not smart and I can't play an instrument and I don't do sports. I'm not much good at art or math or anything like that – I got by in school last year and I'm doing okay this year, but 'okay' isn't 'great' and it's nothing to be proud of. Maybe I'd do well if I tried harder, but I don't. I don't do anything useful with my life, like charity work.

I'm very good at running from my own problems. It's facing up to them that would make me something worthwhile, and when was the last time I ever did that?

I don't even realize I'm crying until I see a teardrop land on the back of Dwight's hand, which is still on my knee. I pull the cuff of the shirt I'm wearing around my fingers and wipe under my eyes.

'I'm sorry.' I don't just mean for crying. I mean for everything. 'For tonight, for making you think I hated you, for not saying anything when Kyle was a jerk to you that first day of school, for kissing you in the library that day, for—'

He clamps a hand over my mouth. 'Stop it. Stop it.'

I push his hand away, but before I can say anything more he's talking again. 'Stop apologizing for things that aren't your fault. We all mess up, okay? Look, Dice, it's . . . Just stop it, okay?'

I can't say anything. The lump is back in my throat and I know that if I try to speak I'll burst into tears again.

So we sit in silence, watching each other, until I feel like I can talk. And when I do, I say, like I always have done, 'Can we not talk about all this right now? Please?'

Dwight sighs. 'Sure. You know where to find me when you do want to, though, okay?'

I nod silently. He hesitates for a moment before leaning forward and kissing my forehead. It's not really a romantic gesture; it's more comforting, telling me that he's there. The corner of my mouth turns up in a smile.

'You can stay here tonight, okay? I'll camp on the couch.'

'No, I can't—'

'Yes, you can, and you will. It's three in the morning. Your parents aren't going to be too happy to be woken up at this hour, I bet.'

'They won't care,' I insist. 'Really. I can't let you stay on the couch. I'll just go home. It's fine.'

'No it's not. Look, I'm not letting you go home in this state. I'll kidnap you if that's what it takes,' he jokes, and I actually do smile at that, 'but I don't want you to be on your own right now. So you can stay here and I'll bunk on the couch.'

I bite my top lip before whispering, 'Thank you.'

He smiles. 'Anytime. Oh, I almost forgot,' he says suddenly, stopping halfway to the door. He turns back and fishes something out of his pocket – my cell and my iPod. 'They were in the pocket of your jeans. Now I'm no rocket scientist, but I *can* tell you that the dryer is not the best place for those.'

I laugh a little, sounding more like my usual self. 'Thank you. Night, Ike.'

And he replies, 'Goodnight, Dice.'

He snaps the light off before closing the door. I wait in silence for a while. I can hear the noise of voices and a video game downstairs; Gellman woofs quietly.

I press a button on my cell phone to bring it to life. The screen lights up, flashing up notifications of missed calls from all sorts of people. Most of them are from Summer, I notice. A fair few from Bryce too. And two from my mom – as always.

There's a text from Mom asking for me to call her when I'm back at Tiffany's. She sent it half an hour ago. I send her a text telling her I'm at Tiffany's. I can explain properly tomorrow, I decide, when we're face-to-face. She'll understand. It's not fair to make her panic in the middle of the night when she should be sleeping.

I send Summer a short reply too, because I feel I have to tell her something. *I'm fine. Sorry. I went home early, couldn't stay. I'll pick up my stuff tomorrow, thanks for picking it up for me. X.*

I decide that, just like Mom, Summer deserves a face-to-face explanation.

I scramble under the covers of Dwight's bed and rest my head on the pillow. My mind is abuzz with too many thoughts to sleep, though, so I just stare blankly at the wall, where there's a faded poster of the periodic table.

I think I'd almost prefer it if I was really upset about the whole thing. But I don't feel much at all. Earlier, I felt like crying because I'm scared of my whole life here as the new Madison falling apart.

I continue to stare at the wall. I feel a little sick, in all honesty.

The truth is, I don't know if I can still be friends with them after this. Especially given how awkward the situation with me and Bryce will make everything . . . It just won't work. But besides that, I don't know if I want to carry on hanging out with them and calling them my friends. Part of me wishes I could just cut myself away from them entirely.

As if it were that easy.

But the rest of me would miss Adam and Ricky

goofing around, and Marcus's occasional sarcastic and witty comment – and Summer, because she was always nice to me, and never made me feel like I didn't belong.

I don't know. I honestly just don't know what to do, or even what I think about this whole thing right now.

I'll have to just wait it out and see what happens. That's all I can do right now. That's the best thing to do.

Feeling a little soothed by that thought, I snuggle down into the bed and close my eyes. The pillow smells nice; gradually I let fatigue wash over me; sleep takes hold of me.

I wake up at seven-thirty. It's hideously early, but considering I only got four hours' sleep, I feel much better. I can hear a dog barking, and I groan sleepily and turn over, mushing my face into the pillow. Gellman must rouse the entire house if he's awake this early every morning, I think.

But I'm awake now, and I know there's no chance of me getting back to sleep. So I haul myself out of bed and run my fingers through my hair. I tiptoe out of the bedroom, just in case the others have managed to sleep through Gellman's racket, and make my way to the bathroom. I wash my face and avoid looking at myself for too long in the mirror – though I catch sight of my hair; it's sticking out at all sorts of angles, so with a sigh I run the faucet again and damp it down a little.

Since I have no clothes other than what Dwight gave me last night, which are creased from sleeping, I go downstairs looking a bit of a mess, in the hope of finding Dwight awake.

When I get to the bottom of the staircase, I hear voices coming from the kitchen, so I guess nobody can sleep through Gellman barking.

Hesitating in the doorway, I see Dwight's mom, Teresa, frying bacon; Cynthia is sitting at the table, talking animatedly. They must be morning people, I think immediately. They're even dressed.

I hope Dwight's mom doesn't mind that I stayed the night. I don't want to put her out or anything. And who knows, maybe she doesn't like me anymore after Dwight and I didn't talk all those weeks.

'Hi,' I say nervously.

'Hi!' Cynthia says brightly, turning to grin at me.

'Good morning,' Teresa says, just as chirpy as her daughter. 'I hope you're hungry. Sundays we always have a big fry-up for breakfast.'

'Starving,' I reply with a laugh, because I'm so relieved that she doesn't appear to bear a grudge.

'Dwight's just gone to walk Gellman,' Teresa carries

on. 'They won't be long. He just gets restless this early in the morning. The dog, I mean, not Dwight.'

I laugh. 'I'm sorry if I'm intruding . . . I just . . .'

'Oh, honestly, dear, don't worry about it. Dwight told me you had a really rough night and needed a place to stay. I won't ask any questions.' I smile, and she continues, 'Did you have a good night at the dance?'

'Yeah. It was great, thanks.'

Cynthia sighs wistfully. 'I seriously cannot *wait* until I'm old enough to go to a prom.'

'I'll let you in on a secret,' I say to her. 'They're entirely overrated.'

A few minutes later the front door opens. 'I'm back!' Dwight yells. I hear Gellman panting, and a second later he barrels into the kitchen and makes straight for his water bowl, dunking his whole face in. Dwight follows him, hanging Gellman's red lead from a hook.

'Morning,' he says to me. 'How're you feeling?'

'Okay,' I tell him, and I'm not lying. 'Thanks again.'

'It's no problem, really.'

Teresa starts to plate up bacon and toast and fried eggs, and instructs us to sit down to eat breakfast, so we do. About halfway through, my cell phone trills from the pocket of the sweatpants I'm wearing.

'Sorry,' I say quickly.

'Don't worry,' Teresa says, waving a hand. 'Go ahead and answer. It might be your parents.'

'Thanks,' I say quietly, and check my cell. It's my mom asking me to give her a call if I need a ride home. I can reply later, I decide, and put my cell phone back.

'So,' Dwight's mom says, 'how's that project you guys were working on coming along?'

'Fine . . .' I say hesitantly.

'Okay,' Dwight says in the same tone. We exchange a brief glance before we continue to eat.

His mom laughs. 'Wow. I can barely get you two to shut up.'

'Yeah,' I joke. 'Come on, Ike, you're barely letting me get a word in edgeways here.'

I catch a fleeting smirk cross his face and he shakes his head at me.

'Ike?' Teresa's tone abruptly catches my attention. She sounds . . . stunned, I guess, is the only word for it. Her eyebrows have shot up too.

'Um . . .' I clear my throat quietly. 'It's my, uh . . . my nickname for him?'

None of them says anything, and I wonder why I feel like I've done something wrong and put my foot in it here. I should say something, but I have no idea what. Teresa looks at her son but he just blanks her out.

Then he says to me, 'I'll go grab your clothes from the dryer so that you can change.'

I don't miss the look he shoots his mother as he leaves. I sit there for a moment wondering what just happened, and then pick up his empty plate and mine, and go to put them next to the sink.

Teresa says, 'Madison?'

I turn around. 'Yeah?'

She pauses, and I see her bite her lip as though she's debating whether or not to say anything to me. I'm expecting her to say 'never mind', but instead she tells me, 'He doesn't let anyone call him that anymore. Ever since his dad passed away he's always hated it. His dad started calling him Ike in the first place, you know,' she adds quietly.

'He . . .' I swallow hard. My tone is apologetic when I say, 'He didn't tell me.'

'No, I don't suppose he would.' Before I can wonder what that's supposed to mean, she surprises me by saying, 'You're good for him, Madison. I'm glad you two are talking again.'

Then there are footsteps behind me, and I turn to see Dwight holding my clothes from last night's party. He smiles. 'Here you go.'

'Thanks.'

I head upstairs to change, asking myself why he let me call him Ike if he hates it so much.

When I get out of the bathroom, I look down the corridor and see movement in Dwight's room. His door is only half closed, so I walk up and say, 'Knock, knock.'

He turns around. 'Hey.'

'Hi.'

We both stand in silence for a long moment and both start talking at once.

'Are you sure you're—'

'Why didn't you tell me—'

We both stop in the same instant too, which makes us laugh. He says, 'You go first.'

'Why . . . Why didn't you tell me that you don't like being called Ike?'

He closes his eyes and presses his fingertips over his eyelids. 'She told you.'

'Yeah,' I reply softly. 'Why didn't you just say?'

'Because . . .' He shrugs and then looks at me with a helpless smile. 'You looked really pleased you'd come up with a nickname for me, and I didn't want to disappoint you. And . . . I don't know . . . I suppose I just didn't mind you calling me Ike.'

'Why?'

He shrugs. 'I don't know.'

I laugh. 'I thought you were supposed to be the genius here.'

He smiles. 'My turn to ask questions now, anyway. How are you?'

'I told you earlier, I'm okay.'

He raises a dubious eyebrow. 'Really?'

'Yes, really,' I say, punctuating my words with a genuine smile. 'Thanks. For last night, I mean. And I honestly am sorry about—'

'Hey!' he snaps, cutting me off. 'What'd I say about apologizing? I told you to stop doing it. Remember that?'

'Nope,' I say. '*Sorry.*'

He chuckles. 'So, do you. . . do you want to hang out here for a bit or go home?'

'I think I'd better head on home. I need to calmly explain to my mom in as few details as possible what happened – I need to get my stuff back from Summer.'

'Okay.' A pause, then: 'You know where to find me if you need me.'

A small smile slips onto my face and I nod. 'Yeah.'

I don't know which of us moves first, but suddenly we've stepped together and we're hugging. That's all. We just hug. It's not like that time at the library when he was comforting me and we ended up kissing. This is entirely innocent, and exactly what I need right now.

I squeeze him tightly before letting go and stepping back. 'Thank you.'

He just smiles and replies, 'I'm glad we're talking again.'

Chapter 38

To say that my mom 'freaks out' when I tell her that I had a fight with Bryce and then caught him cheating on me so I stayed at Dwight's – and, oh yeah, Dwight and I are talking again now – would be a gross understatement.

What surprises me most, however, is how angry my dad is about the whole thing. He's never really gotten mad at Jenna or me, but when I tell him about my night, his neck and ears turn beet red and he starts cussing about 'that boy'.

When I finally escape to my room, I call Summer.

'Madison?' She picks up on the first ring. 'Are you okay? What happened?'

'No,' I say quietly. 'You first, though. What happened at the party? I guess there must've been something going round about me and Bryce.'

'Well, yeah, of course there was. People said that he'd gone upstairs with some other girl, but then they said that you were all over that guy Justin, and that it was you and Bryce getting it on upstairs, but then you bailed and you guys had a fight . . . I don't know. Nobody seems to know what happened. The rumor about you and Justin seemed the popular choice. Tiffany told me she saw you two.'

'I was looking for you guys and he was . . .' I sigh. 'He was just being *nice*. Nothing happened. I think Tiffany just . . . saw what she wanted to see.'

'Anyway. Moving on. What happened with you and Bryce?'

'I went to the bathroom, came out, and he was with some other girl. And you know what he tried to say to me when I left? *It's not what it looks like.* When he had his underwear down to his ankles.'

'Oh my God,' is all that Summer can say. And she repeats it several more times, like a broken record. I wait for her to find some more words. 'You poor thing! You should've called me last night! Do you want me to come over?'

I shake my head, despite the fact she can't see me. 'No, it's okay. This is going to sound horrible, but it . . . it doesn't hurt that much. It should, but it doesn't. And I was planning on breaking up with him anyway, after the fight we had,' I add.

'He doesn't know that, though. That was— Ugh! I

cannot believe he would do that! So you guys had some stupid fight! He didn't know you wanted to permanently break up. Just . . . ugh!'

She sounds angrier than I could ever be about this situation. Maybe it's because she's known Bryce longer and thought he was better than that. Or maybe it's just that she's a good friend and actually cares about me.

'I don't know what to do tomorrow, though. I don't want to see him.' This was what I didn't say to Dwight: that now I'm actually a little afraid of going to school. Because I don't know what everybody will be saying about me, how bad things might be.

'Think of it this way – if you can hold your head up high and come into school after he's been such a—' She follows with a string of swearwords I never wish to repeat again in my life. 'Then you're going to look like the better person.'

'Yeah, I suppose you're right . . .'

'Besides, I'll be there. And I'm sure the girls will understand once you explain it to them. And the guys will too, I bet. It'll be fine, Madison.'

'You don't know that,' I say quietly.

'No. But you have to hope for the best. What have you got to lose?'

* * *

So I take Summer's advice and I get up Monday morning to go to school. I wear a pair of black shorts and a white tank top and toss on my Converse. The only makeup I wear is some eyeliner, and concealer to mask the bags under my eyes. I don't want anything that will stand out too much; if things go badly today, I may want to stick to playing invisible.

I walk to school, because I don't want to be really early. And it goes to plan – I get there about ten minutes before everyone is due to head off to home-room. Nobody is in our usual spot on the bench outside; they must all be inside by the lockers, I think, and so I head inside. I don't bother taking out my ear-phones yet – I like the song that's playing.

Walking through those doors is like walking into a dream.

No, not a dream.

A nightmare.

The corridors are full. I hear everyone talking, even with my earphones in; I pull one out, but all I hear is a cacophony of chatter and laughter. Why is it so busy in here? We still have ten minutes until homeroom. It's never this busy unless it's raining outside, which it isn't right now.

I begin to push past people, but it turns out I don't need to – they part and create a zigzag pathway for me, heads turned towards me. My forehead twitches with a frown. What's going on?

I can feel eyes on me, and I keep my head down. But I can't help but steal sideways glances and, sure enough, everybody's looking at me. And even though I can't quite catch what people are saying, I'm instantly under the impression that they're talking about me.

I turn left to head towards my locker.

That's when it all makes sense.

There are sheets of paper everywhere: scattered over the floor, taped to the lockers, tacked to the walls and the classroom doors . . . The noise stops when people notice me, and they start to whisper instead, as though talking about me behind my back isn't so bad then. My chest begins to cave in and all of a sudden I can't breathe. I just have to make it to my locker.

Just make it to your locker, Madison. Just make it to your locker . . . The way I chant that over and over to myself makes it sound as if my locker is some kind of sanctuary in this place.

I don't care about finding the others anymore. Not even Summer. I can find them later. I just have to get to my locker and hide out in the bathroom for homeroom, and then get to history class and then art and photography. Twenty-five minutes. I can manage that. Twenty-five minutes. That's all.

I make it to my locker and the whole world stops spinning. Everything freezes for one hideous, unending moment.

One of the billions of sheets of paper is tacked onto my locker door, at eye level, by someone who knows just how short I am. I reach up a hand and pull it off. It's a photograph – not the best quality, and a little fuzzy, but it's clear enough to see exactly what's going on.

It's a photo of me and Dwight kissing in the library.

There's no way it can be anything else; no way someone could think it was anything but us kissing. I don't know who took it or why it's on my locker, but that doesn't even matter right now. It doesn't change the fact that this photo is all over the school, and everybody's seen it.

I look up, my head turning slowly from side to side. Then I see him: Dwight pulls the photo taped to his locker off, and his face pales, and I see him gulp. Then it scrunches up as he closes his fist around it. He turns and catches my eye immediately.

I look back at my locker, lowering my hand with the photograph. And, oh look, it only gets better – of course it does.

There are letters scratched into my locker. Not spray painted. Nothing that could be removed or cleaned off or even covered over. The letters are actually carved into my locker, jagged silver scratches that stand out against the colored door.

B – I – T – C – H.

Bitch.

The word pinballs riotously through my head, bouncing around, echoing.

Then I remember I need to breathe, and I take in a shallow, trembling breath. And another. And another and another. Breathe out. Breathe in again. And breathe out. Yeah. That'll do. That's good enough.

The photo in my hand falls slowly to the floor. I stumble back a step from my abused locker. I can't hear anything but whispers and my own hollow, shallow breathing.

'Slut,' someone calls out. And the words don't stop, coming at me from every angle, a verbal attack. 'Oh my God how dare she poor Bryce I don't understand what happened she always seemed so nice I heard she got with that Justin guy you know the one Tiffany brought to the dance poor Bryce I knew she was a bitch freak slut freak—'

And with that, the whispers are suddenly too loud and the words all mash together in my head and I can't handle it anymore.

This is so much worse than what I'd dreaded happening.

I'd never wanted anybody here to find out about the old me. I didn't want Fatty Maddie coming back to haunt me, to ruin the life I've made for myself. I've stayed awake into the early hours more than once, letting various nightmarish scenarios play out in my mind where everybody found out what I used to be like.

But this . . .

This is so, so much worse than I could have ever imagined.

It's not my past coming back to haunt me. This is my present, and it's tearing down everything I've built for myself here. The new Madison's life is crumbling to pieces. And the old Madison has nothing to hide behind now.

I resurrect the walls I spent so long constructing back in Pineford; they're not going to see me cry. I won't give them the satisfaction of seeing that they've got to me, that they've broken me.

I put my other earphone in and whatever music that's playing fills my ears. I hitch my bag up a little higher on my shoulder. And I turn around and walk away.

I don't bother trying to look like I'm trying to keep my dignity, like I don't give a dime what they say or think about me. I keep my eyes focused on my feet as they move steadily, one in front of the other in front of the other, my head down. I just wish I hadn't cut my hair so short; now I have nothing to hide behind.

I feel like I'm growing smaller and smaller inside. I feel as though I'm constricting and hiding away in the most distant recesses of my mind until I'm just a shell moving step by step down the corridor.

This isn't like Pineford all over again.

This isn't like Fatty Maddie who they wouldn't let be invisible.

This is far worse.

Distantly, I hear people talking, gossiping – shouting names at me.

Someone steps in front of me; I see sneakers and the frayed hems of jeans. I stop in my tracks and follow the legs up the torso to their face.

Bryce. My lips form his name but my voice isn't working.

He's saying something to me. I can see his lips moving. I can hear his voice. But my brain's not making the connection between his voice and his words. It's as though I've shut down completely. My mind is too loud, and the rest of me is just – just *there*.

So I look back at the floor and step around him, and keep moving.

Eventually I end up walking into a music room.

There's nobody here. Just instruments and music stands and chairs arranged in curves around the conductor's stand. I pull out my earphones, and then I remember exactly why I became so attached to my music in the first place – it helped drown out all my thoughts when it was so dreadfully quiet, like it is now.

Slowly I wrap my earphones around my iPod and set it on the desk at the front of the room. I drop my satchel on the floor, and I'm still standing awkwardly when the door opens.

'Madison, are you . . . ?' Dwight trails off, and I turn to look at him. His eyes are on me, and they're so full of sadness. He walks closer to me – slowly, cautiously – like I'm some kind of feral animal that might rip his head off at any moment. 'Madison . . .' He regards me warily. 'It's going to be okay.'

Is he serious?

He reaches up to put his hands on my shoulders and I can see he's about to say something – and I just lose it completely. I knock his arms away and shove him back, snapping at him, 'How can you even say that? You have no idea. How is it going to be okay?'

He catches my hands in his and pins them against his chest, immobilizing my pathetically weak arms. I thrash and twist, trying to break free even though I know it's not going to do any good.

I can't breathe. I can't breathe. I'm gulping down air into my lungs but it's not working. I'm no longer fighting him; I'm fighting because I'm struggling to breathe properly. Dwight notices something's wrong because he lets go – but barely. His hands never leave me. He just lowers me to the ground and moves me so my head is between my knees.

Then he says three words.

To anyone else, they might not mean much at all, but to me they mean everything and more, and that's all it takes. His voice is soft and calm, totally collected, and I can practically feel his hushed words brushing against my skin.

'Dice, I'm listening.'

And only then do I stop struggling.

In that moment, I just give up trying to fight.

I collapse against him, and finally, finally my lungs accept the oxygen and I can breathe. Dwight topples a little with my dead weight against him, and twists around so he can sit down with me rather than balancing on the balls of his feet. His arms wrap around me, holding me close.

My body is racked with sobs that don't quite come out. There are no tears running down my face. I wonder why I'm not crying. If ever there was a time for crying, this is it. But there are no tears now.

For once, I find myself wishing I would cry. After you cry, your head aches and your mouth feels gross and your throat hurts, but despite all that, you feel so much better for it – clearer. Back in Pineford, I didn't cry over any of it; at least, I did my best not to. Now, I want to – and I can't.

'Dice,' he breathes in my ear. It's a prompt, to get me to talk to him, to tell him, but it's not just that. It's the way his voice sounds – so comforting, so reassuring – that tells me it's also him letting me know he's there. And despite the fact that I'm crumpled in a shaking heap against him, the verbal assurance that he's there calms me slightly.

'Nobody ever—' My breath hitches and I can't finish the sentence. 'Nobody ever . . . ever told me . . . how hard this was going to be,' I stammer. My voice sounds so broken and hopeless. I feel so completely and utterly pathetic right now.

I still don't cry.

'How hard what was going to be?' Dwight asks me softly.

'This. Life. It's . . .'

'Hard?'

Anger threatens to boil up inside me again; I can feel it in the pit of my stomach. But it doesn't come to anything – the hurt is enough to blot it out. So I sound very half-hearted when I tell him, 'Don't patronize me.'

'I didn't mean— sorry. Carry on.'

It takes me another minute – or maybe a bit longer, I don't know. It would be better if I were crying, I think. Just to make me feel less empty.

I pull at Dwight's arms and he gets the message, squeezing me closer. I put my arms around him now, because I need to know he's not going anywhere. Maybe, if I can stay like this long enough, it will stop me from falling apart.

'I've tried,' I tell him, whispering because I'm afraid to speak too loudly. 'I've tried so hard to make it work, and it just . . . didn't. I tried hiding and being invisible, and that didn't work; so I tried – tried it the other way around. Tried not being invisible. And *it didn't work*.'

Dwight doesn't respond. He doesn't offer any helpful advice; nor does he try to understand. Which is good. He just rocks me and holds me, and he's there, and that's the best he can do right at this moment.

I stare blankly at the logo on his T-shirt, looking at the tiny stitches holding it in place. I trace it with my finger, and take another deep, shaky breath, which I let out in a rush.

Then I say, 'I'm such a fuck-up.'

The hand that's rubbing soothing circles on my back

stills. In fact, Dwight's entire body is motionless for just a moment.

I don't look up, but I feel his jaw moving against my head and I know he's about to say something. And I have a pretty good idea of what it is.

'Save it. I'm not looking for excuses. I'm not asking you to tell me I'm wrong. I'm a mess. I'm not smart or pretty or talented, and—'

I don't want to sound stupid, like I'm wallowing in self-pity; but I think I'll forgive myself, just this once. But he interrupts me before I can carry on.

'Would you stop talking like that?'

Dwight actually sounds . . . angry. As in, really, genuinely angry. And I know that every ounce of that anger is directed right at me, for whatever bizarre reason. He pushes me into a sitting position, his hands gripping my shoulders. His fingers dig into my skin; he's desperate.

'For God's sake, Dice, listen to yourself! You can't just—'

'You're hurting me.'

He drops his hands in an instant. Then his arms are around me again, and the way in which he pulls me close is almost desperate.

'Listen to me.' His voice is rough and low, and there's an edge to it that makes me listen. 'I know it's

435

hard. And you've had it harder than a lot of people. But just because there are people out there who can't see what it's doing to you does not make you a bad person.'

I begin to protest, but he carries on before I can utter a single syllable.

'So people picked on you in Maine and made your life hell. So people ripped down the life you built here and tore you to pieces for kicks. That *doesn't* mean you don't matter. It just makes you one hell of a fighter for not breaking down before.'

I snort. A fighter?

Yeah, right.

A runner, maybe.

I don't realize I said that one aloud until he says, 'Maybe.' *All I need to do is try again*, I think to myself.

'That's all we ever do, though, isn't it?'

'What?'

'We try. And try and try and try and we hope it works out the next time, and just when we think we've got the hang of things and we've done it right . . . everything falls to pieces again. And you know what, Dwight?'

'What?'

'I'm tired of it.'

It's a while before he responds.

I'm crying now. Silently. The tears trickle down my

cheeks, down my neck. My limbs feel heavy. And inside, everything hurts.

I let out a sob and cling to Dwight. 'Just . . . don't go anywhere. Please. Just hold me.'

And he does. He kisses my forehead, leaving his lips there, pressed hard against my skin, and his arms are so tight around me it might hurt if I didn't feel so numb on the outside.

It feels like years later that he speaks.

'Dice, listen. I know it's hard, okay, I know. And I know that people haven't made it any easier for you. And I know it might seem impossible to keep trying, but I know you; I know that you won't let them win, and you'll keep trying. And . . .' He trails off. This time it's my turn to wait and hear what he has to say.

'And I don't want you to give up, because I need you around too. You're like – like a stray dog I've grown attached to.'

'Gee, thanks.'

But it makes me almost laugh, and I feel a little more like myself. Not like the old Madison, and not like the new Madison. Like the Madison I am around Jenna, and Dwight – the Madison who doesn't feel stupid for snorting when she laughs and who openly admits she can be a complete dork and not feel two inches tall by saying so.

'Maybe it's not the best comparison,' he admits sheepishly. 'But it's true. I do need you around.'

The corners of my mouth twitch with a smile. A few minutes later, the tears dry up. My throat feels sore and my head aches from crying. I feel gross, so I know I must look a dozen times worse.

'Just promise me something,' Dwight says suddenly, his voice quiet and very close to my ear.

'What?' I sit up and turn to see him better, wiping my fingers over my cheeks to get rid of the tear-tracks.

'Promise me,' he says steadily, 'you won't think about yourself like that again.'

One of his hands strokes my arm, from my shoulder to my elbow. He reaches the other hand up to cup my cheek so I can't avoid his eyes, which are so intense and sincere right now.

And then, very slowly, I nod.

'Yeah?'

'Yeah,' I breathe in reply.

Even though I'm all gross from crying, Dwight leans his head forward. I tilt my face towards his, a sub-conscious action. I expect him to kiss me, but he doesn't. Instead, we sit there with our foreheads touching, our noses pressed together. His eyelashes tickle the skin below my eyebrow when he closes his eyes.

And as we just sit there in that odd embrace and in that moment, everything begins to hurt a little less, and my mind doesn't seem so loud, and that's when I think that this time when I try, it will be worth trying again.

Epilogue

I spin the tiny silver teaspoon around the mug holding my latte. I still can't stand them – but I had to order something to stay here, and a latte seemed appropriate.

I've been waiting ten minutes for him to come out. I asked the girl behind the counter, and she said he was just clearing up and would be out any minute.

It's a quiet day here. I don't know if that's because it's a Sunday or because it's rainy and most people have stayed in. Most likely the latter: it's that thin, gray, relentless drizzle that just makes it all look so hideous outside.

A door swings open and my head snaps up.

'Yeah! See you Tuesday,' he calls over his shoulder, and then his head turns and his eyes spot me straight-away, sitting at my little table for two in the middle of the room, away from everyone else.

I can't quite read his face. Something between shock and a smile. Slowly he comes over and scrapes out the chair opposite me. He spins it around and sits straddling it. 'Hey,' he says quietly.

I give him a small smile. 'Hey, yourself.'

'What . . . uh . . .' He trails off and shakes his head slightly.

I take over while he tries to decide which question to ask me first. 'How are you?'

'Uh, yeah, I'm – I'm good. It's all good. When – when did you get back?'

'Friday night,' I reply quietly, cupping the hot mug in my palms and lacing my fingers together around it. It's a little too hot for comfort but I don't really care. 'I didn't know whether to call or not.'

He opens his mouth, but then thinks better of it and closes it again. 'How have you been?'

I laugh, but it's not entirely humorless. 'I don't know. Okay, I guess? I'm better. I think after that – that day in the music room, I got everything out. I'm better.'

'Are you coming back to school?' he asks tentatively.

'My parents thought it would be better to just transfer again, but I told them it'd just disrupt my studies. And I also said that I might end up in AP geometry this time, and I don't know about you, but that sounds even worse than AP physics. Plus, you wouldn't be there to drag me through it.'

He laughs.

I missed that laugh.

I missed that lopsided smile too: the way it quirks up higher on the one side; the way his eyes crinkle at the corners when he grins like that.

His hair's gotten longer. You can see the curls are more defined now. His freckles look just the same as ever, though, and his eyes are just as sea-green, and he's just as gangly. I don't think I've changed much either, physically. I got my hair cut a week ago. That's about it.

'That's good, though, isn't it? That you're coming back?'

I nod, looking down at the curls of steam rising from my latte.

It's January now. After that day back at school, Dwight walked me home, and stayed with me, cutting class all day to keep me company until my parents got in. Then I told them everything.

Mom decided there and then that we all needed a break. So I missed the last days of school, and we went to New York to visit my sister. We got back just after New Year. My parents hadn't been sure about sending me back to school, but I want to go back. I feel refreshed. And more than that: I'm determined.

The vacation had helped me put things in perspective too. My whole life doesn't have to revolve around Bryce, Tiffany, and the rest of the popular clique. And I would find other friends. People in my classes. The girls on the track team. Dwight and his friends.

Although, that said, I'd avoided speaking to Dwight, since.

I texted him to explain that I needed space to sort myself out, and he replied *Okay*, and gave me that space.

I knew who'd defaced my locker and put all those pictures up. I had no proof, of course, but I'd seen that triumphant smirk on Tiffany's face that day, and I knew it was her. But with Bryce being Principal Peters' stepson and Tiffany one of his model students, and everybody probably too intimidated by what had happened to me to come forward if they did have evidence, nothing would be done to resolve the situation.

'Did it help?' Dwight asks suddenly, pulling me out of my thoughts. 'Having some space, I mean. Being away from everything for a while.'

I shrug. 'We went to see Jenna. She was really happy to see us.'

'You're not answering my question,' he points out, a note of amusement in his voice that makes me smile.

'It helped.'

He nods, recognizing that this is probably the best he'll get out of me. 'I called a few times.'

I nod. 'Yeah. I . . . I'm sorry. I just didn't know what to say to you.'

'So what – you sent me a text saying that you were going out of town for a few weeks with no other explanation, other than you needed space to think? I was worried about you.'

He reaches over and makes to cup his hands around mine, but I let go of my mug and quickly put my hands in my lap, looking down.

'Dice, you remember what you said to me when you made me go up to the tree house?'

I shrug.

'You told me that there are always people who will help you out even if you don't want to notice that they're there to help you. And you just have to let them help you.'

I roll my eyes and sigh dramatically. 'Well, make me eat my own words, why don't you. Jeez. Have you no pity, Ike Butler?'

But there's a laugh in my voice, and he laughs too, and it's just a nice feeling.

'I'm serious, though,' he says. And he reaches a hand up to touch my chin and make me look at him again. I push his hand away.

'Dice . . .'

'How's your vacation been going?' I ask him. 'And Andy and Carter, are they okay?'

'Sure, they're all right. And it's been fine.' He smiles a little, and I start to pick up my mug again. Dwight's fingers extend across the table towards me, and as they brush mine, I flinch, almost knocking the mug over.

But he catches me and holds my fingers tight. I forget how deceptively strong he can be.

'Let go of me,' I tell him sharply, trying to tug my hand out of his grip.

'Dice, look at me,' he says, and with his other hand he pulls my chin up so I have to look him in the eye. I'm scowling, but that slowly subsides when I see the crease in his forehead that shadows his eyes, and the hurt in his face. 'What's wrong?'

'It's – it's just . . .'

Maybe he doesn't think about me in a romantic way. I know we kissed that one time, and it seemed like he was making little romantic gestures, but maybe I'm wrong. Probably. The time we kissed was just sympathy – him being friendly and me reading it incorrectly.

I don't want to say it and make a fool of myself.

I owe him an explanation, though. And if I make a fool of myself . . . well, I know that with Dwight, at least, I can laugh it off.

'It's just – all the little intimate gestures! I don't know if you're just being nice or if – if they're because you like me or what, but it doesn't matter, because you don't want me around, okay, I just – I don't think I'm good to be with, in that way. Right now, I just want to focus on schoolwork. And – and maybe we shouldn't be friends anymore.'

I blurt the words out before I can stop myself. I'm struggling to put it into words for him, but it feels like it makes sense to distance myself from him. I like Dwight, I honestly do, and I've missed him so much these past weeks. It just wouldn't be fair to him to have me around when I'm so . . . so . . . scattered.

I stand up, and my chair scrapes noisily. 'I should get going. I just wanted to say hi before I go back to school, is all. I owed you that much.'

'Hang on,' he calls after me, and I hear him follow as I make my way to the door. I jerk my hood up over my head. I don't have an umbrella; it wasn't raining this bad when Mom dropped me off on her way grocery shopping.

'Dice, hang on. Madison!'

He catches my shoulder as I step out of the door. 'What, so that's it? Just, "Hey, I'm back, but we can't be friends anymore!" That's it? That's all I get? You just turn up here out of the blue after ignoring all my texts and calls and emails for weeks, and everything's normal until we can't be friends anymore?'

I flounder for a response for a moment.

'You told Summer what was going on. Where you were, how things were going.'

My eyes narrow at him. 'How would you know?'

He stares me down, unfaltering. 'She told me. Marched up to me in the corridor at lunch one day and asked if I knew what was going on with you. I said not really. She met up with me after school and told me the whole story. She was almost as worried about you as I was. She was the one keeping me updated whenever you returned her calls, but not mine.'

I don't reply. I can't. I have no idea what to say, or even what he wants to hear from me at this stage.

Summer left me several voicemails that bordered on hysterical, telling me to call her because she was worried about me, and so I got back in touch. I'd kept her up to date, but I hadn't realized she'd been feeding this information back to Dwight.

I thought I was doing him a favor.

'After everything that happened, everything you went through, and I tried being there for you, and now you're just—'

'I'm a mess, Dwight, okay? Is that what you wanted to hear? I'm still trying to figure out who I am. You don't need to feel responsible for me. And I don't want to have to look at you and see the same expression I catch on my parents' faces when they don't think I'm looking, all right? Worried that I'm still upset. Because I like you, Dwight, I really do, and I don't want to mess it all up again, so it's just best if – if I'm not around you . . .'

I trail off because . . . because . . . well, I don't know why.

It's partly because I'm crying – because I know this is best but I just really don't want to lose him, and my saltwater tears are mingling with the rain that's falling on my face even though we're stood under the awning outside the café. It's partly because I don't know how to finish. And it's partly because of that look he's giving me that's so terribly sad.

We stare at each other for a long time. A car drives past, and then another soon after, but going the other way.

'Dice . . .'

He says my name so softly, so gently, that this time I let him pull me into his arms, and he wraps them around me like he's never going to let me go again, which is an exceptionally nice feeling. I bury my face in his chest, because in my sneakers I don't reach much higher on him. He smells so familiar. It's nice.

He loosens his hold on me slightly, and I look up at him questioningly. Up close like this, I think how unconventionally cute he is, in his nerdy way, especially with all those freckles. And I think how nice it is being held by him, and I can't help the small smile that spreads over my face. And suddenly it doesn't matter what I think might be best for him, because everything he's doing tells me he doesn't want to lose me either. And I'm happy.

He smiles back and kisses my forehead.

But that's not what I want him to do.

So I tilt my head up and go on my tiptoes to kiss him full on the mouth.

Just gently at first, because I don't know if he really wants me to. But after the split second of shock and hesitation passes, he kisses me back with such force it knocks out every bit of doubt I ever had from that first day we met that he might ever like me.

I kiss him back and he wraps his arms tight around me, leaning back so I'm literally swept off my feet. I giggle against his lips, and when he sets me down again, we're in the rain, and it's running down our faces but it doesn't even matter.

School will probably be a nightmare tomorrow; it will probably stay that way for a little while. My reappearance will be a wonderful new topic for everybody to talk about, and I'm sure it'll dredge up the gossip about what happened after the Winter Dance.

Although – if I don't care about them and what they think, then they can't hurt me so much. It worked okay back in Pineford, and I'll have to manage somehow here.

This time, it's better, I think. I was so determined to push Dwight away because I thought that was best, but with his arms around me and his lips on mine, I realize how wrong I was.

I'm not alone, not this time.

I'm not *lonely*.

When we finally break apart for air, Dwight and I just look at each other.

And he says, 'I wouldn't have let you go anyway. I still owe you a surfing lesson.'

He brings his hands up to my face to wipe away the rain, which is a useless gesture, but sweet all the same, and I laugh again, happy – truly happy.

**The first published book by Beth Reekles –
the internet sensation everyone is talking about!**

**Meet Rochelle Evans.
Pretty, popular – and never been kissed.**

**Meet Noah Flynn.
Badass, volatile – and a total player.
And also Elle's best friend's older brother...**

When Elle decides to run a kissing booth for the
school's Spring Carnival, she locks lips with Noah
and her life is turned upside down. But this romance
seems far from fairy-tale and headed for heartbreak
... Will Elle get her happily ever after in the end?

'A deeply compelling, romantic and utterly heart-rending story of first love' *The Bookseller*

Chicago, 1995. Anna is sixteen, and fiercely determined to travel the world.

San Francisco, 2012. Bennett is seventeen . . . and desperately trying to stay in one place.

Their paths were never supposed to cross. But Bennett has the incredible ability to travel through time and space, and suddenly finds himself in Anna's world.

They are inescapably drawn together – but it can never last. For no matter how hard Bennett tries to stay with Anna, his unpredictable gift will inevitably knock him right back to where he belongs – and Anna will be left to pick up the pieces.

40148